# WALLEYE JUNCTION

ALSO BY KARIN SALVALAGGIO

*Burnt River*

*Bone Dust White*

# WALLEYE JUNCTION

Karin Salvalaggio

MINOTAUR BOOKS
NEW YORK

This is a work of fiction. All of the characters, organizations, and events portrayed in this novel are either products of the author's imagination or are used fictitiously.


Printed in the United States of America. For information, address St. Martin's Press, 175 Fifth Avenue, New York, N.Y. 10010.

www.minotaurbooks.com

LIBRARY OF CONGRESS CATALOGING-IN-PUBLICATION DATA

Names: Salvalaggio, Karin, author.
Title: Walleye Junction / Karin Salvalaggio.
Description: First Edition. | New York : Minotaur Books, 2016. | Series: Macy Greeley mysteries
Identifiers: LCCN 2015050421| ISBN 9781250078926 (hardcover) | ISBN 9781466891470 (e-book)
Subjects: LCSH: Murder—Investigation—Fiction. | BISAC: FICTION / Mystery & Detective / Women Sleuths. | FICTION / Mystery & Detective / Police Procedural. | GSAFD: Mystery fiction.
Classification: LCC PR6119.A436 W35 2016 | DDC 823/.92—dc23
LC record available at http://lccn.loc.gov/2015050421

Our books may be purchased in bulk for promotional, educational, or business use. Please contact your local bookseller or the Macmillan Corporate and Premium Sales Department at 1-800-221-7945, extension 5442, or by e-mail at MacmillanSpecialMarkets@macmillan.com.

First Edition: May 2016

10 9 8 7 6 5 4 3 2 1

*Aunt Louise and Uncle Larry,*
*this one's for you.*

# Acknowledgments

I'm lucky to have Felicity Blunt, Kari Stuart, and the rest of the team at Curtis Brown and ICM Partners on my side. You take such good care of me! Thanks also go out to the people at St. Martin's Press and Minotaur for all the hard work they do behind the scenes, especially Elizabeth Lacks, whose enthusiasm and encouragement make it easier for me to do my job. I'm also grateful that my rather clever and cultured friend Alison Lee shared a bit of her art expertise for this book. And I mustn't forget my little family of conscripted editors who patiently waded through my manuscript. Dani, Mom, and Dad, you are my heroes! It goes without saying that my son, Matteo, is also my hero. Without you and your sister, Dani, none of this would be possible. And finally there are all my dear friends who've been with me every step of the way. I love and cherish you all.

*How well I have learned that there is no fence to sit on between heaven and hell. There is a deep, wide gulf, a chasm, and in that chasm is no place for any man.*

–Johnny Cash

# WALLEYE JUNCTION

# 1

The voice coming in over the police radio sounded skeptical.

"Philip Long isn't here. He must have been moved to another location."

Detective Macy Greeley held the steering wheel in one hand and the radio with the other. "He may have gotten out. You need to check the perimeter and start a search. Any idea where the homeowner is?"

"We're looking into it."

"I'm just coming up to the turnoff. I'll be there in five."

In the distance the flashing lights of emergency vehicles and patrol cars bled red, white, and blue into a wash of black sky. The windshield wipers barely had time to snap back into place before Macy was once again driving blind. The view outside the car windows came at her in short bursts—a lonely stand of trees, an isolated mailbox, a farmhouse, a roadside fruit stand. A gust of wind pushed her into the oncoming lane and for a brief time she slid across the slick surface. It was late spring and snow was falling in the Whitefish Range. Summer still seemed a long way off.

Philip Long's phone call had woken her up thirty minutes ago. She'd been dozing in the incident room they'd set up at the Walleye Junction police station where the authorities were monitoring his home's incoming calls. It had been three days since he'd been abducted at gunpoint at a gas station, but his kidnappers had yet to make contact. All the authorities had so far was video footage of two masked gunmen threatening to kill their hostage if he didn't get into a dark blue van. When Philip Long tried to call his home number, it was Macy who answered.

She'd recognized his voice immediately. As far as she knew he was the only Englishman in Montana with a talk radio program. Apparently he had a way of making people sit up and listen. During their brief phone conversation, Macy had hung on his every word.

*I don't know how much time I have,* he said.

*Can you tell us where you are?*

*I've been kept in the dark since I was taken. I really have no idea.*

*Look around. Describe what you see.*

*It's a family home. Maybe two floors with a basement. I'm not sure when they'll come back. I have to go.*

*How many kidnappers are there?*

*I see headlights in the trees. Someone's coming up the driveway.*

Macy's eyes flicked to the digital clock on the dashboard. It was almost three in the morning. A half hour had passed since they'd spoken. If they didn't find him soon somebody else would. Macy checked the sat nav. The police had traced Long's phone call to a residence on the outskirts of Walleye Junction. The first wave of law enforcement officers was already there.

There was no sign of the secondary road she needed to turn onto. Dark windswept trees twisted overhead, the branches arching so far they almost brushed the top of the vehicle. The drainage ditch that lined Route 93 was overflowing. Black water lapped onto the road. She caught sight of what looked like an exit and put on her turn signal.

A figure burst from the trees to her right just as she was slowing down. Macy hit the brakes hard, turning the wheel as the vehicle went into a spin. A pale face. A startled look. Philip Long flew into her windshield and disappeared over the roof as the car started to roll. Glass shattered. The frame buckled. Two and a half times around and the SUV came to a rest on the hard shoulder, its back end suspended above the drainage ditch.

Macy's screams got caught up in a tangle of pain, panic, and grinding metal. She swung her head around as she tried to make sense of what had happened. Still in her seat belt, she was hanging upside down in the cab of the SUV with her hands braced against the ceiling. Her left wrist ached. She held it to her chest and blinked into what was left of the windshield. Outside, the SUV's headlights picked up the trail of rain-soaked debris that had been thrown into the road when the car rolled—broken glass, a notebook, an empty Diet Coke can, her handgun still in its holster, Philip Long's body. She struggled to move, but her seat belt was tight across her lap. She tugged at the clasp. It wouldn't give. Using her legs as leverage, she pushed back hard against the seat and tried again. Metal scraped against pavement as the car lurched back another foot. She swayed from the seat belt as the ceiling buckled beneath her.

"Shit, shit, shit, shit."

Driving rain, whipped up by strong wind, hit her directly in the face. She pressed her fingertips into her eyes and tried to think. She needed to remain calm. Help was close by. They'd get to her in time.

Outside the car something caught her eye. She looked on in disbelief. Philip Long was still alive. He staggered to his feet and swayed barefooted on the empty road. His wet gray hair was matted to his head. He took a tentative step toward her then stopped. The heavy roar of an engine filled the night. A vehicle was approaching. Its headlights hit Philip right between the eyes. He raised a hand and backed away.

Macy turned on the interior light and sifted through the wreckage in the car. The cord for the police radio was tangled on something beneath the passenger seat. She couldn't find her phone.

A motorcycle pulled up just out of her line of sight. Exhaust fumes drifted into the cab. Macy twisted around to get a better look, but all she saw was the driver's heavy black boots. The motorcycle's engine continued to rumble as its driver moved across the road. Her SUV's headlights caught him from behind. Rain poured over his helmet and down his close-fitting motorcycle gear. He knelt to pick up her gun before walking to where Philip Long was standing in the road with his hands up. Philip was yelling something, but the words were warped by wind and driving rain.

Macy's seat belt snapped loose and she fell onto the roof in a heap. Her body felt awkward and heavy. She rolled to her side and crawled through the debris on her hands and knees. She was halfway out the window when the first of two shots rang out.

She slid across the wet gravel on her stomach, the broken glass crackling beneath her. She risked one last look. Philip Long was lying on his side, eyes wide, lips slightly parted. The man turned toward her patrol car just as she dropped into the drainage ditch. The water was ice cold. She dipped below the surface and let the dark current carry her away.

# 2

It was nearly six in the morning and the lamp above the kitchen table was the only light on in the house, but outside the back garden was slowly coming into focus. After several days of heavy rain, the weather forecast was clear for the coming week. Macy pressed her palms against the cool granite countertop and waited for her hands to stop trembling. In the four days since the accident she'd had several nightmares. Her most recent had started as a faithful reenactment of the night Philip Long died. Unable to breathe, she'd tumbled through the fast-moving water in the drainage ditch. She'd woken up believing that she'd died.

Macy held her hands up to the light. There were scratches and bruises all over her body, but it was her hands that told the story best. Her fingernails were snapped off and her fingertips had been rubbed raw from trying to claw her way out of the ditch. The sides had been too steep and the water too fast. If not for the tangled roots of a cottonwood tree, she might not have survived her ordeal. She'd grabbed hold and scrambled onto the hard shoulder of Route 93. The lights of rescue vehicles glowed in the distance. She'd been so cold she'd nearly lost consciousness, but she'd limped toward those lights. She had vague memories of someone wrapping her in a blanket. Macy blinked back tears and reminded herself of what she knew to be true. It was six in the morning, she was in her mother's kitchen in Helena, Montana, and she was very much alive.

Macy returned to the kitchen table. Crime scene photos, maps, and sheets of notes were laid out in a neat grid. She spent a few seconds studying Philip Long's photograph. He was sixty-two and more physically fit than most people half his age. According to the biography on his Web site he ran five miles a day when the weather was fine. During the winter he cross-country skied. While she was recovering in the hospital she'd read most of his recent articles and listened to hours of his radio talk show. He'd had such enthusiasm for life. It was difficult for her to reconcile this man with the one she'd seen on the road that night. In her mind Philip Long was forever swaying, forever afraid, and forever in midsentence. The more she thought about it the more she was convinced he'd been trying to tell her something. In her nightmares she watched his lips move, but all she heard was the pounding of the rain and the roar of that motorcycle engine.

Philip Long had suffered thirty-one separate injuries, ranging from contusions to broken ribs to a fractured skull. It was impossible to say for certain if they were a result of the accident or a struggle with his captors. Aside from a smashed glass coffee table and a broken lamp they'd found nothing up at the house that indicated there'd been a final altercation with his kidnappers. As far as the police could tell, Philip Long was on his own when he escaped the 4,000 square-foot custom-built home on Edgewood Road.

Macy flipped through the information she'd gathered on the homeowner. Ron Forester was a Flathead Valley–based accountant who was serving time for aggravated sexual assault. He'd told the police that the kidnappers had used his home without his knowledge. Macy had watched his recorded interview from her hospital room. He'd held up his hands.

*Nothing to do with me.*

Macy checked the Edgewood Road property's phone records again. In the past three months there'd been no outgoing calls aside from the one Philip Long had made on the night he died. The property's utility records told a similar story. There'd been a spike in usage in the days prior to Long's abduction. The property was about a half mile away from Route 93. There were no neighbors and so far Macy could find nothing to tie Philip Long to the owner of the property. She checked the files again. A local company called Mountain Security was contracted to monitor the house alarm. According to bank records, payments for the service were still being made. Whoever broke in must have known the access code. Macy picked up Ron Forester's photo. The man was a convicted felon. She had no reason to trust anything he said.

"Nothing to do with *me*, my ass," she said.

Macy sifted through the photos of the home's interior. The kidnappers had forced the lock on the back door and cleared out the basement storage room where they'd kept Philip Long. There were Chinese takeaways in the refrigerator, a warm coffeepot, and dishes soaking in the sink. So far they'd found two sets of unidentified fingerprints that couldn't be accounted for.

A large flock of blue jays peppered the dawning sky before settling into uppermost branches of a birch tree at the far end of the garden. Macy glanced at the clock hanging over the kitchen table and frowned. A highway patrol officer was picking her up in an hour. Macy had protested she was well enough to drive back up to the Flathead Valley on her own, but her new boss at the Department of Justice had insisted that it was either a driver or medical leave. Macy gave in. If she wanted Philip Long out of her dreams she needed to figure out what had happened out on that isolated stretch of Route 93. The first thing she had to do was go see the house where he'd been held captive. Photographs weren't good enough.

There was a light step on the stairs and Macy turned to see her mother, Ellen, coming down in her robe and slippers. She wasn't alone. A naturally cautious child, Luke held tight to his grandmother's hand. He was nearly two and half and tall for his age. With his shaggy black hair and aquiline nose, Luke was a dead ringer for his father, former Chief of State Police Ray Davidson, but when his green eyes lit up, he was pure Greeley.

"Mommy!" he said, flinging his arms wide and racing toward her.

Macy smiled through the pain as she bent low to pick him up. The seat belt strap had left deep bruises across her chest and her left wrist ached where it had slammed against the SUV's roof. Ellen put a hand on her daughter's shoulder.

"Please don't put on an act for my benefit. I know you're hurting. Did you take some ibuprofen when you got up this morning?"

Macy groaned as she slid Luke into his high chair.

"Yes, but it doesn't seem to do much good."

"It will take time to heal, but you know that. Anyway, nothing is broken so you'll mend soon enough."

Macy started making faces at Luke. He giggled and grabbed at her nose.

"I wish I had your faith," said Macy.

"Macy, you're stronger than you think. I am grateful they're sending a driver around though. You're not ready to sit behind the wheel just yet."

"Highway patrol officer Gina Cunningham has seventeen years of experience. I doubt she's happy being reduced to a *driver*."

Ellen laughed. "If I get a chance to meet her I'll keep that in mind."

Macy held up the coffeepot. "I just made a fresh pot. Do you want some?"

"Thank you, that would be lovely." Ellen drifted through the downstairs rooms, turning on lights. "Why do you insist on sitting in the dark? It's creepy. And speaking of creepy, are those crime scene photos all over our kitchen table?"

"Sorry about the mess. I'll clear it up in a sec."

Ellen took a quick look. "If I were looking at these photos I'd have every light in the house switched on."

"In my spare time I'm trying to save the planet." Macy swung open the refrigerator door. "I'm making scrambled eggs. Do you want some?"

"No thank you. I'll just have a bowl of cereal." Ellen smiled. "I really like your new haircut. It suits you."

Macy brushed her red hair forward so it framed her face. "I'm not sure I like it this short. I feel oddly exposed."

"Sweetheart, you're being ridiculous. It's shoulder length. Besides, most of the time you'll pull it into a ponytail like you've always done." Ellen brushed a piece of lint from Macy's navy blazer. "You look well. You're starting to get some of your color back." She touched her daughter's cheek. "You even have a few freckles coming through. Must be spring."

Macy turned away from her mother's steady gaze. Ellen was incredibly perceptive and Macy didn't want her to see how conflicted she was feeling. Macy had been offered medical leave. It would have meant more time at home with Luke. It was her choice to return to the Flathead Valley so she could continue investigating Philip Long's kidnapping and murder. Once she was committed to a case she always saw it through. Every file and photo was stored in her head; she'd work every angle until it made sense. She'd failed Philip Long in life. She would not fail him in death.

She bent low so she could look her son directly in the eyes. Fortunately for Macy, Luke wasn't as perceptive as her mother, but she knew there would come a time when she'd have a lot of explaining to do. There were other moms who were home for dinner every night and had weekends off. She wasn't one of them. This wasn't the first time her job had taken her away for days at a time. There were a lot of police departments in rural Montana that didn't have any detectives on staff. As a special investigator working for the state, she was sent where she was most needed.

Macy made a conscious effort to change the subject. She pointed to her mother's yoga mat. It was rolled up next to the kitchen door with her gym bag.

"Are you going to your yoga class today?"

"Yep, it's nice that Luke likes the day care center. It's good for him to socialize."

"It's good for you too."

"I socialize plenty. The girls are coming over for dinner tomorrow night."

Macy smiled. The girls were all in their late sixties and loved playing a dirty game of poker.

"But the girls don't go with you to yoga?"

Macy was pretty sure her mother had met someone. Ellen was taking more care in her appearance and had finally gained back the weight she'd lost after Macy's father died. During a recent shopping trip at the mall, she'd introduced Macy to an older gentleman named Jeff who they'd bumped into in the food court. Apparently, Jeff and Ellen attended the same yoga class. Ellen had been so flustered she'd had difficulty speaking.

"Thank you again for looking after Luke," said Macy. "I couldn't do this without you."

"It's wonderful for all of us. I love that you and Luke are here with me."

Macy ruffled Luke's hair as she handed him an apple she'd cut up into wedges. He was generally quiet but took a great deal of satisfaction in repeating any interesting words he heard, the more inappropriate the better. Macy still forgot and cursed sometimes. It was hard not to laugh when he mimicked her, but Ellen had put her straight on that one right away.

*Don't you dare encourage him,* she warned. *There's nothing cute about a child saying fuck.*

Macy had loved how formal it sounded when her mother said it. *You're right. It's much cuter when* you *drop the f bomb.*

Ellen picked up a photo of Ron Forester's living room and held it up to the light.

"This house is beautifully furnished," said Ellen.

"It should be. It belongs to a rather well-off accountant."

"Accountants do seem to have all the money." Ellen waved a hand over the rest of the images on the kitchen table. "Where was he during all this?"

"He's serving time for aggravated sexual assault."

"Charming."

"I'm interviewing him tomorrow."

Ellen raised an eyebrow. "Where's he being held?"

Macy pulled out a bowl and cracked her first egg. She would not meet her mother's eyes.

"Montana State Prison, Deer Lodge."

"Ray Davidson is also being held there."

"I'm aware of that."

"Have you spoken to him recently?"

"Not since he agreed to plead guilty on all counts." Macy switched on the hob and placed the frying pan on the burner. "I wanted to thank him for not dragging all of us through the courts. Not that it matters much as everyone learned about our affair during the inquiry."

"It wasn't an affair. It was a relationship. He was separated from his wife when you were seeing him."

"Not the second time around."

"Well, he lied to you and just about everyone else. Why didn't you tell me you spoke to him?"

"I knew you wouldn't approve."

"He's behind bars, but you're not safe yet. I know you're still not over him."

Macy kissed Luke on top of the head. "It's difficult to move on when I'm constantly reminded."

"Stop torturing yourself. Luke may resemble Ray, but I really think he takes after your father. We'll dig out the family photos so you can see for yourself."

"Mom, you may not understand this, but I really needed to tell Ray that he did the right thing." She scooped some scrambled egg onto a plate and put it on the counter to cool. "What he did was awful, but he's living a nightmare. . . . They'll never let him out."

"Don't you dare feel sorry for that man. He's corrupt through and through. It's his wife and children who you should feel sorry for."

"His wife has moved the family to Chicago. I hear she's already engaged to a guy she dated when she was in high school."

"Can you blame her for wanting to move on as quickly as possible?"

"No, not really." Macy took the seat next to Luke and started clearing away the case files. "Sometimes I wish I had the option of leaving."

"Running away won't help matters. It's better to stay and work through this. I know it's hard now, but if you continue to do your job well, people will soon forget." Ellen paused. "Are you going to be seeing Aiden when you're up in the Flathead Valley?"

"That's the idea. It's been a while since we've had any time together so it will be nice."

"I told you to take things slow, but this is glacial."

Luke popped a piece of apple into Macy's mouth and howled with laughter when she made a face.

"After everything that's happened I don't know if it's wise for me to date someone in law enforcement again."

"With the hours you work who else are you going to meet, let alone date?"

"This is true."

Ellen smiled over her cup of coffee. "You could always try online dating. I hear there are sites that specialize in single women who are attracted to men in uniform. I'd say you qualify."

Macy laughed and it hurt.

"I'm going to pretend I never heard you make that suggestion." The doorbell rang. "That will be my ride."

Gina Cunningham's hairstyle was short, sharp, and spiked with a grid of golden highlights that reminded Macy of a leopard print. There was nothing subtle about her personality either. She was known for speaking her mind and for this reason Macy was thankful they'd always been on good terms. Gina had said nothing about Macy's recent troubles with Ray Davidson. She'd instead asked after her son and expressed concern that Macy might be trying to get back to work too soon after her accident. As usual, Gina was direct.

*"I hope you don't mind me saying this, but you look like shit, Greeley."*

They arrived at the outskirts of Walleye Junction at around nine in the morning. The site of Macy's accident had been cleared. If it wasn't for a hastily erected roadside shrine, someone could pass by unaware of what happened four nights ago. Gina slowed the highway patrol car for a better look. Stray bits of broken glass sparkled on the asphalt. Skid marks twisted into a question mark. Cards fluttered every time a car passed by and flower bouquets, some still wrapped in plastic and others clearly made of plastic, sparkled in the midmorning light. Pools of melted candle wax dotted the pavement and an enterprising church had left a notice offering its free counseling services for mourners who were in need of spiritual guidance.

Philip Long may have been a divisive figure in Walleye Junction, but he was also a popular one. It seemed his critics had considered him a worthy opponent. Macy had scrolled through the comments sections on various obituaries. One admirer wrote, *Sometimes it takes an outsider to shine a light on our problems* to which someone responded, *Although I respected Philip I always wondered why he didn't return to England if he was so opposed to how we do things over here.*

Seeing a break in the oncoming traffic, Gina crossed over the southbound lanes and pulled onto the hard shoulder. She opened the window and leaned out to get a better look at the messages of condolence left for Philip Long's family.

Macy gripped her hands together on her lap and focused on the middle distance. It was a clear spring day and everything was sharp and new. The cherry orchards were in blossom and verdant evergreen forests coated the surrounding foothills. Higher up, the mountain peaks of the Whitefish Range were covered in a crisp layer of white.

Originally from Texas, Gina had never completely eradicated the twang from her voice.

"There was a serial killer down in Texas who used to leave clues at his victim's roadside shrines."

Gina tore open a bag of Doritos and Macy recoiled at the smell. She felt clammy and feverish. She touched her forehead. It was damp. She opened the passenger-side window and watched a helicopter fly back and forth over the cherry orchards on the far side of the highway. It hovered like a giant dragonfly. Gina put the bag of Doritos on the seat between them and told Macy to help herself.

"Bet the water in the drainage ditch was fucking cold, but I guess jumping in was better than getting shot." Gina glanced over at Macy. "You feeling okay?"

"I need some fresh air."

Macy opened the door at the same time a logging truck passed by. It sounded its horn and Macy shrank back into the vehicle. Gina's hand was on her shoulder.

"You're shaking."

Macy nodded. Gina was being kind and she wasn't going to fault her for it.

"Thank you," Macy said. "I'm a little nervous about being back here, but I guess that's to be expected."

Gina reached for the radio. "Nice to know you're human after all. You do what you have to do. I'll call the folks in Walleye and let them know our ETA."

Macy walked a few paces north along the hard shoulder. The cold wind churned up by passing vehicles slapped at her hair. She pulled it back into a rough ponytail using a band wrapped around her wrist. To her right cars and trucks rumbled along Route 93. To her left dark water gurgled along the drainage ditch. She watched her reflection waver on the dark surface. Macy had looked up detailed maps of the area online. Another hundred yards beyond where she'd managed to escape the drainage ditch, a shunt directed the overflow toward the Flathead River. She knew damn well that she was lucky to be alive. She studied the spot in the center of the road where Philip Long had died. Solving the case would never be enough. She had a feeling his final moments were going to haunt her dreams forever.

Philip Long's roadside shrine had been erected at the base of the exit sign for Edgewood Road. Squatting down low, Macy poked a ballpoint pen among the flowers, pushing them to the side so she could see the cards. People had left children's drawings, sympathy cards, and little notes. On several, the ink ran down paper so damp it was turning back to pulp.

*Ashes to ashes, dust to dust.*

*You will be missed.*

*Godspeed.*

Macy stood up tall and stretched her shoulder. The ibuprofen had already worn off. She needed to take some more but would wait until she'd had something more substantial to eat.

Gina passed a bag of caramels out the open window. "Do yourself a favor and have a few of these. You look like you're about to pass out."

The candy wrapper crackled in Macy's fingers. "This case you were talking about in Texas. When was this?"

"Been years . . . maybe in the seventies. It turned out he was a trucker who was preying on hitchhikers. He'd leave their bodies roadside."

"Not likely he's our guy then."

"Nah, he fried."

The helicopter buzzed nearby. It was just a few yards above the cherry orchard across the highway. Macy turned and watched.

"What the hell is that guy doing?" Macy asked.

"When it rains they use choppers to fan dry the cherry blossoms."

"I did not know that." Macy handed the bag of caramels to Gina and checked her phone. Aiden Marsh was calling. She signaled to Gina that she'd be a few seconds and walked to the front of the vehicle.

"Hey, Aiden," said Macy. "Nice to hear your voice."

"Detective Greeley, I was relieved to hear you're on the mend."

"Oh, I guess you're calling me in a professional capacity."

"Unfortunately, that is the case," said Aiden. "We've found two bodies at a business park midway between Walleye Junction and Wilmington Creek. It looks like they've overdosed."

"Interesting, but why are you calling me?"

"Initially I thought this was routine, but there's a dark blue van with Idaho plates parked nearby. It matches the one from the surveillance video at the gas station where Philip Long was abducted."

"Did you run the plates?"

"It's stolen. The ME took fingerprints and we got a match with what was found at the house where Long was kept. It looks like we've found your kidnappers."

"Have you identified them?"

"Carla and Lloyd Spencer, both lifelong residents of Walleye Junction. They're both addicts. They may have been after cash to buy more drugs."

"There are easier ways to get cash than kidnapping. Can you send me the address?"

"Will do. Where are you now?"

"Standing next to *the* drainage ditch."

Aiden broke character. "Are you okay?"

"Barely."

"Hang in there."

Macy climbed onto the passenger seat and told Gina to head north toward Wilmington Creek.

"Chief Marsh, I appreciate the heads-up," Macy said. "We'll be there in twenty minutes."

Gina pulled out onto Route 93. "Who was that?"

Macy hesitated. She and Aiden had been seeing each other for nearly a year. There was really no reason to be so secretive about their relationship, but she'd only told her closest friends and family and even then she'd been cautious in her remarks. There'd been so much upheaval in her life over the past year. There were times she couldn't decide whether she actually liked Aiden or was just using him as a crutch to get through it all.

Macy dug her hand into the bag of caramels.

"Aidan Marsh," she said, popping one into her mouth. "Wilmington Creek Chief of Police. They found two bodies. Looks like an overdose. Prints match our kidnappers."

Gina's voice went flat. "Job done then."

"You sound disappointed."

"My mother-in-law moved in yesterday to look after the kids while I'm away. Would have been nice to make it worth her trouble and mine. I packed for a week."

"Sounds like you were betting against me solving this."

"Nah, just needed a break. Trying to work and find time for the house, my husband, and the kids is exhausting."

Fields of dark, tilled earth surrounded the small business park. A woman who ran a bakery out of one of the units had spotted the couple lying side by side in the long grass near where she usually parked her car. It didn't occur to her that they might be dead until sounding the horn failed to wake them. She'd been so upset she'd stayed in the car until the police arrived.

Gina parked outside the temporary perimeter the forensic team had set up and offered Macy another caramel before cutting the engine.

"Sweetheart," said Gina. "Are you sure you're ready for this?"

Macy kept her eyes on Aiden Marsh. Though she'd never admit it, her mother was right. There was something about a man in uniform and as usual Aiden's was nicely pressed. He was deep in conversation with the head of the forensics team, Ryan Marshall, but he waved to them as they drove up. Ryan was shrouded in white-hooded coveralls replete with gloves, booties, and dark sunglasses. Most of the time, it was impossible to tell what he really looked like. Macy had taken to pretending that she didn't recognize him when she saw him in civilian clothes. He'd taken to telling Macy to piss off, one of many phrases he'd picked up at an international forensics conference where he'd discovered that his British counterparts liked drinking even more than he did.

When she'd joined the force, Macy had been told Gina could be prickly. Over the years she'd noticed more and more that it was only the men who said this. Macy gave Gina a slight smile and reached for the door handle.

"Thanks for asking, Gina, but I'm good. Let's go do this."

Outside, the cloying smell of sugar drifting from the bakery's ovens hung heavy in the air. As far as Macy could tell there was no smell coming off the bodies. Carla and Lloyd Spencer had not been dead long. They were almost invisible in the tall grass. All that could be seen clearly were their shoes—one pair of sneakers and one pair of cowboy boots. About thirty feet away a couple of women wearing aprons stood in front of the bakery's delivery bay smoking cigarettes.

Macy started with introductions, making a point of shaking both Ryan and Aidan's hands.

Ryan cracked a smile. "What's with the formalities? We haven't shook hands in ten years."

"Maybe I want the pleasure of getting to know you all over again."

Macy pulled on booties and gloves and went over to have a closer look at Carla and Lloyd Spencer. The husband and wife both wore jeans and hooded sweatshirts. Their clothing wasn't threadbare, but it was well worn. It was also dry. They'd not died in the rain that had fallen during the night. Carla Spencer was an attractive woman, but the same didn't hold true for her husband. Lloyd looked a little worse for wear. Deep lines traced the contours of his face and his teeth and his hands were stained sepia from tobacco.

"So what do you think, Ryan?"

"I think we found your kidnappers so we can all go home."

"What killed them?"

"Probably heroin, but they may have been cooking prescription drugs and injecting them. The toxicology screen will tell us what we need to know. The male was a heavy user. Lots of needle marks."

"And the female?"

"Nothing I can see aside from the puncture wound that killed her. She appears to be in much better health."

Aiden cleared his throat. "Macy, I ran a check. Carla has been in a rehab program for a couple months and Lloyd is on a waiting list." He turned to Ryan. "Any estimate on time of death?"

Macy spoke first. "If the bodies haven't been dumped here I'd say between six and seven this morning."

Ryan nodded in agreement. "Nice work, Greeley. I suppose you'll be wanting my job next."

Macy was tempted to look smug for Ryan's benefit but kept a straight face.

"Their clothing is dry," Macy said. "It stopped raining at around six and the bakery manager arrived at seven. Was anyone else here yet?"

"Nope," said Aiden. "She was the first to arrive. She noticed the van and then the bodies."

"Do Carla and Lloyd Spencer have family in Walleye?"

"Chief of Police Lou Turner is arriving any minute. He should know."

"I'm going to have a chat with the manager of the bakery," said Gina. "See if I can find out anything else."

Aiden pointed out the woman in the apron wearing a baseball cap. "She's pretty shaken up. Go easy on her."

Ryan yawned deeply. "See if you can get me some doughnuts and a cup of coffee. I could just about murder for a plain-glazed." He started walking away. "I'm going to arrange transport for the bodies. I'll make sure there's a rush put on the toxicology screen."

Macy turned her attention to Carla and Lloyd Spencer again. They were lying with their arms by their sides, palms up. Since it was probably drugs that killed them it was difficult to believe they'd have the wherewithal to die in such similar poses. She squatted down low. There were no apparent signs of struggle. With a gloved hand she lifted Lloyd's cowboy boot. There was gravel imbedded in the back of the heel. The same was not true of Carla's trainers. Macy pivoted and looked at the van. It was about ten yards away.

"I think they died in the van. Lloyd was dragged across the pavement and Carla was carried."

"You don't think this is an accidental overdose?" said Aiden.

"I'm not ruling it out, but they've been moved. Could mean they died a little earlier this morning. It certainly points to a third party. There may have been someone else involved in Long's kidnapping." Macy peeled off her gloves. "We'll have to wait for an autopsy report to tell us more."

As she stood up her vision blurred. She reached for Aiden and he was there.

Aiden kept his voice low. "You okay? You're looking a little pale."

"I'm not going to lie. I'm struggling."

He righted her and let go. "I'd give you a hug if I could."

"I appreciate the sentiment."

"Are you sure it's a good idea going back to work so soon?"

Her eyes flicked to Gina. "Don't worry, I'm in good hands."

"Should I be jealous?"

"Most definitely. Gina's a hottie."

"If you don't need me here I'm going to head off. There's a meeting I have to get to."

Macy walked him to his vehicle. "So," she said, checking to make sure that no one was in earshot. "I'll see you later on tonight?"

"Just give me a shout when you're free and I'll come pick you up at your hotel."

"Do you still feel like making dinner?"

"Heading to the river now. Hopefully, I'll catch something."

"I thought you said you had a meeting."

"I do. The mayor is coming with me." He raised his voice so he could be heard. "It was a pleasure seeing you again, Detective Greeley."

"Are you kidding me?"

He leaned in and spoke in a whisper. "How was that for acting?"

"I wouldn't give up your day job just yet."

Police Chief Lou Turner pulled into the parking lot in his SUV as Macy was peering in the front windows of the stolen van. She'd been told on more than one occasion that Lou had a wicked sense of humor and liked nothing more than to fish and hang out with friends he'd known since childhood. Macy couldn't imagine it. Since they'd met in the hours following Philip Long's kidnapping he'd hadn't smiled once, but then again, she could hardly blame him, given the circumstances.

Lou asked after her health before turning his attention to Carla and Lloyd. He stared at them for a long time before speaking.

"I can't say that I'm surprised that they ended up this way, but I am a little taken aback that they were involved in Philip's kidnapping."

"Did they have any children?"

"An older boy in his teens from Carla's first marriage and two younger ones who are in foster care. There's extended family, but no one was able to take them in."

"That's sad."

"Carla was trying to stay clean though. Last time we spoke she seemed determined to get her kids back."

"I want to know where Carla was attending rehab. Her therapist might have some insight. It's also possible that Carla met someone there that she shouldn't have." Macy tilted her head to the stolen van. "The vehicle still needs to be processed."

"I just got off the phone. More crime scene techs are on their way."

"I've been through Philip Long's archived shows. Recently he was pretty vocal about the growing threat of the militias in Montana. Any possibility of a connection?"

Lou Turner sighed. "Carla and Lloyd's only claim to fame was when some obscure blog characterized their militia group as being a potential domestic terrorist threat, but I don't think those idiots did their research. Anyone with half a brain would have seen them for what they were. Carla and Lloyd were all talk. I'm not saying Lloyd wasn't a mean bastard, but he kept it in house. More of a bully than a defender of democracy."

"Philip Long went out of his way to provoke a lot of people. He went so far as predict the emergence of a breakaway territory. Something he called the *Third State*. He said it was his duty to expose these groups before it was too late," Macy said.

"A big part of Philip's job was chasing ratings so don't take everything he said too seriously. Sure there are people in the valley who are involved. Some of them are among my friends, but I can't think of anyone who's far gone enough to try something like this."

"That may be so," said Macy. "But he's received a lot of hate mail in the past few weeks."

"Then why kidnap him? There are more subtle ways to get someone to shut up when you don't like what they're saying."

Macy decided to change tack.

"Lloyd and Carla may have died of an overdose, but it looks to me like the bodies were moved. There's gravel imbedded in the heel of his boots and their positioning looks posed. We'll have to wait for a report back from the crime scene techs to be sure." She paused. "Do you think Carla and Lloyd Spencer could have pulled off Long's kidnapping on their own?"

Lou walked toward the bodies for a closer look. "They didn't exactly pull it off. Philip almost got out alive and they're both dead. We'll look closely at the militia angle though. We're going through Philip's hate mail and the comments left on the radio station's Web site. If Carla or Lloyd made any threats we'll know soon enough."

"Do either of them ride a dirt bike?"

"You got me there. We'll have to check."

"We'll need to search their home."

Lou patted his shirt pocket. "A warrant has already been issued. I've got a unit keeping an eye on things over there. Just waiting for more manpower." He took off his sunglasses and rubbed his eyes. "You know, the motive could have been financial. Philip Long was as close to a celebrity as you can get around here. Maybe they thought he was loaded. We'll have to interview the family members and look into Carla and Lloyd's financial situation, but odds are they were heavily in debt."

"Is there a connection between them and Ron Forester, the homeowner?"

"At three hundred dollars an hour, I doubt they could have afforded Ron's accountancy services. Lloyd was an unemployed roofer and although Carla once held a good job with a tech company, she's spent the last year delivering pizzas."

"I'm interviewing Philip Long's wife tomorrow," said Macy.

"His daughter Emma arrived in town today."

"It took a while for her to get here."

"I spoke to her briefly," said Lou. "She says she only found out about her father's death because she called home wanting to speak to him and got her mother instead."

"Her mother didn't call her?"

"Nope."

"Wouldn't you characterize that as odd?"

"Definitely out of character for Francine, but I've always seen Emma as a bit of a wild card. Among other things she has a rep for running away from funerals."

"Sounds interesting. I'll have to ask her about that."

Lou cleared his throat. "By the way, the toxicology screen came back on Philip Long. He had heroin in his system."

"Considering the extensive injuries to his body, it's impossible to tell what was going on in that house. They may have used it to sedate him. Did he have a history of drug abuse?"

"Not to my knowledge, but maybe so. It's not exactly something people advertise." Lou Turner glanced over at the bodies again. "I need to notify the family and set up some interviews."

Gina walked over and shook the chief's hand as Macy introduced them. Gina held open a box of doughnuts, but neither Macy nor Lou wanted one.

"The manager of the bakery doesn't seem to know anything," said Gina.

Lou Turner pointed to the cameras mounted on the wall beneath the eaves.

"Did you ask her about the security cameras?"

"They're only there as a deterrent. The owners quit maintaining them a few years back."

Macy took off her sunglasses and polished them with the hem of her shirt. "Lou, if it's okay with you, Gina and I will go out to the house where Long was held. I really need to see it firsthand."

Lou jotted something down on a sheet of paper and handed it to Macy. "This is Carla and Lloyd's home address. Meet you there when you're done at the other house, around two?"

"That works for us. See you then."

# 3

Pulling over on a rough bit of road heading north toward the Canadian border, Emma Long checked the map. She leaned the tangled folds against the steering wheel and peered over her glasses every few seconds, studying the view. In the distance, the lonely silhouette of her hometown rose out of the landscape, and on either side of the car a patchwork of farmland rolled away like a quilt, flattening out across the wide valley, before giving way to high, crystallized peaks. But distant memories confused her sense of place. The scale was wrong and Walleye Junction's skyline wore an imperfect smile; in her absence someone had knocked out a few teeth.

Another mile on she realized what was missing from the view. The steeple from Walleye Junction's biggest church and the brick tower that marked the entrance to the town's cinema were both gone. Along with a rusted water tower and radio mast, they'd once formed the modest skyline that stood tall in her memories. In the years of her exile, her hometown had only made the national news once. In 2008 a gas line exploded on Main Street, punishing Jesus and celluloid in equal measure. The church, where she cursed quietly during prayers, and the cinema, where as a teenager she'd had her first fumbled sexual encounters, were both flattened in the explosion.

As she was about to take a right turn onto another farm track, a long-legged dog darted into the road. She yanked the steering wheel hard, clipping the animal on its hindquarter. It disappeared from sight and she skidded to a halt inches before the hard shoulder gave way to endless rows of cherry trees. Emma dipped her head to the steering wheel. For a few seconds she couldn't move. Her hands trembled when she put the car in reverse and backed away from the edge of the shallow ditch that cut into the soil following the orchard's boundary. A Winfrey Farm truck drove up just as she was opening the door. An old uneasiness took hold and she struggled to find her feet, standing up slowly and acknowledging the man sitting at the wheel with a tentatively raised hand. Technically speaking, she was on private land. She knew the owner, but they were not on good terms. The man remained in his truck, talking on his phone. She wondered what he would do when he found out her name.

A flatbed truck drove by, honking its horn and raising a cloud of dust. The smell of cherry blossoms rose up from the fields. Above the call of crows, she could hear the steady ticking of her car's motor. She pointed to the orchard and waved the man over. He nodded and put down the phone before exiting his vehicle in a way that seemed purposefully intimidating—straight backed, no smile, and checking his phone again before fully acknowledging her presence.

Their shared history snapped open like a pocketbook. Emma held her hand to her mouth, while her wide eyes said everything her lips could not. Nathan Winfrey was flesh and blood once more. His metal-framed sunglasses concealed his eyes. He looked her up and down, his face giving nothing away. This bothered her. She couldn't tell what kind of man he'd turned out to be.

"Welcome home," he said, his feet growing roots in the gravel where he stood.

Emma struggled to come up with a simple response. "I hit a dog," she said haltingly, once again pointing to the orchard. "It came out of nowhere."

While Emma peered over the side, ready to close her eyes at any hint of blood, Nathan jumped the narrow ditch without a second thought. He was already kneeling next to the dog before she had a chance to focus.

He shook his head, removing his hat in that dramatic way they do in movies. There was a bit of a smile on his face. "Em," he said softly, using the nickname she once loathed. "You're gone for twelve years and the first thing you do when you come back is run over Caleb's dog?"

The word *fuck* hung in the air between them like a swarm of blackfly. Emma never meant to say it out loud, but the sentiment escaped before she could snatch it back. Caleb Winfrey wasn't someone she wanted to see again. The dog stood up and looked around like it was lost before taking a few tentative steps toward the road.

"Will he live?" she asked hopefully.

"Yeah," he said, coaxing the dog to follow him back to where Emma was standing. "Looks like he's a little dazed though. I'll run him to the vet to be sure there's nothing more serious." He pushed his hair back off his face and put on his hat. "I'll tell Caleb that I found him here."

"You don't have to cover for me."

Nathan interrupted her. "You know it's for the best, so don't worry yourself. Damn kamikaze dog has had a death wish for years." He turned and looked her full in the face, removing his sunglasses for the first time. "Would be funny if you were the one to take him out."

Emma rubbed the tears from her eyes. "This doesn't feel like fun."

Nathan cocked his head to the side and watched her for a few moments. "I'm surprised you're only just getting here."

"Not as surprised as I am," she said, looking everywhere but at him. "I only found out what happened yesterday."

"I am sorry about your dad. Philip was a good man."

Her eyes settled on cherry blossoms. It was difficult to speak.

"How is your uncle anyway?" she asked.

"Caleb's in a nursing home. His health has deteriorated over the last few years. Two strokes so far." Nathan lowered his voice. "His memory comes and goes."

"I know we had our differences, but I wouldn't wish that on anyone. How are your mom and dad?"

"Fine. Fine." He squinted into the sun. "You know nothing around here changes much."

Emma pointed to his truck. "It looks like you're in charge of the farm now. That's something."

"By default. With Lucy gone there was no one to take over the business. I'm still a little surprised he's entrusted me to run things."

"You were like a son to him."

"Yeah, I guess so."

"I thought farming was what you always wanted to do," she said.

He looked to the horizon as if he was checking the weather. "You know what they say about being careful what you wish for."

Emma leaned against her car. She was vaguely aware of how she must have appeared. She raked her brown hair back from her face and fought the urge to straighten her blouse. There was a coffee stain running down one leg of her jeans. She'd been driving for twenty-four hours straight, dosed up on a tightly wound rotation of Red Bull and coffee. It was only a matter of miles before she collapsed.

"It's weird being back here after so many years. The distances are huge and yet everything feels so small."

"You'll get used to it by and by." He paused. "You talk to the police yet?"

"I've barely talked to my mother. Have you seen her lately?"

"Sometimes. Since she retired she and my mom spend more time together so I hear stuff. She volunteers down at the homeless shelter her church set up."

"Walleye has homeless people?"

"It's just a bunch of losers. As far as I can tell they're all on drugs."

"I wasn't expecting that."

"I think more come our way because of the shelter. It's not very Christian of me to say this, but I don't feel they deserve charity." He gave her red hatchback a quick glance. "Where are you living now anyway? It seems to be a different place every time I ask."

"San Francisco, but it's only temporary."

"You always wanted to get away from here."

Her voice was flat. "Not as much as you wanted to stay."

"Thought I might stop by your house this evening. We could talk. There's that business with Lucy. I feel there are some things that need to be said."

Emma pursed her lips. "Not sure that's a good idea. I don't know what things are like at home. Can I give you a call and let you know?"

"That's okay, I understand. Maybe another time then."

"I'm not blowing you off, Nathan. It's just that things have been strained between my mom and me for years. I don't know what to expect. I was actually thinking of staying at a hotel."

"You can't mean that. Your mother needs you there with her. I've heard she misses you." He gestured toward Walleye's broken skyline. "You go on now. She must be expecting you."

Emma hesitated, picking at a loose thread on her sleeve, watching the garment unravel between her fingers. "Yeah, I guess I better go. I haven't called her since I was in Spokane. She'll be worrying."

Nathan put a hand on her shoulder and leaned in so he could look her in the eye. "I want you to get in touch if you need anything. It may seem like you've been away a long time, but people still talk about you."

Emma's voice was sharp. "I bet they do."

"It's not like that. They're grieving. They want to know you and your mom are okay."

Emma kicked a dirt clod and nodded; speaking was impossible. Leaving him standing on the edge of the farm track, she set off toward the main road that cut through town. The last time she'd seen Caleb was at Lucy's funeral. Emma had been just shy of eighteen when she left town less than a week later. She glanced out the window. One side of Main Street was as she remembered it. The feed store, diner, the police station, and other businesses looked pretty much the same as they always had. The explosion had flattened the other side of the road, where there was now one long, ugly strip mall and a modern building made of glass, steel, and brick that took up a whole city block. Traffic was heavy and cars crammed into parking spaces. Walleye Junction had thrived despite her predictions to the contrary. At a traffic light, she took a left, heading four blocks up to her childhood home.

Pristine white and perched on a lawn of vivid green, the house she grew up in looked like it was recently unfolded from a pop-up book. Emma pulled into the driveway just as her mother, Francine, stepped out onto the front porch flanked by two women who looked vaguely familiar. They greeted Emma with hugs and quiet words before leaving with promises to return the next day. Francine clasped her daughter's hand, not letting go until they'd crossed the threshold and disappeared into the small, two-story time capsule. Flower arrangements were scattered about the living room and cards of condolence filled the mantelpiece. Otherwise, everything was as Emma remembered it, only smaller.

Emma fought the urge to hunch down low to avoid banging her head, even though there was a good foot and a half of clearance between her and the ceiling. She stepped lightly and spoke in a reverential whisper. She stared at her father's leather recliner. It didn't seem possible that something she remembered as brand new could have aged overnight. She didn't mean to say anything, but her thoughts pushed their way into the world.

"Mom, why didn't you call me sooner?"

"Pardon?"

Emma faced her mother. Francine gripped hold of the door frame with whitening knuckles. She looked as if she was about to collapse.

"Mom," said Emma, softening. "Here, let me help you."

Francine mumbled into a wadded-up handkerchief as she was led to the sofa.

"It's been so upsetting. I didn't know what to do."

"I feel awful. I should have been here to help you."

Francine shook her head hard. Her hair had come loose from where it had been pinned. Gray tendrils fell around her round face. Her makeup wasn't fully blended into her cheeks, but she'd dressed with care in a light gray pair of trousers and pale blue cardigan.

"I didn't think you cared anymore."

"Don't say that."

"I'll say it as I see it."

Emma had no answer. At some point Emma had gotten tired of being asked when she was coming home, and Francine had gotten tired of asking. After that, there wasn't much left to discuss during their phone calls. Her mother no longer came to see Emma so her father traveled alone. Despite his pleas to the both of them, the stalemate had lasted nearly six years.

"Well, I'm here now," said Emma.

"But you'll be gone tomorrow."

"It's been a long drive and I'm exhausted. I'm going to lie down for a while."

As Emma started to get up, Francine made a move to grab her daughter's hand. She seemed to want to say one thing, but then said something else.

"I didn't have time to make up your bed."

"I can manage. Do you need me to get you anything?"

Francine closed her eyes. "That won't be necessary. Some friends are arriving soon. I'm being well looked after."

Emma's parents had kept her bedroom exactly as she'd left it. Faded posters of forgotten pop stars and snapshots of childhood friends covered the walls. Photos of Lucy Winfrey were everywhere. Wading pools to ponies to prom—the entire arc of her friend's short life had been captured on Polaroid film. A framed picture of Emma and Nathan taken at their senior prom was on the dresser. She picked it up and traced a finger across their young faces before turning it around so she couldn't see it. On the bookshelf she found yellowing copies of teen magazines and paperbacks standing like soldiers in neat rows. She read the titles, flipping through the ones she still cherished, finding the odd phrase that took her back in time. A strip of photos fell from *A Handmaid's Tale*. They were taken in the photo booth in the foyer of the old cinema. Wrapped around each other behind the curtain, she and Lucy smiled into the camera. Nobody could see them in there. It wasn't the first time Lucy had tried to kiss her. They were in the tenth grade.

Emma went to find some bedding in the hall closet but ended up wandering into her parent's bedroom instead. Emma had vague memories of her mother's excitement when it was redecorated ten years earlier. An entire phone call had been spent discussing paint colors. Along with one of her father's white shirts, a dark suit hung from the closet door. Several of his ties were stretched across the bed. She picked up a blue one she remembered him wearing and held it up to the light. Downstairs the doorbell chimed. She put the tie around the collar of the shirt and left the room. Voices drifted up the stairwell. Her name was mentioned more than once.

"It was a long drive," said Francine. "Emma has gone up to rest."

The voices dropped to a whisper.

Emma went back to her room and quietly shut the door before climbing into the unmade bed. As soon as she closed her eyes miles of darkened highway came racing up to meet her. Her heart thumped wildly every time she imagined drifting out of her lane. Sleeper lines rumbled in her head. Headlights flashed in her eyes. She pulled the thin coverlet over her head and cried.

# 4

Macy stood in the doorway of the small storage room in the basement of Ron Forester's home, where Philip Long had been held captive. It had no windows, and other than a single mattress that had been taken from an upstairs bed, the room had been stripped down to its concrete floor. The storage boxes that once filled the space were stacked in the hallway. The door had recently been fitted with a padlock. Macy touched it with her gloved hands. It hadn't been forced and other than the smashed eyeglasses that were found on the steps and some broken furniture in the living room, there was no sign of a struggle.

"How do you think he managed to get out?"

Gina shrugged. "Maybe Lloyd and Carla were so off their heads they forgot to lock the door."

"It does appear that he walked out unchallenged." Macy glanced at the crime scene report. "They found his prints on the telephone in Forester's home office."

"Makes sense. It's right at the top of the basement stairs." Gina pointed out one of the wooden steps. "This where they found his broken glasses."

Macy trudged up the wooden steps with Gina following close behind.

"The medical examiner thinks he may have stepped on them. There were shards imbedded in his foot."

Ron Forester's vast mahogany desk took up half the space in the ground-floor office. French doors led out into the front garden. A small herd of elk grazed at the edge of the lawn; a calf stood in the shadow of one of the females. Dappled sunlight broke through the forest canopy. Macy focused in on the shadows. There were more elk moving through the trees. Behind her she could hear Gina opening and shutting desk drawers.

"It looks like most of the stuff has been cleared out already," said Gina.

Macy picked up the phone on the desk. Black powder coated the keypad and handset. When Philip Long dialed his home number the call went straight through to the police. He'd hesitated when he heard Macy's voice.

*Francine,* he'd said. *You need to . . . who is this?*

"I wonder why he called his wife first," said Macy. "He was practically blind without his glasses. Dialing 911 would have been a lot easier."

"If he was frightened he wouldn't have been thinking straight."

Macy put the phone down and turned to the French doors again. The keys were still in the lock. Philip Long's bare feet had left clear prints in the grit coating the covered wooden porch.

"A few seconds could have meant the difference between living and dying, but instead of running he called his wife."

"They were married for nearly forty years," said Gina. "Maybe he felt compelled to let her know that he was okay."

Most of the elk herd had migrated into the middle of the lawn, but a bull stood in the shadows beneath the trees. Their heads all shot up at once. They stared off into the woods that lined the western edge of the property before turning tail and running hard in the opposite direction. Macy watched for a few more seconds, but whatever had spooked them stayed hidden.

"Gina, how long have you been married?"

"Eight years this summer."

"That's impressive."

"He also works in law enforcement. I guess it helps."

"Would you have called him first?"

Gina looked up from where she was kneeling in front of an open drawer. "Hell no. I would have run."

"Same here."

Macy opened a low filing cabinet. Ron Forester kept meticulous records. There were several files documenting client entertainment events. She pulled out a recent one labeled Client Summer Party.

"I've already seen Ron Forester's client list," said Macy. "They're all high end. Doctors, lawyers, that sort of thing. Quite a few of them testified on his behalf. There seem to be a lot of people who think he was set up."

"Forester was tried and convicted of aggravated sexual assault. Until I learn otherwise I'll stick with the verdict on record." Gina slid open another desk drawer. "Maybe Lloyd did some maintenance work for Forester. Didn't Lou say that he used to be a roofer?"

"I haven't come across his name, but we should check it out. He or Carla may have been employed indirectly by someone Ron contracted to work for him." Macy put the party file on the desk. Along with a guest list there was an invoice from a catering company. A plastic sleeve contained a tightly bound stack of thank-you cards. "He hosted a lot of big client parties here. We should look at this catering company. They may have taken on temporary help."

Gina stood and stretched out her back. "There's nothing in the desk."

Macy untied the bundle of thank you cards and flipped through them. "From the tone of the thank-you notes I'd say he was on very good terms with his clients, especially their wives. All these seem to be written by women."

She held up one for Gina to see.

*Ron, Thanks again for throwing such a wonderful party. I'm so sorry we didn't have time for a quiet moment, but I love the idea of getting together for dinner. Sadly, Hal is away next month on business so he won't be able to join us. Shall we say Thursday the 11th? Until then. Julia xxx*

Gina smirked. "Not exactly subtle."

Macy put the file in an evidence folder. "She wasn't the only one. Cross-referencing his client list with the people that attended his parties on a regular basis will tell us who he was closest to. Maybe someone on that list held a grudge against Philip Long."

Gina switched off the light and shut the door behind them. "The only interesting thing the search turned up upstairs was some empty prescription bottles on the floor in the master bathroom. Lloyd's prints are all over them. He probably raided the medicine cabinet as soon as he got here."

"The home has been empty for a few months so I'm surprised no one beat him to it. Vicodin, Percocet, and Xanax are worth quite a bit on the street these days." Macy headed toward the stairs. "I'm going to go have a quick look upstairs anyway. Why don't you start on the kitchen?"

The king-size bed looked a little lost inside the vast master bedroom. Other than two bedside tables and a large flat-screen television, it was the only piece of furniture. The west-facing windows were at least twenty feet high and through the trees she could just make out the Flathead River. The plush cream-colored carpeting appeared to be new and other than a slight indentation on one of the pillows, the bed didn't look as if it had been slept in. The forensic team had checked for fibers, but aside from those belonging to the owner and those of a cleaning lady he'd once employed, it had come up clean. She knelt down at the foot of the bed to get a closer look. It was possible that Ron Forester had left the impression in the bedspread months earlier. It was barely noticeable. She checked the electrical socket beneath the bedside table. The alarm clock's plug had been pulled out. The forensics team had already dusted it for fingerprints. They'd found nothing.

The master suite bathroom was lined in white marble and the shower was so large you could park a small car in it. She flipped the mirrored cabinet doors open one by one, peering at her reflection when she was done. During the winter her freckles almost disappeared, but there were a few poking through. She combed loose strands of red hair back into the ponytail. Under the bright overhead lights she could clearly see the fine gray hairs that were just beginning to appear at her temples. She frowned. She barely had time to brush her hair, let alone get it colored.

Macy wandered downstairs where she found Gina staring into a Sub-Zero refrigerator.

"Anything edible in there?" asked Macy. "I'm getting hungry."

"Nothing I would eat. There is a considerable quantity of Red Bull if you're interested."

Macy peered over Gina's shoulder. Red Bull was lined up along one shelf in perfect rows.

"That looks like enough caffeine to keep you awake for a month."

"You'll be delighted to know that Ron Forester alphabetized his condiments."

"That's a career first," said Macy.

"They're past their sell-by dates by months so I assume they've been here all along." Gina poked at the half-empty takeaway containers. Noodles were spilling out the side and the refrigerator shelf was stained with sweet and sour sauce. "Carla and Lloyd Spencer were never going to win any Good Housekeeping awards."

Macy walked past a sink full of dirty dishes and countertops covered in grease. What looked like spilled cornflakes was in fact the remnants of a bag of corn chips that had been strewn across the counter. Two triangles of burned toast sat alone on a plate.

The double-height windows that ran along the western side of the living room were coated with fine dust. According to initial findings, Carla Spencer and her husband, Lloyd, had slept on the downstairs sofas, but Carla's DNA and several fingerprints had been found in an upstairs bedroom as well. A dining chair was tipped on its side and an alabaster Buddha had been used to smash the glass coffee table. There was also an overturned lamp near the fireplace. The stained-glass lampshade had shattered in the fall. Gina walked around the back of the sofa for a better look.

"I don't understand why the crime techs made such a big deal about this lamp," said Gina. "It looks like someone tripped over the cord."

"Say there was a struggle. Why would someone throw a stone statue through a coffee table?"

"It looks like someone got pissed off and decided to trash the place."

"Since we didn't find Philip Long's fingerprints anywhere in this room, I'd say that's a pretty likely scenario."

Macy stared down at the unfinished solitaire game spread out on the dining table, impulsively checking the remaining playing cards in the stack.

"Only a few cards away from winning," Macy said, flipping through them three at a time.

Gina held up the empty playing card box. Its plastic sleeve was still attached. "Brand new and available in thousands of retail outlets. Not a single fingerprint."

Macy kept seeing moments of order amid the disorder. It was starting to make her think she was missing something or someone.

"Carla and Lloyd Spencer's prints are all over the house, so why not here?" Macy held up a crime scene photo. "This is what the playing cards looked like before they dusted them. Every one of them is perfectly aligned." She gestured toward the open plan kitchen. "Meanwhile there are unwashed dishes in the kitchen sink, congealed food left on the stove, and wet towels on the bathroom floor."

"Do you think there was someone else in the house?"

"I keep going back to that night on the road. I'm not sure an unemployed drug addict could have pulled off something like that. Whoever killed Philip Long was in complete control."

"Could it have been Carla?" said Gina. "She was motivated. She wanted her kids back."

Macy closed her eyes for a second. "All that motorcycle gear on, I really can't say for sure if it was a man or a woman." She hesitated. "I'd say the killer was slim and of average height. For lack of a better word I'd say he or she moved with grace."

"Both Carla and Lloyd Spencer were thin. How tall was the shooter? I think you said around five nine."

"I was hanging upside down in the dark, so five nine was a guess at best, but I'd swear that they were a few inches shorter than Philip Long. We need to find out if Carla and Lloyd rode motorcycles. Philip was chased through the woods on a dirt bike. That takes some skill. Plus there's the placement of their bodies. I'm convinced someone moved them." Macy tapped the envelope of crime scene photos against the edge of the table. "So, for argument's sake let's say that there's a third party. Why did he need help from a couple of drug addicts?"

"Maybe he's an outsider. They'd have local knowledge."

"Then how did they meet him?"

"Buying drugs is a dangerous business. Every time you score you're putting yourself at risk."

"So, a dealer who is at home on a bike."

"It could be gang related."

Macy made a face. "God, I hope not. The bike gangs running heroin through Montana originate out of state. We'd have to bring in pretty much every law enforcement agency known to mankind." Macy turned her back on the solitaire game. "I think I've seen enough. We should get going."

Gina held up the car keys. "Where to next?"

Macy checked the time.

"Let's grab some lunch before we head up to meet Lou at Carla and Lloyd's place. I'm starving."

"Are you sure you don't want some leftover Chinese?" asked Gina.

"Not even if it's alphabetized."

They found Lou Turner in the Spencer's garage looking over a dirt bike that appeared to have been recently driven off a showroom floor.

"Detective Greeley," asked Lou. "Could this be the bike you saw that night?"

Macy shook her head. "I don't know. It was out of my sight line. We lifted some tire impressions though. Might be able to find a match that way." She knelt down to take a closer look. "This looks like it's been cleaned recently. Who's the owner?"

"Carla's teenage son, Sean. Turns out he's quite good on a bike. Lots of trophies in his room."

"I wonder how he is with a gun," asked Macy. "How old did you say he was?"

"Old enough. He turned nineteen in March."

"Have you brought him in?"

Lou gestured toward the empty driveway. "His truck is gone and it doesn't look like anyone has been home for a few days. I've put an APB out on him."

"Do we have a phone number for him?" asked Gina.

"Yep, but he's not answering," said Lou. "We found a few pay-as-you-go phones in the house so it's possible he's using one."

"Did you get anything off them?" asked Macy.

"We'll see, but I wouldn't hold your breath. They appear to have been wiped clean." Lou started walking toward the house. "They're bagging everything in the house worth taking—two computers so far, but they're ancient. We found a thick folder containing Lloyd Spencer's medical history. Until seven years ago he was fully employed. Then he rolled his quad bike up near Darby Lake and messed up his back. He could barely walk without a cane. No way he was riding that bike."

"What about Carla?"

"We'll interview her friends and family. Someone should know."

"Did you find the gear the shooter was wearing? I've been looking into different makes. I think a company called Alliance probably manufactured it. It's pretty high end and has a distinctive logo."

"Plenty of gear inside the house, but so far I don't think they've found anything made by Alliance."

"Sean could have dumped the gear," suggested Gina.

"Then why not get rid of the bike too?" said Lou.

"The fact that it's so clean is suspicious," said Macy. "How many teenagers do you know who take such good care of their stuff?"

Lou led Macy and Gina to the side entrance of the house. "Sean Spencer may be the world's only exception. Compared to the rest of the house, his room is rather well kept."

Macy slipped on a pair of shoe coverings before entering the one-story ranch house through the kitchen door. The smell of spoiled food was so strong she covered her mouth. The queasiness that had hit her so hard on the drive up from Helena was back. She stepped around what looked like engine parts and nearly tripped over a pile of discarded pizza boxes. There wasn't a square inch of the kitchen and living room that wasn't covered with clutter.

"It sure looks like the family went downhill in a hurry," said Macy.

Gina opened a cupboard and a box of cereal tumbled out.

"Carla may have been in rehab, but if this house is anything to go by I'd say she was losing that battle."

"Macy," said Lou. "I spoke to the head of the center where Carla attended counseling. She's expecting your call."

"Did she have any insight?" asked Macy

"She said it wouldn't be the first time they've been fooled by an addict. Carla was also attending a twelve-step recovery group that meets in the church on Main. I'll get the name of her sponsor."

"Might be worth attending a meeting to see who shows up," said Gina.

"I'll see what I can do," said Lou. "They have a tendency to scatter when law enforcement arrive."

Macy could see nothing but sadness. She picked up a child's drawing. Five stick figures stood in front of a brightly painted house. The two smallest figures were almost identical except one was pink and one was blue. Carla Spencer had a crayon red mouth and long golden hair.

"Whoever is fostering the younger children needs to be informed," said Macy. "Sean may try to make contact."

Lou found a remote control and turned on the television. There was only static.

Ryan entered the living room, looking flustered. "It will take us ages to process this mess." He handed Lou a stack of unopened bills. "Internet and cable have also been disconnected. We're lucky they still have power."

"Anything aside from the discarded cell phones that strikes you as interesting?" asked Macy.

"I've been working in Sean's room." Ryan led them down a dark hallway. "The boy was obsessed with three things—bikes, girls, and keeping a well-ordered world."

"Two out of three are normal," said Macy. "Anything else?"

"A couple drawers have been cleared out and there's no laptop. Our boy may have left in a hurry."

"Are you sure there was a computer?" asked Lou.

"Cables are still there," said Ryan.

Sean's room didn't fit in with the rest of the house. The first thing Macy noticed was that the door could be locked from both the inside and the outside. The bed was made with care and the remaining clothes in the dresser were folded neatly. Posters of everything from dirt bikes to heavy metal bands covered the walls. Trophies he'd won in competitions filled a low set of bookshelves.

Macy picked up a framed photo.

"Is this Sean?" she asked. "He looks about ten years old here."

Lou nodded. "Yes, that's him."

Sean was a dark-eyed boy with a shock of black hair and an easy smile. He stood with an older man who had his arm draped casually around the boy's shoulders. The background was filled with mountains and motorcycles. There was definitely a family resemblance. Macy turned over the frame and took the picture out. There was no writing on the back.

"I see a family resemblance. Could this be Sean's real father?"

"Not sure," said Lou. "There's no father listed on his birth certificate and for the past ten years Sean has used Lloyd's surname."

"And before that?"

"Carla's."

Macy pointed to a collage of snapshots that was taped to the wall. Blue eyed and sparrow thin, a bleached-blond female with a quirky fashion sense pulled a selection of purposefully awkward faces in many of the photos.

"Do we have any idea who this girl is?"

Lou peeled off a photo that was above Macy's line of sight and handed it to her. "This one has Xtina xxx written across the bottom. Could be short for Kristina. Doesn't look like your typical local girl."

"We should check his school anyway," said Macy. "She might have been there at the same time as Sean."

Ryan held up a framed high school diploma. "Sean graduated a year ago. He's due to start school at Montana State University in Bozeman this fall. Seems like he was trying to rise above all this. It would be a shame if he was involved."

Lou Turner placed the photo of Kristina into an evidence bag. "He probably took a year off school to earn some money. He sure as hell wasn't going to get anything from Carla and Lloyd."

Macy gazed at the carefully organized desk and couldn't help but think of the solitaire game. Future university student or not, Sean was starting to look interesting.

She glanced up at Lou. He seemed deep in thought. "We need to find Sean," she said. "Have you started interviewing friends and family yet?"

Lou nodded. "It's a large and unruly clan. I'm afraid we've got a rather packed schedule this afternoon."

Carla Spencer's older sister, Donna, lived with her husband in a mobile home that was parked within yards of Route 93. Macy left Gina in the car so she could start making some inquiries over the phone and went in to meet them on her own. They'd both been on disability for years. Donna sat in a reclining armchair elevating her swollen ankles. The bedroom door was ajar and through the opening Macy could see the flickering light of a television screen.

"Jay's tired," Donna said. She straightened the gray sweatshirt that kept riding up her belly. "If you want to talk to him, you'll need to come back tomorrow." She took a sip of the coffee Macy had prepared and grimaced. "Needs more sugar."

Macy was perched on the narrow sofa. She'd had to lean forward to avoid the three cats that were lying on the top of the backrest catching the afternoon sun. The home was clean but cluttered. Stacks of everything from hubcaps to newspapers to overstuffed garbage bags were squeezed into every available crevice. Beyond the back fence eighteen-wheelers passed within twenty feet of the home, rattling the dishes stacked next to the sink.

"Donna," said Macy, eyeing what looked like cat hair floating in her coffee. "When was the last time you saw your sister?"

Jay shouted from the bedroom. "Every time Carla's rent was due she'd come here asking for money."

Donna rolled her eyes. "Jay, keep your trap shut. That's family business."

"Actually," said Macy, putting her cup down. "That's the type of thing we need to know."

"My sister and her husband overdosed on drugs. What business is their financial situation to you?"

"As we're in the middle of an active investigation I'm not at liberty to say."

Donna pursed her lips. "Six months ago they tried to get us to take their kids off them. Like we have any room here. We can barely feed ourselves on our disability checks. No way we could have afforded a bigger place."

"The state has since put them into care," said Macy.

"Oh, I know all about that. It was me that let the police know how bad things had gotten over at their place. Imagine being so obsessed with getting your next fix that you're willing to sell your kids."

Macy's pen floated in the air. She'd thought she'd heard it all, but apparently not.

Donna sniffed into a tissue. "When Lloyd wasn't using he was mean as fuck. Those kids needed to get out of there. I warned my sister that it was either Lloyd or her babies and she chose Lloyd. There was no way she was ever going to get clean with him still living there."

The bedroom door opened and Jay stood in the threshold. He had tubes coming out of his nose and wheeled an oxygen tank with him into the room. Macy moved up to make room for him on the sofa. The cats scattered as soon as he sat down. His hair was thin and gray and he smelled strongly of cigarettes and alcohol. Open sores covered his wrists. He yanked down his shirtsleeves to hide them.

"I thought I'd better get in here before Donna mouths off and says something she regrets later," he said.

"You're one to talk," said Donna.

"Well," he said, breaking into a toothless smile. "At least I'm not all talk."

Macy tried again. "What kind of money were they asking for?"

"Last time it was three grand," Jay snorted. "Seriously, where in the hell did they think we were going to get that kind of money?"

"To be fair," said Donna, shifting her weight one buttock at a time, "Carla was really broken up when she lost her kids. I heard she got herself into a recovery program. I was hopeful it was the kick up the backside she needed."

Jay rubbed his nose. "Serves them right losing their kids. They don't deserve them. Not after what happened."

"That's enough, Jay. We're talking about my dead baby sister here."

Macy tapped the table with her pen. "Did something happen that we need to know about?"

"Nah," said Jay, adjusting the tubes going up his nose. "Nothing specific. Same shit, different day, near as I can tell. Always fucking everything up."

"Did Carla ride a dirt bike?"

Donna frowned. "She once did a fair amount, but it's been years ago now. Sean is the one who rides. Took after his father, which considering what a loser Carla turned out to be, is just as well."

"Do either of you know where we can find Sean?" asked Macy.

Donna looked at Jay and Jay shrugged.

"Our son, Kyle, might know," said Donna "When things got rough at home Sean crashed at Kyle's place. Might be there now."

Macy handed Donna a pen and a pad of paper. "Do you mind jotting down his details?"

Donna wrote with a firm hand. "I'll give you his work number as well. He's been away in Missoula visiting friends, but he arrived back today. Good boy, that one."

Macy held up a photo of Sean's girlfriend, Kristina. "Do either of you recognize this girl? She may be in a relationship with Sean."

Jay and Donna took turns looking at the photo. Jay frowned and Donna squinted.

"Carla didn't say anything to us about her," said Donna.

"Did Sean get along with his mother?"

"They fought, but considering the situation with Lloyd, that's hardly surprising. I know he loved his mother, but there was only so much he could take. Sean learned not to rely on Carla a long time ago. He brought his brother and sister here on more than one occasion."

"What about his relationship with Lloyd?"

Jay coughed into his hand. "Lloyd beat him up pretty bad a couple of times."

"Did anyone report it?" asked Macy.

The pair remained silent and Macy guessed that was a *no*.

"Did Sean have much contact with his real father?"

Another shrug from Jay. "Scott knew to stay clear of that house."

"You know him?"

"Not well. It's been a good ten years since I saw him last."

"Got a last name?" asked Macy

Jay shook his head and Donna remained tight-lipped.

Macy gathered her things. "I really appreciate you taking the time to speak to me." She handed a business card to both Jay and Donna. "I'll be in touch. Please let me know if you hear from Sean."

Macy sat alone at a table near the coffee shop's front windows watching the entrance to Flathead Valley Security, where Donna had said her son Kyle worked. Situated in a strip mall that ran along Main Street, the company was wedged between a Mexican restaurant and a dry cleaner. The door opened and a slightly built man with blond hair stepped out with two females. Both women gave him long hugs. He smiled as he spoke to them, but his expression darkened once he set off across the road. Dressed in a polo shirt and pair of freshly pressed chinos, he had the air of someone who took life seriously. Macy noted that his posture was slightly askew. His left shoulder drooped. According to his parents, Kyle Miller was twenty-nine, but Macy would have never guessed it. Kyle didn't look old enough to buy a beer.

The woman behind the counter joked with him.

"What's gotten into you? This isn't your usual time."

Kyle gestured toward the only occupied table. "Client meeting."

"Sweetheart, you go on. I'll bring your coffee over."

Macy rose from her chair and held out her hand. "Thank you for coming to meet me."

He winced. "Sorry," he said, rotating his shoulder and making a face. "Do you ever get frozen shoulder?"

They sat down across from each other.

"On occasion," said Macy. "It's awful."

"It's from sitting at a computer all day. It's been worse than ever this spring."

"Do you take anything for it?"

"Addiction runs in my family. Medication is not an option."

"I'm sorry. This must be difficult for you."

He reached for a napkin and pressed it to his eyes. "You have no idea. We've had near misses in emergency rooms, interventions, incarcerations." He paused. "And now this."

"I heard your parents have had issues in the past."

"They're okay now, but I have to be vigilant. My mother is finally off her meds, but Dad still slips occasionally. He has a problem with the bottle. I've been working with them. We pray together. I'd like to think it helps."

Macy gave him a small smile. "You sound more like a minister than a computer engineer."

"I guess you could call it social engineering. I like to help out in the community where I can. Mentoring, sponsoring at AA, that sort of thing. I'm worried about what I'm seeing."

"And what are you seeing?"

"Now that the government has realized they've got a crisis on their hands they're handling it all wrong. They're cutting off the supply of prescription painkillers without funding programs that could help people who've become addicted to opiates. People are turning to heroin instead." He took a deep breath. "It's incredibly frustrating."

"There's been a spike in heroin overdoses throughout the country."

"Is that what killed Carla and Lloyd?"

"We believe so."

"Carla was in rehab. I was so hopeful she'd turned a corner."

Kyle looked up at the approaching waitress and smiled as she handed him a mug of coffee the size of his head.

"Thank you." Kyle took a sip of his coffee. "This is my only addiction."

"I like to live dangerously. I mix it up with a little Diet Coke."

"Now, that is living on the edge."

"Kyle, when did you last speak to your aunt and uncle?"

"Carla came by a couple weeks ago. She apologized for Lloyd showing up the day before asking for money and then went and did the same thing. The only difference was that Lloyd threatened me with physical violence and Carla used emotional blackmail."

"Did they give any indication that they might be planning something?"

Kyle raised an eyebrow. "Like a suicide pact?"

"No, like a kidnapping."

He took a quick glance around the room before lowering his voice.

"Excuse me," he said, leaning in close.

"Kyle," she said, keeping a close eye on his reaction. "Your aunt and uncle were involved in Philip Long's kidnapping and murder. Their fingerprints are all over the house where he was held and the stolen van that was used in his abduction was parked near their bodies this morning."

"That's crazy. They wouldn't—"

"I realize that it's a lot to take in, but we really need your help."

He raised his voice. "Where's Sean? Is he okay?"

"I was just going to ask you that."

He made a sudden move for his pocket and Macy almost reached for her gun. Oblivious, he pulled out a cell phone and tapped in a message.

"Sean will call me back right away. We've always been close."

"Would he have confided in you if he was worried about his parents?"

"I hope so. I'd like to think he trusts me. I gave him a key to my new place so he could come use it whenever things got too rough at home. When I got back from Missoula this morning, I could tell that he'd stayed over." He frowned. "He didn't leave a note though."

"Was that unusual?"

"Sean is always compensating for his parents' behavior. Generally speaking he's very well-mannered."

"Did Sean use drugs?"

Kyle hesitated. "Not in the past, but I've been worried about him for a while now. He has a new girlfriend. She seems the sort who could get him a lot of trouble."

"You've met her?"

"Briefly. I think her name was Kristina, but she goes by Xtina or something silly like that. Sean said she was an event planner."

Macy raised an eyebrow.

"My reaction exactly," said Kyle. "The girl looked more like a prostitute than someone who would plan a wedding."

"Did you catch her last name?"

"No, but she had an accent. Sean said she was Latvian. Not a lot of those in Montana."

"I imagine not. We found a lot of guns stashed up at Carla and Lloyd's house. I take it Sean learned to shoot."

"We all learn to shoot around here. It doesn't make us criminals." Kyle picked up his cell phone and stared at his screen. "Sean is a good kid. He would have never gotten involved in something like this."

"Do you know anything about Carla and Lloyd's militia group?"

Kyle smirked. "I don't like to speak ill of the dead, but you're not giving me much choice here. My aunt and uncle weren't the brightest of souls. Sean told me about the meetings they were having up at the house so I made sure I was around for one. It was just a bunch of drug addicts who seemed more intent on getting another fix than organizing an insurgency."

"Was Sean involved in the group?"

"He was drawn to it when he was younger, but he soon saw it for what it was. Not that his opinion mattered. Lloyd insisted that he go to the meetings."

"Kyle, it's important that you let me know the minute Sean contacts you. We have reason to believe that Carla and Lloyd Spencer had an accomplice. We'd like nothing more than to rule Sean out."

Kyle ran his fingers along the edge of the table. "What makes you think there was someone else?"

"I'm not at liberty to say. Do you know if Carla was any good on a dirt bike?"

He rubbed his right shoulder with his left hand. "How do you mean?"

"I understand she used to have one, but she's not ridden recently. Do you know anything about that?"

"I saw her on a dirt bike a few weeks back. She seemed pretty competent to me."

"Where was this?"

"Out on the trails near the footbridge, north of town."

"That's a pretty isolated area."

"There's a lot of homeless camping out that way. My church group goes out every week to distribute food and clothing. I focus on getting counseling for anyone who has addiction issues."

"Was Carla competent on the bike?"

"It's pretty rugged down that way. I'd say she had to be."

"Who was she with?"

He hesitated. "I'm not sure. The guy was wearing a helmet. I wasn't introduced."

Macy pulled an image of the Alliance logo out of her file.

"Does this logo look familiar to you? Could either Carla or the man she was with have been wearing gear with this logo on it?"

"Maybe," said Kyle. "Hard to say. It all looks the same to me."

"Do you ride a motorbike, Kyle?"

"Not for a long time. Wiping out on one is what messed up my shoulder in the first place."

"I understand you've spent the past week in Bozeman."

"Actually, it was Missoula. I was visiting friends." He picked up his cell phone again. "I'm guessing you need proof."

"I'm afraid so."

Kyle wrote down a few names and numbers on a napkin and handed it to Macy.

"Thank you, Kyle. I appreciate your cooperation."

"You're just doing your job."

"Do you know if Sean has had any contact with his real father recently?"

"Scott showed up in Sean's life just long enough to give Sean an idea of what he'd been missing when he got stuck with Lloyd as a stepfather," said Kyle. "As far as I know, Sean hasn't seen him since he was ten."

"Do you know Scott's last name? Sean may have tried to get in touch with him."

"I really don't think Sean had anything to do with this."

"We just want to speak to Sean," said Macy. "At this point he's not a suspect."

"His father's name is Scott Walker."

"Is that all you have?"

"That might be all there is. He's a survivalist who lives off the grid."

"They never make my job easy."

"I imagine not."

Macy checked her notes. "How long have you worked at Flathead Valley Security?"

"Since I finished university, so going on nine years now. I mostly deal with their computer systems. Because most of the properties are so isolated we have remote monitoring in place twenty-four seven. There's always some bug that needs fixing. We also do private security for events, banks, that sort of thing. You should see the size of some of the guys we employ. They make me look like a boy scout."

"Have you ever had any dealings with a company called Mountain Security?"

"They're our main competition in the valley."

"Do you share information?" asked Macy.

"Not if we want to keep our jobs. As far as my boss is concerned Mountain Security is the enemy." Kyle rolled his eyes. "There's a lot of testosterone floating around over there at the office—ex military, ex cops. They all seem to think this is Mogadishu or something. Our crime rates are lower than the national average, but you wouldn't know it from how they're always going on."

"Even New York's crime rate is dropping."

"If this keeps up we'll all be put out of business."

"I somehow doubt it will come to that."

Kyle checked his watch. "I sure hope not. I need this job. I'm still paying off my student loans."

Macy started gathering her things.

"I'd like you to keep what I've told you about Lloyd and Carla's involvement to yourself for the time being."

"That won't be a problem," said Kyle. "I'm in no hurry for this to become public. It's been difficult explaining my family in the past. I can only imagine what people will say this time."

Aiden picked Macy up at her hotel room at half past nine. She was so tired she'd nearly canceled, but something told her she'd better make the effort.

"I've only just got back from doing interviews. I haven't even had a chance to take a shower."

Aiden put his arms around her. "You are kind of smelly."

She pressed her cheek into his freshly washed T-shirt. "And you smell annoyingly clean. Laundry detergent is such a turn on."

"I'll remember that for next time," he said, taking her bag and leading her to a pickup truck she didn't recognize.

"You've bought a new truck."

"Not so new. It's got over twenty thousand miles on it. Picked it up at a dealership in Collier."

"I know the one," said Macy. "Does Toby Larson still own it?"

"Yeah, I got his whole song and dance. He's quite the salesman. Gave me a good deal though."

"That's not surprising. He likes to keep law enforcement happy."

"That's why I went there." Aiden opened Macy's door and placed her bag in the backseat. "Are you still hungry?"

"They ordered in pizza at the office, but I resisted."

"Good girl."

Macy checked her messages as she settled into her seat. Ryan had sent her an e-mail. He agreed that Carla and Lloyd's bodies had probably been moved but wanted to run some more tests to be sure. She watched Aiden as he scanned the screen of his own phone. His eyes lit up and he burst out laughing.

"What's so funny?" she said.

He shrugged. "It's nothing. Just something the guys at work said. Not fit for female consumption."

Macy noticed that his forehead was flushed red. She pressed her finger to it and the skin went white. "Looks like you caught some sun."

"That's pretty much all I caught."

"No fish."

"Nothing worth keeping. I picked up a couple of steaks." He switched on the radio. "I hope that's okay."

"I never complain when someone offers to cook dinner."

He tuned the radio to a local music station but kept the sound down low. "We can talk about the case. I know it's all you've got on your mind."

"It takes time to process everything."

"Feel free to process out loud."

"I want my gun back. I hate to think that someone could use it again."

He squeezed her hand. "This isn't your fault."

"I ran over an innocent man before he was shot to death with my firearm."

"Your gun was in the glove compartment. You couldn't have known it would end up in the middle of Route 93."

Macy closed her eyes for a second. "Sorry, but there are only so many technicalities you can get away with in life. This isn't one of them."

"I get it. I'd feel the same way if I were you, but at least you know the perpetrators are dead."

She checked the rearview mirror out of habit. All she could see was the white glow of a pair of trailing headlights.

"I'm not so sure."

"I thought things were looking pretty straightforward. Carla and Lloyd kidnap Philip Long hoping to make a quick buck and when it all goes wrong they take the easy way out."

"There may have been a third party involved in the kidnapping, and

Carla and Lloyd's deaths are a little more suspicious than we first thought. Their bodies were moved, and I'm not convinced either one of them had the skills needed to pull off what happened the night Philip Long was murdered."

He glanced over at her.

"About seven years back Lloyd injured his back in a quad bike accident," Macy said. "He couldn't have ridden the motorbike, and only one person has seen Carla on a bike in the past ten years."

"I noticed an APB was out on their son."

"It looks like he cleared out a few days ago. He stayed at his cousin's place, but the trail goes cold after that."

"Could be a coincidence."

"He's got a dirt bike and a shelf full of trophies," said Macy.

"He must be fairly young though."

"He's nineteen."

"Does anyone in the family know where he's gone?" asked Aiden.

"Half the family is in rehab or recovering addicts and the other half are using. There have been a couple of other accidental overdoses and a suicide. It's depressing as hell. Aside from Sean's cousin, Kyle, they all seem to be on disability."

"Was Sean using?"

"Seems he was clean in more ways than one. His room was a world apart—completely different from the rest of the family home. I can't imagine what it would be like to grow up in a place like that. I'd have never felt secure."

"I've seen it before," said Aiden. "Kids in those situations can become obsessed with creating order. It's their way of coping. More often than not they're the ones who are looking after their parents and not the other way around."

"He graduated from high school last year and was due to start university in Bozeman this fall. Looks like he took a year off to make some money."

"Did someone speak to his employer?"

Macy nodded. "He was a parts runner for Midas. The manager said he was a perfect employee. Handed in his notice two weeks ago."

"Did he say why he was quitting?"

"Nothing concrete, but the manager did get the impression that things were stressful at home. Lloyd showed up a few times asking for Sean. They argued about money. On more than one occasion Lloyd called his stepson an ungrateful little shit."

"Sounds like he left empty-handed."

"Also sounds like they wouldn't have worked well together," said Macy.

"But you've got to admit that Sean has motive and opportunity. University is expensive."

"At one level it makes sense, but on another I don't see it."

"How do you mean?"

"Philip Long's killer didn't hesitate. It was the most cold-blooded thing I've ever seen in my life. It's difficult for me to reconcile what I saw that night with what I know about Sean. He's a nineteen-year-old kid from Walleye Junction who was saving up for university."

"Have you interviewed Philip Long's wife? Maybe there's a connection between the Spencer family and Philip Long we don't know about."

"I'm stopping in tomorrow. The militia angle also needs to be explored further. It turns out Lloyd was a caller on Philip Long's radio program a month ago. He took issue with Long's views on the private militia movement. The ensuing argument got ugly."

"I can only imagine," said Aiden.

"I'm paraphrasing here, but I believe Lloyd said something like *show your face around here saying that sort of crap and I'll make sure you've got shit for brains*."

"Nice."

"A regular Cary Grant. He didn't give his real name, but the Spencer's home number showed up on caller ID."

"They didn't think that through very well."

"By the way, Lloyd and Carla's cell phones are missing. The ones we found at their house were temporary pay-as-you-go and they've been wiped clean."

"Maybe they weren't so stupid after all," said Aiden.

Aiden exited Route 93 and headed toward Wilmington Creek. Instead of turning on Main Street, he took a back road that passed in front of the town's high school. The school marquee announced an upcoming high school basketball game against Walleye Junction.

"Growing up here in the valley, did you ever come across Emma Long?"

He made a face. "I've heard some stuff about her, but she was quite a few years behind me in school so we never met. There was a rumor going around that she was gay. People said some pretty unkind things."

"You've got a good memory."

"Since the news broke about her father people have started talking again."

"Which is probably why she's not lived here since leaving high school." Macy held back a yawn. "It may not even be true."

"Who knows? Apparently, she used to date the high school quarterback. Apparently, he's still heartbroken. Blah blah blah."

"Sounds like a soap opera."

"Speaking of which, how are you holding up?" asked Aiden. "Everyone being nice to you at your new job?"

"No, not everyone."

"You're going to have to let me know if someone's ass needs kicking."

"Thank you for the kind offer, but I can kick ass all on my own." Macy took his hand. "All joking about ass-kicking aside, I've brought this on myself. I'm a walking, talking cliché. Affair with married boss, child born out of wedlock, single mom."

"It's going to be rough. No matter what the facts are, some people will only see the story they want to see."

"I don't even blame them," said Macy. "I'd feel the same way if I was looking at the situation from the outside. Getting involved with Ray was incredibly stupid."

"But getting a confession out of him was incredibly brave. You put yourself out there when you didn't have to. The right people will remember that."

It was almost ten when Aiden pulled into the driveway of his one-story home. A trailer holding a drift boat was backed into the front yard. Macy grabbed her bag and stepped outside. They both stopped to admire the boat.

"Nice landscaping. Marsh. Very classy."

He pulled her along to the house. "In these parts that qualifies as a lawn ornament."

Twenty minutes later Macy stood in the living room wearing a pair of baggy sweatpants and one of Aiden's T-shirts. Her hair was still wet and she'd not bothered with makeup. The wooden floorboards felt cool and clean against her bare feet. Aiden was working in the kitchen. His back was to her and he'd not heard her come in. Jazz was playing on the stereo. She picked up the remote control and turned down the volume. Aiden's voice filled the room.

"Don't tell me that you don't like John Coltrane?" He handed her a glass of red wine. "I thought you might be needing this."

Macy took the glass of wine and lied. "John Coltrane is fine. It's just a little loud."

"I can change it if you like."

She noticed that he'd gone to the trouble of setting the dining room table.

"I've brought no wine and I'm wearing a pair of baggy sweats. What on earth do you see in me, Aiden Marsh?"

He kissed her for a long time. "You're talking to a guy with a fishing boat parked on his front yard. As far as I'm concerned you always look great." He kissed her again. "Taste great too."

Macy put her glass aside and leaned into his chest so she could listen to his heart. Same sound, different man. The fact that he and Ray both listened to Coltrane was irrelevant. Aiden was different. Very different. She'd never met someone so ready to keep the peace. It even bothered her sometimes. On occasion she'd found herself being contrary for the sake of it, but he'd never taken the bait. He'd laughed and told her to grow up.

He kissed the top of her head.

"What's going on in that pretty little red head of yours?"

She lowered her voice. "I was just wondering when dinner was going to be ready."

"That's entirely up to you."

"In that case," she said, locking her expression in neutral. "There's something important we need to discuss."

He hesitated. "Is this about the case or is this about us?"

"I'm afraid it's about us."

He held up his glass of wine. "Should I pour something stronger? If I'm going to get dumped I want to be drinking something manly like whiskey."

"Don't be ridiculous. I'm the whiskey drinker in this relationship."

"Okay," he said, pulling away. "A beer then."

She held on. "Don't go. This was just getting interesting."

She stood up on tiptoe and they kissed again.

He smiled. "Are we about to have breakup sex?"

"We'd have to break up in order for that to happen."

"In that case, Macy Greeley, will you break up with me?"

She poked him in the ribs. "You haven't even let me tell you my news."

"I was trying to avoid that. You're kind of scary when you're serious."

Macy nodded. "Very scary."

"Should I sit down for this?"

She pressed her palms against his chest and held them there. "I have a feeling you'd prefer to take it lying down."

"You should know that I'm seconds away from throwing you over my shoulder and carting you off to my bedroom caveman style."

She grabbed a fistful of his shirt and pulled him closer. "You have to be gentle. I'm still a little bruised."

"I'll keep that in mind. So what's this big secret?"

She stood on her tiptoes so she could whisper in his ear.

"You know that lingerie you saw online," she said.

He gazed up at the ceiling like he was giving it some thought. "I tend to see a lot of lingerie online," he said. "You'll have to remind me."

She pulled up her sweatshirt a few inches to reveal the black camisole she was wearing underneath.

"I may have come empty-handed," she said, sliding back into his arms. "But I'm wearing very nice underwear."

# 5

Emma and Francine ate supper at the kitchen table, reheating a casserole a neighbor had left earlier in the day. Above the clatter of cutlery, they talked around their grief, not quite ready to claim it as their own. A radio played gospel, and the occasional car bathed the front of the house with fractured light before disappearing with a soulful whoosh. In the hall, the old clock marked time, and as the hour grew later the walls pressed in on Emma. Her mood shifted along with the boundaries that separated her from Walleye Junction. She'd walked away, but now the town was closing in on her, making it seem like she'd never left. With Francine in her shadow, she drifted around the house like a restless spirit, laying on hands, trying to find some connection to the past that didn't hurt like hell.

Standing by her bedroom window staring out into the darkness, Emma couldn't help but think that she'd come full circle. All these years later and she had more questions than ever. The familiar ache of loneliness sat alongside her grief. She couldn't see a way past it.

She made up her bed with the sheets her mother had left on the chest of drawers. The picture of her and Nathan was once again facing the world. In a bid to keep the peace with Francine she left it where it was. By habit she reached for her laptop, but then changed her mind. That world could wait and for that matter so could her boss.

She sifted through the clothing in her suitcase, dropping stacks of neatly folded shirts and trousers into empty dresser drawers. She hung up the black dress she'd brought for the funeral. It was still encased in the plastic sleeve from when she'd had it dry-cleaned in Chicago two and a half years ago. It was made from wool. The last funeral she'd attended had taken place in the snow. If she was still grieving for a man she'd only known for a year, there was no hope of ever getting over the loss of her father. She made her way downstairs, taking care to avoid the steps that had always squeaked.

Earlier Emma had awoken from her afternoon nap to the sound of a ringing telephone. It was so shrill and old-fashioned that it had taken a few seconds for her to realize she was no longer dreaming. She'd staggered onto the first-floor landing to answer it. It felt odd to handle a phone that was still attached by a cord. She was pretty sure it was the same one her parents had owned when she was in high school.

*"Hello,"* she'd said, using the script she'd learned as a child. *"This is Emma Long. May I ask who is calling please?"*

Emma had waited, but there'd been no response.

*"Hello, is anyone there?"*

A girl had laughed.

*"Hello?"*

More giggling. *"What do you call a lesbian with fat . . ."*

Emma had hung up before the girl could finish speaking. For a long time she'd stood on the landing feeling like someone had punched her in the gut.

It was cooler downstairs than it had been in her bedroom. Emma turned on some lights and made her way into the kitchen. Her father's old coat was on a hook near the back door. She slipped it on. She hadn't expected it to smell so familiar. For a few seconds she had a strange sense that her father was standing right behind her, but other than her reflection in the windows, Emma was alone. There wasn't one single visible light outside. The darkness had weight to it. The silence was unnerving. She glanced over at the door leading onto the back porch. She knew it was locked but checked anyway.

Her father had used the sunroom as an office for as long as Emma could remember. Built along the western side of the house, it baked in the summer and was unbearably cold in the winter, but her father had always prided himself on his ability to transcend the elements. Kerosene heater humming by his side and snow falling heavily inches away, he'd sit bundled up at a desk that looked out over the side yard.

Sitting cross-legged on the floor, Emma sifted through the files he'd gathered for his radio program on the growing number of militia groups in Montana and in the United States as a whole. He'd scribbled in the margins and highlighted sections of newspaper articles that interested him. There didn't appear to be any notations that indicated what he'd been working on more recently, which was odd given how excited he'd been when they last spoke. He'd been convinced that it was the story that would finally bring his radio show national attention. She'd told him to be careful what he wished for. He'd told her to relax.

*It's my job to worry, not yours,* he'd said.

Emma went through the books on the shelf, scanning the pages for hidden scraps of paper and photos. One section was filled with books on how to write a novel. Pages were bent back or marked with bits of colored tape. Her father had always fancied himself a spy novelist. Emma had lost track of how many of his first chapters she'd read. She ignored the stacked boxes of unfinished manuscripts and tried the desk drawers and filing cabinets. After that she was on her hands and knees crawling on the floor, searching beneath the furniture and behind it. She didn't find what she was looking for. Her father's private journal wasn't where he once kept it, and he hadn't hidden it in any of the other places she remembered from when she was a child. She sat back in the desk chair and swiveled it full circle several times. Emma was twelve the first time she'd come across the journal in one of her father's desk drawers. She'd been hoping to find some spare change for the ice-cream van. Instead she found a thick, leather-bound book containing all of Walleye's dirty little secrets.

The journal had notes on everyone from the high school principal to the head librarian to the police chief. Family trees had been carefully drawn with dates of births and deaths included. He'd taken down details and recorded the intimate secrets of almost everyone he knew or met in passing. Emma had found a page on her middle school principal. Ms. Ashford had once posed naked for *Playboy* and was having an affair with a married man who taught history at the high school. The man who headed the chamber of commerce had been meeting the mayor's wife for trysts at a motel outside of Kalispell for years. In the margins of another page her father had written—*possible that the mayor's children are not his own*. Emma couldn't help herself. Every time she'd had a chance she'd snuck into her father's office for another look. She'd been reading about a woman named Sue who grew cannabis in her back garden when her father arrived home earlier than expected. As far as she could remember it was the only time he'd ever yelled at her.

Fifteen years passed before Emma saw the journal again. She and her father had been having lunch at the café in the Marina District in San Francisco when he'd set it down on the table between them.

*Emma, I shouldn't have yelled at you for reading this.*

*Dad, I was twelve and I was in the wrong. Anyway, I'd rather have an explanation. Why do you spy on people? It's not normal.*

It was the first time she'd ever remembered hearing her father stutter.

*It's . . . it's a compulsion I have. Have . . . have always had.* He'd laid his hand flat on the journal's cover. *The more I know, the safer I feel.*

*Don't you think you're taking the idea that knowledge is power a step too far?*

*Don't be like that.*

*Don't be like what?* Emma had asked.

*I'm trying to make you understand something quite fundamental about me and you're dismissing it out of hand.*

*So what if you're a little paranoid. You're fine.*

His eyes had welled up. *Sweetheart, I'm not just a little paranoid. I'm worried I've lost all sense of proportion. I used to be able to shut it off for periods of time, but not anymore.*

*Have you thought of going to speak to someone?*

*I wouldn't be able to trust anyone.* He'd hesitated. *That's why I've come to you.*

She'd tapped the journal's cover with her finger.

*You should destroy this thing.* She'd gestured to the southern tower of the Golden Gate Bridge. It was emerging out of the dense fog like a rampart. *We can do it today. We can throw it off the Golden Gate Bridge.*

He'd looked embarrassed when he spoke again. *Emma, I can't do that. It makes me feel safe.*

She'd grown increasingly wary as she watched him clutch the journal tightly to his chest. Emma wasn't used to seeing her father like this. He was her one constant in the world—the one person who tied her to where she came from. She'd tried to meet his eyes, but he kept looking away.

*Dad, it isn't making you feel safe anymore. I can tell you're anxious just looking at you.* Emma had tried a different tack. *A lot of people you care about would get hurt if it ever fell into the wrong hands. You should get rid of it for their sakes.*

He'd shaken his head hard. *That's . . . that's not going to . . . to happen.*

*Are you sure? I found it when I was twelve and I wasn't even trying.*

A week after her father had returned home to Walleye Junction Emma received a text.

*Emma, I know you're worried so I wanted to put your mind at ease. I've found a safe place for the journal. No one will ever find it. Dad x*

A shallow, glass-fronted cabinet hung on one wall of her father's office. Her father had called it his curio for crows. The wooden recesses held everything from buttons to bits of twisted metal to coins. He'd started feeding the neighborhood crows when he moved to Walleye. In return they left him gifts at the feeding table and in the birdbath. At some point they started following him wherever he went. He'd found their presence reassuring, but her mother had thought otherwise.

*I swear they're waiting for me to drop dead so they can pick me to pieces.*

Her father had laughed. *Imagine the gift they'll bring if you do.*

Emma opened the cabinet's glass doors and poked among the bits of twisted metal, glass, and plastic. When she was a child she believed they were lost treasure. All Emma saw now was junk. Some of the objects were dated with Magic Marker, but others were left to tell their own story. One of the compartments contained an assortment of buttons and another had nails. Emma sifted through a selection of keys. She recognized a locker key from her high school. The red plastic handle had been gnawed on. One of the keys looked brand new. She held it up to the light. There was some writing on the green tag, but she couldn't make it out.

At the sound of a car pulling up outside Emma returned the items to the cabinet and shut the glass doors. She went to the front window and moved the curtains aside a fraction so she could see outside. It took a few seconds for her eyes to adjust. A string of black crows perched like musical notes on the power lines that ran along the road. A shadow moved across the lawn, disappearing briefly beneath the low splay of tree branches. In the dim light she couldn't make out who it was. There was a quiet knock at the door.

"Who is it?" she asked.

"Emma. It's me, Nathan. I know you're up. I saw you in the window."

She kept her voice low. "This isn't a good time."

"It can't wait. We need to talk."

"Tomorrow."

"Please, Emma, it's important."

She unlatched and unlocked the door. She could smell beer on Nathan's breath and he was a little unsteady on his feet. His smile was at half tilt. She couldn't help but think they'd both been here before.

He reached for her. "Emma, I can't believe you're really here."

Emma stayed behind the half open screen door. "Please keep your voice down. My mother is sleeping."

He smiled. "Just like high school."

She frowned. "Exactly like high school."

"Hey," he said, slipping his hands into his pockets and looking sheepish. "I'm not here for anything. I just want to talk. There were things that were said and done. Stuff I'm sure both of us would like to take back." He shifted his weight. "It's been on my mind a lot lately."

"Nathan, this isn't really a good time."

He held up his hands. "I'm not leaving this porch, Emma. I'll stay here all night if I have to."

Emma stared at him for a few seconds. Where there were once sharp angles there were now soft curves. Where there was once an air of entitlement there was now a look of resignation. She stepped back and opened the door for him. It had been twelve years since they were a couple. If he wanted to talk that was fine, but she would not let him bully her. She was stronger now.

Emma led him into the kitchen. Beyond the back windows acres of cherry blossoms glowed under a pale moon. She'd not been in the garden since she arrived.

"Let's go out back," she said.

They sat on a cushioned bench that faced north. On a clear day the Whitefish Range dominated the view. To the east the Flathead River, still heavy with snowmelt, rumbled through the valley like a locomotive. Emma felt the pockets of her father's coat and pulled out the key she'd found in her father's office.

"What's that?" he said.

"Just something I found in my father's office. Can I get you something to drink?"

"Nah, I'm good." He stared out toward the orchard.

"Admiring your handiwork?" she asked.

He nodded. "The lawyer handling the family's affairs says I can move into Caleb's place since it's vacant."

Beyond the orchard, Caleb Winfrey's farmhouse was a dark silhouette. The distance had diminished with time. It felt uncomfortably close. Emma tried not to picture its unlit rooms.

"How do you feel about that?" asked Emma.

"It's a nice house, but it's got too many ghosts. Lucy and her mother were hard enough work when they were alive. Can't imagine keeping company with them now."

"Surely, you don't believe in ghosts."

He lifted his chin a fraction. "No, but I believe in memories and there's no escaping them when I'm in that place."

Fearing he was right, Emma averted her gaze, setting her eyes on the Flathead River instead. The moonlit water passed in and out of shadow. Emma really wasn't ready to talk about what had happened in Caleb Winfrey's house.

"I can't get over my room," she said. "It's like time stood still. My mom kept everything."

He put his arm around her shoulder and pulled her in. "How you holding up?"

Emma tried to shrug him off, but his arm didn't budge. She chose her words carefully.

"Things are difficult with my mom. I get the sense that she'd rather not have me here."

He took a moment to gather his thoughts. "Francine is in shock. She'll come around if you give her some time."

"I know this sounds weird to say out loud, but I don't feel I've earned the right to grieve."

Nathan twisted around to look at her. "What on earth is that supposed to mean?"

"My relationship with my father was a weekly phone call and a yearly pilgrimage to meet him in some soulless hotel." The dull ache in her chest made speaking difficult. "If I didn't make more effort when he was alive, what right do I have to miss him now?"

"Em," he said, pressing his lips to the top of her hair. "You haven't changed a bit. You still overthink everything. You have every right to grieve. Philip was your connection to this place, to everything that makes you who you are today."

The coarse fabric of Nathan's shirt chafed against her cheek. She slid out from under his embrace and sat up, making a point of stretching out her back.

"I'm so stiff from the drive."

He kneaded her shoulders hard enough to make her want to cry out.

"You have a chance to make things right with your mom," he said. "You were close once."

"She really resented my leaving Walleye."

"Can you blame her?"

He'd raised his voice and she matched his tone note for note.

"I just wish she understood why I had to go. My dad did."

"I hated you for a long time," said Nathan. "The way you left things . . . it wasn't right."

She almost told Nathan that she still hated him sometimes but decided to keep that to herself.

"I still hate Lucy," she said.

"I pity her. She was messed up."

Emma wiped her eyes with the sleeve of her father's jacket. She'd not realized she was crying.

"Nathan, do you remember Lucy's mother's funeral?"

"Beverly died when we were in the fourth grade. That was a long time ago."

"But, you must remember it."

Nathan remained silent for a long while. He kept his hands clutched in his lap when he finally spoke.

"I remember little things. I'll never forget seeing my uncle Caleb cry. I didn't think men did that. And little Lucy was so fierce in her grief. My mother had to hold her down to get her in that dress."

"You looked so serious in your suit."

"I had to read a poem in front of half the town." He laughed. "I was scared shitless."

"Lucy and I weren't even close friends back then. Our mothers were always forcing us to do stuff together, but we didn't get along."

"She was a tomboy and you were a princess." He held up her well-manicured hand. Her fingernails were long and painted pale pink. "Some things never change."

"Everything changes."

He intertwined her fingers with his one by one. "Anyway," he said. "I always thought it was weird that she picked you out of the crowd that day."

"At the church I gave her some candy to make her feel better. Next thing I know, I'm standing graveside at the heart of the Winfrey clan. At some point Lucy grabbed my hand." Emma shook her head. "I didn't realize what she was up to until she started running."

"She tried to get me to come with her, but I wasn't having any part of it."

"It was the middle of March. We could have died from exposure."

"But you didn't. You got her back home safe and sound."

"It wasn't easy," said Emma. "She fought me every step of the way. If I'd known that the next ten years would be more of the same I might have left her out there."

"Half the town was out looking for you. Caleb had just lost Beverly. He was angry and worried all at once."

"Lucy told me that she was running away to find her real father."

"She was always throwing stuff like that in Caleb's face. I don't know why he put up with it."

Emma shivered and Nathan noticed.

"Do you want to go in?" he asked. "You must be cold. It's freezing out here."

"I should try to sleep. I've been so wired since I got here."

"I'll keep you company," he said. "Better than you sitting up all night by yourself."

Their hands were still intertwined. His palms were heavily callused.

He kept his voice low. "Do you ever regret leaving?"

She pulled her hand away as she stood up.

"Emma?" he said.

"Sometimes, but it's rare."

Emma kept her father's coat on even though the house was warm. She filled the kettle with water and switched on the burner.

"I'm making some tea. Do you want some?"

"Coffee would be nice."

She opened the cupboard. "There's only instant."

"Coffee is coffee."

"We could argue that point all night."

"I'd rather not."

She placed their mugs on the table and sat opposite him. "I'm surprised you haven't settled down with someone yet."

"It will happen eventually. What about you?"

"I'm not really interested," she said.

"Don't you want to have kids?"

"I'm not crazy about the idea."

"Come on. Everyone wants kids."

She was careful to enunciate every word. "Maybe I'm not everyone."

He watched her from across the top of his coffee mug. "I suppose that's possible."

"My mother actually implied I was getting past my prime."

"She's probably worried because you're on your own."

Emma turned around. "How did you know that?"

"News trickles through. I also heard you had some sort of breakdown."

"That's a gross exaggeration. I went through a bad patch. Not quite the same thing." She put her cup down, being careful to line it up with the flowered pattern on the tablecloth. "Three years and two cities later I'm cured."

"You sure move around a lot."

"When my company makes a new acquisition they send in a team to handle the transition."

"So, you fire people."

"I have to figure out how to make things work more efficiently. Generally speaking we try to keep people in their jobs."

"We're so different," said Nathan. "It's hard to believe we dated for three years."

"If you want proof it's all in my room. It's a shrine to high school romance. There are pictures of us everywhere."

He took hold of her hands again. "Emma, I was joking. I don't need any proof."

She made a real effort to look him in the eye. "I am sorry for how I went about things. I should have been straighter with you. The last year I was here was difficult."

"I could tell you were just biding your time until you could leave again. I'm not going to lie. It hurt."

"I thought things with Lucy would have calmed down a bit while I was away in England during our junior year, but it was worse when I got back. It felt as if I had to prove I was her friend over and over again." Emma closed her eyes briefly. "She just kept raising the bar. It was like she was punishing me for going away. She couldn't see past Walleye."

"Lucy started partying a lot the year you were away. People were saying she was getting into some pretty freaky shit. Got so bad Caleb took away her car keys so she couldn't go out."

"That wouldn't have stopped her. When Lucy wanted something she generally got it."

"Apparently," he said, raising his voice. "She wanted you."

Emma looked down at her hands. He held them so tight it was starting to hurt. She kept her voice even.

"That stuff she wrote about me in her journal. I swear it never happened."

"You needed to say that twelve years ago . . . it's a little late now."

For a long time neither of them spoke. Outside the world had slipped into shadow. Insects clung to the kitchen windows looking for light. A strong easterly blew through the orchard, stirring the fragrant cherry blossoms and rattling the little house.

"Nathan," she said, noticing her whitening fingertips. "Could you please not hold on so tight? I'm starting to lose circulation."

Nathan slid his hands into his pockets and watched as Emma gathered their cups.

"Is that all you've got to say for yourself?" he asked.

"I am sorry," she stuttered. "A lot of things . . . I mean I should have handled things differently. I was young. If I could do it all over again, I would."

Nathan pushed his chair back with such force it nearly toppled. "You never said a word when Caleb said all that stuff about you. You just took it."

"That's because I blamed myself. Lucy spoke to me the day she died. She begged me to come up to the house that same night." Never taking her eyes off Nathan, she carefully placed the cups in the sink. "I took my time and she took her life."

"You couldn't have known that would happen."

She folded her arms across her chest. "I knew she was capable."

Nathan walked to the back door and stared out into the night.

"It was a long time ago. Maybe we should all try to move on."

"What do you think I've been doing all these years?"

He placed his hand on the doorframe. "Running away isn't the same thing. You could have stayed and helped clean up the mess Lucy left behind. Everyone found out what was in her diary. I ended up looking like a fool."

"You were at Lucy's funeral. You saw what happened. And talk about not saying a word. You should have stuck up for me then and there, but you didn't."

"A funeral isn't the time or the place for that sort of talk." He stood over her. "I think you were looking for an excuse to leave for good and Caleb gave you one."

"Your uncle humiliated me in front of the whole town and you make it sound like I had a choice."

"There's always a choice. You just made the wrong one."

She turned away. "I'm going to bed. You can let yourself out."

Nathan grabbed her by the arm and swung her around to face him.

"Don't speak to me like that," he said.

"Nathan," she said, pulling away. "I'm not eighteen. I'm not going to put up with this shit."

"You have no idea how much you hurt me."

"Nathan, I understand you're upset, but this isn't the way to deal with it."

"I'm sorry," he said, holding his hands up in defeat. "I don't understand what gets into me sometimes."

"We were close for a long time. I know it's hard to let go, but you have to. It isn't healthy that you're still hung up on what happened between us all those years ago."

Nathan pulled her into a deep hug and pressed his lips to the top of her head. His words were muffled.

"I replay what happened at Lucy's funeral in my head sometimes. I should have said something. Now it's too late."

"It may have always been too late," she said, closing her eyes and letting him hold her.

Feeling more trapped than loved, Emma stood perfectly still. She feared he'd try to kiss her if she didn't make a move soon. She didn't know what she'd do if that happened. There was always doubt lingering inside her. She'd left him and Walleye far behind, but she couldn't put her hand to her heart and swear she was happier for going. She felt so worn through with sadness that she couldn't think straight. It would be easy to vanish into their past together, but she knew that she'd only end up leaving him all over again. Nathan hadn't changed and neither had she. She could still string him along and he was still willing to follow her lead. He really had every right to hate her. She pulled away.

"Nathan," she said. "You should go before we do something stupid."

"I'll call you tomorrow," he said, letting her go and walking away.

Emma listened to the front door shut softly in his wake.

"I guess you know where to find me now," she said.

# 6

The director of the Flathead Valley opiate-addiction program led Macy into a small conference room where the center's counselors had gathered to discuss the patients under their care. The east-facing windows were full of morning light and a coffee machine bubbled away in the corner. Julia Price was a heavyset woman with round cheeks and frizzy gray hair. She offered Macy a chair near the window.

"I'm sorry to interrupt the meeting," Julia said to the room, gathering the folds of her flowing skirt and taking a seat at the head of the conference table. "Detective Macy Greeley has some news she needs to share with us."

"Good morning," said Macy. "I understand that Carla Spencer has been receiving treatment here for some time."

A man with a slight frame and short-cropped hair held up his hand. "Carla Spencer is my patient."

"Merle Hepworth?"

"Yes," he said, his eyes shifting to his case files. Carla's was on top. "I have an appointment with Carla later this morning. We were just discussing her progress. She missed group therapy this week."

"Was that unusual?"

"She's had perfect attendance thus far."

"What did her therapy involve?"

"Weekly one-on-one sessions and group therapy. She is also required to attend four twelve-step Narcotics Anonymous meetings per week."

Macy made a few notes. "Was she on methadone?"

Julia Price spoke again. "We find that buprenorphine is more effective for treating withdrawal symptoms. Patients can't get their medication if they don't attend their meetings."

Macy pointed to the stacks of files in front of each counselor. "How many patients are treated here?"

"At the moment we're maxed out at one hundred patients each. The wait time for a place in the program is up to three months. The good news is that we have funding to hire four more counselors so we're expanding."

Merle raised his hand again. "May I ask what this is all about?"

"I'm afraid that Carla Spencer and her husband, Lloyd, died from an apparent drug overdose early yesterday morning."

"Painkillers?"

"We're pretty sure it was heroin."

Merle dropped Carla's file on the table. "I really thought we were making progress."

"We're not ruling out foul play."

"You think she was murdered?"

"We have reason to believe a third party was involved, but it still may have been accidental. The medical examiner should have more information by this afternoon. I need to know about the other patients who attended her group therapy sessions. We'll be speaking to her twelve-step sponsor as well. At this point I just want to know if there was anyone Carla Spencer was friendly with. They may have insight into why this has happened."

"I'm sorry," said Merle. "These are my patients. I can't give you their names without a court order."

"Fair enough," said Macy. "Don't name names. Was there anyone in the group who worried you? They may have had previous convictions. They may have also missed sessions in the past couple of weeks."

He nodded. "I've got a name in mind."

Julia Price picked her way through the stack of files in front of Merle.

"Joel Edwards," she said, holding the file up in the air. "He's just been kicked out of the program for violating parole. He failed to check in with his case officer two weeks running."

Merle sat back in his chair. "How come I wasn't notified?"

"I only received the e-mail a few minutes ago."

Macy wrote down his name. "What's the story on Joel Edwards?"

Merle scratched his neck. "He attempted to rob a doctor at gunpoint when he was off his head on a cocktail of Oxy and Xanax. After serving his sentence he started using again. When he was arrested on a possession charge the courts said it was the drug treatment program or prison."

"Did you notice if he and Carla were close?"

"Yes, they were pretty tight. I know they went for coffee a few times after the sessions. He was struggling, but I got the impression Carla was really pulling for him. She seemed to be completely focused on her recovery, which makes her death even more upsetting. She was on buprenorphine. She shouldn't have been craving."

"But she missed a session."

"She called to apologize so I arranged for her to pick up some at the pharmacy."

"Is it common practice to prescribe such strong medication without seeing the patient?"

Julia Price answered. "We have patients who travel more than two hours each way to reach this center. Cars break down. Medicaid vans don't show up. We can't punish a patient unduly when they have a legitimate excuse for missing a meeting."

"What was Carla's excuse?"

Merle looked at her file. "Her husband and son had a physical altercation. She didn't feel it was safe to leave them alone together in the house. Her attendance had been perfect up to that point so I gave her the benefit of the doubt."

"Did she talk about her husband in her therapy sessions?" asked Macy.

"She wanted to leave him but didn't see how she'd ever manage. I got the impression she was scared of him. He was still using, which made her recovery particularly challenging."

"Is it common for addicts to move from painkillers to heroin?"

"Unfortunately, yes," said Julia. "As both are opiate based it's a natural progression and now that prescription painkillers are becoming more difficult to obtain it's becoming a real problem. Heroin used to be the type of drug you only found in urban areas, but now it's in the suburbs, our schools, and in rural communities. It's cheaper but far more dangerous. The plus side of prescription painkillers is that you know exactly what dosage you're getting."

Macy started gathering her things. "You've been incredibly helpful. I wish I could have brought you better news."

Julia walked Macy to the door. "We've had to develop some pretty thick skin working in this business. Thankfully, we've had quite a few success stories recently, so I would like to think that we're finally turning a corner."

Macy shook her hand. "Thank you for all the work you're doing here. I'm sure it's making a difference."

As she made her way back to the police station Macy peered in the window of a children's toy shop on Main Street, making a note to stop in when they were open to pick up something for Luke. She'd been wondering how her son would feel about spending more time in the Flathead Valley. Aiden had invited them to stay for a couple of weeks over the summer. Macy had made a point of explaining exactly what having a two-and-a-half-year-old living in the house would mean. Luke couldn't be left on his own. They wouldn't be able to go to Murphy's Tavern until two in the morning. They'd also have to forgo mountain biking, rock climbing, and sleeping in. Aiden had said he didn't mind, but Macy wasn't convinced he was ready for fatherhood, temporary or otherwise.

With the exception of his job, which he took very seriously, Aiden seemed to move through life with very few constraints. The truth was she didn't really understand why Aiden was so prepared to give up freedoms she sometimes wished she still had. Luke may have been three hundred miles away and well cared for, but Macy never lost sight of the fact she was his mother. It colored every decision she made. She worried constantly that she wasn't good enough so she overcompensated. At the moment Luke came first and her job came second. She wondered how Aiden would feel about third place.

A car horn sounded and Macy turned to see Gina beaming at her from behind the wheel of her patrol car.

"You need a ride to the station?" asked Gina.

"It's only another block. I think I can manage."

Gina revved the engine. "I'll race you."

"Lou's not going to take kindly to you speeding down Main Street."

"Lou's a pushover."

Macy's ribs ached when she laughed. "Okay then, you're on."

Gina was waiting for Macy on the front steps. She'd spent the morning tracking down Sean Spencer's friends. Most of them had still been in bed when she'd showed up at their doors.

"It's amazing how much teenagers sleep," said Gina.

"Was it worth the trip?"

Gina held up a list of microbreweries in Montana.

"One of his friends came through. He said Sean was interested in getting a job at a microbrewery in Bozeman to make money while he was in school. He got the impression that Sean was heading down there this week."

"Why microbreweries?"

"Apparently, it's something Sean has always been into."

Macy scanned the list. "There are at least fifty breweries listed here."

"Yeah, but some are circled, so I'll start there. Any luck at the drug treatment center?"

"Maybe, but it's best that we discuss it inside. Probably should run it by Lou as well."

"I spoke to him a few minutes ago. He's making a stab at finding Sean's real father. Apparently, Scott Walker has a place south of Darby Lake. Lou said he'd be out of cell phone range for a while."

Gina and Macy sat across from each other at the two desks they'd been assigned. Gina's was covered in empty food wrappers. She held up a box of doughnuts.

"Hungry?"

Macy said she'd already eaten. "There was a guy named Joel Edwards in Carla's therapy group. Apparently, they were tight. It may be a coincidence, but Edwards has missed the last two meetings with his parole officer."

Gina was already typing. She leaned in and studied the screen. "There's an APB out on him. Sounds like a nice guy. He did a short stint in prison for armed robbery."

"He robbed a doctor at gunpoint." Macy glanced at her watch. "We're kind of pressed for time. When are we supposed to interview Ron Forester?"

"I told the associate warden we'd be at the prison at around half past three."

"We're going to have to split up again then. I'll drive myself over to Philip Long's house to interview his wife while you find out what you can about Joel Edwards and the microbrewery lead on Sean Spencer. Once I'm done we'll head south to Deer Lodge."

Gina hesitated before handing Macy the car keys.

"Are you sure you're okay to drive?" said Gina. "You were in a serious accident. Nobody around here is going to blame you if you're still a little shaky behind the wheel."

"Gina, you worry too much. I'll be fine."

Macy parked Gina's patrol car in front of the home Philip Long once shared with his wife, Francine, and fought the urge to crawl under the dashboard and hide. The confidence she'd felt upon leaving the police station had vanished at the first intersection. The light had turned green, but instead of moving she'd sat staring out the front windshield. It wasn't until someone behind her sounded a horn that she'd started off again. In her haste she'd nearly run over a pedestrian that hadn't cleared the crosswalk. Thankfully, she'd been wearing sunglasses so no one could see she was crying.

Macy picked up her cell phone but stopped short of dialing. At some point she'd started calling Aiden whenever she was in trouble. She closed her eyes for a few seconds. Ray had never been there when she needed him so it still surprised her when Aiden answered the phone. She wasn't sure what was normal anymore. Before she met Ray she wouldn't have asked anyone for help. She would have just got on with it. Macy reached over and grabbed her laptop and case notes from her bag. She was already late so a few more minutes wouldn't hurt. The last thing Francine Long needed was a detective unraveling on her doorstep.

Macy scrolled through her e-mails, stopping on the ones that related to Philip Long's case. She frowned. The tire tread impressions found near the crime scene didn't match those on Sean Spencer's dirt bike. It didn't mean Sean didn't kill Philip Long. It just meant that he would have had to use another bike. Macy slid her computer into her bag and checked her reflection in the mirror. Nothing could be done about her appearance. She put her sunglasses back on to hide her bloodshot eyes. If anyone asked she'd say she was suffering from allergies.

The modest two-story bungalow was separated from the street by a bright green lawn lined with colorful borders. A Cadillac Escalade boxed in an older sedan and a red hatchback. On closer inspection the house was showing signs of disrepair. Paint peeled from the woodwork and thin lightning-shaped cracks ran down the plastered walls. Philip Long may have been a local celebrity, but he wasn't wealthy. According to financial documents, they'd recently taken out a second mortgage on their home.

Macy pressed the bell and waited. Footsteps followed. The young woman who greeted her wore an expensive-looking cream silk blouse, a pair of dark blue trousers, and ballet flats. Her dark hair was pulled up in a tight ponytail and she was worryingly slim. Macy wouldn't have called her pretty, but she was striking.

"Hello," said Macy, pulling out her badge. "My name is Detective Macy Greeley. Francine Long is expecting me." She watched as the woman inspected her badge.

"I apologize that I'm a bit late," said Macy.

Instead of answering the woman opened the screen door a fraction further and stepped outside. The wind whipped up, catching a few loose strands of her hair. She brushed them away before squaring her shoulders. She spoke with authority.

"There have been people stopping by all morning. My mother is exhausted."

"You must be Emma," said Macy, extending her hand. "I admired your father greatly."

"That's kind of you to say." Emma flicked her blue eyes to the door. "I need a minute to compose myself. You can go on in if you like."

"I can wait."

Emma folded her arms tightly across her chest. "You may regret it. I'm not great company at the moment."

"I heard you've only just returned to Walleye Junction after a long time away."

"It's been twelve years."

"Have you seen your parents in that time?"

"I saw my father a couple of times a year. My mother less so."

"You live in San Francisco?"

"Yes," she said, sounding exhausted. "It was a long drive."

Emma walked along the porch and stared out at the view of the mountains.

"My mother isn't just upset. She's confused. I'm worried there might be some underlying health issue."

"Could that be why she didn't contact you?"

Emma turned to face Macy. "That's the story I'm telling myself.

We've had our disagreements in the past, but she'd have never shut me out of something as important as this."

Macy gestured toward the driveway. "Is that your Escalade?"

"Not even if I had all the money in the world. The hatchback is mine." She tilted her head toward the house and frowned. "My mother has company. Her old boss has stopped by with his third wife. I know my mother can't stand the thought of having the woman in the house, but she's still doing her level best to make them feel welcome. The strain is beginning to show though. They've been here for nearly an hour."

"I need to speak to your mother on her own."

"It will be a good excuse to get rid of them. They may mean well, but they're only making matters worse."

Dr. Whitaker handed Macy his business card before taking charge of introductions. Macy recognized him from billboards along Route 93 where he loomed over the highway wearing a benevolent smile, lab coat, and stethoscope. According to the billboards, Dr. Whitaker could perform miracles. Macy felt he inspired far less confidence in the shiny blue tracksuit and tennis shoes he was wearing. His wife Sharon was a crisp-looking brunette who wore a string of polished pearls that matched her smile. While he appeared to be in his mid-sixties, Sharon was thirty at best. She clutched a smartphone in her well-manicured hands like it was a lifeline and glanced down at the screen every time she thought no one was looking. They were very tan so Macy imagined they spent a lot of time on vacation.

Dr. Whitaker and his wife had positioned Francine Long between them on the sofa. She was as gray as they were golden. Silver threads of hair fell around her finely wrinkled complexion. She wore no makeup and her blue eyes were raw from crying. She barely acknowledged Macy when she was introduced. The doctor and his wife stood as Francine made a move to get up.

"I'll just be a couple of minutes," she said, gripping Dr. Whitaker's outstretched hand for balance. "I want to freshen up."

Francine exchanged awkward hugs with her guests and in turn they promised to stop in again. Offers of help were made more than once and the latest Mrs. Whitaker provided instructions for reheating the casserole she'd left on the kitchen counter. Apparently it was gluten free.

Macy accompanied Dr. Whitaker and Sharon to the door. A tall man of considerable bulk, the doctor loomed over Macy when he spoke.

"If you think of anything that we could do for Francine could you please let us know," he said. "She is very dear to us."

Sharon clutched a tissue tight in her hand, but her eyes were bone dry. "We cut our vacation short when we heard the news about Philip."

"We couldn't sit on that cruise ship a moment longer knowing what Francine must be going through." Dr. Whitaker shook Macy's hand again. "The poor woman."

Emma opened the front door. "Thank you so much for stopping by to visit with my mother." Once outside, they hovered on the porch. Macy could hear bits of their conversation.

*It's so good that you're here with your mother in her time of need.*

*Where else would I be,* asked Emma.

The doctor's voice boomed. *How long has it been? Twelve years? That whole tragic business with Lucy seems a lifetime ago now. I'm sure everyone has forgotten.*

Upstairs floorboards creaked and a toilet flushed. Downstairs the screen door snapped shut and Emma wandered into the room looking sad and angry at the same time.

"Would you like a drink?" she said, heading for the kitchen. "I found something at the store that looked like coffee."

"Only if it isn't any trouble."

Emma talked to Macy through the open door. "You're not from around here are you?

"No, I was born and raised in Helena. I still live there, but as a special investigator working for the state, I generally go wherever they need me."

"You must put in a lot of miles."

"Too many to count. It's a big state."

"How do you take your coffee?"

"Molten."

"My specialty."

Macy stood in the middle of the living room that looked as if it was lifted straight from the pages of a 1960s Sears catalog. The small flat-screen television appeared to be the only nod Philip and Francine had made to recent advancements. The sofa was covered in a pale blue fabric that matched the floor-to-ceiling curtains. Despite its age everything was in good order. She ran her eyes over a set of bookshelves that stood behind a reclining leather chair. Philip Long enjoyed spy novels. Macy picked up a well-thumbed classic by John le Carré from a stack of books that sat on a low table.

*"Magnus Pym, ranking diplomat, has vanished, believed defected. The chase is on: for a missing husband, a devoted father, and a secret agent. Pym's life, it is revealed, is entirely made up of secrets."*

Macy sensed she was being watched. She turned toward the stairs.

Francine Long had changed her clothing. She wore a mustard-yellow dress that was cinched in at the waist and had a hem that fell below the knee. Her hair was no longer hanging loose. It was now pulled back into a neatly pinned bun.

"My husband was the reader," she said, taking the book from Macy and putting it back in its original position. "Once his nose was stuck in a book there was no distracting him."

Francine rearranged the cushions before sitting down in an armchair with a floral print. Macy positioned herself on the sofa and dug a business card out of her bag for Francine.

"I'm sorry to intrude at such a difficult time, but I thought it best that I stop by and introduce myself properly."

For a few seconds Francine's face was twisted in grief. She spoke softly.

"I'm not sure how I'll be able to help. I really can't understand . . ."

Emma walked into the room carrying a tray. She touched her mother's shoulder. "Mom, I've made you tea and coffee. I wasn't sure what you wanted."

"Tea is fine."

Macy thanked Emma for her coffee. It was so thick she imagined a spoon would stand upright in it.

"Mom," said Emma. "Do you want me to stay while you speak to the detective?"

Francine barely nodded. Her eyes darted around the room eventually landing on her late husband's empty leather chair. Emma brushed past it on her way to the sofa.

Macy slid her notebook out of her bag and took a moment to gather her thoughts. She'd have to take this slowly.

"Thank you again for speaking to me," said Macy. "I know it's a difficult time, so I want you to tell me if you're tired. I can come back."

In a gesture reminiscent of her daughter, Francine squared her shoulders. "I'd rather know what's going on. All this uncertainty is difficult. I'm worried . . ."

Macy almost reached out and touched Francine's arm, but then thought better of it. Francine Long struck her as someone who could crumble at the slightest sign of kindness.

"I'll speak to Lou Turner if you feel you need someone keeping an eye on things here," said Macy. "I know he's having regular patrols monitor the house."

"Thank you," said Francine, her eyes moving to her daughter Emma. "I'd . . . we'd appreciate that."

"We're following various leads, but as there is no clear motive for your husband's kidnapping and murder, the investigation could take some time." Macy paused. "I'm not at liberty to tell you everything, but I will tell you what I can. I'm afraid that some of the information I'm going to give you today is going to be distressing."

Francine pulled a cushion to her chest and shut her eyes.

Macy chose her words with care.

"Yesterday morning a local couple was found dead from an apparent drug overdose. The responding officer became suspicious when he noticed that their vehicle matched the description of the one seen the evening your husband was abducted. The crime scene investigators collected fingerprints and they were compared to what was found at the house where your husband had been kept. There was a match."

Francine's cornflower blue eyes snapped open. "Who were they?"

Macy held up a pair of DMV photos. "They've been identified as Carla and Lloyd Spencer. Do those names sound familiar?"

"No," said Francine, firmly shaking her head.

"I need you to take your time. You have to be sure," said Macy.

Francine pressed a tissue to her lips and shook her head again. Macy checked her notes.

"Carla and Lloyd Spencer have lived in Walleye Junction all their lives. You could have come across them in any number of ways. Lloyd was a roofer. Maybe he worked for you and your husband at some point? Carla has held various jobs. She has worked as a tech consultant and as a waitress at the IHOP. More recently she delivered pizzas."

Receiving no response, Macy pulled out a picture of Sean Spencer and placed it on the table.

"What about this young man?" Macy said, pointing to the image. "He finished high school last year."

Francine picked up the photo. It trembled in her hands. "Who's this?"

"This is their son, Sean Spencer. He left town a few days ago and we're having difficulty tracking him down."

"Do you think he—"

"At this point we just want to question him. We have no physical evidence that links him to any of the crime scenes."

"But he's so young."

"He's nineteen."

"I'm sorry," said Francine, handing the photo back. "I do not know these people."

Macy left the photos on the table where Francine could see them. Emma picked up the photo of Carla and stared at it. "Do they have extended family in the valley?"

"Carla's sister lives here with her husband, Jay. They have a son named Kyle."

"Kyle Miller?"

"You know him?"

"I went to school with him," said Emma. "I guess you could say we were friends. As I recall he was quite bright."

"I interviewed him yesterday."

"He never talked about his family," said Emma. "We all knew things were difficult at home."

"They still are," said Macy. "As far as I can tell, Kyle is the only one holding down a job. Carla and Lloyd Spencer both had histories of drug abuse. They were heavily in debt and in danger of losing their home. It is possible that they kidnapped your father for financial gain."

Emma frowned. "But that's ridiculous. There are plenty of people around here with far more money than my parents."

"As I said before, without knowing their motives for kidnapping your father, it's difficult to move forward in a focused manner." Macy glanced at Francine. "I understand from Lou Turner that your husband feared reprisals following a series of programs he'd done on the growing numbers of the private militias in this part of the state."

Francine nodded. "There have been threats. On a few occasions Philip was confronted in public. I thought he should get a gun for protection, but he wouldn't listen."

Emma dismissed her mother's comment. "Buying a gun would have gone against everything dad believed in."

Francine mumbled something under her breath that Macy didn't quite catch.

"Mom, I'm aware that I haven't been here for twelve years, but I still spoke to him once a week. He wasn't ever going to change his stance on gun ownership."

Macy looked from daughter to mother. In unison they took a deep breath and dipped their heads. Their hands were folded in the same way on their laps. Their mouths held the same hard line. They were at odds and yet so similar. Macy started to speak again and two sets of blue eyes zeroed in on her.

"Then I guess it would come as a surprise to both of you that Philip applied for and received a gun license three months ago. He owned a registered handgun."

Francine stared at Macy. "That's not possible. He would have told me."

"Have you come across any firearms here at the house?"

"I had no idea." Francine glanced at her daughter. "Did he say anything to you?"

Emma looked lost. "Not a word."

"It's possible he decided to take the threats seriously but didn't want to alarm you," said Macy.

Emma picked up Lloyd's photo. "Do these people have ties to any militia groups?" she asked.

"Carla and Lloyd formed their own group two years ago. Lloyd called your father during one of his shows. His language can only be described as colorful."

"Did he threaten to harm my father?"

"Most definitely."

"So that's it then," said Francine. "It's over. You found who did it."

"There are still unanswered questions," said Macy. "We searched the van and Carla and Lloyd's home but have yet to find the murder weapon or your husband's laptop."

"They could have thrown that stuff in the river or buried it," Francine said, her voice going up an octave. "What other questions do you need answered?"

Macy waited a few seconds to answer. It could be that Francine was right and there were no other questions left to answer, but Macy wouldn't let it rest until she was sure.

"We need to be absolutely certain there weren't others involved. Lloyd Spencer was physically incapable of riding a motorcycle, and so far only one person has admitted to seeing Carla on a motorcycle in the past ten years. The conditions were treacherous the night your husband was killed." Macy kept her voice steady. "Winds were gusting at sixty miles per hour and rain was pouring down. It would have taken a lot of skill to ride a bike off road on a night like that."

Francine sat forward. "Was it you in the police car?"

"Yes, ma'am. I'm afraid it was."

"Then you saw everything," said Emma.

"Unfortunately," said Macy, "the motorbike was out of my field of vision and the rider was wearing a helmet, making identification impossible. We've been able to establish the brand of gear the rider was wearing from the description I gave of the logo, and we know the bike cut through the cherry orchard between the house and Route 93 because we found tire tracks." Macy leafed through her file until she found a picture of Philip Long's broken glasses. "We found these up at the house. His vision would have been greatly impaired the night he died. I believe he ran out onto Route 93 in an attempt to flag down a passing vehicle but misjudged the timing." She lowered her voice. "I tried to stop."

"I saw pictures of the accident in the paper." Francine's voice also faded. "You're lucky to have survived."

Macy hesitated before telling them the results of the toxicology screen. Francine was exhausted and Emma looked like she was ready to bolt.

"The medical examiner ran a routine toxicology screen, and I'm afraid we've had some worrying results." Macy took a deep breath. "Heroin was found in your husband's system."

Francine pressed her hands to her face. "My husband never took drugs. Dr. Whitaker tried to prescribe something for the pain after Philip had knee surgery, but he insisted on getting through without them."

Emma's voice was tight. "My mother is right. They would have had to force him."

"That is one line of inquiry," said Macy. "I just wanted to rule out the possibility that he might be using. There's been a rise in heroin abuse in the area over the past few years. There's a lot of it coming through the state on its way to the Bakken oil fields in North Dakota."

Macy looked from daughter to mother. Francine had closed her eyes again. Her face looked serene, but there was nothing relaxed about her posture. Emma's face was in profile. Tears were streaming down her cheek.

"I'm sorry, I don't feel well," said Emma as she got up from the sofa.

Macy stood with her. "You have my card. Please get in touch if you have any questions."

"I'm going out back," said Emma. "Please come see me before you leave."

Francine flinched at the sound of the back door slamming shut. She smoothed her dress and took a deep breath.

"Emma has been away a long time. It's difficult having her here."

"I'm sorry to hear that."

"I'm afraid we're both too stubborn for our own good."

"But you still stayed in touch."

"Yes, but it wasn't the same. We used to talk once a week and meet up a couple of times a year." Francine leveled her blue eyes on Macy again. "To really know someone you have to spend more time together than that. After a while I gave up trying to make it work."

"You stopped going to meet her?"

"I decided enough was enough. In my opinion her reasons for staying away were unfounded. It was time for her to grow up and come home."

Through the back windows Macy could see Emma walking across the yard. Sunlight filtered through pollen and dust. Macy checked the time. It was coming up to midday. Francine cleared her throat.

"A few years ago there was an incident in Chicago," said Francine. "I should have put my feelings aside and gone to be with her, but I stayed here. Now I don't know that we'll ever be able to make it right again."

"May I ask what happened?"

Francine looked like she was lost. "Pardon?"

"You said there was an incident in Chicago."

Francine nodded vigorously. "Emma's boyfriend died of a brain hemorrhage."

"That's so sad."

Another nod. "He fell and hit his head during an altercation with a group of youths who'd been trying to steal Emma's purse."

"I'm sorry to hear that," said Macy.

"All for a handbag. Emma can afford to buy a hundred more with the salary she makes and yet he decided to take a stand. I didn't go to the funeral."

"Did your husband go?"

"Philip was always there for Emma when she needed him."

Macy made some notes. There'd been a hint of anger in Francine's voice. It seemed she was jealous of Emma's close relationship with her father. Everyone interviewed thus far had described the marriage as a happy one. Maybe there were cracks there.

Francine put her fingers to her lips. "I'm not sure why I told you all that. It's not something I tell anyone. She's had a tough few years, but she's pulled through."

"When did you last speak to your daughter?"

"Is that relevant?"

"I'm just trying to get an impression of how much she'd have known about what was going on at home."

"It would have been six years in November." Francine took hold of the cushion again. "Emma continued to talk to her father once or twice a week, but I'd always make myself scarce when she called. He'd tell me her news. I never asked what he said about me or Walleye."

"That's okay. I'm sure Emma will let me know if anything was said that could be of help." Macy paused. "Mrs. Long, your husband had a reputation for being very argumentative when he was on the air. Did this carry through into everyday life?"

Francine almost smiled. "Everyone in town knew that Philip would go out of his way to be contrary if he thought it would get a rise out of someone. It was always in jest, but I suppose it's possible that he could have upset someone. At times he could be relentless."

"I've listened to his radio program. He seemed to enjoy getting under people's skin."

"I sometimes wondered what he saw in me. I'm not the argumentative sort. I'd make peace with the devil if it meant I could have a quiet life."

"You retired from your job recently."

Francine's voice broke. "I was the receptionist at Dr. Whitaker's practice for thirty-four years."

"That's a long time."

"When I started, there was only him and a part-time nurse." Francine frowned. "After he expanded things got a little crazy. Now it's a dozen full-time staff, security at the door. They were very patient with me. I never did get to grips with the computer system."

"It was nice of Dr. Whitaker to come see you. It seems like a lot of people are looking after you."

Francine's eyes shifted to the front windows. "It's a real comfort."

"You look like you could use a rest," said Macy. "Perhaps I could stop by again sometime soon? I'd like to keep you abreast of developments."

Francine picked up Macy's business card and stared at it for a few seconds before rising to her feet. "Please, tell Emma that I've gone to take a nap."

Macy found Emma sitting on an old swing at the far end of the backyard. Beyond her a low wooden fence marked the property boundary. A dozen crows gathered on the lawn. They were cracking apart peanut shells with their sharp beaks.

Eyebrows in a knit, Emma's thumbs were flying over her smartphone's screen. She didn't look up when she spoke.

"My boss has no shame."

Macy plunked herself down on the second swing and pivoted around so she faced the Whitefish Range. Gray clouds had settled in on the lower slopes, but the highest peaks sparkled in the midday sun.

"Seems to be a lot of that going around," said Macy.

Macy was dreading the long drive down to the town of Deer Lodge, where Montana State Prison was located. She knew damn well that the trip had nothing to do with the case she was working on. Ron Forester's interview could be done via video link. She was going because she wanted to see her old boss, Ray Davidson. In his case a video link wouldn't do. She needed him to look her in the eye and say he was sorry.

Emma apologized for taking so long. "I just need to finish this e-mail and I'm all yours."

Macy told her to take as long as she needed. In truth, she wasn't in a hurry to get to her next destination. The only place she really wanted to be was at home with her son. She scrolled through the pictures of Luke that were stored on her phone and reminded herself for what seemed the millionth time that he was happy and well looked after. Macy gazed out into a cherry orchard that stretched out in a precise grid. Sunshine shot through the delicate white blossoms, scattering light and shadow across the neatly tended earth. At the far end of the orchard she could just make out a farmhouse and some outbuildings. The Flathead River ran along one side. The big black cottonwood trees lining its shore rustled in the breeze.

Emma shoved her phone into her jacket pocket. "While I'm here my boss wants me to look into investment opportunities. How tacky can you get?"

Emma got up from the swing and walked to the back fence where a wooden gate was secured with a latch. Someone had made a daisy chain and fixed it to the top of the metal crossbars. Emma touched the petals lightly with her fingertips.

Macy went and stood next to her. "Your work?"

Emma shook her head. "My second cousins stopped by yesterday with their mother. It must have been them."

Emma opened the gate. "Do you feel like taking a walk?"

"Are we trespassing?"

"It's okay. I know the owner."

"After you then."

They followed the fence line until it butted up against the shores of the Flathead River. Emma had her hands tucked deeply into the pockets of the thin coat she was wearing. Her long brown hair fell across shoulders that curved a bit too far inward. When they reached the shore, Macy stayed well back and watched as Emma picked through the dense undergrowth that edged the fast-moving river. In places the wash had submerged trees up to their lower branches. Emma stopped a few feet from the water and pointed out a small raised clump of land that was stranded in the middle of the river. The remnants of a tree fort clung to the branches of a battered tree. The current was so loud Emma had to yell.

"In the summers I used to spend a lot of time out there."

Macy couldn't look at the slate gray water without remembering what it was like to tumble through the drainage ditch in darkness. She focused on the abandoned tree house and the endless blue sky that framed the distant hills. She almost warned Emma to be careful, but instead mumbled something about Walleye Junction being a wonderful place to grow up. Emma picked up a rock and threw it into the churning water before turning back to join Macy.

"I feel stupid for coming home," said Emma. "For some reason I thought my mother needed me."

"Have you always had a difficult relationship?"

"I wouldn't describe it as difficult. Until a few years ago I thought she understood my reasons for staying away from this place." Emma headed east along a path that cut between the cherry trees. "I take it you know the whole story."

"I heard you have a reputation for running away from funerals."

"Makes it all sound so quaint."

"Quaint seems to be what this place is all about."

Emma pointed to the farmhouse. "My best friend, Lucy Winfrey, used to live over there."

"*Winfrey* as in Winfrey Farms?"

"That's the one. Do you know it?"

"I've eaten the cherries. Does that count?"

"It's all that counts. We used to call Lucy's father the cherry king, but we didn't mean it kindly. Caleb was rather obsessive." Emma frowned. "His nephew, Nathan, seems to be in charge now. Anyway, to make a long story short, Lucy's mother, Beverly, and my mother became close. They put a gate between the properties so it would be easier for them to visit each other without having to drive all the way out to the main road. Lucy and I would get dragged along, but we didn't really get on. She was an odd child who was always getting into trouble. I, on the other hand, was already working too hard at being perfect."

"So what changed?" asked Macy.

"Lucy's mother died when we were nine. I honored Beverly's wishes by making a special effort to look after her daughter. Caleb wasn't the most affectionate of fathers and Lucy didn't have many friends. At the church service I offered her candy in an effort to comfort her. When we got to the cemetery she came and found me. When she ran off, I went after her."

"How far did you get?"

"Not very," said Emma. "It was March and there was a lot of snow on the ground. It felt like a long way though. I called my dad from a gas station about five miles south of Walleye."

"I think you're shortchanging yourself a bit there. Around here five miles is quite a distance at that time of year."

"Thankfully, we were dressed for it."

"Your friend was very young," said Macy. "Losing her mother would have been tough."

Emma glanced up at the farmhouse. "There was and is a lot of sadness in that house. I did my best to keep Lucy afloat, but in the end it was a weight I couldn't carry. She died from a drug overdose when we were eighteen."

"Prescription drugs?"

"There was a mixture of Vicodin and OxyContin in her system, but they weren't hers. No one is sure how she got them."

"Sadly, prescription drug abuse is a big problem these days. Was it an accident?"

Emma shrugged. "Cause of death was ruled accidental, but I don't see how that's possible seeing that they found a partial print on the syringe."

"She may have been sharing needles."

Emma's voice rose. "I didn't even know she had a habit. Apparently, the cops found enough of a stash to conclude she was dealing. Lucy was supposedly my best friend and I didn't know her at all. What does that say about me?"

"It's an issue I've been dealing with as well. It makes me wonder if I can trust anyone."

"Well, you're a cop. Paranoia comes with the job, doesn't it?"

Macy smiled. "Yeah, I guess it does. Could it have been a suicide? Was there a note?"

"Oh, there were lots of notes, but Caleb made sure they weren't presented as evidence. I can't say that I wasn't grateful. Lucy left a trail of destruction. Anyway," Emma said, looking Macy full in the face. "It's hard being back here. It's all getting dredged up again."

"That can be a good thing," Macy said, thinking of her upcoming meeting with Ray. "You may have to face your past full on if you want to get it out of your system."

Emma stopped walking about twenty yards from the Winfrey farmhouse. The building had an abandoned look about it. The curtains were drawn and it didn't appear that anyone had been home for some time.

"Lucy's father, Caleb, is in a nursing home," said Emma. "The locals probably think the place is haunted."

"Why's that?"

"Both Beverly and Lucy died in there. By Flathead Valley standards that's pretty spooky."

"Emma, I need to ask you a few more questions about your father."

"I'm not sure how much I can help." Emma turned her back on the farmhouse and started toward home. "I hadn't spoken to him in a few weeks."

"Was that normal?"

"No," said Emma. "We were pretty good at keeping a once a week routine, but it was never a set time. Two weeks ago there was nothing, but it was really busy at work so I let it be. When the same thing happened this week I called my mother."

"How did he seem the last time you spoke?"

"He was excited about a new story he was researching for his show, but he wanted to do a bit more work before he told me about it. He was always careful about getting things right. While he found great pleasure in exposing the misdeeds of others, he never took liberties with the truth. He did imply that there'd be a lot of fallout when the story broke."

"Your mother says she didn't know what he was working on."

"That's odd. My parents normally talked about everything. What about his computer?"

"There's nothing on it except the research he'd done for stories he's already covered, the last one being the program on militia groups from a few weeks ago. Judging by what we've found so far it doesn't look like he's been doing any research for the past two months."

"Could he have had another computer?"

"That's what I'm thinking, but we've searched the house and his office at the radio station and have found nothing," said Macy.

"Maybe he had it with him when he was kidnapped. Have you asked my mother?"

"She told Lou Turner that she knew nothing about another laptop."

"Anyone else's parents and I'd say that was possible, but my mom and dad were close. If there was another laptop she would have known about it."

"You've been away for a long while," said Macy. "Things may have changed. Your mother didn't know that your father bought a gun."

"I suppose so." Emma picked a blossom from a cherry tree and crushed it in her fingertips. "You saw my father die."

"I wish I could have done something."

"Odds are we're never going to know what was really going on."

"I'm going to do my best to figure it out." Macy took out her phone and scrolled through the recent messages. Gina was trying to reach her. "Emma, I suggest you try to get your mother to talk more about what your father was up to over the past couple of months. There might be something important that she's forgotten."

"I'll go through his papers as well."

"I thought we'd seen everything."

"There are boxes of stuff in the attic," said Emma. "Some of it dates back years. There's always a possibility that he stashed something up there."

"You'll let me know if you find anything?"

"I'd appreciate if you did the same for me."

Macy hesitated. "This investigation could take some time. Are you going to be able to stick around?"

"Provided I find some interesting investment opportunities for my boss, that won't be a problem."

# 7

Gina looked up from her computer screen and cracked a smile. "I got us on a flight to Deer Lodge. The associate warden at the prison is arranging for transport when we arrive at the airport. If all goes well we'll be back here in time for a late dinner."

"I owe you a drink," said Macy. "I wasn't looking forward to the drive down there."

"Neither was I. My back is killing me." Gina sat up a little taller and stretched. "They're expecting us at the airport in the next half hour so we'd better get moving."

Gina had the homepage of the Montana Brewers Association Web site opened on her computer. Macy leaned in so she could get a better look.

"Any luck tracking down Sean Spencer?"

"Sean is keeping a low profile, but his girlfriend, Xtina, has been partying her way through various social media platforms."

"Can we please call her Kristina? I can't say Xtina without feeling ridiculous."

"Kristina it is then. According to what I've read online, she plans raves for a living."

"Sean told Kyle Miller she was an event planner."

"That's a bit of a stretch."

"Has Sean used his phone?" asked Macy.

"Nada. Ditto on his bank card. No sightings on his truck." Gina scrolled through the list of brewers. "I do have one solid lead that puts Sean in Bozeman. He interviewed at a brewery near the university campus."

"Bridger Brewing," Macy said, pointing to the screen. "I know that place."

"Apparently, it's a good one. Sean put in an application for a bar staff position. The manager liked Sean but didn't hire him. He wasn't too impressed that he brought his obnoxious girlfriend along to an interview. His words, not mine."

"Was it Kristina?"

"The manager didn't get a good look at her because she kept to the far end of the bar, but he could hear her just fine. He thought she may have been drunk or possibly high. He sent over a screen grab from their security cameras." Gina opened the image on her laptop. "It's definitely her."

Macy stared. "She's practically mugging for the camera."

"Still have no idea what her real name is. Xtina, Kris Kringle, and Kiss Kriss are the online personas I've found so far. She's Latvian and may be here illegally. Anyway, I've handed the whole mess over to the tech guys. Hopefully they'll be able to figure it out."

"When did Sean interview at the brewery?"

"Yesterday morning. No way he could have been around when his parents died."

"Could we get an address for him in Bozeman? He must have put something on the job application."

"It's a house twenty miles from town. Local law enforcement is heading there now." Gina snapped the laptop shut and handed Macy a paper bag. "I picked up some lunch for us."

"What, no meal service on the flight?"

"Flying on the state's dime, we'll be lucky if that plane has wings."

. . .

Macy woke from her nap just as the twin-engine aircraft began its descent. She peered out the window. Huge circular hay fields patterned a wide valley that followed a course south along Route 90. To the west, snowcapped mountains flanked Deer Lodge, a town of three thousand residents. It had once been a major transportation hub, but that came to an end when they closed the railroad down. Since then its largest employer had been the Montana State Prison.

Macy nudged Gina awake.

"Are you sure someone is picking us up? We could always grab a taxi."

Gina yawned. "Don't worry. The associate warden assured me that someone would be at the terminal waiting for us."

Macy opened Ron Forester's file and read through what she already knew. He'd been an accountant for nearly twenty-one years. His client list included mayors, city council members, doctors, and lawyers. They may have stood up for him in court, but Macy was pretty sure they would have abandoned him to his fate once he was convicted of assault.

"I feel guilty," Macy said, closing the file.

"Why's that?"

"My home in Helena is only an hour away from Deer Lodge."

"Try not to think about it."

"I can't help it. I miss my son."

"Well, we all have somewhere we'd rather be." Gina paused. "Are you still set on seeing Ray?"

"Yep," said Macy, feeling less confident than she sounded. "That's the idea."

"Why are you bothering? If I were you I wouldn't want to be anywhere near that son of a bitch."

"Somehow, I feel I owe it to my son. He is Luke's father."

"I think you're carrying guilt that isn't yours to carry," said Gina. "Ray is the one who committed the crime, not you."

"He confessed, but he's yet to show any regret. He's only sorry he got caught."

Gina gave Macy a harsh look. "Are you waiting for some sign of remorse?"

"I guess I want him to be the man I once knew and respected."

"That's not going to happen. Not where he is anyway. They've got him in solitary twenty-four seven. His fellow inmates want him dead, and the guards aren't too fond of him either." Gina brushed some crumbs from her trousers. "I heard his request for a transfer to a privately run prison has been denied three times. No one is in the mood to make his stay more comfortable."

"Every time I feel sorry for him I imagine what it was like dying in that fire."

"You should do whatever it takes to get you through, but don't go there. It will only drag you down."

Macy picked at the water bottle's label. "What are people saying about me?"

"Macy, you really shouldn't go there either."

"I can't help it."

"You need thicker skin. Whether you like it or not, people are gonna talk. Getting involved with Ray was a mistake, but anyone with a pulse can see how it could happen. I met my husband on the job. It was a rocky start. We're damn lucky it worked out."

"Why's that?"

Gina looked away. "Because he worked nights and I worked days. It was a long time before we really had a chance to get to know each other."

Located a few miles west of the Deer Lodge Airport, Montana State Prison was a sprawling compound that housed nearly fifteen hundred inmates. A local patrol officer met Macy and Gina at the airport terminal. Outside the car windows the landscape was flat and gray. Clouds hovered low over vast tracts of land where family homes appeared to be as rare as trees. Macy sat by herself in the backseat listening to Gina and their driver make small talk. The medical examiner in Helena called just as the prison's perimeter fence was coming into view.

"Macy," said Priscilla. "The tox screen results are rather alarming. Both Carla and Lloyd died of a massive heroin overdose. Lloyd's blood contained 1.58 milligrams per liter. Carla's levels were slightly lower, but it was still three times what is generally considered to be a lethal dose.

"Wow. That does seem high."

"They would have had to shoot up around 240 milligrams to come close to these levels. It's not unprecedented, but I personally have never seen anything like it."

"Any chance it was a mistake? Were there other drugs in the system that might have impaired their judgment?"

"Lloyd Spencer's blood alcohol level was 0.12 so maybe, but since he was an alcoholic I doubt he would have been impaired even at those levels. Other than the heroin, his wife had buprenorphine in her system at levels consistent to what her therapist prescribed. There was a single puncture wound on Carla, but Lloyd looks like he was shooting up on a regular basis. We only found Carla's prints on the syringe, so it appears she administered the fatal dose that killed her husband before turning the syringe on herself. I don't believe that's what happened though."

"There was a third party?"

"Yep. I think Ryan already told you that you were right about the bodies. They were moved. We've confirmed that the gravel found embedded in the heels of Lloyd Spencer's shoes came from the bakery's parking lot. Looks like he was dragged and she was carried. We've found evidence that they died in the van and were positioned on the verge. It throws into doubt the theory that this was accidental."

"There was no obvious sign of struggle."

"Carla has hand-shaped bruises on her upper arms. She was restrained at some point before she died."

"It could have been Lloyd. He was known for being physically abusive."

"Handprints are too small to be his."

"Any transfer?" asked Macy.

"Whoever handled the bodies was using gloves. By the way, there was trauma to the area near Carla's right temple. I could only see it once I removed her hair. It's possible that a gun was pressed tightly against her skull."

"My gun?"

"Might be. If we find the weapon we can check the muzzle for Carla Spencer's DNA. Unless it's been wiped clean there should be plenty."

"Thank you, Priscilla. Let me know if you find anything else."

By the time they were led into the associate warden's office, Macy and Gina had been waiting for over two hours. Macy sat down in the seat that was offered and smiled politely, but inside she felt like screaming.

Even though it was warm in the room, Alex Finley wore a navy field jacket zipped up to his neck. He apologized for keeping them waiting before sitting down across from them. His hands were shaking. Seeing that his guests noticed, he smiled nervously.

"I've just come from the prison hospital," he said, clearing his throat. "There's been an incident."

Macy almost asked if Ray Davidson was involved, but Gina spoke first.

"Ron Forester?"

The assistant warden blanched. "He was involved but is thankfully okay. According to early reports, a prisoner attacked people out in the exercise yard at random."

Macy kept her voice steady. "When did this happen?"

"Earlier this afternoon."

"Was Forester singled out?"

"I seriously doubt it. There were a couple of other prisoners who faired far worse than him. The prisoner who attacked him was shot dead by guards." He lowered his voice. "There was a lot of blood."

"Did you find the weapon?" asked Gina.

"A utility knife blade had been embedded into a toothbrush handle. We do all we can to keep the place secure, but they're mighty resourceful."

"You seem confident the attack was random."

"Forester has been here a relatively short time, but he is already well liked. It's difficult to imagine someone having a grudge against him."

"Why's that?" asked Macy.

"He is affable, generous . . . does what he can to help out. He tutors inmates who are nearing their release dates—how to do tax returns, manage household bills, stay out of debt, that sort of thing. He also spends a lot of time working on his appeal."

Gina looked through her notes. "How could this happen? Wasn't Forester housed with minimum security prisoners?"

"That was normally the case, but there was a fire. Nearly thirty high security prisoners were shunted out into the yard." He spread his hands. "The perpetrator died on the operating table so we may never know the reasons behind the attack. He was a lifer. Might be he decided that he'd had enough."

Macy gazed out the window toward the watchtower they'd passed on the road in.

"What sort of injuries did Forester sustain?" asked Macy.

"Defensive wounds, mostly to his hands. We pride ourselves on running secure facilities. Thankfully, incidents such as this are rare." All business again, the assistant warden opened a folder. "I understand you've put in a request to speak to Ray Davidson as well."

Macy hesitated. "I'm hoping he'll have some insight. With his vast knowledge of private militia movements in the state, he may have some information that could help us with our investigation. Will it still be possible to see him?"

"We're pretty much in lockdown at the moment, but I've made an exception as it's official business. There's a conference room next door you can use. He's there now. My assistant will make sure you have everything you need. If you'll excuse me, I have to get back downstairs and meet the forensics team."

"What about Ron Forester?" asked Macy. "Will we be able to meet with him as well?"

"He is still receiving medical treatment, but he should be available in the next hour. Will you be able to wait?"

"That won't be a problem," said Gina.

The sleeve of his jacket pulled away as he reached out to shake their hands. The cuffs of his white shirt were soaked with blood. He turned a deeper shade of pale.

"I've not even had time to change yet."

Ray sat at the conference table dressed in an orange prison jumpsuit staring down at his handcuffed wrists. Since Macy last saw him, he'd grown a beard and lost a considerable amount of weight. She pressed her back against the closed door and watched him. There were so many different things she wanted to say and do at once, all of them conflicting. Keeping well away, she skirted the edges of the room as she made her way to a window that overlooked the exercise yard. A forensics team had started processing the scene. The assistant warden stood on the edge with his hands in his pockets speaking to a few prison security officers wearing dark sweatshirts and camouflage trousers.

"When I heard there'd been an incident I was afraid it was you," she said.

Ray looked up at her and she didn't look away. She walked to the table, pulled out the chair opposite him, and sat down. It took a few seconds before she was able to speak.

"Logic dictates that I should hate you, but that reaction tells me I still care. Why do you suppose that is?"

He put his shackled wrists on the table and leaned forward a fraction. She wasn't bothered that he didn't respond. She knew exactly what she wanted to say.

"There was a time when you were everything to me. You recruited me out of university, you were my mentor, my boss . . . my confidant. And when we eventually started seeing each other, I'd like to think that we were happy. I want to believe that Luke was conceived by two people who were in love, that you were and are capable of love."

Ray blinked.

"Your son is getting on nicely by the way. As you know, he'll be three in December." She reached into her bag and pulled out the sheaf of photos she'd printed off. "These are for you."

She spread the 8 by 10s out on the table in the same way she would if she were asking someone to identify a suspect. She watched Ray focus on each one in turn, his expression growing harder every time Luke smiled up at him.

Macy rested her chin in her hands. "It's fortunate Luke is still so young. I haven't had to explain where his father is."

"Don't."

"Don't what, Ray?"

"He doesn't need to know I exist." With difficulty, Ray gathered the photos and pushed them back across the table. "And I don't need to be reminded of what I've lost." He looked up at her. "So that goes for you too. I don't want you coming here."

"You could have refused to see me."

Ray stared up at the ceiling. "It's not that simple. I couldn't not see you."

"I'm having a hard time getting past you."

"You should have given me a way out. A little warning . . . a loaded gun." He rubbed his eyes. "It would have saved the state a lot of time and money."

Macy flinched. "You know me better than that. Regardless of my feelings for you, I wasn't going to let you take the easy way out."

"And yet here you are. Sitting in this room with me. Right now. Admitting that you still have feelings for a convicted felon. Admitting that you can't bring yourself to hate me." He slumped forward and rested his chin in his hands. "Maybe, just maybe it's better to keep that sort of thing to yourself."

Macy slipped her hands in her pockets and made a conscious decision to keep them there. She drew the line at touching him.

"I believe in being direct," she said. "If I feel something I say it."

"What are you feeling now?"

"Fear."

"Why are you afraid, Macy? You're a free woman. You can walk out of here anytime you like." He held up his handcuffed wrists. "I can't hurt you."

"I can't walk away when you're in my head. I keep thinking that I should have seen the warning signs, that I missed the point when I could have saved you."

"Careful Macy, it sounds like you're developing a God complex. Maybe that new job of yours at the Department of Justice is going to your head."

"I'm far from God. If anything I've been humbled." She caught his eye. "How did you know I changed jobs?"

"My lawyer told me. It was a wise career move. They'll give you far more autonomy than I ever did."

"It's a good team of people."

"If you're set on rebuilding your reputation you may want to keep away from doing any internal investigations. How's your boss?"

Macy almost smiled. "Pleasant. A little dull."

"I'm sure you'll find he's more difficult to please than you realize."

"You know him well?"

"Well enough." Ray yawned. "He knows his limitations so he surrounds himself with people who can make up for them. If he took you on it's because he feels you have potential."

"Nice to know, but I'm not here to talk about my new job."

"And here I was hoping I'd successfully changed the subject."

"Ray, you were a brilliant man, and I was one of the few people close to you. If I knew what was going on, I would have intervened. I'd like to think you would have listened to me."

"You're giving yourself far too much credit. I wasn't in the mood to listen to anyone."

"Are you listening now?"

He raised his wrists again. "I don't have a choice."

"You've never shown remorse. Why is that?"

Ray didn't answer.

"I know you're sorry for all you've lost, but are you sorry for what happened in that fire?"

"It's not as simple as that, Macy. Either way I'd have lost everything. One stupid mistake and I was fucked."

"I'll take that as a *no*."

"I only wanted to silence her. She wouldn't—"

"Fall into line like I did? I was so gullible, wasn't I? Your bright-eyed ingénue, ready to take a bullet in more ways than one." Macy paused. "You asked me why I'm afraid so I'll tell you. I'm afraid that I've been wired so well to expect disappointment that it's now my default position."

Macy gathered her son's photos and stood up from the table, slamming the chair into place as she turned to go.

"I wasn't a born cynic. You made me into one." Macy opened the door. "And do you know what, Ray? It sucks. It really sucks."

Ron Forester looked more like a boxer than an accountant. Both his hands were heavily bandaged and a strip of tape bridged his swollen nose. His deep-set eyes were shadowed with black and blue hues. Someone had placed a plastic cup full of orange juice on the table in front of him. He leaned forward so he could sip it through a straw.

"I hope you guys will put in a good word for me," he said.

Macy feigned concern. Ron Forester was convicted on charges of aggravated sexual assault. Nothing she said would make any difference.

"I'll do what I can," she said.

"The woman who accused me of assault has a history of psychiatric problems. It should have been disclosed in court."

"Do you have a court date for your appeal?" asked Macy.

"Yes, but it's taking too much time." He held up his bandaged hands as evidence. "I nearly died out there today."

"Do you have any reason to believe you were singled out as a target this afternoon?"

He shook his head. "As far as I can tell it was some random nutcase.

You never know what's going to cause offense in here. You can be staring off into space and some asshole will accuse you of looking at him funny."

"I need to speak to you about what happened at your home on Edgewood Road."

"I'm not sure how much more I can add."

"I understand that you went through photos from the scene with the detectives who first interviewed you."

"They left one hell of a mess."

Macy slipped out several photos of the kitchen, including one of the contents of the refrigerator.

"In general would you say that you are a fairly neat person?"

Ron Forester sifted through the photos. He stopped and stared at the photo of the inside of his refrigerator. "I'd say I'm average." He pointed to the photo. "That's not my Red Bull."

"Anything else that's odd about the photo?"

Ron leaned in. "The Chinese takeaway?"

"The rest is yours?"

He shrugged. "I suppose so. I've had other things to worry about. Is there something important that I'm missing here?"

"Does anything look like it's not where you normally put it?"

He stared again. "It's too neat."

"Would you be surprised to learn that your condiments are now alphabetized?"

Two eyebrows rose in unison. "I didn't do that."

"What about the cleaner you used? Had she ever done anything like that?"

"God, no. I think I'd have fired her if she'd wasted her time organizing my cupboards."

Macy showed him several photos of the contents of his cabinets.

He laughed and winced at the same time. "It's like a scene from *Sleeping with the Enemy*."

"So you don't alphabetize your spices either?"

"Hell, no."

"Do you know anyone who has these sorts of tendencies?"

"No one I can think of."

"We're pretty sure you've had some kind of contact with the perpetrators. They knew the code for your alarm system."

"I already gave the guys that came to interview me a list of anyone who may have known the access code."

"Everyone has checked out so far. You were with Mountain Security?"

He nodded. "For years. I assume they do background checks on their staff."

Macy thought about what Kyle Miller had said about Flathead Valley Security employees all being ex-military or ex–law enforcement. Mountain Security had a similar employee profile.

"We checked," said Macy. "There's no known connection between the security company and the kidnappers."

"You know who did it?"

"Carla and Lloyd Spencer were found dead yesterday morning. We've come to believe they were involved." Macy placed their DMV photos on the table in front of him. "Do you know them?"

He stared at Carla's photo. "I can't place her, but she sure looks familiar."

"She worked at a waitress at the IHOP."

"The IHOP?" he said, looking insulted. "Give me some credit."

"For the past year she's delivered pizzas."

He tapped his bandaged finger on the photo. "That's it. I only remember because I think it's the last time I actually had fun. Some friends came over and we ordered pizza. One of my guests had drunk a bit too much. He invited her in."

"How long did she stay?"

"I'm not sure. She was still there when I went to bed."

"I need his name."

"Could be awkward. He's married."

"We'll be discreet."

"Bob Crawley."

Macy made a face.

"You know him?" asked Ron.

"We've met."

"Then he's probably made a pass at you," he said.

"It was in a professional capacity."

"That wouldn't have mattered to him."

"His wife wasn't too pleased the last time we spoke, either."

"I hope you nail him for this," he said.

"I thought he was your friend."

"Now that I'm in here I know exactly who my friends are." He glanced down at his bandaged hands like he was contemplating counting the number of friends he had on his fingers. "It turns out I don't have any."

Night was falling as the prison's well-lit perimeter faded in the rearview mirror. The road heading into town was empty save a pinprick of red taillights in the distance. Following a round of polite introductions their driver had gone quiet. Gina had her hand wedged deep in a bag of potato chips.

"We missed our flight so I've initiated Plan B."

Macy closed her eyes. Driving all the way back to Walleye Junction held no appeal.

"Does Plan B involve a glass of red wine?" asked Macy. "I still owe you a drink."

"Sadly, no, but I'll take a rain check on that. I've rented a car. We're driving to Helena. We'll get a flight from there in the morning."

"You'll have to spend time with your mother-in-law."

"She's not so bad in small doses. To tell you the truth I think I resent her sometimes because she's there with the kids when I can't be. Anyway, I suspect I'll arrive just as she's heading up to bed."

"Luke will be sound asleep by the time I get home."

"Wake him up. A little anarchy never hurt anyone."

"Honestly, I'm not sure I'm up for the anarchy. I'll see him in the morning. Did the Bozeman police find anything at the address Sean listed on his employment application for the brewery?"

"Looks like he used a random address. The homeowner said he'd never heard of Sean Spencer."

Macy pictured Kristina's face captured on the security footage. There'd only been one camera at the entrance to the microbrewery, and it almost seemed like she'd gone out of her way to find it.

"What is going on with that kid?" said Macy. "He and his girlfriend go out of their way to advertise their location and then disappear into the night."

"They could be leading us on a wild-goose chase. For all we know they're back in the Flathead Valley."

Macy let herself in the front door and locked it behind her. Her mother was sitting on the family room sofa. As usual she had a book in her hand.

"Hi Mom," said Macy, taking off her jacket and hanging it on a hook.

Ellen put her book to one side and took off her reading glasses. "I wasn't expecting you tonight."

"We were at Montana State Prison all afternoon. The interviews took longer than expected so we decided to come back to Helena instead."

"You must be exhausted. There's a bottle of red open on the counter."

"Thank you, I'll go pour myself a glass." Macy noticed her mother's glass was nearly empty. "Would you like a refill?"

"No thank you, I've had my one for today."

Macy wandered into the dimly lit kitchen and poured a large measure of red. She'd fallen asleep in the car and was still feeling disoriented. She sifted through some mail that had been left on the counter. The only thing that stood out was the letter from Ray's eldest daughter, Nicole. She carried it into the living room and set it down on the coffee table next to her glass of wine.

"There's some leftover pasta in the refrigerator," said Ellen.

Macy settled down on the sofa next to her mother. She took a sip of her wine but left the letter unopened.

"I wish I'd waited," said Macy. "Gina stopped at a fast food Mexican restaurant for dinner. The woman likes her junk food."

"She likes her opinions as well. In those five minutes you left us alone yesterday morning she shared her thoughts on everything from gay marriage to the value of a college education. For the record, we disagreed on both counts."

"She's never been shy about letting folks know what's on her mind."

Ellen glanced at the coffee table. "I see you found Nicole's letter," she said.

Macy closed her eyes. It was the fourth letter she'd received from Ray's daughter since her and Ray's past relationship became public. Macy wasn't convinced any sort of correspondence was healthy for either of them, but during a brief phone call with Nicole's therapist, Macy had been told that it was a good idea for Nicole and her half-brother Luke to form some sort of relationship.

*Nicole is convinced that Luke is the only positive thing that has come out of this difficult time. As part of her ongoing therapy, I've encouraged her to reach out to you.*

*Does her mother know about this?*

*Unfortunately, her mother has washed her hands of the situation.*

Ellen placed her empty wineglass next to the envelope. "Are you going to open it?" she asked.

"I'm afraid to."

"Remind me what the last one was like."

Macy stared into space. "Four pages of teenage angst. She pretty much called me every name in the book and then some. I couldn't finish reading it."

"If she's following a pattern then this one will be an apology."

"I told her therapist that I wasn't willing to do this any longer if the verbal abuse continued."

"What did the therapist say?"

"She didn't seem to think my discomfort was equal to Nicole's. Apparently, Nicole has been self-harming for some time but has recently graduated to slitting her wrists."

"How does this kind of thing happen?" said Ellen. "I remember her being such a happy little girl."

"Ray told me that you could see the moment she changed by looking at family photos."

"How old was she?"

"Twelve. They were camping in Yellowstone Park. He and his wife had a huge fight in front of the girls. Nicole was never the same. The snapshots from the trip are like before and after photos. Healthy one day. Nervous wreck the next."

"She was old enough to understand that her parent's problems were serious," said Ellen.

"You have to admire her single-mindedness. She practically destroyed herself trying to keep the family together."

"Wouldn't it be nice if she directed that same energy outward instead of inward?"

"I'm not so sure about that," said Macy, taking another sip of wine. "It's pretty negative energy."

Macy checked the return address on the envelope. It had been sent from the therapist's office in Chicago. It had been agreed that neither Macy's nor Nicole's home addresses would be revealed.

"I don't like that she's fixated on Luke," said Macy. "The girl is as manipulative as she is unstable. Unless there's some real improvement I'm not letting her near him."

"You won't get any argument from me on that front. How was today? Did you go see Ray in the end?"

"Ray doesn't want me to visit anymore. He told me that he didn't want Luke to know he exists."

"That's probably for the best."

"Luke is going to find out eventually. I can't protect him forever."

"We've been over this a hundred times," said Ellen. "Luke is the most loved up child I've ever met. He'll be fine."

Macy squeezed her mother's hand. "I know I don't say thank you often enough. I wouldn't have been able to get through this without you. You've been amazing."

"You'd have been fine on your own."

"I wouldn't have been able to work."

"You would have had to cut back for a few years, that's all."

"Doesn't really work that way in law enforcement. There are no half measures."

"Well," her mother said, rising to her feet. "It's all academic. I'm here so all is well. Are you going to bed soon?"

Macy held up her glass. "I'm passing out as soon as I finish this."

Ellen snatched the letter off the coffee table before Macy had a chance to pick it up again.

"I'm taking this with me," said Ellen. "Regardless of its tone, I doubt it's good bedtime reading."

The hallway light illuminated the soft curves of Luke's face. Macy watched him from the doorway for a few minutes before sitting on the edge of his narrow bed. She bent over and kissed his forehead. He stirred but did not wake. She removed one of his hands from beneath the blankets and pressed it to her cheek. It felt like a hot stone. She had no idea what she'd say to Luke when he was old enough to ask about his father. As far as she was concerned, the Ray she knew was dead. She didn't think she could breathe life into him if she tried.

Macy stretched out on her side and rested her head on Luke's pillow. Her cell phone buzzed in her pocket. It was Aiden, probably checking to see if she was okay. She started to answer then stopped. Aiden could wait until morning. She draped her arm across her son and closed her eyes.

# 8

Francine Long sat perched in the passenger seat of her daughter's hatchback with her handbag resting against her chest like a shield.

"Your car is so small," said Francine. "Don't you feel vulnerable sitting down so low?"

Emma put the car in gear and backed out of the driveway.

"Finding parking is difficult where I live. I don't have much of a choice."

"You wouldn't be able to drive this car here during the winter."

"I wasn't planning on it."

Francine checked the time. "After all the trouble Father Kevin has gone to organizing the service I'd hate to be late."

"The church is less than five minutes away. We'll be fine."

"We're expecting a high turnout so parking will be difficult."

"Then it's a good thing I have a small car."

Francine pointed to a narrow side street. "Take a right up here. Traffic will be heavy on the main road. We'll go the back way."

"We could have walked," said Emma. "The fresh air would have been good for you."

"No, it's better this way. I feel safer."

Emma almost reminded her mother that she'd just said that she'd felt unsafe but decided it best she keep that one to herself. She peeked in her review mirror. A patrol car trailed them at a discreet distance.

Francine held her hand up to the vent. "Can we turn the heat on? I'm a little cold."

"It should warm up in a minute." Emma paused. "Since I arrived home I've been thinking a lot about Lucy. I guess it's easier than thinking about Dad."

"She used to come see me quite a bit the year you were away. Nine times out of ten she'd arrive at the back door in tears. She and Caleb fought all the time. If the wind direction was right we could hear them shouting."

"Nathan said she had been getting up to all sorts of stuff," said Emma.

"That may be so, but at first she just seemed to be at a loose end. She'd always bring over her sketchbook. That girl was always leaving stuff behind. I think it was her way of keeping a foothold in our lives. There's a whole folder of her work up in the attic somewhere. A few months after you left for England I showed some of Lucy's drawings to Dot."

Emma clutched at various childhood memories. Finding nothing that pointed her in Dot's direction, she nodded vaguely.

Francine sighed. "Surely, you remember Dr. Whitaker's second wife, the one before Sharon? Dot used to be a nurse at the doctor's practice."

"Tiny yet formidable."

"That's the one."

Dot had organized the art fair that took place alongside the Cherry Harvest Festival every autumn. A self-taught artist, she favored big blousy still lifes and paint-by-number style pastoral scenes. In the summer months she could be spotted with her easel positioned anywhere there was a scenic view. In the winter she disappeared into her art studio up at her house. She had a gallery on Main and her little pictures, as she liked to call them, sold well among visiting tourists. One of Dot's paintings hung above the fireplace in Emma's parents' home. Emma had tried to get her father to admit that he secretly hated it, but he was unusually polite when it came to Dot's artwork.

Emma cleared her throat. "Does Dot still paint pretty pictures?"

"Pretty isn't really her thing these days."

"Don't tell me she's gone to the dark side."

"She's had a rough time."

"When did she and Dr. Whitaker split up?" asked Emma.

"Eight years ago."

"Did she keep the McMansion?"

"Among other things. She also still has a share in the doctor's practice." Francine managed a smile. "I bet that keeps Peter on his toes."

The Whitaker's home was an eight-thousand-square-foot edifice built into the hills overlooking Walleye Junction. The gated property had a long, winding drive, six bedrooms, and an indoor swimming pool that doubled as a dance floor when the retractable cover was put in place. The Whitakers' parties were legendary. Emma pictured Dot holding a cocktail and a cigarette while she danced on the diving board.

"It's funny how memory works," said Emma. "Five minutes ago I couldn't recall Dot's face, but now it's like it all happened yesterday."

"Hopefully, there are some good memories stored away in there," said Francine. "I think you sometimes forget that you were happy here for a long while."

If Francine hadn't been directing her every move, Emma would have driven past the multistory glass and brick fronted building without guessing it was a church. After the gas main explosion destroyed half of downtown, the church expanded into the empty lot where the cinema had once stood. It now took up one city block. Her father had joked that the parishioners were under the misguided impression that being seen from heaven was the next best thing to being there. In recent conversations, he'd been more withering in his criticism. He'd taken to calling it the church that pain built. He'd always been critical of organized religion, so Emma hadn't been surprised by his remarks. She'd warned him not to let Francine hear him say things like that.

The municipal parking lot was a block east of Main Street. Emma backed into a space between two pickup trucks that were jacked up higher than her car's roofline. The community park and public library were directly across the street. Caught in the dense leaves of overgrown trees, the light coming off the streetlights barely touched the wide sidewalks. Long shadows fell across the infield of a baseball diamond. The field was empty aside from a few young girls who loitered near the dugouts wearing shorts and crop tops. Their sharp laughter cut through the noise of traffic. Emma watched them for a few seconds before going around the car to open her mother's door.

Francine was searching her bag for tissues.

"The prayer service was a thoughtful gesture, but I don't know how I'm going to manage this."

Francine's cheeks were damp with tears. Emma fished a packet of tissues out from the glove compartment and handed them to Francine.

"Let's just stay here a minute," said Emma. "They're not going to start without us."

Francine stared out the front windshield. "I should have come to see you in Chicago when you were in a bad way. I'm sorry."

Emma couldn't think of what to say. She didn't want to talk about what had happened in Chicago. She glanced over at the park. The girls were running up and down the sidewalk. Their bare legs and midriffs shone stark white in the glare of the passing headlights.

"It was pride that kept me away," said Francine. "Your father was so angry with me. I'm not sure we were ever the same after that."

Emma pictured the high hill overlooking the town where Daniel had grown up—a grid of streets, a town square, and the furniture store that had been his family's ancestral home. These were the things that were pointed out to Emma and Philip as they waited for the service to commence. No one wanted to talk about how Daniel had died.

"Never question how much Dad loved you," said Emma.

"He was keeping secrets." Francine stared straight ahead. "I thought that maybe he was having an affair."

"What would make you suspect such a thing?"

"It was just a feeling I had."

"There was something else going on. He bought a gun. For some reason he was afraid. It wasn't an affair."

At the sound of screaming, Emma turned toward the park. Arms stretched wide and laughing hysterically, the girls ran across the street. A car horn sounded. Brakes squealed. A man shouted.

"I think it might have been Dot," said Francine, pressing a tissue into her cheeks. "She's gotten so glamorous since the divorce. I feel like a frump standing next to her."

"Don't say things like that. You're beautiful and Dad loved you. He would have never done something like that. Besides Dot's been your friend since before I was born."

"You didn't see her when she set her sights on Peter. People around here seem to forget that he was still married to his first wife when Dot started working as a nurse at the practice. He had two young children and another on the way. Dot didn't give them much thought. Why am I any different?"

"Mom, please, don't do this now. You're only making yourself upset."

"I don't know what's come over me. I used to trust people."

Emma held out her hand. "Your friends are waiting at the church. You'll feel better once you're there."

Emma felt like she was standing in front of a wall of photographers. Every face was the pop of a flashbulb. Every flash set off a cascade of memories. She didn't have time to think. She shook hands with people who said that they remembered her fondly and endured lingering hugs from those who claimed to know her well. It took her and her mother twenty minutes to walk from the street to the church foyer where administrative offices were partitioned behind plate glass and floating stairs led up to the upper landing and smaller meeting rooms. A stained-glass archway some twenty feet in height framed an enormous set of oak doors that opened wide onto the seated congregation. Emma took a deep breath. The predictions of a large turnout had been correct. There was a discreet sign directing visitors to the ladies' room. Not since high school had she been so desperate to hide in a stall.

An older woman pulled Emma into a long hug. She smelled of

perfume and hairspray. Her skin was powdered, her glasses crystal clear. She held Emma away from her, clutching her forearms with strong hands.

"It is so good to see you again."

Emma stared at her blankly, not remembering. "It's nice of you to come," she said cautiously.

The woman placed a warm hand to Emma's cheek. "You were such a joy to teach."

Emma smiled. Perhaps her mother was right after all. It was too easy to forget that she'd once been happy in Walleye Junction. She remembered her classroom, sunlight streaming through tall windows and desks in neat rows. Lucy was next to her, cracking jokes, making her and Nathan laugh.

Dressed in a suit and wearing his trademark benevolent smile, Dr. Peter Whitaker held the lectern with both hands. The overhead lights reflected off his silver hair as his eyes swept across the congregation.

"To be truly blessed is to be blessed with a sense of purpose, a clear understanding of why we're here and how our faith might bring us closer to both God and our goals. Philip Long may not have understood God, but he understood purpose. A true crusader in our midst, he not only took on the big headline-grabbing issues but also the humbler concerns that dogged our daily lives. If you met him on the street and he asked how you were, it wasn't some empty platitude that would be followed by a hollow wish for you to have a nice day. Philip was a man who stopped and listened and then listened some more. Before you knew it, you'd find yourself buying him a cup of coffee. And if you were really lucky you'd get to buy him breakfast as well."

He waited for the congregation's laughter to die down.

"Today our community mourns the loss of an individual who made it his mission to expose the darker side of our humanity so that the light in all of us might shine a little brighter. Tonight we pray for his wife, Francine, who I've known these many years, and his daughter, Emma, who has at long last returned to her home here in Walleye Junction." The doctor paused again. "I think I speak on their behalf when I thank the people who helped organize the prayer service this evening. It will be a long time before this community heals, but events like this bring us one step closer. Some of you have been invited to a small reception upstairs. I apologize to those of you who will not be able to attend." He looked around. "We really had no idea so many people would come, otherwise we would have made arrangements for a larger venue. I'm sure Francine and her daughter thank you from the bottom of their hearts. Perhaps we could just have a few moments of quiet contemplation before calling this gathering to a close."

Emma sat in the front row next to her mother, clutching a program she'd been handed as they'd been swept into the hall. Emma couldn't see Dr. Peter Whitaker through her tears. She reached into her bag, but her mother was there first. Francine held up a tissue. In her trembling hand, it waved like a white flag. Emma said a quiet thank-you and pressed it to her eyes.

In the row behind her two women were whispering.

"Are you going to the reception?"

"Of course I'm going. I've been making canapés all afternoon."

"It's nice that Emma is here for her mother."

The second woman lowered her voice further. "She's too thin. A strong wind and she'd snap."

Emma and her mother rose to their feet, as Peter made his way off the stage. Peter and Francine hugged for a long while. Emma thought it was nice to see her mother smile again.

"Thank you, Peter," said Francine. "That meant a lot to me."

Peter held tight to Francine's hand. "Whatever you need, Francine. I'm here for you."

Emma risked a quick look behind her. She didn't recognize the two whisperers, but noticed that Peter's ex-wife Dot was two rows away. Her shiny blond bob looked as if it had been chiseled from marble. She stared at Emma for a couple of seconds before turning to the woman next to her. Nathan was standing with a group of people who were making their way toward the big oak doors. She hoped he wasn't attending the reception. He'd been sending her text messages saying he wanted to see her again. Two days in Walleye and old patterns were already setting in. Keeping her eyes down, she fell into conversation with one of her mother's friends as they made their way out of the hall and up the stairs to the rooftop reception room.

Emma stood next to the floor-to-ceiling windows that overlooked a floodlit terrace. The moonlit peaks of the Whitefish Range glowed in the distance. The sloping glass ceiling reflected the guests below. Most of the hair was gray and everyone seemed to be holding a glass of wine. Despite the sweeping views the room felt as if it was hermetically sealed. The cloying scent of sweet perfume was thick in the air. Emma felt a headache coming on. She sipped her glass of white wine and smiled as people came up to say a few words.

Emma searched the sea of heads for her mother. Francine was on the far side of the room having what looked like an intense conversation with Dot Whitaker. Emma placed her glass down on a passing tray. She'd had enough. She'd wait for her mother in the foyer. Halfway to the door she stopped short as an elderly man fixed his eyes on her.

Caleb Winfrey had aged. A tall man, he was now stooped, half bent over as if he'd been out in a gale for too long. She caught sight of his cane. She could plainly see the white-knuckled strain in the supporting hand. That slender piece of wood was all that was keeping him up. It made her want to kick it out from under him. Rheumy-eyed and bald, his dry lips scraped together as he worked his thoughts into words. The room quieted around them. They were being watched. Emma squared her shoulders. She was prepared this time. She waited patiently. This was her day.

Caleb opened his mouth but stopped short of speaking. A mist fell across his features. His eyes drifted over her face. As they went blank, he blinked. His voice had lost its bluster.

"Do I know you?" he said.

Emma didn't know how to respond. She stared at Caleb and Caleb stared back. She didn't want to be rude, but she didn't want to remind him of her name either. The crowded room continued to hold its breath, but the sustained hush had grown awkward. Someone coughed. Nervous laughter followed. A woman Emma didn't recognize sidled up to Caleb and took him by the arm. She was heavyset and looked as stable as a buttress. Those pearly-white knuckles relaxed as Caleb's grip on the cane loosened. The mouth cracked into a smile. Emma didn't wait to be introduced. Head down, she retreated. It felt like she was walking beneath a loaded sky. She imagined a web of cracks forming in the glass ceiling. It was only a matter of time before it shattered.

With her head in her hands, Emma sat on a small sofa that was tucked into a deep alcove. The foyer was to the right and a corridor that led to a rear exit was to the left. Hiding in a bathroom stall had been her first choice but there'd been a line of women waiting there. She couldn't pretend anymore. She wanted to be alone in her grief. She missed her father. None of this made any sense without him.

Emma had spent the afternoon searching his office. She'd found the damning receipt for the 9mm handgun and several rounds of ammunition wedged between a picture frame and the wall. Its existence proved Emma and her father had drifted further apart than she realized. Emma couldn't understand why he hadn't told her mother. It wasn't in Francine's nature to be smug. Despite her ardent support for the NRA and Second Amendment rights, she'd been proud of her husband's stubborn resolve to remain a pacifist. She would have found no pleasure in his change of heart. She'd cried when Emma showed her the receipt.

*"I don't understand,"* she'd said. *"Why did your father think he needed a gun?"*

Emma leaned her head back against the cushions and waited for the increasingly familiar feeling of vertigo to pass. She needed to calm down for her mother's sake. In another fifteen minutes the reception would end and she could go home. She wanted to hide in her childhood bedroom. She wanted to wake in the morning thinking it was all a bad dream. That split second of peace would be worth all the pain that followed.

Somewhere an outer door must have opened. The air along the corridor felt noticeably fresher. There were faint sounds of traffic. She started reading the notifications on a bulletin board that hung on the wall opposite. She stood up when she saw Nathan's name.

It seemed Nathan was engaged.

She read the notice twice to be sure she had the right Winfrey. Nathan was due to marry Cynthia Phelps in a month's time. Back in high school Cynthia was a girl with a generous mouth and a less than generous spirit. There'd been rumors that she and Nathan had slept together after Emma had gone to live in England during their junior year. Emma's friends had let her know about the stories that were going around. Nathan had denied everything in a long distance call that must have cost him a fortune and Emma had let him think that she believed him. Sometimes she felt she'd stayed with him during their senior year out of spite. She knew she was leaving. It was just a matter of time before he was the one who got hurt. Other times she'd felt that she'd stayed with him because she was too eager to please.

Emma heard footfalls. Someone was standing in the unlit end of the corridor below an exit sign. All she could see was the dark shadow of a man. Emma stepped away.

"I'm sorry to frighten you," he said, walking into the light and extending his hand. "It's been a long time."

"Kyle?" she said, taking another step back.

He smiled. "You remember me?"

"Your aunt and uncle . . . The police came to the house."

Kyle shoved his hands deep in his pockets. "I can't tell you how sorry I am."

There was a strange fluttering in her chest. Breathing hurt. She almost sank down onto the sofa but decided it was best to stay standing.

"I don't know what to say to you." She raised her voice. "I'm so angry."

He tipped his head to the back door he'd only just entered. "Would you like to go get a coffee? We could talk."

"What?"

"We don't have to talk about what happened. We can talk about old times instead. It will help you get your mind off everything."

She almost laughed but started crying instead. "Kyle, that's kind of you, but I'm here for my mother. She needs me here."

This time Kyle backed away. "Of course. I understand." He shook his head. "God, I'm such an idiot."

Emma didn't disagree.

"Where's your mother now?" he asked.

"There's a reception upstairs in one of the rooftop rooms. I couldn't . . . Anyway, I've been loitering out here."

"You loiter well."

"Pardon?"

"I said you loiter well."

"I know what you said, I'm just trying to figure out what you meant by it."

"Just that you look great. You're just as beautiful as you were back in high school."

Emma stared at him. She was trying to decide if she was being overly sensitive or he was being completely inappropriate. She almost said *pardon?* again but stopped. She really needed to quit trying to please everyone. It wasn't her job to make the world a happier place.

"Kyle, you know what your aunt and uncle have done?"

He gave her a slight nod.

"So, you can appreciate that I might not want to spend time with their nephew. You do get that, don't you? I don't want to be rude but this seems kind of obvious. You're making me uncomfortable, Kyle. Do you understand?"

Kyle held up his hands. A rash had traveled up his throat and was spreading onto his cheeks. Emma suddenly had a flash of him in high school. He'd been terribly shy but kind. He'd been one of the few to write to her following the scene Caleb made at Lucy's funeral.

*You're a good person, Emma. Always remember that. Stay in touch. You're one of the few people around here I feel close to.*

He started stuttering and it was like they'd never left those classrooms.

"I . . . I . . . I . . . just want you to know how sorry I am. Carla . . . Lloyd . . . they were bad . . . people."

Emma watched him for a few seconds. He'd been one of those kids who hid out in the library, book smart but almost incapable of holding a conversation with anyone outside his close circle of friends. Nathan's crowd had singled him out on occasion. They'd been unnecessarily cruel and Emma hadn't intervened as often as she should have. Kyle had changed over the past twelve years. For one thing, he'd filled out. They'd both been teased a lot in high school. His and hers stick figures had been etched into their lockers and scribbled on their notebooks.

"I'm sorry, Kyle. I shouldn't take this out on you. You were always nice to me back in high school."

"You were always good to me too."

"You're the only reason I survived AP biology. The fetal pig incident still haunts me."

"Speaking of haunting," he said, glancing at the notice board. "Nathan is getting married to Cynthia Phelps."

"I saw."

"She's had her eye on him since high school."

Emma shrugged. "That feels like a lifetime ago."

"If you'd stayed in Walleye it would feel more like a life sentence."

Emma noted Kyle's jacket and tie. They looked new. This was a man who spent his childhood wearing castoffs.

"Can't be all that bad," she said. "You look like you're doing okay."

He stood a little taller. "I get by."

"This must be an impossible situation for your family," she said, fumbling in her bag and handing him her business card out of habit. "This whole thing . . . I just don't know how to act. Plus, being back here again. It's confusing." She gestured toward the foyer. It was starting to fill up with her mother's friends. The reception must have ended. "Anyway, I have to go."

Kyle tucked her business card into his pocket. "We used to meet in the library every Tuesday. There was that table that everyone said was jinxed, but we sat there anyway."

She could see him clearly now, sitting at a study table far back in the stacks, his face twisted with concentration, his glasses looked thick enough to stop bullets.

"You don't wear glasses anymore."

He held out his hand and this time Emma took it.

"Corrective surgery," he said, looking her straight in the eye. "It's really good to see you again, Emma."

Emma felt a blush creeping up her neck. She turned away. Her mother was in the foyer. She was talking to Dr. Whitaker.

"It's probably best that my mom doesn't see you."

He kept to the shadows. "Don't worry. I know when to make myself scarce."

Emma and her mother sat in the living room staring at the television. The news was on but neither of them was paying much attention to what was happening on the screen.

"Emma, promise me that you'll forget what I said about Dot. It was just some crazy notion that's been running through my head. I don't know what came over me."

"You've been under a lot of stress. It's understandable."

"Dot and I talked a long while this evening. She was a real comfort."

"That's nice," said Emma. "Out of curiosity, what did she think of Lucy's artwork?"

"Artwork?"

"You told me you showed her some of Lucy's drawings."

"Oh, you lost me there for a second." Francine took a sip of her tea. "She thought Lucy had potential. When she took her on as an assistant I was hopeful the Whitakers would be a positive influence."

"I didn't know Lucy worked for Dot."

Francine sank down further into her chair. "She'd been fired by the time you came back. To tell you the truth, it was an awkward situation. I'd introduced her to Dot."

"Do you know what happened?"

"I assume they fell out because of Lucy's behavior. She'd become erratic. She was showing up at the back door day and night. Always asking for money. Your father spoke to Caleb because we were worried. The visits stopped after that."

"Did the police ever find out where she was getting the drugs she was selling?"

"Not that I know of. Your father was so upset. You know how he feels about that sort of thing."

"Mom," Emma said, sitting forward in her chair. "There's something you need to know about dad. He—"

Francine held up her hand. "I decided a long time ago that I didn't want to know the details about your father's past drug addictions."

Emma retreated. "You've known all this time?"

"I didn't have much choice but to accept him despite his failings. Your father waited until the morning we got married to tell me. I had had an inkling he was keeping secrets."

"It must have been a shock. You couldn't have suspected he was addicted to heroin."

"Not in my wildest dreams. He'd hinted that he'd come here to Walleye Junction to escape his past. To tell you the truth I thought he was running away from the law. I was young then. A bit of a romantic. The idea didn't bother me as much as it should have."

"Do you think he told you everything?"

"Yes, I had faith in him. He swore that he'd never use again, that he loved me more than any drug." Francine paused. "I guess he didn't love me enough. If he was using drugs again it would explain his recent behavior."

"He did love you, Mom. More than anything."

"It wasn't enough."

"I don't think we should tell the police about this. There's still a chance he was forced to take it."

"Your father was a good man. I don't want him to be remembered like that. People won't understand. All they'll see is the word *addict*."

Emma started to cry. "I miss him."

They sat quietly for a few minutes. The weather forecast for the next few days called for sunshine and temperatures in the high sixties. Francine stared at the screen.

"Your father spent most of his life trying to make amends for his misspent youth. You should have seen him in the months after Lucy died. He was so angry that he hadn't done something sooner."

"Sometimes," said Emma. "I feel like Lucy's death was my fault."

"She wasn't your responsibility."

"I promised to look after her."

"Emma, you were only nine years old when Lucy's mother died and Beverly, bless her heart, had no right to saddle you with a burden like that."

"It wasn't all bad. For a long time we were close, like siblings."

"Yes," said Francine. "But she was always holding you back. You really did your best by that girl. If it weren't for you and Nathan, she would have been completely friendless."

"I didn't think you understood."

"It was your father who set me straight. You know me . . . all unicorns and rainbows. I used to only see the good in people." Francine frowned at something on the news. An inmate at the Montana State Prison had been shot dead by guards after he assaulted several prisoners. "I don't anymore."

"There's still a lot of good out there. You could see that this evening at the church. It was a nice service. I talked to so many people who care about you."

"They care about you too."

Emma looked down at her hands. Many of those same people had been at Lucy's funeral. Caleb's words had been met with stunned silence. Not one of them had spoken out against him.

"I guess that's nice to know," said Emma.

"They're concerned. They thought you were looking unwell."

"I was feeling faint."

Francine sniffed into a tissue. "It's not surprising. You run miles every day and yet you eat hardly anything."

"That's not why I was feeling unwell."

"You're too thin. It's just like when you were in high school. It worried me then. It worries me now."

# 9

Bob Crawley sat at a table in Walleye Junction's police department's only interview room. His hair was as blond and boyishly cut as it had been when they'd met the previous summer. He stood as Macy entered the room.

"Detective Greeley," he said, giving her a firm handshake and holding on for a few seconds too long. "Always a pleasure."

She arched an eyebrow. She didn't like this game but decided it was best to play along for the time being.

"We have to quit meeting like this, Mr. Crawley. People are starting to talk."

He laughed. "Let them."

"Please," she said, gesturing to his empty chair. "Have a seat."

Once the attending officer left the room she explained that the interview was being videotaped and read him his Miranda rights in full.

"I already understand my rights," he said. "I have a law degree."

"Which makes it even more essential for us to do this by the book." Macy's smile wasn't genuine. "I have your previous statement here. You were interviewed in relation to a serious incident that took place in Ron Forester's home." She handed him the written statement. "I want you to read this over carefully and tell me whether there's anything you'd like to add."

Bob slipped on his glasses. "No," he said, passing it back. "It's all there. Rob is a good friend. I've spent time there. I've provided you with my fingerprints for elimination purposes."

"You were asked specifically about the alarm code."

"Ron gave it to me years ago. He's not all that original. It's his ex-wife's birthday. Margot was a classic Scorpio."

"In your statement you say that you were with Ron Forester the last time you entered the property. You spent the evening playing poker and eating pizza."

"That is correct."

"It has been reported that you were drinking heavily."

"That is also correct."

"Did you spend the night?"

"I did."

Macy showed him a floor plan of Forester's house. "Could you indicate which room you stayed in?"

Bob pointed out an upstairs guestroom.

"That's interesting."

"Why?"

"We found your DNA and fingerprints in that room."

He shrugged. "It's where I slept."

"The room has been thoroughly cleaned on several occasions during the past year."

"Then Ron should probably fire his cleaner."

"Since the evening other guests have stayed in that same room and yet there is no trace of their DNA and fingerprints." She gestured to his original statement. "Are you sure you don't wish to add something? It wasn't just your DNA that was found in that room."

Bob Crawley took off his glasses and rubbed his eyes.

"Does the name Carla Spencer mean anything to you?" asked Macy. "We found your business card in her possession."

"I'm sorry. The name doesn't sound familiar."

Macy placed Carla's photo on the table.

"She delivered the pizzas on the night you stayed at Ron Forester's house."

Bob picked up the photo and stared at it.

"I was drunk. It was mutual. What's going on here? Is she claiming I assaulted her?"

"What's the nature of your relationship with Carla Spencer?"

"It was a one-off thing."

"We have your DNA in an upstairs bedroom and alarm records show that the property was entered on five separate occasions after Ron Forester began his sentence at Montana State Prison. We have so far been unable to account for these late night visits. Did you meet Carla Spencer at the house?"

Bob spent a few seconds thinking things over before he answered.

"Take your time," said Macy. "It's important that you get this right."

"Yes, I brought Carla up there. I fail to see why this is relevant."

"Did you tell her the alarm code?"

"I might have."

"Answer the question."

"Yes," said Bob. "I told Carla Spencer the alarm code."

"Mr. Crawley. You are aware that we are investigating a very serious crime. A man was kidnapped and held at the Forester house before he was murdered. You have withheld valuable information that would have aided our investigation."

"Don't be so dramatic. Carla delivered pizzas. What on earth does she have to do with any of this?"

"Can you account for your whereabouts the night Philip Long was murdered?"

"I was with my wife."

"I'll need to have her confirm that."

"There's no need to bother her with this," said Bob. "You can check with my staff."

"I'm not in the mood to be accommodating. You've wasted police time and may have contributed to the death of three individuals."

"You've got to be kidding me."

"Carla used the alarm code you gave her to access Ron Forester's property," said Macy.

"She was involved in the kidnapping?"

"She was aided by her husband and an unknown accomplice."

"If she's saying I was involved, she's lying. I barely knew the woman."

"She's not saying anything at the moment. Both Carla and her husband are dead, which leaves you, Mr. Crawley."

"I was with my wife," he insisted.

"That doesn't mean you weren't involved."

"I didn't even know Philip Long. Why on earth would I do such a thing?"

"That's what I have to figure out," said Macy. "You lied to us about your relationship with Carla so now we have to figure out if there is anything else you're lying about."

"I only lied because I didn't want anyone to know I was sleeping with her."

"Do you ride a dirt bike, Mr. Crawley?"

"On occasion. I have a few up at the house. You're welcome to have a look."

"We don't need your permission. We have a warrant." Macy checked the time. "They should be serving it right about now."

"You can't be serious."

Macy stared at him. Her smile was long gone. "It is up to the DA to decide whether you're charged with obstruction. Going forward I advise you to be very cooperative. I also recommend that both you and your wife are tested. Carla was a drug addict who's probably been sharing needles for years." Macy called the attending uniformed officer back into the room and ended the interview. "Please escort Mr. Crawley to his home. We may need him to answer further questions while we're searching the property."

Gina handed Macy a printout of an e-mail as they walked down a hallway that ran the length of the police station.

"This may be nothing," said Gina. "But I thought you should see it."

Macy noticed the date. It had been sent to Lou Turner two days earlier.

"How come we're just seeing this now?" asked Macy.

"Manpower. There are only so many tips we can follow up in a day, so we have to prioritize."

The e-mail opened with a question. *What really killed Philip Long?*

"Do we have any idea who sent this?"

"The tech guys are trying to establish its origin, but the e-mail account was shut down right after it was sent. It looks like it bounced around a few servers before landing in Lou Turner's in-box."

The Word document that was attached to the e-mail consisted of a list of eighty-two names. Accompanying the names were a few sentences, which described the circumstances of their deaths and listed the dates they died and their birthdates. Macy flipped through the pages. Some of the deaths dated as far back as five years. The only indication of the e-mail's source was a roughly drawn image. Three slashed lines formed a capital letter *A* that was enclosed by a circle. There was no further explanation.

Macy frowned. "The Circle-A is a symbol used by anarchists."

"I didn't know Montana had anarchists."

Macy checked over the list of names again. "It looks like everyone on this list died from accidentally overdosing on prescription painkillers. Are they local to the Flathead Valley?"

"No, nine lived in Idaho, five were from North Dakota, and at least ten were residents of Wyoming."

"This isn't a problem that's unique to this area. Last I heard more people die from prescription drug overdoses than traffic accidents." Macy handed the printout back to Gina. "Carla and Lloyd overdosed on heroin. I'm not seeing a connection."

"Carla Spencer was forced to administer a lethal dose to herself and her husband. It wasn't accidental. It was murder." Gina pointed to the list of names. "Maybe this is more of the same."

"Eighty-two murders? Not sure I have the stamina for that sort of investigation."

"What should we do with this e-mail?" asked Gina. "We don't have the resources to follow every lead."

"Get someone to cross-reference these names with doctors, clinics, and hospitals. The state coroner should have data from all the counties. Pick a few at random and see whether there was any suspicion surrounding their deaths."

"I'll talk to Lou about getting someone on it. If not, I'll do it myself. How did the Crawley interview go?"

Macy's mood darkened. "He admitted to meeting Carla at Ron Forester's house but denies any connection to the kidnapping and murder. He says he was with his wife the night Philip died."

"He sounds like a total prick."

"He's a charming prick. Despite everything, it's hard not to like him."

"Your buddy Aiden Marsh has a team searching Crawley's residence now. I hear it's a nice place," said Gina.

"I had the pleasure of visiting last summer . . . same story, different woman."

"You have to wonder why his wife puts up with it."

"There's no way of knowing what goes on in their marriage," said Macy. "I'm sure it's complicated. I'll interview her this afternoon, but I doubt she'll give me any insight. Meanwhile, we've got to find Sean Spencer. Any news?"

"Nothing. It's like he's gone underground. His girlfriend is another story. Some buzz has been building online. There are rumors going around that she's planning one of her raves here in the Flathead Valley sometime during the next week. From everything I'm hearing from Sean's friends, he and Kristina are practically inseparable. If we find her, we should find him."

"A rave would make a nice change. I'm in the mood for a little fun."

"Speaking of fun," said Gina. "How were your ten hours in Helena?"

"Too brief. I had breakfast with my son, but he wasn't at his best. My mother thinks he might be coming down with something. Did you manage to escape your mother-in-law undetected?"

"She caught me just as I was sneaking out the door this morning. She thinks it's my fault that my husband is getting fat."

"You need to remind her what year it is."

"I did. I just wasn't as gentle as I should have been. I'm afraid it was handbags at dawn."

"What did your husband have to say about it?"

"Nothing. He hadn't returned from pulling a nightshift. I spoke to him though. He's not feeling well either. Maybe the flu is going around."

"I hope not. My mother has her hands full looking after Luke as it is. Have you spoken to Lou today? Do you know if he managed to track down Sean Spencer's real father?"

"I did. Scott Walker has been laid up with a broken leg for the past few weeks. He's not our guy."

"Has Sean been in touch with him?"

"Walker says he hasn't, but Lou isn't convinced he's telling us the truth. There's still nothing concrete on Joel Edwards's whereabouts either, but we did find out that he used to be a member of a militia group."

Macy gave Gina a blank look. "Sorry, remind me who Joel Edwards is. I'm a little slow today."

"He's the loser Carla met in rehab."

"Right. No address for him?"

"He lived out of his car."

"Okay, chase the militia lead and see if he has any affiliation with Carla and Lloyd Spencer's group."

Macy checked her phone. There was a missed call from Aiden.

"It's Aiden Marsh," said Macy. "I'd better call him back. There may be news from the search up at the Crawley residence."

"I'll be at my desk if you need me."

Macy went outside and sat at a picnic table situated on a patch of lawn near the station's back door. She closed her eyes and tilted her face to the sky.

Aiden sounded like he'd been running. "Macy, I think you should get up here."

"Have you found something?"

"Maybe. It looks like someone tried to destroy some evidence."

"The bike gear."

"Yep. It's mostly ashes, but the Alliance logo is visible."

"Was it in the house?" asked Macy.

"No, there's an outdoor fire pit near the river. It's only a ten minute walk away from the house."

Macy hurried back inside the police station. "Is it on the Crawley property?"

"Yes, but anyone with a boat could access that section of river."

"Do they know when that fire pit was last used?" she asked Aiden.

"According to the ranch foreman it would have been sometime last fall."

"Has Crawley been seen down there?"

"There's a lot of staff that work in the house and on the grounds. We've not had time to interview all the potential witnesses."

"What about the wife? Crawley says he was with her the night Philip Long died."

Aiden's voice sounded strained. "Bob lied. Charlotte says he was out."

"Why would Bob Crawley be involved in something like this? He's got plenty of money."

"Maybe the story Long was researching had something to do with Bob Crawley's software company."

"We really need to find Long's computer."

"You coming up this way?"

Macy checked the time. "I'll get there as soon as I can. Give me a shout if you find anything else."

There were several patrol cars parked along the Crawley's poplar-lined driveway and one forensic team van backed up next to the garages. The three-story windows on the east side of the house reflected the cloud-choked slopes of the Whitefish Range. A strong wind whipped Macy's hair into her face. There was shouting coming from inside the house. Charlotte Crawley was letting everyone know exactly how fed up she was with her husband's behavior.

"Robert, you're an idiot. That woman was a drug addict for fuck's sake. Your behavior has put the whole family at risk."

Macy stepped inside at the same time Bob Crawley was being led away in handcuffs. He stopped walking as he came alongside Macy.

"I didn't do this," he said.

"You come up with a solid alibi and I just might believe you."

Charlotte Crawley was tall and had an athletic build. Her auburn hair was loose and she was dressed casually in jeans, a T-shirt, and flip-flops. Her dark eyes fell on Macy and stayed there.

Macy had the distinct impression that she was being carefully assessed as she moved through the house. There were a few crime scene techs working in Bob Crawley's office. She took a quick peek inside.

"Anything of interest?"

"We're checking his computer now."

"Let me know if you find anything."

Macy glanced over her shoulder. Charlotte Crawley was still watching her. The crime scene tech noticed.

"I don't think she likes you."

"Does she like anyone?" asked Macy.

A shrug. "She seemed to be pretty chummy with Aiden Marsh."

Macy fought the urge to throw daggers right back at Charlotte. Aiden was friends with the family. There was no reason to suspect anything, but that didn't stop her mind from going into overdrive. You'd have to be blind not to notice that Charlotte Crawley was an incredibly attractive woman.

"Where is Police Chief Marsh now?" asked Macy.

"Not sure. Last I heard he was heading outside to the garage to talk to Ryan about the off-road bikes that are stored there."

. . .

Macy found Charlotte staring into an open refrigerator. Her expression hadn't softened.

"Charlotte Crawley?" said Macy.

Charlotte slammed the refrigerator shut.

"Can't you people just go already?"

"Your husband may have been involved in a serious crime. We're not going anywhere until we've searched the entire property." Macy paused. "It could take a while due to the size."

"The unexpected downside of having a large home."

"I doubt it's ever listed as a potential problem in the property brochures."

"Who are you anyway?" Charlotte asked. "I feel like I've already talked to pretty much everyone who works in law enforcement in this part of the state."

Macy didn't bother trying to shake Charlotte's hand. She pulled out her badge and held it in the air between them. "My name is Detective Macy Greeley, and I've been sent here from Helena to lead the investigation into Philip Long's kidnapping and murder. I have a few questions."

"I'm sorry, but I don't have time to talk to anyone else."

"I'm afraid you need to make the time."

"None of you understand how difficult this is. I have to make arrangements for my children. If the press gets wind of what's happened it's going to be all over the news."

"I appreciate how disruptive this is for your family, but I have to insist." Macy tipped her head toward the outside terrace where some tables sat next to the pool. "Let's go sit outside. You look like you could use some fresh air."

Charlotte pulled her hair back into a ponytail with a band that had been looped around her wrist. There was a pack of cigarettes on the table. She took one out and lit it with difficulty. She didn't look like someone who smoked regularly. Macy decided it was better to get right to the sharp end of the conversation.

"When did you first learn about your husband's affair with Carla Spencer?"

"This isn't easy to talk about."

"It never is, but the sooner you talk the sooner you're free to go."

Charlotte looked down at the table.

"I hadn't been feeling well for a while. I was scared. Cancer runs in my family, so naturally I went to see my doctor." Charlotte laughed nervously. "It turns out I'd contracted hepatitis C."

"And you're sure it was from your husband?"

"It's the only thing that made sense. I hired a private investigator. He sent me some photos of my husband and Carla Spencer in various stages of undress. You're welcome to see them."

"Did you confront him?"

Charlotte stubbed out the cigarette without smoking it. "I was in the process of filing for divorce, so I was advised to keep what I knew to myself for the time being."

"When you spoke to Chief Marsh earlier you said that your husband was out of the house on the night of Philip Long's murder. Are you absolutely sure that is correct?"

Charlotte barely nodded.

"Were there any other unexplained absences over the past couple of weeks?"

"He'd go out sometimes and not come back until late. It wasn't unusual. If you need the dates and times I have them. . . . Now that I know the truth about what's been going on behind my back, I've been keeping a diary."

Macy scribbled a few notes. "Did your private investigator discover anything else about your husband that could be of interest to us?"

Charlotte tried to slide another cigarette out of the pack, but her hands were shaking too much. She crushed the box in her fist and threw it aside.

"There were other women. With the exception of Carla they were all quite young." Charlotte breathed deeply. "It's really fucked with my confidence. I'm forty-four this year. I can't compete with an eighteen-year-old."

"You shouldn't have to."

"But it seems that's precisely what I've been doing for the past few years." She pressed a tissue to her eyes. "I'll send you the file."

"I'm sorry," said Macy. "This must be awful. I really appreciate your cooperation."

Charlotte gazed out across green rolling hills and pine forests. Beyond the trees, the Flathead River flowed slow and wide.

"You'd think that all this would have been enough for anyone," said Charlotte.

"How long have you been married?"

"Sixteen years in August. I don't know how I'm going to tell the children."

"You're stronger than you realize. You'll find a way."

"Aiden said you were nice. That I should be nice to you." Her eyes fell on Macy again. "Sorry about earlier. I'm not usually such a bitch."

"Under the circumstances I wouldn't think too highly of other women either."

"Other women aren't really the problem though, are they? Bob had lost respect for our marriage. Once that happened we really didn't stand a chance. Anyway, it's done and I don't want to talk about *those* women anymore."

Macy handed Charlotte a packet of tissues she had in her bag.

"I need to ask you about a fire pit that's down near the river. Do you recall seeing anyone burning trash there recently? The ranch foreman says it's not been used since last fall."

Charlotte yanked her hair out of its band and twisted the elastic loop in her fingers. "I walk the dogs down there sometimes, but I can't say I've noticed anything unusual."

"Has there been any change in your husband's behavior over the past few weeks?"

"We've been fighting a lot, but that's been coming from me, not him. He seems his usual gregarious self. It almost made me feel guilty about the bomb I was about to drop in his lap."

"We're having some difficulty understanding why your husband would have been involved in Philip Long's kidnapping. Have there been any problems with your finances?"

"My lawyer hired a forensic accountant to go through everything. I've been assured that our finances are in good order."

"Do you know if your husband has had any professional or personal dealings with Philip Long?"

Charlotte shook her head. "We listened to his radio program sometimes, but as far as I know Bob has never met him." She paused. "What happens now?"

"Your husband lied to us about where he was on the night of the murder. Unless he comes up with an explanation for his whereabouts he will remain in custody. There are several motorbikes in the garage. A couple of them are specifically for riding off road. How often does your husband use them?"

"He and my eldest son go out sometimes. I can't say I approve. As a family we seem to spend an inordinate amount of time in emergency rooms."

"Where are your children now?"

Charlotte glanced at her watch. "They're at school. I'd appreciate it if you were done by the time they get home."

"We'll do our best, but it might be a good idea to delay their return for as long as possible."

"Am I free to go? I'd like to go pick them up. I could take them out somewhere for dinner."

"That would probably be a good idea, but before you go I'd like you to send me the information your private detective gathered on your husband. It will be interesting to see if any of the other women are connected to the case."

Aiden and Macy walked along a trail that cut across the low hills on the western side of the Crawley's property. Clouds moved across the sky at dizzying speeds. At the moment the sun was shining through and it was the warmest it had been since Macy had arrived in the Flathead

Valley, but the distant horizons told another story. A storm was coming. Before the path dipped down to a dense stand of pine trees that bordered the river, Macy turned and gazed back up at the house. She couldn't imagine how someone could get bored with the view.

"If someone burned that bike gear down here I think the smoke from a fire would have been seen up at the house," said Macy.

"Crawley could have done it at night. It might explain why he left the job unfinished."

"He's not a seasoned criminal so there's lots of scope to screw things up. I noticed you were speaking to his wife, Charlotte. You've socialized with the Crawley family so you must have some insight. What's your take on the wife? Is she angry enough to land her husband in it?"

"You think she might be lying about him not being here?" asked Aiden.

"Considering how he's behaved, she has every right to be angry. She's been meeting with lawyers, forensic accountants, and private detectives. She already knows she can screw him financially. Getting sole custody of the kids would be an added bonus."

"You have a point, but I don't see Charlotte doing something like that. She's a good person. Besides, someone has tried to destroy evidence. He has no alibi so there's every reason to think it was Bob."

The ground beneath the trees was thickly carpeted with pine needles. Crime scene tape wound through the woods, blocking off a clearing of about thirty square yards. In the center thick logs that had been split lengthwise served as seating for a fire pit. The far side of the clearing opened up onto the shores of the Flathead River.

Macy dipped under the crime scene tape and stood next to the empty fire pit. The contents had already been collected and bagged as evidence. At the sound of voices she turned toward the river. A boat drifted downstream. Two men sat holding fishing rods while another one steered the boat. One of the men shouted hello and Macy waved back.

"You were right," said Macy. "Anyone could access the property from this stretch of river."

"It's illegal to come ashore, but I doubt that would have been a deterrent if someone was trying to set Bob Crawley up." Aiden pointed upstream. "There's a public boat launch about two miles from here."

"How far downstream do you have to go before you can access the river again?"

"It's about four miles. During the high season a bus runs between the two sites."

"It would have been risky," said Macy. "The beach is visible from the river. They may have been spotted setting the fire."

"Not necessarily. It's still a little early in the season for fishing and people really don't use this stretch of river for float trips until late June. I think there was greater risk of being discovered by someone coming down from the house."

Macy took a moment to think. "They could have burned the gear somewhere else and deposited the remnants in the pit. On and off the boat in a matter of seconds," she said.

Aiden walked out to the water's edge and picked up a stone. "I realize this is all theoretical at this point, but if Crawley is innocent, who do you suppose he's covering for?"

"Charlotte Crawley hired a private detective to keep an eye on Bob. She just sent me the list of women Crawley was sleeping with." Macy scrolled through the e-mail message. "I see five names, including Carla Spencer's. It might be that he couldn't bring himself to admit to being with one of them. Providing a proper alibi for the night of Philip's murder would have saved his family a lot of grief. If he is innocent, it's hard to believe that he didn't have the foresight to realize this."

Aiden skipped a flat stone across the river's surface. "Considering your history with Ray, I'm surprised this kind of behavior surprises you."

"I seem to have a blind spot."

"Open your eyes, Macy. Men are assholes."

She made a face. "Aiden, are you trying to tell me something?"

He threw another stone. "Maybe."

"What do you mean by maybe?"

Aiden brushed his hands clean on his trousers and turned to face her.

"I guess I want to know how serious I should be taking us."

"I'm not sure," said Macy.

"I think it's time you made up your mind."

"Where is this coming from?"

"I don't like having to hide that we're together. It makes it feel more like an affair than a relationship. Sometimes I think you'd rather people didn't know because you're not sure if it's something you really want."

"It's been a difficult year. I thought you understood."

"I thought I did too," said Aiden. "But you're going to be back in Helena soon. Lately, it seems like it's a little of something or all of nothing."

"I'm sorry. I honestly didn't know you felt this way." She tilted her face up to the sky. It had gone from blue to black in a matter of minutes. "Are you free this evening? We could talk."

"Sort of depends on Bob Crawley. We really should go question him again." He stood next to her. "Sorry to bring up personal stuff at work."

"It's okay. There's nobody down here but us."

"Truth is, I don't know how this thing between us can ever work. I'm tied to my job here and you've got your mom and Luke back in Helena. Neither of us are the type of person who would walk away from something this good, but there has to be some promise of a future. I feel like I'm treading water when I'm with you."

Macy put her palm flat to his chest. She often felt as if she was barely staying afloat. She had no idea he was feeling the same way.

"Aiden," she said. "I feel like this is my fault. I'm coming out of a situation that was never normal. I think I've forgotten how to do this."

"It's not just you. I'm not sure what I want either. I just think that this rarified air we're living in isn't good for us."

"We'll talk tonight. I promise."

The shadows beneath the trees had deepened. Gusts of wind shook the upper branches. The river seemed to swell in the dying light. Thunder rumbled in the distance.

"It's going to rain soon," said Aiden. "We'd better get going."

"Give me another minute. I feel like we should have a better look around the perimeter."

Macy pulled a small flashlight from her bag and took one last walk around the clearing. She pointed toward some trees a dozen feet farther along the shoreline. The light had caught on something reflective.

"Do you see that?" she said.

"It looks like a children's fort."

Built from sawn-off branches of pine trees held together by silver duct tape, the small lean-to was barely visible in the dense undergrowth.

"Crawley's kids must have built it."

Macy pulled away a couple of branches and peeked inside. A blond-haired doll was wrapped up in a baby blanket. She picked it up and inspected it carefully.

"This doll must belong to one of the kids."

"Three boys and one girl," said Aiden. "I think it's safe to assume it's Annabel's."

There was an empty yogurt container on the ground.

"Look at the expiration date," said Macy, holding it up to the flash-light's beam. "Annabel was here recently."

"It doesn't mean she saw anything."

"The fort is less than thirty feet from the fire pit. We need to talk to her."

Macy slipped everything into a plastic evidence bag.

Aiden frowned. "Do you actually think that doll is evidence?"

"No, but if it's someone's favorite doll I don't want it to get wet."

The tall grass whipped at their legs as they climbed the path from the river basin up to the house. To the north, lightning threaded through the dark sky.

Macy had to yell to be heard above the driving wind.

"It's hard to believe the sun was shining a few minutes ago," she said.

"This is Montana. You can have all four seasons in a day."

"Maybe we should quit our jobs and move somewhere warm."

"I think we both love it here too much to leave."

With all its lights on, the Crawley's house hovered over the valley like a spaceship. The first time she'd visited she'd thought it blended into the landscape. Now she wasn't so sure. It was out of scale. It was too much and yet it wasn't enough.

"I know what you mean," she said, taking a moment to look north, where the storm clouds were massing. There was another lightning strike, but this one was closer. "It is beautiful up here."

He put his hand to her lower back and guided her up the hill.

"This probably isn't the best time to commune with nature. We're going to get struck by lightning if we stay out here much longer."

Ryan was waiting for them in the garage. They stood in the open door and watched hailstones pelt the parked cars. Ryan scrolled through some images of tire impressions on his tablet. He had to yell to be heard over the racket.

"We've got a match on the tire impressions from one of the bikes, but it's a popular brand so not exactly damning evidence. I've taken trace samples from the treads to see if there's anything specific that will tie it to the area where Philip Long was murdered."

"Anything of interest in the house?" asked Macy.

"Nada. We've had a look at his laptop though," said Ryan. "Turns out Daddy Crawley was into sugar."

Aiden frowned. "Sugar Daddy Web sites?"

"Looks like he is running his own private University of Montana scholarship program."

Macy gave Ryan a sharp look. "I know when you're exaggerating."

"Not by much. He is a member of a couple of Web sites that specialize in matching financial donors with disadvantaged coeds. It's called an arrangement." Ryan smiled. "We just don't know how much he's donated."

"What happened to getting a job at a local coffee shop to pay your way through school?" asked Macy.

"A minimum wage job isn't going to cut it these days," said Ryan. "These sites have become more popular than anyone could have ever foreseen."

"Remind me to start saving up for Luke's education."

Aiden pulled up the hood of his jacket before making his way back to the main house. "I wouldn't worry about that," he said. "Your mom has already opened an account for Luke. I'm going to have a quick word with guys inside. I'll be back in sec."

Ryan raised an eyebrow. "I had no idea Aiden was so well acquainted with your family's finances. Anything you want to tell me that I haven't already figured out?"

"That obvious?" asked Macy.

"Only to the initiated, but don't worry, your secret is safe with me—unless you want me to be the bearer of glad tidings. I love a happy ending."

"Then you should stick to musicals." Macy noticed that Gina's vehicle was gone. "Have you seen Gina?"

"Something came up, and she had to head back to Helena. I thought I'd give you a lift, but it looks like Aiden is already giving you a ride."

"Ryan, that's quite enough."

"I've been staring at tire treads all afternoon. You have to let me have some fun."

"It's been fun, but I'm not feeling humored. I'm feeling anxious. Aiden just told me that he wants to know where our relationship is going."

"Oh dear," said Ryan. "That will mean you have to talk."

"He's looking for clarity."

"How do you feel about that?"

Macy closed her eyes. "Cloudy."

"Not exactly a position of strength," said Ryan.

"What should I do?"

"You have great instincts. Use them."

"I'm not sure if I trust them anymore."

"How long has it been since you were in a proper relationship?" Ryan held up a hand. "Ray and that redneck paramedic from Collier don't count."

Macy sighed. "Six and half years."

"And you want to walk away from someone you actually like who is willing to give it a go?"

"I do sound like an idiot when you put it that way."

"I'm always here for you when you need to be reminded." Ryan paused. "But in all seriousness, don't rush into anything. You've had a tough year. Aiden may seem like a safe bet, but he'll come with his own set of issues. We all do. Take an honest look at why you're hesitating and go from there."

Macy scrolled through the women listed in Charlotte Crawley's e-mail.

"Where on earth does Bob Crawley find the time and energy for all this extracurricular activity?" asked Macy. "Doesn't he have a company to run? Millions of dollars to manage?"

Aiden checked the rearview mirror before pulling into the outside lane.

"Charlotte deserves better."

"This is interesting," said Macy, rereading the information to make sure she had it right. "This girl is barely eighteen. Unbelievable. It gets worse."

"What?"

"Stacy Shaw attends the same high school as the Crawley's eldest son."

"That's sinking pretty low."

"If Crawley was with her on the night of the murder it could explain why he's unwilling to provide an alibi."

"Age of consent is sixteen so he's okay from a legal standpoint, but I doubt that would matter in the court of public opinion. But is an affair with an eighteen-year-old girl enough of a reason for him to risk a murder charge?"

"If he's innocent maybe he's hoping he'll get off for another reason."

"That's a pretty risky strategy."

"He's screwed either way," said Macy.

"Another angle we could look at is blackmail. If he's messing around with a girl from his son's high school, he would have made himself vulnerable. He's got a lot of money. Might be that Carla and Lloyd threatened him with exposure if he didn't cooperate. It's only a hunch, but maybe you should lead with his affair with Stacy Shaw when you question him."

Bob Crawley was waiting in the same interview room where he'd met Macy earlier in the day. Macy was a little surprised he hadn't contacted his lawyer yet. She switched on the recording equipment and read him his rights again. It was all beginning to feel a little too familiar.

"Mr. Crawley, you weren't with your wife the night Philip Long was kidnapped and murdered. If you do not provide us with a sound alibi you will be charged. Do you fully understand what's at stake here?"

Bob scratched at the rough patches on his cheeks. His eyes were bloodshot.

"I didn't kidnap or kill Philip Long. I stand by what I said earlier," said Bob. "I've never even met the man."

"Where were you the night of the murder?"

"I can't say."

Macy pulled out a photo the private investigator had taken. Bob Crawley and Stacy Shaw had been meeting regularly at a motel south of Collier. He'd not waited until they were safely inside before putting his hands up her skirt.

"Do you recognize the person in this photograph?"

Bob Crawley stared at the image a few seconds before closing his eyes. His skin had a gray pallor. It looked as if he was going to be sick.

Macy placed a few more photos on the table between them. She could only imagine how Charlotte Crawley felt when she'd first seen them.

"So how did you and Stacy Shaw meet?" asked Macy. "Did she come up to the house to hang out with your son and end up getting to know his daddy instead? Or was there a chance encounter at a parent-teacher evening at the high school? There are just so many possibilities. Each one more inappropriate than the next."

He shook his head vigorously. "It was nothing like that. She was registered on a Web site I use. After exchanging a few e-mails we met at Murphy's Tavern in Collier. I assumed she was at least twenty-one. She'd lied and said she was a junior at the University of Montana."

"How long before you knew her real age?"

"I've done nothing illegal."

"She's barely eighteen and attends your son's high school," said Macy. "You must be scared shitless that this might come out."

"Where did you get these photographs?"

"Your wife gave them to us. It turns out she's not as understanding as you thought, but I guess everyone has a breaking point." Macy had saved the most damning photograph for last. It was taken with a telephoto lens. Stacy Shaw straddled Bob in the front seat of his car. The Walleye Junction High School gymnasium could be seen in the background. "Just so you know, I've reached my breaking point too. No more fucking around. I need to know where you were the night of the murder."

Bob turned the last photo over. "I was with Stacy."

"All night?"

"Between ten and three."

Macy didn't need to check her notes. She knew that Philip Long had died shortly before three in the morning. She was there.

"Mr. Crawley, you're going to have to provide proof that you were together. Where did you meet Miss Shaw?"

"Same motel as before. It's the Valley Inn near Route 93."

"Did anyone see you together?"

"Maybe my wife's private detective was hiding out taking photos."

"Not that night. Did the manager see you?"

"Stacy checked us in."

"You better hope Stacy Shaw backs up your alibi. There's only so much more of your bullshit I can take."

"This doesn't need to go any further than this room."

"Your wife is free to do whatever she likes with these photographs. Ms. Shaw probably has her own plans. Maybe they'll both sell their stories to the press. Wouldn't be the first time that's happened."

Macy put the photos aside and placed the evidence bag containing the doll on the table.

"Do you recognize this doll?"

He turned the bag over in his hands. There was a tightening around his eyes. His voice caught.

"It belongs to my daughter, Annabel."

"Were you aware that it was missing?"

"Yes, she's been having trouble sleeping. We've been looking everywhere."

"Could you be more specific about the time frame of when it went missing?" asked Macy. "We found it near the fire pit by the river on your property. It may be that your daughter saw something she wasn't supposed to while she was playing down there. If you weren't involved in Philip Long's kidnapping and murder, someone is taking measures to set you up."

"Charlotte and I realized something was amiss three days ago when our daughter wouldn't settle down for the night. The doll is very special to her. I'm surprised she left it somewhere."

"Are you aware that your children have built a fort down by the river?"

"They're not supposed to be down there on their own."

"Which is probably why Annabel didn't tell you where to find the doll. The fort is only thirty feet from the fire pit. It's possible your daughter may have seen something."

Aiden backed his patrol car into his driveway and nudged Macy awake. She'd drifted off in midsentence somewhere between Walleye Junction and Wilmington Creek. She was pretty sure she'd been rambling incoherently about her thoughts on everything from marriage to having more children to long-term commitment. Aiden kissed her lightly on the lips.

"Rise and shine, beautiful," he said.

Apparently, she had yet to say anything that put him off. She eased out of the seat. For some reason her back and chest were hurting more than they did a couple of days after the accident.

"I'm sore all over," she said.

"Might want to take something before turning in."

"Thanks," said Macy. "But I think I'm going to try to manage without."

Aiden's house was as clean and well-ordered as it always was. She tried to picture the chaos that would result when Luke arrived on the scene. There was no doubt that Aiden had become accustomed to having things in a particular way. She'd caught him tidying up after her on more than one occasion.

He put his arms around her and she leaned into him.

"Do you want a drink? I could open a bottle."

"I'd have one glass and pass out."

He headed for the kitchen. "I've got orange juice."

"Actually, I'd love a glass of water."

"So," he said, handing her a glass and leading her to the sofa. "Have you given any thought to what I said earlier?"

She settled her head on his shoulder and they stretched their legs out onto the coffee table. She made a point of holding his hand.

"Aiden, I'm not very good at this."

"Take your time."

"I'm afraid I've been badly trained in relationships. I have a long history of dating *unavailables*."

"That's ironic."

"Why is it ironic?"

Aiden kissed the top of Macy's head. "I have a long history of being an *unavailable*."

"Is that what broke up your marriage?"

"Apparently, my heart was never really in it. My ex-wife's words, not mine, but she was probably right."

"Then why did you marry her in the first place?" asked Macy.

"She gave me an ultimatum and instead of walking away, I married her. I'd never been in love before. I thought that maybe it was as good as things would ever get, that it was enough to really care about someone."

"She shouldn't have forced your hand. You can't make someone want to stay."

"Which brings us to us. I need to know what's really going on in that head of yours."

Macy placed her hand on his chest.

"I'm afraid it involves Ray. The fallout from that relationship may never go away."

"Dating a sociopath is never a good idea."

"I didn't know that when we started seeing each other. Nobody did."

"I could have told you," said Aiden.

"I wouldn't have listened."

"Macy, are you really over him?"

"I'm no longer in love with him if that's what you're asking."

"Then what do I need to worry about?"

"I wasn't joking when I said I'd been badly trained in relationships. When I was with Ray I rarely asked for anything because the answer would always be no. I learned to pretend I was independent until I really was independent. I lowered my expectations, then lowered them again. It was a very lonely four years, but I convinced myself that it wasn't. It was that fucked up."

Aiden brushed away her hair and kissed her on the forehead. His voice sounded lazy and slow.

"So," he said. "What do you want to do?"

"This isn't going to be easy."

"I know."

"I'm not promising anything, but I want to try."

"Are you sure?"

She nodded. "So, what do we do now?"

"We make plans. It's that simple."

"Kalispell has a branch office," said Macy. "I could look into the possibility of a transfer."

"That's a start."

Macy's phone buzzed and she fished it out of her pocket.

"I have a missed call from Gina," she said, rising to her feet. "I really need to speak to her."

Macy drifted to the kitchen and opened the refrigerator out of habit more than hunger.

"Gina, it's Macy," she said, poking through a selection of readymade meals before shutting the door. "Is everything okay in Helena?"

"Yeah, it's all fine now. My mother-in-law slipped and fell down the stairs."

"That's terrible. Is she okay?"

"She's dislocated a shoulder and is pretty bruised. Thankfully, my kids were here when it happened. Her blood pressure was super low when the paramedics arrived so a delay could have been fatal. Just a sec." Gina covered the mouthpiece for a few seconds and all Macy could hear were muffled voices. "Macy, are you still there?"

"I'm here."

"My husband is taking off a few days from work to care for his mother, and it looks like my sister-in-law is willing to step in to look after the children, so I should get back up to Walleye soon."

"Gina, there are plenty of people working this case. You should take all the time you need."

"I don't see how hanging around here is going to help. It's going to be a full house."

"What happens when your husband goes back to work?"

Gina paused. "I'm not sure. I'm either going to have to come up with a more permanent child-care arrangement or find some way to cut back on my hours. Having my mother-in-law move in whenever we're stuck isn't working."

"Makes me realize how lucky I am to have my mom around to look after Luke."

"You do seem to be able to come and go as you please. How are you holding up?" asked Gina. "I'm supposed to be looking after you, not the other way around."

Macy sat down on the coffee table in front of Aiden. His eyes fluttered but didn't open. Being with Aiden would mean leaving Helena. Without her mother providing full-time child care, she didn't see how she'd manage the hours she worked as a special investigator. She'd have to cut back or change jobs.

"I'm fine," said Macy. "Just trying to sort through some issues I'm having."

"Are you talking about work or your personal life?"

"I work a lot of hours. They're pretty much the same thing."

"If you ever want to talk, you know where to find me."

"Thanks, Gina. I appreciate that. Let me know when you're heading back this way."

# 10

A dozen crows fought over the remnants of a gopher snake that had been flattened by a passing car. They scattered as Emma came running up the road. She stopped on the sidewalk outside her home and paced back and forth with her hands on her hips. She was struggling to catch her breath. The air was cold and sharp, and at five thousand feet above sea level, it was also much thinner than what she was used to back in San Francisco. She glanced up at her mother's bedroom window. The curtains were still drawn.

A lone bicycle came from the direction of town. The girl peddling it appeared to be in her early teens. The bike lurched sharply every time she hurled a newspaper onto a driveway. She said a breathless good morning as she threw a newspaper in Emma's direction. Emma smiled as she returned the greeting, but inside her heart was racing. She hadn't expected to see her picture on the front page of the local paper. She slid the rubber band off the folded paper to reveal the rest of the article about her father's murder and the ongoing investigation. There was a photo of Emma alongside the text. It was a corporate shot pinched from her employer's Web site. She looked at the story's byline and frowned. It was the second time she'd seen Nathan's fiancée's name in print. Emma skimmed the article and was relieved to find that other than a brief biography cut and pasted from her company's online profile, she was barely mentioned. On the third page there was a short piece on Carla and Lloyd Spencer's death that highlighted their ongoing fight with addiction. Their link to her father's kidnapping and murder was still being kept out of the papers.

By the time Emma went inside, she was shivering from the cold. She nudged the thermostat until the heating came on and made a quick cup of tea. Carrying it in one hand, she ascended the stairs as quietly as possible. The door to her mother's room was cracked open. A sliver of lamplight cut across the landing. Emma almost knocked but stopped when she heard her mother's voice. It sounded like she was on the phone. The words needed context to make sense.

*"I don't know what more I can do . . . she doesn't know anything."*

A floorboard creaked beneath Emma's feet.

"Emma?" her mother called out, "Is that you?"

Emma poked her head into her mother's room. Francine was fully dressed and sitting on the edge of the unmade bed. There was no phone in sight. Leaving her cup of tea on a table in the landing, Emma wished her mother a good morning and stepped inside.

"I couldn't sleep so I went out early for a run," said Emma.

Her mother blinked up at her.

"Mom, are you okay?" she asked, her eyes searching the rumpled folds of the bedspread for a phone. "I thought I heard your voice. Were you on the phone?"

Francine looked nervous.

"I was talking to myself," said Francine.

"Since when do you talk to yourself?"

"It's your father's death. I can't accept it." Francine twisted a tissue in her hands. "It's all the things I should have said. I keep thinking that somewhere along the way I could have done something differently."

"Mom, I'm here now. I want you to talk to me. I want us to be close again."

"You go take a shower," her mom said, reaching down to smooth the bedspread. "I'll make us some breakfast."

Emma and Francine sat across from each other at the kitchen table. Francine hadn't stopped speaking since Emma came downstairs, but it was all nervous chatter. The newspaper was sitting in full view on the counter. It was opened to the article about Carla and Lloyd Spencer.

"Mom, we need to talk about what was going on with Dad. It may have been drugs, but it also may have been something else. He must have confided in you about what he was working on."

Francine put her fork down next to her plate. She'd yet to touch her food, but she still dabbed her lips with her napkin.

"Philip said nothing," said Francine.

"You expect me to believe that you knew nothing about what he's been up to over the past two months."

"It's the truth."

"He bought a gun. It goes against everything he stood for. You've been together for nearly forty years. It's not something he would have kept secret."

"Don't you think I know that?" Francine's blue eyes were clouded with tears. "He'd become so withdrawn over the past few months. Whenever we went out he kept saying that we were being followed. Emma, there was never anyone there. *It's just those crows,* I'd tell him. *They follow you everywhere.*"

"You said he was talking to Dot?"

"I told you to forget what I said about Dot. I spoke out of turn. What happened to your father is making me paranoid."

"But don't you see now that he could have been right," said Emma. "Someone may have been following him. We need to find out what he was working on."

"We need to let the police do their job."

"I can't just sit here and do nothing."

"Emma, promise me that you'll stay out of it. I need to know that you're safe more than anything right now."

Emma softened her tone. There was no reason to worry her mother.

"I'm sorry, Mom. I'll promise to stay out of it if that's what you want."

"Thank you. I know it's hard for you to let other people take charge. It's not in your nature."

Emma checked the time. It was just coming up to eight. There were hours of daylight ahead of her and she had no idea how she'd spend them. Sitting in her mother's kitchen wasn't an option, but neither was meeting Nathan for lunch. He'd sent her a text saying that he wanted to talk. Emma couldn't think of anything she wanted to say to him that didn't involve rehashing unresolved issues that dated back to high school. She focused in on her mother again.

"I hear that you volunteer at a homeless charity."

"After years sitting behind a receptionist's desk, I wanted to do something that mattered."

"You worked at a doctor's office. I'd say that mattered."

Francine fingered the handle of her coffee cup. There were tears in her eyes.

"That's kind of you to say," said Francine. "It didn't always feel like that. Your father was always the one with the cause. I was the one with the paycheck."

"There's nothing wrong with earning a living. I don't remember there being any homeless people in Walleye when I lived here."

"The downturn in the economy hit families around here hard. Even if they managed to keep their homes, a lot of people couldn't afford the upkeep. The charity raises money for repairs, but some of the houses are uninhabitable. I went out to do an inspection a couple weeks ago. A family has been without running water for the past six months and their roof has so many leaks they all sleep in one room."

"Nathan told me that it's mostly drug addicts."

"I really don't have time for Nathan Winfrey's opinions. It's that kind of attitude that makes it difficult for us to raise money. If we even suspect someone of using we turn them away."

Emma took a sip of her coffee. "What do you do there?"

"I help with administration and fund-raising. I know most everyone in this part of the valley. If you shake people hard enough money starts spilling from their pockets. It turns out I'm good at shaking."

"Did dad ever help out?"

"He'd come along when we were fixing up properties." Francine half smiled. "The men would get so competitive on the job site."

"Kind of dangerous if they're armed with hammers. I don't suppose Nathan ever lent a hand."

"I tried to get them to help out, but neither he nor his uncle Caleb wanted any part of it." Francine folded her hands in her lap. "When did you speak to Nathan?"

"He came by the other night when you were sleeping."

"I think you made a lucky escape with that boy."

"How do you mean?"

"Back in high school there was all this talk of marriage. I know he's your friend so I don't want to speak ill of him, but your father and I didn't think it was a good idea."

"You never said anything."

"You were—you are—so headstrong. We worried that you'd dig your heels in if we showed our disapproval. Besides it wasn't even something we could put our finger on. We just didn't like him."

"He wasn't who I thought he was. I just didn't see it until it was too late."

"Nathan was one of the reasons your father and I insisted you study in London during your junior year. We were hoping you'd break up, but when you came back you were a couple again."

"I was just biding my time." Emma lifted her chin. "You know he's moving into Caleb's house. If we'd stayed together I'd only be a few hundred yards away."

"I think you misunderstand me sometimes. I supported your decision to move away and have a career. I just couldn't understand why you stayed away for so long. I know that stuff Caleb said was very upsetting, but it was so long ago now. Besides, he's just one man and a very unpleasant one at that. If people thought they could get away with it, they would cross the street to avoid shaking his hand. And who cares if people thought you were gay? Around here pretty much anything is okay as long as you go to church." Francine paused. "You do go to church?"

"Every Sunday," Emma lied.

"Good girl."

"It's amazing that you still have faith after what has happened."

"It comes and goes," said Francine. "I've had a lot of support over the past week. Even Dr. Whitaker's evil third wife risked coming to see me. She usually steers clear of Dot's friends."

"With good reason. You threw her casserole away. I saw it in the trash."

"I doubt she cooked it anyway."

Francine pulled a set of keys from the pocket of her sweater and set them on the table.

"What's this?" asked Emma.

"The keys to Caleb's place. Philip had been keeping an eye on the house since Caleb was moved into the nursing home. I want you to give them back to Nathan. I don't want the responsibility."

Emma picked up the keys and turned them over in her hands. There was a metal heart with the letter *L* engraved in it. It felt strange to be holding something that once belonged to Lucy.

"I came across some homeless people when I was running this morning," said Emma. "They were living in tents out near the footbridge."

"I didn't think to warn you. Locals steer clear of that area now."

"You just told me that the homeless were mostly families."

"Yes," said Francine. "But there are also addicts and people suffering from mental health issues."

"So these guys were one or the other."

"I'm afraid so. We're not heartless. We offer them counseling and a hot meal. Sadly, most are unwilling to get help. It's the war veterans that really break my heart." Francine rose from her chair, leaving her untouched food behind. "Come with me. I have something to show you."

They spread the contents of Lucy's art portfolio out on the living room floor. The work wasn't as accomplished as Emma remembered. Among sketches of landscapes and farm animals were a half dozen portraits of Emma that dated back to when they were in high school. She didn't remember sitting for them. They had a voyeuristic quality.

She picked up a portrait that Lucy must have done while Emma was sleeping. She held it up for Francine to see.

"Since we know what was going on in Lucy's head at the time, this is kind of difficult to look at," said Emma.

Francine sifted through the pile. "I remember them being better than this."

"I was thinking the same thing."

The last sketch was more abstract than the others. The pen strokes were heavy. In places the paper had torn under their weight. A man stood with his back to the viewer. It appeared to have been set at night.

"Do you think it's a picture of Caleb?" asked Emma.

"Looks too broad to be Caleb."

"He's carrying a suitcase. Maybe it's a visitor." Emma held it up to the light. It looked more like a toolbox than a suitcase. "I thought I might go over and have a word with Dot Whitaker."

"I told you to ignore what I said."

"This has nothing to do with Dad. I want to ask her about the time Lucy worked for her as an assistant." Emma leaned back against the coffee table. "Maybe if I work through some of my issues it will be easier to come back here to visit more often."

For once her mother didn't disagree.

Dot's house wasn't as impressive as Emma remembered. The façade was a confused combination of different architectural styles. Corinthian columns were never meant to butt up against redwood cladding, and the large portico topped with Greek statues was completely out of place in northern Montana. Emma parked next to a fountain where a statue of a scantily clad nymph poured water into a pool filled with water lilies. Emma had dressed well for the occasion, in a tailored jacket and skirt, but her complexion was pale in the rearview mirror. She dabbed on some blush and puffed out her cheeks. She was tired of people telling her she was too thin. It was one of the last things her father had said to her. They'd been in the check-in line at San Francisco International. There was a section of wall covered with mirrors. They'd stood side-by-side studying their reflections.

*I'm worried about you, Emma. You're far too thin.*

She'd given her father a defiant look.

*I'm eating enough,* she'd said. *You saw me at lunch. A whole hamburger. I even had French fries.*

*It's not adequate given how much you exercise.* He'd squeezed her hand. *Promise me that you'll look after yourself better. You're going to get ill if you keep this up much longer.*

The sound of Dot's doorbell echoed through the house. Emma waited under a covered porch that ran across the front. Cushioned benches were set in alcoves that overlooked the sloping lawn. She spotted Dot coming along the drive from the direction of her studio. She wore an oversized flannel work shirt that was covered in paint and smelled of turpentine. She greeted Emma with a smile as she slipped off a pair of worn-looking clogs.

"I lost track of time," Dot said. "Were you waiting long?"

"I've only just arrived."

Dot led Emma into the high-ceilinged entryway and pointed to some open double doors. "I'll just be a second. Please wait in the living room."

Emma had expected dark paneled walls and heavy brocaded furniture, but instead the room was upholstered and painted various shades of white. A series of framed oil paintings hung on one of the walls. Emma walked over for a closer look. She was surprised to see Dot's signature at the bottom of all of them. Francine had spoken the truth. Dot had gone over to the dark side.

The paintings featured a young girl on the cusp of womanhood. Rendered in intricate detail, the girl's face was partially hidden behind a veil of jet-black hair highlighted with a few strands of white. An eye was visible in one painting, red lips in another. Her nose was small and turned slightly upward. Her eyebrow was arched and razor sharp. Emma scanned the paintings several times, but the varying parts of the girl's face failed to make up a whole. In the first painting the girl was squeezed into a red dress with a Peter Pan collar. She sat on the steps of a mobile home, peeling a shiny red apple with a hunting knife's long serrated blade. Her bare feet were filthy and a sharp-eyed crone hovered behind the screen door. Though the girl faced the viewer, only her lips were visible. In another painting she wore a red hospital gown, but this time she held a bloody heart in one hand and the knife in the other. Her hair hung over her face like a veil. All you saw was one eye. In the third painting the girl had changed into a red baby doll nightie. She stood in profile at a locked gate speaking to an old man who carried red roses in one hand and a Bible in the other. Snow was falling. In the next painting the same girl ran barefoot through woods covered in snow chased by footprints that couldn't possibly be her own. In the final painting she walked toward the viewer wearing a red coat and matching boots. Her hair whipped across the front of her face. In the background the mobile home burned orange and red against a black sky.

Emma studied each of the paintings carefully. Everything from the hair to the grit beneath the young girl's broken fingernails had been rendered with precision. The hyperreality touching on the surreal reminded Emma of Andrea Kowch's work. There was a story in there somewhere, but Emma couldn't figure out what it was. She was so engrossed she didn't hear Dot enter the room.

"Do you like them?" asked Dot.

"Yes, very much," said Emma. She stepped away and stood next to Dot. "They seem to be a modern take on Snow White, but I don't recognize all of the references. The author Angela Carter comes to mind, as does the work of Andrea Kowch and Andrew Wyeth."

"Oh, this is no fairy tale. Grace Adams is very real. I was so inspired by the girl's story that I felt compelled to make something more of it. Hence the paintings."

"Who is she?" asked Emma.

"Grace grew up in Collier, but I don't think she lives there anymore. Fascinating story. When her mother was murdered it was as if Pandora's box suddenly opened up. Who knew there was such evil in that town? It turns out a network of pedophiles and sex traffickers had been operating there for years."

"And this girl was at the center of all of it?"

"She's one of the lucky ones," said Dot. "As far as I know she's still alive. When the news broke it was all anyone talked about. Other people may have been attracted to the sensationalized stories but I was fascinated with the allegorical nature of the crimes. Here is a story that has been told since the beginning of time." Dot pointed to the old man and girl standing at the gate. "There is death and there is the maiden. As she draws her first real breath of freedom he stands ready to snuff it out."

"This is so different from the paintings you used to do."

Dot straightened the frame closest to her. There was a wistful look in her eye.

"I used to paint for approval. Now I paint for myself."

"Do you still have your gallery?"

"Only to support other local artists. I show my work on occasion, but it is no longer for sale."

They had lunch at a table in the conservatory. The room was filled with dappled light. Two gray-haired cats lounged on a settee that was bathed in sunshine. Despite Emma's protests, Dot poured them both a glass of white wine.

"Humor me," Dot said. "I don't like to be seen as someone who drinks alone."

Emma took a sip. "Thank you," she said, holding the glass up to the light. "I'm very impressed with how you've moved on with your life."

"My divorce from Peter was just the kick up the backside I needed. I was finally free to do as I pleased. I hear from your mother that you've not settled down yet."

"She thinks it's the only thing that will make me happy."

"Surely, you don't buy into that nonsense."

"I did for a time," said Emma. "Now I'm not convinced. I have married friends who are incredibly happy, and I have married friends who are incredibly good at faking they're incredibly happy. They all seem to think I have a fabulous life, so I guess I'm good at faking it too."

"I suppose there's a Mr. Right lurking out there somewhere."

"You make him sound like a stalker."

"Maybe a stalker would suit you. The magazines say you should keep an open mind."

"Duly noted," said Emma. "What about you? I'm surprised you kept the house after the divorce. It must have a lot of painful memories."

Dot stared at Emma for a few seconds too long. It was that same dark look Emma had seen at the church service.

"Dot?"

Dot softened her gaze. "Sorry, I was a million miles away. That happens to me sometimes. I'll be looking at one thing but thinking about another. There's a series of paintings I'm working on. Ideas come and go. What were you saying?"

"I was asking you about keeping the house after the divorce. It must have a lot of painful memories."

"Staying on has been a challenge, but this is where I raised my children. I want them to be able to come home to the house where they grew up. It requires a lot of upkeep so I've had to fight hard to make it work."

"How are your children?"

"All grown up now. You were in school with my son Alex as I recall."

"I've not thought of him in years."

"He's not fared as well as my eldest two, but he's doing all right in his own way. He's a huge disappointment to Peter—his father. I take a more pragmatic view."

Emma tried to picture Alex as a man but couldn't see it. He'd been one of the lost boys back in high school.

"That's really all you can do," said Emma.

"Anyway, I may not have moved on from the house but I've changed it as much as I could. Made the corners less sharp, so to speak. Peter was a big fan of mahogany. I painted everything white." Dot's hand fluttered toward a large wall unit. The brush strokes were visible. "Anyway, you didn't come here to ask me about my home furnishings."

Emma placed her folded napkin neatly next to her plate.

"Since I can't deal with what happened to my father I've decided to obsess on something else."

"And what is the object of your obsession?"

"I'm afraid it's Lucy Winfrey. After all these years it's time I finally tried to figure out what happened to her."

Dot picked up the bottle. "I think you're going to need more wine."

Emma paused while Dot poured. Emma hadn't realized that she'd nearly drained her glass. She made a mental note to slow down.

"My mother mentioned that Lucy used to work for you."

"I'm surprised you didn't know," said Dot.

"It turns out there were quite a few things I didn't know about Lucy. She was one person when I left for England and an entirely new one when I came back. In eleven short months she'd turned into someone almost unrecognizable."

"Had she always kept things from you?"

Emma smoothed the white tablecloth.

"Not at first," said Emma. "We were getting on fine until the spring of our sophomore year. Lucy was very resentful. She thought the sole purpose of the trip I was planning to England was to get away from her."

"Was it?"

"It wasn't central to the reason I was going, but I did consider it an added bonus. Lucy was my best friend. We were incredibly close, like sisters I suppose, but it was a friendship that was shaped by constant drama. With Lucy it was all or nothing. Sometimes it was too much." Emma drank some of her wine. "Anyway, it wasn't just her. I was suffocating here."

"What have you got against Walleye Junction? It's pretty much like every small town I've ever visited. I doubt you've found a much better life beyond the county line."

"Things with my boyfriend were also difficult. The expectation was that we would get married. I wasn't ready for that, but living in a place as small as Walleye made it difficult to move on. All I knew was that I wanted out. Going away seemed easier than breaking up."

"Are you talking about Nathan Winfrey?"

"Yes," said Emma. "He was my boyfriend for over three years."

"So, it wasn't Walleye that was getting you down, it was the Winfrey family."

"Seems that way."

"Nathan and my son Alex were part of the same crowd. They got into a lot of mischief together and I'm convinced Nathan was behind most of it. He tried to make out that he was an all-American boy, but he could be a bit of a shit. Alex avoids him now. Blames him for a lot that went wrong."

"I'm sorry to hear that."

"Anyway, the Winfrey family is a strange little clan. Too many cherries in their diet," Dot laughed. "Too many tarts."

"Do you think Lucy was a tart?"

Dot waited a few seconds before answering. "I heard things about Lucy, but then again I also heard things about you. That stuff that Caleb said at the funeral. It was all anyone talked about for years."

"It wasn't true."

An eyebrow shot up. "Not even one little bit?"

"Lucy and I were close, but not in that way."

"She really was an odd little bird then," said Dot. "I heard she wrote about your sexual intimacy in great detail."

Emma didn't want Dot or anyone else to know how much it still stung. She kept her voice steady. She even smiled.

"Lucy made it all up," said Emma. "It never happened."

"Don't worry," said Dot as she reached over and squeezed Emma's hand. "I believe you. I saw another side of Lucy when she worked for me. I take it that your mother told you that it ended badly."

"Yes, but she didn't know why."

Dot leaned back in her chair and sipped her wine.

"It all seems a long time ago now," said Dot.

"Was it drugs?"

"I'm sure that was a factor. She probably needed the money. At first it was little things that were missing, like jewelry. I started to think it was Alex or the housekeeper." Dot's fingers fluttered again. "You start to lose your trust in the people around you. Once that goes it's hard to get back."

"Lucy was stealing from you?"

Dot swallowed some wine. "Among other things."

"She'd been asking my parents for money. It got so bad my father went to speak to Caleb."

"Caleb didn't have a handle on things. Lucy's downfall really rattled that man's sense of superiority, which is probably why he lashed out at you. He needed someone to blame, otherwise people might have looked closer to home."

"Do you think Caleb had something to do with her death?" asked Emma.

"No, not directly, but he is a difficult man. God knows what Beverly saw in him. She was one of the most carefree women I've ever met. I was genuinely surprised when she settled down with him. Makes me think that she'd already realized she was ill. Caleb may have been an old curmudgeon but he was solid. And I give him full credit. He really looked after Beverly when she was dying." Dot swirled the contents of her glass. "It was Lucy that he couldn't love. You know, I never once saw Caleb show that girl any sign of affection."

"In a way that's not surprising. Lucy was difficult to love."

Dot's eyes widened. "You didn't like her."

"It's more complicated than that. I loved her like a sister, but I didn't particularly like her as a person. She could be very needy. There were times when I really hated her."

"And you felt the same way about Nathan, didn't you?"

"Yes."

"Tell me, Emma," Dot said, leaning in. "Do you still stay with people who make you unhappy?"

"I've taken it to the other extreme. I now walk away with alarming regularity."

"Do you think you stuck with Lucy out of obligation?" asked Dot.

"Habit, obligation, and a complete lack of imagination. When I was young my world consisted of two houses and the cherry orchard in between. I didn't realize there would be more choices in my future."

"It's a shame you had to leave town under such a cloud."

"I should have stayed and confronted Caleb, but I have a feeling it would have been useless. He wasn't interested in my side of the story. And in a way I guess I should be thankful. He burned my bridges for me."

"Have you ever thought of speaking to Caleb now? I could go over to the nursing home with you."

"I saw him last night. I can't confront a man who's lost his hold on reality. It would be cruel."

"He didn't remember you?"

"It's fine. I'd rather be forgotten."

"So, Emma," Dot said, placing her hands on the table. "If not Caleb, who are you going to scream at about the past?"

"I can't think of anyone who's worth troubling myself over."

"You could yell at Nathan. He's still around."

Emma smiled. "I can't confront a man who's lost his hold on reality. It would be cruel."

Dot laughed so hard she almost choked on her wine. "You must have heard that he's marrying Cynthia Phelps."

"I hope for his sake that she's changed since high school. She could be very cruel. She especially liked to single out Lucy."

"Cynthia's interviewed me a couple times for the local paper. Believe me when I say she's no Terry Gross. Anyway, you could run laps around that girl with your blinders on."

"Cynthia is welcome to Nathan. I'm not interested."

"Shame. It would be nice to have you around."

"Not on those terms. I've changed," said Emma, saying her vows aloud. "I'd never go back to that."

"It would be nice if you came to see your mother more often. She really needs you now."

"My mother fluctuates between pushing me away and wanting me close. I'm not really sure where I stand at the moment."

"That's sounds very familiar to me," said Dot. "Your mother and I aren't as close as we once were. We did have a nice chat at the prayer service though. We'll see."

"I'm trying to put her behavior in the context of what's happened, but it's difficult to think clearly. My father's death has really hit us both very hard."

"Of course it has."

"It turns out that my mother has been anxious for some time. She thought my father was hiding something." Emma watched Dot carefully. "She believed he was having an affair."

Dot's eyes widened. She put a hand to her chest.

"With me?"

Emma nodded.

"That explains so much," said Dot.

"I'm sorry, but I have to ask if it's true?"

Dot looked sad. "No, of course not. Your father and I were good friends. He's been very supportive. It's been difficult being alone. There are always so many little decisions that need to be made. I may have leaned on him a little too often. I never meant to cause offense. Poor Francine."

"You're not angry?"

"No, not at all." Dot folded her napkin and put it beside her plate. She looked close to crying. "I'm frustrated. Because I'm on my own some people view me as a predatory female. Women have a tendency to hide their husbands from me. Then there's the gossip. If I'm seen with a man people assume I'm sleeping with him. I'm sure you've faced the same thing."

"Sadly, yes."

"So much for the sisterhood."

"Did my father tell you what he was working on when he died?" asked Emma. "The police think it might be linked to his kidnapping, but his laptop is missing and he never confided in my mother."

"I'm sorry, but I can't help you there. We didn't really talk about his work." Dot hesitated. "I'm not sure you're aware of this, but your father loved to gossip. That man seemed to have his finger on every pulse in the valley. He had such a wicked sense of humor."

"I miss him."

"Me too. He was a good man."

Emma noticed the time. She'd promised to meet Nathan. If she didn't leave right away she was going to be late.

"I'm sorry," she said, reaching for her handbag. "I'd better get going."

"Do you need to be somewhere?"

"I'm meeting Nathan."

"Sounds dreadful. Call and cancel. We can go for a walk in the garden instead."

"I've already canceled three times."

"Then once more won't hurt. Besides," Dot said, pointing out Emma's empty wineglass. "You've had far too much to drink. It will be a while before you're fit to drive."

# 11

Stacy Shaw's mother stared at Macy through the half open door with a blank expression on her face. Macy held her badge a little higher.

"Mrs. Shaw, do you have any idea when your daughter will be home?"

The woman peered over Macy's shoulder. She'd borrowed Aiden's pickup truck, and it was blocking the narrow country lane. The sun was rising in the sky. It was coming up to nine in the morning.

"Is Stacy in trouble?" asked Mrs. Shaw.

"No, ma'am. I only want to ask her a few questions."

"That's what the cops who stopped by yesterday evening said. Seems like there's more to it if you're already back again this morning."

The woman grew in stature as she stepped out onto the porch. Close to six feet tall and painfully thin, she wore a flannel shirt and jeans. The little hair she had was hidden beneath a red checked bandana. The laces of her heavy work boots trailed behind her as she walked the length of the porch. She tapped a pipe on the railing before pulling a bag of weed out of her shirt pocket.

"That had better be medical grade," said Macy.

Mrs. Shaw held up the bag for Macy's inspection.

"I've been worried about Stacy," she said.

"Is there something specific that's been worrying you?"

"She's got money coming in from somewhere." Mrs. Shaw broke off some of the bud and pressed it into the bowl of the pipe. She struck a match. "She says it's from babysitting, but I know that's a lie. Nobody pays that well."

"We already have a list of her friends at school. Do you have any idea who else she's been hanging out with?"

Mrs. Shaw leaned against the railing. She looked younger out in the light. One eye was green, the other blue. She took a long hit from the pipe and held it in. Macy silently counted the seconds before Mrs. Shaw exhaled.

"A couple of weeks ago, I went into town to collect a bedside table someone dumped in an alleyway." Mrs. Shaw tipped her head to the barn. "I restore furniture for a living so I'm always looking for castoffs. I'd just finished loading it up into my van when I saw a woman making her way along the pavement. It was dark, but there was something familiar about her so I waited. When she got closer I realized it was Stacy. She was so dressed up I almost didn't recognize my own daughter."

"What was she wearing?"

"A tight-fitting dress and heels. She doesn't have those kind of clothes here at the house so she must have gone somewhere to change. I said hello, and she looked at me like I wasn't there. Got into a car and was driven away." Mrs. Shaw's voice trailed off. "I've not had much to say to her since then."

"What kind of car was it?"

"It was a big dark SUV, navy or black I suppose. I couldn't tell the make. It had been parked there when I pulled up. I thought it was kind of weird as it wasn't the type of place you normally find nice cars."

"Did you see the driver?" asked Macy.

"I'd assumed it was empty, but then the high beams went on at the same time I tried talking to Stacy. Couldn't see much of anything after that." She held the pipe up again, but spoke before she took another hit. "I really wish I could tell you more."

"Did you ask your daughter who she was with that night?"

"When she came home the next day I tried to get through to her, but it turned into a screaming match. Needless to say, I didn't get anything out of her."

"When was the last time you saw Stacy?"

"She was here a few nights ago but didn't stay long. The school called. She's not been there either."

"Does she have her own car?"

"Her dad went out and bought her one when she turned sixteen. I told him to wait until she improved her grades, but he thought differently. No matter what I say or do, I end up looking like the bad guy."

"Is her father here?" said Macy.

"No, he's working in the oil fields in North Dakota. Won't be home again for a few months. It really breaks my heart. You know, she used to be the sweetest little girl, loved school, stuck close to home. Now she's this angry stranger who stomps through the house slamming doors. I've been ill the past year, and she's barely noticed."

"Does she do drugs?"

"It would explain the change in her personality. She can be manipulative and cruel. It's not how I raised her, but it's how she turned out."

Lou Turner called Macy into his office at the rear of Walleye Junction's Police Department. He slid a bundle of papers across the desk.

"There was another one of those anonymous e-mails last night," said Lou. "Looks like it's from that same group of anarchists that sent us a list of people who died of accidental overdose."

The e-mail opened with a question. *What's taking you so long to figure this out? People are still dying.*

"Have you had time to have a look?" asked Macy.

Lou took a sip of his coffee. "The e-mail had several attachments. One was a Word document that summarizes several cases involving doctors who've been convicted for doing anything from dealing prescription drugs to running pill mills to exchanging painkiller prescriptions for sexual favors. The other documents are PDFs of the original newspaper articles. It's all there in that pile in front of you."

"Any of the doctors from Montana?"

"No, this is nationwide," said Lou.

"What are they trying to tell us? Weren't the overdose victims listed in the first e-mail mostly from Montana?"

Lou nodded. "Maybe we've got the same sort of problems around here, but we just don't know it yet. The tech guys are hopeful they'll find something in the attached Word document that can indicate the source. Gina was looking into that first e-mail. Do you know if she found anything?"

"I'm not sure how much progress she's made. I'll give her a call."

"Where is she?" asked Lou. "She's usually in the office before me."

"She had to return to Helena. I can't guarantee that she'll be coming back."

"That's a shame. She knows her shit. How are you getting around?"

Macy held up Aiden's car keys. "I borrowed a car."

Lou sat back in his chair. "These e-mails aren't feeling like a hoax. They're citing real cases. We just have to figure out how it all comes together."

"Do you think we're being drip fed Philip Long's last story?" asked Macy.

"It's a bit of a leap, but I suppose it's possible."

"I've listened to his archived shows. It's just the type of issue he'd try to tackle. He's had numerous conversations with callers about prescription drug abuse."

"It would mean that someone got their hands on Philip Long's missing work."

"Carla's son, Sean, is a possibility. His girlfriend, Kristina, has that whole hacker-girl vibe going on. Might as well fit in a bit of anarchy on the side."

"I didn't realize such a vibe existed," he said.

"Kristina has the tech guys in Helena running around in circles. As far as we can tell, she doesn't exist outside of social media."

"If it is Sean who's behind these e-mails, he needs to quit dicking around and turn himself in." Lou rubbed his eyes. "This social media stuff is so far outside my experience I'm not sure what to do with it."

"It's possible that Carla called Sean for help. If Philip Long had his laptop with him when he was abducted, it would have had his files on it. Maybe she shared the files with Sean and Kristina. You said Carla used to work in the tech industry. Downloading them onto a USB memory stick would have been easy."

"But why would she do that?"

"I can only guess," said Macy. "I was told Carla was frightened of her husband. He may have bullied her into going along with the kidnapping and she was having second thoughts."

"All this speculation is interesting, but it's getting us nowhere. If Sean is too scared to come home, he's free to call us. Meanwhile, Bob Crawley is sitting in a cell, and there's plenty of physical evidence that puts him at the crime scene. I say we charge him with kidnapping and murder and go home for the day." Lou sat back.

"Tempting as that is, we'll have to hold off for a few hours. I'm heading up to see his wife now," said Macy. "She has given us permission to interview the children. She's suddenly very focused on clearing her husband of any involvement."

"Yesterday she wanted his head on a post. What changed her mind?"

"She says it's for their children's sake, but I have a feeling it's more to do with market forces. Bob Crawley runs a publically traded company. News of his arrest got out yesterday evening and the value of the stock fell by twenty percent when trading opened this morning. A continued free fall would reduce the bottom line in any financial settlement she hopes to receive in a divorce."

"Nothing like a wife with a vested interest. Any word on Stacy Shaw?"

"I spoke to her mom. Stacy hasn't been home for three days."

"The officers that went around to Murphy's Tavern to ask about Crawley found out that Stacy Shaw has been a regular there for the past six months."

"Stacy is Crawley's alibi," said Macy. "Without her he's in trouble."

There was a knock on the door. A uniformed officer stepped inside and apologized for interrupting them.

"They found Joel Edwards's car parked illegally in an alley off Main Street. Looks like it's been there since yesterday. From what they can tell, he's been sleeping in the backseat."

"Impound it and have a couple of uniforms canvass the area. He should be close by." The officer left and Lou rubbed his eyes. "I wonder what Joel is up to. You know that his disappearing around the same time this all went down could be a coincidence."

"All the same, he knew Carla as a friend. It would be nice to interview someone who may have some insight into what happened."

"I hear you," said Lou.

Macy picked up the printout of the e-mail. "Mind if I keep this?"

Lou nodded. "I thought we'd all meet tonight for a dinner at my place to talk things through. It would be nice to get everyone in the same room. I invited Aiden Marsh as well. Gina would be a bonus, if she's back in time."

"Sounds like a good idea. Can I bring anything?"

"Just yourself. My wife is expecting us at seven."

"Sounds like a summons."

"That's because it is," said Lou. "Don't be late."

Lined up according to age, Adam, Finn, and Annabel Crawley sat on the living room sofa staring at Macy with varying levels of interest. Their mother, Charlotte, had kept them home from school. The unexpected day off had made them anxious rather than elated. They knew something wasn't quite right. The arrival of two police officers didn't ease their troubled minds. They seemed less bothered by the absence of their father. The eldest of the three had spoken briefly to introduce himself as Adam. His eyes searched out his mother before announcing that his daddy was away on business *again*. Annabel was holding her rescued doll tightly. She'd cried when Macy handed it to her. Between tears she smiled up at Macy like she was the patron saint of lost toys. Meanwhile, the middle one looked suspicious. Finn was not going to be swayed by Macy's shiny new detective badge and friendly demeanor. Something was amiss, and he didn't like it one bit. The eldest of Bob and Charlotte's four children was up in his room. Between slamming doors, Macy had heard music pumping out into the upstairs landing. The fourteen-year-old didn't have anything to add to the conversation so he'd barricaded himself in his room. His parting shot had been directed at his mother.

*Mom, you and dad always fuck up everything.*

Macy had been left feeling winded on her behalf. Charlotte Crawley was present, but sat a discreet distance away where the children couldn't make eye contact. After reassuring them that she loved them no matter what and that they should always tell the truth, she'd gone quiet. There were signs of stress in her face though. Before setting off from Walleye Junction, Macy had spoken to Charlotte on the phone. Charlotte was worried. Annabel had had another difficult night of interrupted sleep. When pressed by her mother she'd hinted at some dark episode that had occurred down by the river.

Macy gave the children another reassuring smile before introducing them to Margaret, a developmental psychologist who consulted for the state. After spending an hour talking through strategies with Charlotte, they'd agreed that it was okay for Macy to take the lead, but Margaret had been firm.

"Children are very impressionable, so no leading questions. Let them tell their version of events. If I feel they're getting stressed I'm going to intervene."

The interview was being videotaped. Macy had already caught Adam mugging for the camera. She had the impression that he would be the most cooperative of the three children and as he was nearly nine it was probable that he was the most reliable witness sitting on the sofa. She started with him first.

"Adam, when did you build that fort that's down by the river?"

Adam verbalized every thought that came into his head. There was a planning stage that had gone on for a few days prior to making a start. Materials were gathered. Schedules coordinated. Twice Finn conferred with his brother through whispering in his ear.

Adam brushed his younger brother off. "We built it last Saturday morning."

"It's a nice fort," said Macy. "Did you have any help?"

"Annabel kept watch."

"Why did you need Annabel to keep watch?"

Another whisper from Finn was followed by a quick turn to check with his mother. Charlotte told him that it was okay. She wasn't angry with them. Adam looked down at his hands.

"We weren't supposed to be down there on our own," said Adam.

"Why do you suppose that is?" asked Macy.

"Dad says in the spring the river is really high because the snow is melting. It's dangerous."

Macy glanced down at her notes. There was the unmistakable sound of rushing water in her head. She suddenly felt cold. For a few seconds she said nothing.

"Did you go near the water?" she asked.

"Only to throw stones," said Adam. "I swear we didn't go in."

"Did anyone from the house see you down there?"

"Daddy came looking for us, but we hid in the fort."

"Did you watch him?"

"Yes, ma'am."

"What was he doing?"

"He was calling our names. He left after a few minutes."

"Did he do anything else?"

"No, ma'am."

"Did anyone else come looking for you?"

"No, ma'am."

"Did you ever see anyone else down there?"

Annabel sunk her face into her doll's hair. Her voice came out in breathless whisper.

"There were two men," said Annabel.

"Anna, we're not supposed to tell," said Finn, finally breaking his silence. "They said they'd hurt us."

Adam put his arm around his younger brother's shoulders.

"It's okay, Finn."

This time it was Finn who shoved his brother's arm off.

"You don't know that," said Finn.

Macy handed Annabel a tissue. She was crying again. From the corner of her eye, Macy caught sight of Charlotte. She had her face buried in her hands.

"Finn," said Macy. "Would you feel safer if those men were in prison?"

Finn nodded.

"Would you like to help us catch them?"

"Yes, ma'am."

Adam was sitting on the edge of his seat, looking eager. He almost raised his hand to speak. Macy reached out and touched Finn's knee very lightly.

"I'm going to let Adam tell us what happened. Is that okay with you and Annabel?"

Annabel stood up. "I want my mommy."

"That's fine, sweetheart. Go sit with your mommy." Macy smiled at Adam. "Adam, you can start whenever you're ready."

"Do you want me to tell you about the whole afternoon or just the part when we saw the men?"

"Why don't you start the story right before you saw the men. What were you and Finn and Annabel doing? Picture it in your head if it helps."

"We were playing in the woods. We'd been in the fort, but then we wanted to go explore. Annabel stayed behind because her doll was taking a nap."

Finn whispered something in Adam's ear.

"We were looking for animal tracks," said Adam.

"Did you find any?"

"Yes, ma'am."

"Where were you looking for them?" asked Macy.

"In the trees near the path. We could see the river and the fire pit from where we were tracking animals. Finn saw the boat before I did. We watched them bring it ashore."

"What kind of boat was it?"

"A canoe."

"Do you remember the color?"

"Brown, I think."

"What did the men do?"

"They got out of the canoe and looked around. Their faces were covered with masks like we use for skiing when it's really cold. They had a plastic garbage bag. They emptied it in the fire pit."

"Is this when they saw you?"

Adam shook his head. "Annabel was in the fort. She didn't know they were there. She came out and they saw her." He started speaking faster. "They were calling to her to come over and see them so I shouted that they should come get us instead. Me and Finn started running and they both came after us. One was slower because he had a limp."

"Did they catch you?"

"Yes, ma'am. The faster one grabbed Finn, so I stopped too. He told us if we told anyone we saw them, they'd come find us again. They knew where we played."

"Did they hurt you?" asked Macy.

Finn pulled up his sleeve. There was finger-shaped bruising around his forearm. His eyes were wide and anxious.

"He pulled my arm behind me like he was going to break it."

"I bet that hurt. Are you feeling better now?"

Finn rotated his shoulder.

"It's just sore."

Macy returned her gaze to Adam.

"Did you go back for Annabel?"

"We waited until they left and then we went to find her, but she wasn't down at the fire pit anymore. She'd run back to the house. We found her hiding in her closet."

"You were all very brave," said Macy. "Do you think you could tell me a little bit more about what they looked like? I know their faces were covered but maybe you remember what they were wearing."

"Same sort of stuff people always wear for fishing."

"So, aside from the masks it looked like they were out for a day of fishing?"

"Yes, ma'am."

"Finn, do you remember anything else?"

Finn thought for a few seconds. "He and the other man argued."

Adam frowned. "I don't like this part."

"Adam," said Macy. "It's important you tell me everything."

"The man who caught Finn wanted to throw us in the river, but the man with the limp said he didn't want to kill us. He said that we were well-behaved kids and would do as we were told. He made us promise that we wouldn't tell."

"You kept your promise for a long time."

"Yes, ma'am, but we've all been really scared. 'Specially Anna."

"Do you think it would have been better to tell your mommy and daddy right away?"

"Anna wanted to, but we wouldn't let her."

Lloyd Spencer had walked with a pronounced limp since he'd wrecked his quad bike. He'd been involved in the kidnapping so there was a distinct possibility he was one of the two men who'd tried to dump evidence on the Crawley property. Macy wanted Finn's arm photographed. It was a long shot, but the finger-shaped bruise on his arm might match the one found on Carla.

"There's another thing you can help us with," said Macy. "I want you to try to remember what you wore on that day. It would have been cold down by the river. Maybe it was a fleece or a jacket or even a baseball cap—"

Finn interrupted her. "I was wearing my favorite sweatshirt. It's upstairs if you want me to get it."

"Has it been washed?"

Finn's face darkened. "Mommy's not supposed to wash it."

"Do you mind if I borrow it for official police business? I promise to take good care of it."

"I suppose so," said Finn.

"I'm also going to have a special doctor come up to the house and take pictures of your arm. Would that be okay?"

Finn said yes.

Macy took out a sheet of paper and wrote down her name and phone number in very large print.

"This is my phone number," said Macy, hoping it would reassure them. "I'm going to give it to your mommy. If you're frightened or you remember something about the men in the canoe, I want you to have her call me. Can you do that?"

Adam raised his hand. "Do you think you'll catch them?"

"Would it make you feel better to know that we may have already caught one of them?"

"Which one?"

"The man with the limp. So that just leaves one more for me to find."

Finn raised his hand this time. "Will there be a reward if they both get caught?"

Macy's heart was breaking, but she managed to smile. Annabel was asleep on her mother's lap and the two boys were slumped back on the sofa looking past Macy toward the windows. After a rainstorm that had lasted through the night the sun was shining again. Macy could tell they were anxious to go and play.

"I don't know about a reward, but do you know what I'm going to do?" said Macy. "I'm going to make sure the top policeman in Montana sends you a letter to say thank you. Would you like that?"

Adam nodded and Finn spoke.

"Can he send us a medal?"

"You never know," said Macy. "I'll certainly put in a good word for you. Can you guys do something for me in return?"

"Yes, ma'am."

"I want you to listen to your parents."

"Yes, ma'am."

"They're right about the river. It is very dangerous this time of year."

Macy sat at a table at the back of the café eating a sandwich. The first of the two e-mails they'd received anonymously was open on her computer. Reading the short biographies that accompanied the list of people who'd died after taking prescription painkillers wasn't any easier the second time around. She'd grown too used to seeing people as statistics. These people had led full lives. They'd left loved ones behind. Some had died incredibly young.

A twenty-two-year-old law student who'd recently been prescribed Vicodin following knee surgery went to bed on Christmas Eve and never woke up. He'd not realized that he wasn't supposed to consume alcohol in combination with painkillers. A young mother who suffered from chronic back pain for years was found unconscious in her car outside her children's school. After her doctor had cut back on her dosage she'd found physicians in Wyoming and Idaho who were unaware of her medical history and wrote her prescriptions. She never regained consciousness and died in the hospital two days later. A fifty-five-year-old man named Nelson had been left crippled after years of working in the oil fields. He died after ingesting a deadly combination of antianxiety drugs and several opiate-based painkillers, all of which had been prescribed by the same doctor. A few of the patients listed had histories of drug abuse and mental health problems, but most were people who'd gone to see their physicians after suffering an injury or having an operation. They were in pain and needed help. Their ages ranged from nineteen to seventy-two. Some were students or housewives while others were retired or held down regular jobs. None had criminal records.

Gina had sent the list of overdose victims to various agencies, including the Centers for Disease Control and Prevention, asking if the deaths were suspicious, but had so far only received a preliminary reply from the state coroner's office in Helena. None of the prescription overdose deaths in Montana had been ruled suspicious, but they had noticed something interesting about the list. People who die of accidental overdose on prescription medication often abuse drugs that were not prescribed to them. What made this list of overdose cases different was that all the victims were in a doctor's care at the time of their deaths and that they had all been prescribed Schedule II pain medication such as Vicodin, OxyContin, and methadone.

Macy heard Ryan before she saw him. The teenage girl behind the counter looked as bored as he looked bothered. He was careful to annunciate every word.

"Large, four shot, extra hot soy cappuccino with foam so dry it flies."

The girl held a paper cup and pen aloft.

"I'm sorry you'll have to repeat that."

"Large . . . four shot . . . extra hot . . . soy . . . cappuccino with foam so dry it flies." He pointed to her pen. "Aren't you going to write that down?"

"That won't be necessary. Name?"

"Ryan."

"Can you spell that please?"

"Seriously? There's no one else here."

"Humor me."

"R.Y.A.N." He pointed to Macy's table. "I'll be with the redhead in the corner."

The girl had already turned her back on him. "Must be her lucky day."

Ryan plunked himself down in a chair across from Macy. Over the last year he'd grown a beard, and now that it had filled out he'd taken to changing the style on an almost weekly basis. Today he was sporting the beginnings of a handlebar mustache.

"How did you find this place?" he asked.

"I interviewed Carla Spencer's nephew here a few days ago."

"They actually stock decent coffee." Ryan glanced up at the approaching barista. "Let's hope they know how to make it."

Ryan stared at the cup she'd placed in front of him. There it was. Ryan was now Bryan. He frowned.

"I even spelled it for her."

"Does it matter?" asked Macy.

"Of course it matters. Do I look like a Bryan?"

"Maybe you should taste it before passing judgment."

Ryan sipped and sipped again.

"This is surprisingly good," he said.

"Does that mean we can call you Bryan now?"

"Macy, sometimes I forget just how hilarious you are."

"I didn't invite you here to amuse you. Have you had a chance to look at the e-mails I forwarded?"

He held up a hand. "Work can wait. What's going on with you and Aiden?"

"I'm not sure. At present I'm trying to adjust to some level of normality, but it turns out that I'm pretty fucked up."

"I wouldn't let that worry you. We're all a little fucked up."

"You speak the truth. I told him I'm willing to give it a go, and seconds later I was already regretting it."

Ryan stirred his coffee. "You shouldn't mess with Aiden's head like that. Why did you say you'd give it a go if you weren't sure?"

"I honestly don't know." Macy checked her notes. "Let's get back to the case. Working seems to be the only thing that keeps my head clear."

"Seems you need to work on yourself too."

Macy tried to change the subject again. "Have you even looked at those e-mails?"

"Briefly. I was cc'd in the e-mail the coroner sent this morning."

Macy took a sip of coffee. "I'm afraid that I need a crash course on prescription drug abuse."

"We prescribe enough painkillers in this country for every adult to be on round-the-clock meds for four weeks. It's a man-made epidemic that—"

Macy interrupted him.

"I know the statistics already." Macy pointed to the e-mail that listed the overdose victims. "What makes this list interesting is that aside from a few glaring exceptions, these weren't people you'd ever suspect of having drug problems. They died after being prescribed painkillers by their doctors."

"Did you read the articles that accompanied that second e-mail?"

Macy nodded.

"Then you know that not all doctors are nice people. Several have been convicted for illegally dealing drugs to their patients and there are others who have been done for handing out prescriptions in exchange for sexual favors. In 2007 the pill mills running out of Florida accounted for forty-seven of the fifty-three million OxyContin doses prescribed. The amount of money that's been changing hands is staggering."

"Do you think the same thing might be happening here in Montana?" asked Macy.

"Anything is possible, but there are a whole myriad of factors that you have to take into account before you start pointing fingers at doctors. It's incredibly difficult to assess a patient's pain levels. Patients who have become addicted to opiate-based painkillers will lie to get what they want. They'll visit multiple doctors. They'll give doctors a bad rating if they aren't prescribed the drugs they want."

"There's a prescription drug registry in place here in Montana. Doesn't that stop people from being able to go to different doctors for multiple prescriptions?"

"Yes," said Ryan. "But that only started recently, and it's still not linked to other states, so patients are free to head out of state if they want to."

"What about the patients who aren't addicted? Why are they dying when they're taking the prescribed dosage?"

"Opiates are incredibly powerful painkillers, but over time they lose their effectiveness by as much as thirty percent. People take more to ease their symptoms without realizing that the drug's ability to slow vital functions, like breathing and heart rate, hasn't been reduced. The more you stack your medications, the more likely you'll eventually make a mistake. Mix in a little too much alcohol or anxiety medication and it's like playing Russian roulette. For every fatal overdose there are thirty visits to the ER. It's a very dangerous game."

Macy tapped the sheet of paper. "Lou and I think this may have been Philip Long's story. He may have dug up something on a specific doctor or doctors. Like you said, there's a lot of money involved. They wouldn't have wanted this story to get out."

"We need to find out who prescribed the medication in each of these cases. I wouldn't be surprised if it was a relatively small number of doctors. There's been a lot of stuff in the press recently, and the government is cracking down. More and more physicians are shying away from prescribing opiates to their patients."

Lou Turner's home was within walking distance of Macy's hotel so she left Aiden's pickup truck in the parking lot and set off on foot. She was looking forward to a home-cooked meal and a conversation that didn't revolve around work. Lou's wife was an obstetrician based at Collier County Hospital. She wasn't Macy's doctor when Luke was born there two and half years earlier, but was working on the ward at the time. Macy was halfway to the home Lou shared with his wife when Emma Long's car slowed down next to her.

"Do you need a lift somewhere?" she asked through the open window.

Macy spied a bag of groceries on the passenger seat. Cupcakes and cookies were spilling out of the top. Emma reached over and placed it behind the seat.

"I'm not going very far," said Macy, finding it amazing that Emma could eat junk food and remain as thin as she was.

"Really, it's no trouble," said Emma. "Besides, there's something I need to tell you."

The passenger seat was tipped forward at an unforgiving angle. Macy found herself sitting straight up, her knees almost to her chest.

"Sorry," said Emma. "My mother was in the car last night. She's very, shall we say, particular."

Macy pushed the seat back and adjusted the angle.

"How is your mother?" Macy asked.

Emma put the car in neutral and placed her hands on her lap.

"There was a special prayer service yesterday evening at that big church on Main Street."

"The glass and steel box?"

Emma nodded. "When my father called it the church that pain built, I thought he was referencing his disdain for organized religion, but he may have been referring to the building's design. There are lots of sharp angles."

"How was the service?"

Emma thought for a moment. "I think it helped. My mother seems calmer."

"I'm sorry to have missed it. I meant to go."

"That's all right. Law enforcement was well represented."

"I'm heading to Police Chief Turner's house now."

Emma wouldn't look Macy in the eye.

"I've been thinking a lot about how my father was acting the last time I saw him in San Francisco." Emma picked up a magazine that was stashed in the seat pocket and waved away a wasp that was threatening to come in the open window. "If I'd known it was the last time I was going to see him, I'd have paid more attention."

"Was there anything about his behavior that was alarming?"

Emma was slow to answer. The silence went on.

"Emma," said Macy.

Emma looked up, startled.

"You were going to tell me about your father," said Macy.

"I'm sorry. This is hard to talk about."

"I doubt Lou will be upset if I'm a little late," said Macy, dismissing the warning that Lou had made earlier about being on time.

"My father was always paranoid, but in the last few years he got much worse. We spoke about it on his last trip out to see me. I was a little worried that he might be losing his mind."

"Did you discuss it with your mother?"

"I got the impression from my father that Francine already knew that he was struggling, but no, we didn't discuss it." Emma's voice remained steady but rose in volume. "And now I find out he was keeping secrets from her. He didn't tell her what he was working on. He bought a gun without her knowledge."

"Have you found anything in his notes?" asked Macy. "You said you were going to have a look."

"I didn't find anything suspicious among his archived papers, but I did find a receipt for the gun and ammunition he'd purchased hidden in his office. I can't find the gun, and there's not so much as a scrap of paper about what he might have been working on."

"You said he'd always been paranoid? How did it manifest itself? Was he ever violent?"

"No, he was never like that," said Emma. She stared straight ahead as she spoke. Her eyes were dry, but it looked as if she might cry at any moment. "My father liked to give the impression that he was laid back, but he always felt better when he was in control."

"That's not an easy way to live."

"I'm afraid he took it to a whole new level," said Emma. "He was obsessed with keeping track of people. He gathered information, eavesdropped on conversations, and followed people, if necessary. Everything he discovered was written down in a journal."

"I'd like to see it."

"That's just it," said Emma. "I can't find it anywhere. I've practically torn the house apart, but it isn't there. I'm afraid someone may have taken it. It's possible my father spied on the wrong person."

"Did your mother know about the journal?"

"I don't think so, based on what my father told me. I only found it because I liked to snoop when I was younger."

"Why didn't you tell me about it before?" said Macy.

"I didn't think there was anything to it until I realized it was missing. I live in big cities where people live in relative anonymity. Here it's different. It's easier to cause offense. It's harder to make things right."

"Do you know anything specific that was in it?"

"I'm sorry, but I was twelve when I last read it. I don't remember specific names. There was a lot about affairs, marital problems, and financial dealings."

"It does provide us with another possible motive or motives. I'll definitely keep it in mind."

"Have there been any developments in the investigation?"

"Nothing significant. We're tracing the whereabouts of a fellow addict Carla Spencer met in rehab. He has a history of violence and hasn't been seen since before the kidnapping. So far we've been unable to track down Carla's son, Sean, either. There are some other leads, but we need to follow them through before we know if they will amount to anything."

"That's not much, is it?"

Macy closed her eyes. Emma was right. Macy reached over and dug the printout of the anonymous e-mails out of her bag. It wouldn't hurt to show it to Emma. There might be someone on the list of overdose victims who was familiar to her.

"We're getting e-mails from an anonymous source," said Macy as she handed Emma the sheaf of papers. "The first one is a list of patients who live in this region who have died from taking accidental drug overdoses over the past five years, and the second is a link to various articles about doctors who've been found guilty of dealing drugs. We're beginning to think that someone is sending us your father's notes. Did your father discuss any of these issues with you? There's been quite a bit in the press recently. It must have come up in conversation."

Emma flipped through the pages slowly. "He was definitely interested. I remember speaking to him about it at length, but he never gave any indication that he was researching the subject specifically."

"Do any of those names look familiar to you?"

"It's a long list."

"Please, take your time."

"I'm sorry," said Emma when she eventually handed the e-mails back to Macy. "None of the names are familiar to me."

A patrol car approached them from behind. Macy checked the rearview mirror and recognized that it was Aiden at the wheel. Macy checked the time. She was going to be very late for dinner if she didn't get moving.

"Emma," said Macy. "Your father's murder may not have anything to do with the journal, but it's probably a good idea that it's found so we can rule it out."

"Believe me," said Emma, putting the car in gear. "I'm looking everywhere."

Macy started to scroll through the text messages on her phone. "I've got Lou's address somewhere in here."

"Don't worry," said Emma. "I know where the Turners live."

Macy was surprised to see Gina open the front door to Lou Turner's house. She held a glass of wine in one hand and a serving bowl in the other. She laughed.

"Don't look so shocked, Macy. You didn't think you'd get rid of me that easily, did you?"

"How's your mother-in-law?"

"She's camped out on the sofa for the foreseeable future."

Macy stepped inside and closed the door behind her. The entryway was cluttered with coats, boots, and sporting equipment. Both of Lou's sons were in the army and stationed abroad, but his daughter lived close by with her husband and young children.

"Where is everyone?"

"Lou and Aiden are out back dealing with the barbecue. Lou's wife was called into work. One of her patients went into premature labor." Gina peered over Macy's shoulder. "How did you get here? I thought I saw a red hatchback through the kitchen window."

"Emma Long gave me a lift."

"How's she doing?"

"All things considered she seems okay."

"I hear she's pretty tightly wound."

"She has good reason to be."

The back deck overlooked a meadow choked with wildflowers. Farther on a lake shone like glass in the evening light. The air was still but cool. Lou wore an apron he'd purchased while on vacation in Italy. Michelangelo's sculpture *David* had never looked more out of place. Lou put his barbecue tongs aside and poured Macy a large glass of white wine.

"Aiden was just telling me about the fishing lodge he's going to build when he retires." Lou clinked his beer bottle against Macy's wineglass. "Do you fish?"

Macy caught Aiden's eye. "My dad used to take me. I can't say I enjoyed the fishing, but I loved spending time with him."

"That makes a nice change. I always went with my boys. My daughter was never interested."

"My brother had a difficult relationship with my father," said Macy. "It wouldn't have been safe for them to be alone together. Hunting was definitely out of the question."

"That bad?"

"Legendary."

"Do you still go with your dad?" asked Lou.

"Sadly, no. He passed away three years ago."

Lou held up his beer. "Well, here's to your father. I'm sure he'd be very proud of you."

Macy focused on the placid waters of a lake. There was a canoe moored next to a wooden dock. She couldn't help but check the color. It wasn't brown like the one the Crawley children had seen. Her father had owned a drift boat and a couple of kayaks that had been towed to every campsite they'd ever visited. Macy's fondest memories were of being with him on the water, summer and winter.

"Thank you, Lou," Macy said, smiling even though she wanted to cry. "I'm sure my father would have loved it here. You have a beautiful home."

Lou turned his attention to the grill. "I have my wife to thank for that. When we met I was happily living in a mobile home. Aiden, you should take Macy out for a bit of fly-fishing."

Aiden leaned against the handrail. "I'd be happy to, but I'm not sure it's her thing. Didn't you once say that your father was into ice fishing?"

Macy shrugged. "He was from Minnesota. It's how he was raised, but we did a bit of everything. Anyway, I'd love to have a lesson."

Lou handed Aiden the tongs. "I'm leaving you in charge so don't screw this up. I'm going to go check and see how Gina is getting on in the kitchen."

Macy stood next to Aiden.

"I think Lou is onto us."

He ran his fingertips across her knuckles.

"Is that a problem?"

She squeezed his hand. "I will admit it's a little scary."

"For me too."

They ate under the covered porch that had an outdoor fireplace at one end. A fire was blazing, but it was still cold. Lou loaned Macy a thick fleece that must have belonged to one of his sons. The shoulders fell at her elbows.

"I spoke to Emma Long today," said Macy. "She thinks her father had been acting strangely for a while before his death."

"Did she elaborate?" asked Aiden.

"Apparently he's always liked to pry into people's private lives. He wrote down what he found in a journal. She doesn't remember the specifics, but there was a lot about extramarital affairs and financial dealings. The journal's missing."

Gina raised an eyebrow. "Something like that could really piss someone off."

"That's my thinking," said Macy.

Lou served Macy some salad. "What about prescription drug abuse? Had Philip Long ever mentioned if he was doing a story?"

"He was definitely interested in the subject, but never said that he was investigating it specifically," said Macy. "Emma has been looking through his archived papers to see if he may have stashed something there, but so far she's come up with nothing. She did find receipts from a gun shop in Collier hidden in his office, though. Her mother, Francine, is a fully paid member of the NRA, so Emma is surprised her father was so secretive."

Gina poured herself another glass of wine and offered Macy a refill. Macy held her hand up. Aiden was sticking with beer so Gina passed the bottle to Lou.

"I don't think Emma Long has seen her parents often enough to be a good judge of what's been going on in their marriage. People grow apart," said Gina. "Lou, what's Emma's story anyway? I get the impression that she left Walleye Junction under a cloud."

"More like a tornado."

Macy stared down at the plate. She didn't feel comfortable gossiping about Emma Long. She knew what it felt like to be the object of people's curiosity.

"Are Emma's past troubles relevant to the case we're dealing with now?" asked Macy.

"It's been twelve years, so I don't see how." Lou was still wearing his apron. It looked as if Goliath had gotten in a few blows after all. Barbecue sauce was smeared across David's marble chest. "A couple of weeks before Emma finished high school, her friend Lucy Winfrey died of accidental overdose. Lucy had started getting into trouble in her junior year and it escalated from there. Drug possession, drinking, truancy . . . you know the drill. Most kids survive their rebellion. She didn't. Emma was the one who found Lucy's body. As I recall there was a mixture of Vicodin and OxyContin in her blood. She'd taken some intravenously and the rest she swallowed. We found cash and a considerable stash of painkillers in her room. I think the estimated street value back then was between four and five grand. There was an unidentified partial fingerprint on the syringe, but otherwise we found no indication of foul play."

"What about the fingerprint?" asked Aiden. "There could have been someone else there that night."

"Lots of addicts share needles and the medical examiner figured she qualified as one. That partial has always bothered me though," said Lou. "Once in a while I run it through the system. So far there's been no match."

Gina started to open another bottle of wine. "Lou, why did Emma get blamed for Lucy's death?"

"Caleb read his daughter's diaries. He was a little shocked to find that Lucy had carefully documented a long-standing sexual relationship with Emma Long."

Macy raised an eyebrow. "I imagine that didn't go down well."

"Caleb is and was very conservative both religiously and politically. He publically shamed Emma at Lucy's funeral. Caleb pretty much told everyone that Emma was a predatory lesbian who'd used his daughter for years. He blamed her for Lucy's death."

"No wonder Emma has stayed away for twelve years," said Macy.

Lou went on. "We all stood there like idiots. Emma left town a few days later. Skipped her high school graduation ceremony and everything that went with it. She was class valedictorian that year."

Gina frowned. "Was there any truth to what was written in that diary?"

"Who knows?" said Lou. "It was all just so weird."

"Did you figure out who was supplying Lucy with drugs?" said Macy.

"There was a full investigation," said Lou. "We established that she'd been dealing to high school students here in the valley, but someone out there must have targeted her in the first place. She would have been bringing in a lot of money. Back then it was rare to come across such a large stash."

Aiden had been pretty quiet all evening. Macy couldn't tell if he was tired or feeling as awkward as she was. He wadded up his paper napkin and dropped it on the table.

"It may be worth looking into Lucy Winfrey's death again. Carla and Lloyd Spencer were both addicted to painkillers as well." Aiden turned to Macy. "Has Lucy Winfrey's name come up in Philip Long's murder investigation?"

"Only in conversation with Emma Long."

Lou sat up. "Did Emma think there was a link to her father's death?"

"Only in that their deaths were both tragic. I get the impression she's still haunted by what happened to her friend. Finding her body couldn't have been easy." Macy hesitated. "I suppose Aiden's right though. It is worth looking into further. There's a latent fingerprint on the syringe. We'll start there."

"The e-mails we've received only listed people who died while under a doctor's care. That wasn't the case with Lucy Winfrey," said Lou.

Macy agreed. "Lou, I'm sure your instincts are correct, but I'd still like to go through the case file. It shouldn't take long to rule it out as a possibility. By the way, I spoke to the state coroner in Helena. They're cross-checking the patient files for us. By tomorrow I should have the names of all the Montana-based doctors that prescribed medication to the patients who died. There may be someone who's written prescriptions for multiple patients. Not that that's necessarily a problem for them from a legal standpoint. None of the deaths were seen as suspicious."

"Any sign of Bob Crawley's alibi, Stacy Shaw?" asked Aiden.

"Nothing," said Gina. "We're monitoring her bank accounts, social media platforms, and cell phone, but there's been no activity."

"Now that I've interviewed his kids I'm convinced Bob Crawley wasn't involved, but I'd still like to speak to Stacy Shaw," said Macy. "She couldn't have picked a more opportune moment to fall off the face of the earth. It's really slowed down the investigation."

"So, you don't think Bob is our guy," said Gina.

"His kids were very convincing. They saw two men plant evidence on the Crawley property. I'm almost positive one of them was Lloyd Spencer."

"And the other?" asked Gina.

"We've got finger-shaped bruises on a child's arm that are similar in size to the ones that were found on Carla's body. We also have a sweatshirt that may have trace DNA on it. Lab techs are going over it now."

"Could Sean Spencer have been the other man?" asked Aiden.

"We know he was in Bozeman the morning his parents died," said Macy. "Whether he was up on the Crawley property with his stepfather remains to be seen."

"Sean has been living off thin air for a while now," said Gina. "Tech guys have hit a wall. No one knows where he is. According to social media accounts, his girlfriend, Kristina, organized one of her raves down near Bozeman a few days ago, which may have been why they were there. The police are investigating a party that took place in an abandoned warehouse."

"Any arrests?" asked Aiden.

"Nope, but a few kids ended up in the hospital."

Lou poured himself another glass of wine. "Do you ever feel like you keep cleaning up the same mess over and over again?"

"All the time," said Gina.

"Oh," said Lou. "I finally spoke to Joel Edwards's parole officer. They'd discussed his progress in the drug rehabilitation program. Joel mentioned Carla a couple of times. Said she was being really helpful with his recovery."

Macy spoke. "Did he give you any more background?"

"It's a pretty sad story. Addiction seems to run in the family. When his sister died of an accidental overdose a couple of years ago, he spiraled downward pretty quickly. Parole officer thinks he has a death wish."

"He's suicidal?" asked Macy.

Lou thought for a few seconds. "Hard to tell. He may just like to take risks. According to his parole officer, he's stopped breathing in emergency rooms on three separate occasions."

Gina frowned. "He was convicted of attempting to rob a doctor for drugs at gunpoint. You'd think he'd have spent more time behind bars."

"The judge took the view that he needed to be treated, not incarcerated," said Lou.

"It was armed robbery," repeated Gina.

"As I recall there were extenuating circumstances," said Lou.

"Does his parole officer have any idea where Joel might be?" asked Macy.

"There's a homeless camp north of town, near the river," said Lou. "We're sending in a few units at first light. If he's there we'll find him."

"Didn't you impound his car?" said Macy. "Might be hard for him to make it back out there without it."

"The car is indeed impounded. Ryan promised he'd have a look at it tomorrow."

"I think I'm going to head off now," said Aiden. "It's been a long few days."

Macy started gathering plates. "I'll walk you out."

Aiden pulled Macy into his arms as soon as they were out of sight of the house. They leaned back against his patrol car.

"I'm tired," he said. "Much as I'd like to see you tonight, I figure it's best if we go our separate ways."

"I'll have to drive Gina back to the hotel anyway." Macy glanced at the front porch. There were shadows moving about the kitchen. "Not sure how long it will take to extract her."

"She does seem to be knocking back the wine this evening."

"Oh, let her have her fun," said Macy. "I think she's been having difficulties at home."

"Marital problems?"

"No," said Macy. "Her husband seems to be a saint. I think she's exhausted from trying to work and raise a family. There are only so many hours in a day."

Aiden held her a little tighter.

"Are you worried about how you'll manage working without your mother here to look after Luke?"

"I am."

He hesitated. "You could cut back on your hours, maybe even try something new."

"I could."

"But you won't."

Macy stepped away from Aiden so she could look him in the eye. "Aiden, I love my job. If we're going to commit to a future together we have to figure out a way to make it work as well."

"So, no compromise?"

"I'm leaving my life in Helena behind, I'd say I'm compromising enough already."

Aiden took her hand. "I think we're too tired to talk about this now."

Macy didn't disagree.

He kissed her good night.

"I should get back inside before Gina opens up another bottle," said Macy. "We'll talk tomorrow."

Macy's cell phone rang as she was opening the door to her hotel room.

"What's wrong, Lou?" asked Macy. "Did Gina run off with your favorite bottle of wine?"

Lou didn't laugh. "I apologize for the late call, but there's been a development."

Macy let her bag slide off her shoulder onto the bed. She wanted to follow it, but had a feeling she should remain standing.

"I've received a call from Kalispell PD," said Lou. "They found Stacy Shaw. She's staying at a hotel just outside of town. According to the clerk the room was booked for a week in Stacy Shaw's name and paid for in cash."

Macy wrote down the address. "I'll head down there now."

"I appreciate that," said Lou. "I've had a few too many glasses of wine to be much use to anyone this evening."

"No worries. I'll let you know if I find out anything of interest."

Macy opened a Diet Coke she'd stashed in the hotel room's mini fridge and stared out the window. Streetlights lit up Main Street like a stage, but once she hit the city limits she'd be on a very dark road. The drive to Kalispell would take her past the sight of the accident. She pictured Philip Long swaying barefoot in the driving rain. He'd been trying to tell her something that night. She needed to figure out what he'd wanted to say. Macy fished Gina's car keys out of her pocket and contemplated making the drive on her own. Bringing along Gina was out of the question as she'd drunk even more wine than Lou. Macy took a sip of Diet Coke and decided it was best that she not call Aiden. She really wasn't up to having a serious conversation, and the drive to Kalispell would give them too much time to talk. She grabbed her bag and headed out into the night.

The landscape spun away in a succession of billboards and road signs. Macy kept her eyes on the road, but her mind was elsewhere. There was definitely something solid about her relationship with Aiden, but try as she might, she couldn't picture a way around the obstacles that were blocking their way. She'd have to move out of her mother's home in Helena. She'd have to hire a stranger to look after her son. Her career would suffer. She'd have to compromise. They'd not talked about kids. Aiden might want to have more children. She wasn't sure how she felt about that.

Halfway to Kalispell, Macy came to a stop and put on the emergency lights. A few dozen elk stood frozen in the glare of the headlights. She shut them off and waited. First a trickle, then a flood; the herd edged across the highway cautiously. At one point her vehicle was surrounded by hundreds of them. Their hooves clattered on the pavement and steam rose from their snouts. They peered into the windows as they bumped and brushed against the side of the car, their dark eyes wide and anxious. Macy sat back in her seat. There were no other cars coming or going. She closed her eyes and drifted off to sleep. She awoke to an empty highway.

After so much darkness, the town of Kalispell glowed like daybreak. The navigation system directed Macy to an exit north of town. The road narrowed as it wove through stands of solid looking pines. She caught occasional glimpses of putting greens and fairways so finely mowed they shone like glass in the starlight. She passed by the clubhouse and hotel as she followed the route to the condominiums that dotted the grounds. She was looking for number sixty-eight.

Stacy Shaw had refused to leave her bedroom in the two-story condominium set in the woods next to the thirteenth hole.

"I haven't broken the law," said Stacy. "The room is paid for, so I'm staying."

As she wasn't a suspect but only a witness, Macy couldn't fault Stacy's logic, but that didn't stop Macy from wanting to kick some sense into the girl.

Bob Crawley had been right about one thing. Stacy Shaw looked much older than eighteen. She was lying back on her bed wearing a white terrycloth robe. Her long brown hair fell across her shoulders. Her makeup was thick but flawless. She didn't seem to have any sense of shame. She'd been alone with two male police officers for nearly an hour and hadn't thought to get dressed. Macy picked a bottle of nail varnish off the table. It was a drugstore brand.

"Stacy," said Macy. "Who's paying for all this?"

Stacy looked bored. "Online he goes by the name Max. He likes playing golf, is married, and has a preference for brunettes."

"That's not a lot to go on."

"It's enough."

"Maybe if you were meeting for a cup of coffee, but that's not what's going on here. You do realize that you've agreed to spend a week with a complete stranger in a hotel room." Macy lifted the curtain and looked outside. "The clubhouse is at least a mile away. No one would know if you were in trouble."

Stacy's eyes flicked to the silent television screen. A music video was playing. They'd agreed the television could stay on, but the volume was to remain off.

"I don't care that you have a problem with my lifestyle," said Stacy. "I'm not doing anything wrong, otherwise you would have arrested me."

"When exactly was Max supposed to meet you here?"

"Three days ago. He sent me a message saying that he was running late but that I should stay here on my own. Between spa treatments, I watch television and order room service. It's paradise." Stacy stretched out on the bed like a cat. "And it's all paid for."

"Do you have any other photos of Max?"

"Just the one from the Web site. I already gave it to these guys."

"It must be kind of boring sitting here by yourself."

Stacy checked her fingernails. "I have to be here when he arrives."

"Your mother is worried about you."

"As you can plainly see, I'm fine."

"We need to talk about your relationship with Bob Crawley," said Macy.

"I don't know anyone named Bob Crawley."

Macy showed her a photo.

"Oh, him," said Stacy,

"What name did he give you?"

"Steve."

"When was the last time you saw *Steve*?"

"That's none of your business."

"Bob aka Steve is going to be charged with murder if he can't account for his whereabouts. He says he was with you on the night in question."

"What date did he give you?" asked Stacy.

"I'd rather you tell me."

Stacy rolled her eyes as she held out her hand. "Hand me my phone."

Macy tossed the bejeweled smartphone to the girl.

Stacy scrolled through the dates in her calendar. "The last time I saw him was Tuesday the twelfth of May. Is that the date you were thinking of?"

"Yes, it is. I'll need details."

Stacy sat back against the pillows again. Her terrycloth robe hung open, exposing one of her breasts. Macy told her to straighten it, but Stacy ignored her.

"Steve likes role-play," said Stacy. "Cheerleader, naughty schoolgirl, that sort of thing. On the night in question I pretended to be his son's school friend who needed a lift home, which was of course our little joke. We did it three times if I recall—"

Macy interrupted her. "Stacy, that's enough. I want to know where you met Bob Crawley and how long you were together."

Stacy checked her phone again. "The Valley Inn south of Collier. I checked us in at ten. He left sometime after three. I stayed until morning."

"And you're sure Steve and Bob Crawley are the same man?"

"I have no doubt whatsoever." Stacy reached for the hotel phone on the bedside table. "Are you hungry? I could order us some room service. The kitchen stays open all night."

"Thank you, but I've already eaten."

Macy took one last glance around the room. She'd looked into renting vacation homes in the Flathead Valley that weren't nearly as nice as this. A two-bedroom condo on a golf course must cost at least $500 a night.

"Is it normal for guys you meet online to be so generous?"

Stacy picked up the remote and flicked through the channels.

"All the time," said Stacy. "I've actually stayed in nicer places."

"Stacy, I need your attention for a few seconds longer."

Stacy laughed at something she saw on television. It was a scene involving an animated horse. It cut to a commercial and she turned to face Macy again.

"I'm all yours."

Macy set her business card down next to the bottle of nail polish.

"At the moment this may seem like a great way to live, but things will change. I want you to call me if you get into trouble."

Stacy held Macy's gaze as she flicked the card off the bedside table with her manicured finger. It fluttered to the floor.

"I'll take that under advisement," said Stacy.

# 12

The ski resort's main restaurant had been refurbished since Emma had last been there. Outside the windows, the Whitefish Range blushed pink in the east and the dark silhouette of the ski lift hovered over the grass-covered slopes to the west. She found a table in the bar a discreet distance away from the entrance and hung her jacket and scarf on the back of a chair. She sat down and tried to relax. She'd counted on it being quiet in the off-season, but there was a wedding party staying at the resort and the bar was crowded. The cocktail waitress who eventually spotted her wove through the tables with a sour expression plastered to her face.

"What can I get you this evening?"

Emma ordered a glass of white wine from the menu.

"Anything to eat?"

"Maybe later. I'm waiting for someone."

There was a shout and one of the bar stools crashed to the floor. The waitress said something Emma didn't catch.

"Pardon?" said Emma.

"Watch out for those guys," the waitress said. "They've been drinking since noon."

"Charming."

"I hope you're not here for a quiet meal."

Emma risked a quick glance at the bar. They were all big, bearded, and wearing oversized T-shirts. A couple wore ball caps. None were steady on their feet.

"It will be fine," said Emma.

"Well, let me know if they give you any trouble. I'm looking for an excuse to chuck them out."

Emma scrolled through her e-mails, taking occasional glances toward the bar and the double doors. Nathan was running late, but since she'd delayed their meeting four times she didn't feel she was in any position to complain. She pictured him sitting down to dinner with Cynthia. She'd be discussing the wedding while he was planning his escape. A shadow fell over her table. The man didn't wait for an invitation. He pulled out the empty chair and sat down.

Emma barely looked up from her phone. "That seat is taken."

"I think you should come join us for a drink at the bar."

"I'm waiting for someone."

He turned and hollered to his friends. "She's waiting for someone. What do I do now?"

Emma answered for his friends but kept her voice low. "Your friends think you should go back to the bar and leave me alone."

He tried to snatch her phone from her hands. "What's so interesting on that thing anyway?"

She glared at him. "I want you to leave."

"I like it here."

She grabbed her bag and he grabbed hold of her arm.

"Where you going?"

Emma pulled away. "Let go of me."

One of his friends intervened. "Joe, what's wrong with you? Can't you take a hint? She's not interested."

Joe let go of Emma's arm and turned to the window to sulk.

"Sorry about that," said the second man. "He's had a bit too much to drink."

"No harm done," said Emma, leaving her glass of wine untouched. "I was just leaving."

"It's getting dark. Can I walk you out to your car?"

Emma slipped on her coat. "Thank you, but I'll be fine on my own."

Emma walked alone through the dimly lit parking lot clutching her car keys. A pickup truck was parked a few spaces away from her hatchback, but otherwise there were few cars. For a second she thought it might be Nathan's. As she drew near she saw the sign for Flathead Valley Security on the door. She breathed a sigh of relief when she saw that someone was sitting in the driver's seat. She turned at the sound of footsteps. The drunken man who'd come to her table had followed her outside. His arms were held up in a gesture of surrender. She told him to stay where he was. He thrust his thumb in the direction of the hotel bar.

"I was just awful . . . awful back there." He staggered a few feet farther. "I need to apologize."

Emma pulled her car door open. "That's not necessary. I'm fine."

"Don't be that way. The guys gave me a hard time. I need to say sorry."

"I don't need your apologies. I need you to get away from me."

He lunged forward and grabbed hold of the door before she could shut it. He stunk of cigarettes and whiskey. His red face was inches away.

"Look, I just want to say . . ."

The man's head snapped to the side and for a brief moment, he slumped into Emma's lap before an arm locked around his neck and he was dragged away.

Emma stumbled out of the car after him. At first she couldn't understand what she was seeing. The man was facedown on the pavement. Kyle Miller stood over him kicking him again and again. His blond hair had fallen across his eyes and his mouth held a determined line.

"Kyle?" said Emma. "Stop it! That's enough!"

Breathing heavily, Kyle backed off. Blood poured out of his nose. He wiped it with his sleeve before rounding on the man again. He tried to swing his leg forward, but Emma caught Kyle by the arm and pulled him away. Kyle spit up a stream of blood.

"You're hurt," said Emma, leading him to her car.

Kyle pinched his nose. "It's nothing. The asshole caught me with his elbow."

Emma popped open her trunk and grabbed a roll of gauze from a first aid kit. She held it up to Kyle's nose.

"I can do that," he said.

"He just wouldn't take no for an answer," she said, checking to make sure the man was still lying prone on the pavement. "I don't want to think what would have happened if you hadn't come along."

"He's just some stupid drunk."

Emma shook her head. "I used to think Walleye Junction was the safest place on earth."

"By most standards it still is," Kyle said, tilting his head forward. Blood puddled beneath him. "Didn't you used to live in Chicago?"

Emma barely said yes.

"Well, Walleye Junction is like a trip to Disneyland compared to a city like that."

Emma tried to have a closer look at Kyle's face. "You should have that checked out. It looks broken."

"Emma, it's only a nosebleed."

"You can never be too careful."

Kyle pulled the gauze away. "Look, it's stopped bleeding. I'm fine."

Emma risked walking closer to the man who'd followed her out into the parking lot. He was lying quite still on the asphalt. She nudged him with her foot and he rolled to the side and moaned.

"We should get out of here before someone comes outside," said Emma.

"I haven't done anything wrong," said Kyle. "I'm not going anywhere."

Kyle leaned against the side of her car and she joined him.

"I wasn't expecting that from you," she said, gesturing to the man.

"How do you mean?"

"You're a guy who used to spend all his time hiding out in the library. I've never seen this side of you. You beat the crap out of him."

He hesitated. "That makes two of us."

"Not your usual MO?"

"Far from it. I don't know what came over me. One minute I was writing an e-mail and the next I was pulling him off you."

The man on the ground moaned and Kyle told him to shut up. Headlights swept across the dark parking lot. A pickup truck sped toward them, coming to a stop a few yards away. Kyle tilted his chin.

"It's your boyfriend coming to the rescue."

"Nathan isn't my boyfriend," said Emma.

"I hear he's told Cynthia he's having second thoughts."

"That has nothing to do with me."

"I think you'll find that it has everything to do with you," said Kyle.

Nathan studied the man lying on the ground.

"He still breathing?" asked Nathan.

Kyle spit out some blood.

"Only because Emma called me off."

Nathan laughed.

"What's so funny?" asked Kyle.

"Nothing. Everything." Nathan turned to Emma. "Sorry, I'm so late. Were you coming or going?"

"I was going." Emma pointed at the man sprawled across the pavement. "He followed me outside."

Nathan nudged him with his foot.

The man told Nathan to fuck off.

"I'd say he's still breathing." Nathan glanced over at the hotel. "Should we go back inside?"

"He's got a lot of friends in there," said Macy.

"Maybe not a good idea then."

"I'll deal with this," said Kyle.

"Are you sure?" said Emma. "I don't want you to get into trouble. I'll tell them what happened."

"Don't worry. It's—"

Nathan interrupted him. "Let it go Emma. It's his job. He's a glorified mall cop for fuck's sake."

Emma remembered the pickup truck that had been parked nearby. There was a logo for a security company on the door.

"Kyle, is that why you're here?"

Kyle started stammering. "Why . . . why else would I . . . I be here?"

Nathan laughed as he slung his arm around Emma's shoulder.

"Now there's the Kyle I remember. I knew he couldn't have changed that much."

"Nathan," Emma said, shifting out from beneath his arm. "We're all adults here. Please try to keep up."

Kyle started to walk toward his pickup truck.

"Hey, Kyle," said Nathan, following close behind. "No hard feelings. I know you're having a rough time." His voice was singsong. "I heard about your aunt and uncle."

Kyle turned and stood toe to toe with Nathan. The top of his head barely reached Nathan's chin.

"I think you'll find that I've got no feelings for you whatsoever."

"You see, Emma," said Nathan, keeping his eyes locked on Kyle. "It's all fine. I say we go for a drive. We can come back to pick up your car later."

"I don't want to leave my car here," she said. "You can follow me."

"Depends on where we're going."

"Are you worried your fiancée might see us together?"

"No, not at all," Nathan said. "I'd like to go someplace quiet that's all. We have a lot to talk about."

The man who had followed Emma was sitting up. He had a pained expression on his face. He poked around his chest with his fingertips.

"I think you broke my ribs," he slurred.

Kyle knelt down next to him. "I think you'll find that you did that when you fell down the steps. Nod if you get my meaning?"

He nodded.

"Now get the fuck out of here before I call the cops," said Kyle.

They watched him weave across the parking lot. Emma put a hand on Kyle's arm and he shrugged her off.

"Emma," said Kyle. "I said I'd deal with this."

"I just wanted to thank you."

Kyle turned and spit up some more blood. "There's no need. It's like Nathan said. I'm just doing my job."

Emma drove through the foothills above Walleye Junction with the glare of Nathan's headlights reflecting in her rearview mirror. The gates to the municipal cemetery were wide open and inside the grounds a few lampposts illuminated a path that cut a straight line from east to west. Emma fished a flashlight out of the glove compartment and tested it before grabbing a bag full of groceries and a bouquet of flowers off the passenger seat. She started up the main path while Nathan loitered beneath old iron gates.

"Is this quiet enough for you?" she yelled.

"Emma, what in the hell are you playing at?"

"I want to pay my respects to Lucy. I didn't get a chance the last time I was here."

"This sort of thing is best left to daylight."

Emma kept walking. "Lucy is dead. She won't care what time it is."

Nathan kept still. "It's too dark. You'll never find her grave."

"Do you really think I'd forget where she's buried?"

Emma hurried up the gravel path. There was a bench halfway across the cemetery. She stopped there to wait for Nathan. He walked at an easy pace with his hands thrust deep in his pockets. She shined the flashlight in his eyes and laughed nervously. He grimaced, but she didn't move the light.

"Emma," he said, a hand up to shade his eyes. "What's gotten into you? Have you been drinking?"

Emma started walking again. "I used to come up here with Lucy. We'd have picnics on Beverly's grave."

"That's just weird."

"Lucy had a morbid fascination with death. She talked about her mother all the time."

"Maybe with you, but not with me."

"I went to see Dot Whitaker today."

"Oh yeah," he said, stopping to read an epitaph on a headstone. "What did the old lush have to say for herself?"

Emma waited for him again. "Why are you always so mean?"

"I'm not being mean. I'm just saying what everyone around here is afraid to say. I'm kind of surprised you don't remember what she was like."

"As I recall she liked to have a good time. That's not against the law."

"I was pretty tight with her son, Alex. She was always hitting on his friends. Got so bad he didn't invite us to his place anymore," Nathan said.

"I don't remember that."

"You don't seem to remember a lot of things."

"I remember that Alex was high most of the time. Hardly a reliable source."

"Did you ever wonder where he got all those pills?"

"You think Dot gave them to him?"

"Who else?"

"How about his father? Dr. Whitaker? He was the one with a prescription pad. Women always get blamed for everything." Emma paused. She was tempted to tell Nathan that Dot had suspected him of leading her son astray but decided it wasn't worth it. "Whatever happened to Alex?"

"He found Jesus in a big way. He holds revival meetings in some tent outside Collier. Haven't seen him in years."

Emma gave Nathan a quick glance. "It's amazing how you can be so close to someone, but then it's like you hardly knew each other at all."

"Are you talking about us?"

Emma swung the flashlight's beam across the headstones.

"Maybe."

She climbed a short flight of stone steps, but Nathan stayed where he was.

"Is that really how you feel?" he asked.

Emma kept her eyes on the row of grave markers in front of her. "I'm afraid so." She started to count to herself as she walked west. If Beverly was the fifteenth headstone along the row, Lucy was the sixteenth. "Lucy and Beverly are somewhere along here," she said.

"What did I ever do to you?" asked Nathan.

Emma stopped in front of a large marble headstone that looked as if it had been recently cleaned.

LUCINDA WINFREY,

LOVING DAUGHTER AND FRIEND.

EARTH HAS NO SORROW THAT HEAVEN CANNOT HEAL.

She dropped the grocery bag she was carrying on the ground between Beverly and Lucy's graves. A box containing a cherry cheesecake tumbled out. She unwrapped the flowers and leaned them against Lucy's headstone.

"I found Lucy and Beverly," said Emma. She touched Beverly's headstone lightly with her fingertips. Her voice broke. "I'm afraid it's not good news. They're still dead."

"Emma," said Nathan. "I asked you a question."

"I'm well aware of that. I'm just trying to decide whether it's worth answering."

"You make out like I was some sort of monster."

Emma set the flashlight down on the grass.

"Nathan, I want you to take a good look at me and I want you to tell me what you see."

He hesitated. "I see a beautiful woman."

Emma spread her arms wide. "Do you think I'm fat?"

"Don't be ridiculous. If anything you're too thin."

"In high school I actually weighed ten pounds less than I do now."

"That's hard to imagine."

"Try."

"Why are you bringing this up now?" asked Nathan.

"You used to tell me I was too fat."

"I didn't."

Emma insisted. "You did."

"I don't remember."

"You told me I was fat. You told me I was ugly. You even told me I was stupid. I had a 4.3 GPA and weighed a hundred and five pounds. I still have issues because of the way you treated me." Emma sat down on Lucy's grave and started taking things out of the shopping bag. "Now do you remember?

"It was a joke."

Emma looked up into the night sky. She'd been planning this conversation for years. It had played out in a myriad of ways. Never had she imagined that Nathan would say the whole thing was a joke. Emma turned to face him. She wanted to scream but wouldn't give him the satisfaction of losing her temper.

"A joke doesn't last for three years," she said. "You were my boyfriend. You professed to love me. You should have been the person who made me feel better about myself, but instead you undermined me at every turn. Was it part of some long-term strategy? If you made me hate myself then I'd be too insecure to leave?"

"Come off it, Em. You're making too much of this. It was years ago."

"And now you're marrying Cynthia Phelps," said Emma. "Back in high school you used to say she was fat too. You even told jokes about her. She must have outweighed me by at least fifty pounds. I'd look in the mirror and wonder how much more weight I had to lose before I'd be good enough for you."

Emma carefully placed the cakes, cookies, and candy bars in a row in front of her. Her plan was to work from left to right. She tore the wrapper off the box of chocolate muffins and stuffed one in her mouth. She spoke between bites.

"I'm going to eat all this."

Nathan bent down and picked up a packet of Twinkies.

"I didn't think they made these anymore," he said.

"There were times I felt so ugly I wanted to kill myself," she said.

Nathan slid a Twinkie out of its clear plastic packaging and smelled it.

"They still smell the same as they always did," he said. "How is that even possible?"

Emma got up on her knees and snatched it from his hand. "Buy your own fucking Twinkies."

Nathan turned away. The flashlight cast long shadows across the grass. Tiny insects flew in its path.

"I don't know what to say."

Emma tossed the half-finished Twinkie to the side and reached for the cheesecake.

"There's not much you can say," Emma said, ripping open the box. "The damage is done."

His voice broke. "I really hated that you didn't need me. I still hate it."

"Nathan, I don't even know how to respond to that."

"For what it's worth, I am sorry," he said. "I don't like to think that I've made you miserable all these years."

"It's not your fault anymore," said Emma. "I took ownership of my issues a long time ago."

Nathan fell back on the grass and stared up into the trees. "I want to go back. I miss high school. My whole life was ahead of me. It felt like anything was possible."

Cherry topping coated her fingertips. She reached over and wiped them on his T-shirt. Nathan tried to take hold of her hand, but she pulled it away too quickly.

"I think you're the only person on the planet who's ever confessed to missing high school," she said.

"Back then I was *the* man. People respected me," said Nathan. "After graduation I was just *a* man."

"Open your eyes, Nathan. That's how the world works. No one cares that you were the varsity quarterback at Walleye High. You need to get over it. You also need to stop putting people down to make yourself feel better."

"I don't do that."

"You did it to Kyle earlier this evening."

"Kyle is an asshole," said Nathan. "After what his aunt and uncle did I'm surprised you let him near you."

"Kyle's not responsible for what happened. Near as I can tell he disowned them years ago. How do you know his aunt and uncle were involved? So far it's been kept out of the papers."

"Cynthia writes for the local paper. She knows things."

"I hope she's not been telling anyone else. The police don't want people to know yet."

Nathan stood up and walked a few feet away.

"I really can't believe you're defending Kyle Miller," he said.

"How do you figure that?"

Nathan looked as if he was about to start laughing. "His family for starters," he said. "He was never going to amount to much."

"Kyle's done surprisingly well considering his background."

"What's wrong with you, Emma? He's not done squat. He's a security guard for fuck's sake."

"Nathan, can't you see that he didn't have the advantages we had. Your uncle's business practically landed in your lap. If Lucy was still alive you'd be working for her now."

"Even by your standards that's a pretty bitchy thing to say."

"What do mean by *your* standards?"

"Sometimes you come off as pretty damn cold-hearted."

Emma started gathering up the discarded packaging. The last thing she wanted was an argument with Nathan. She wasn't even sure why she was defending Kyle. Like Nathan, he was a ghost from her past. Neither one of them was worth all this trouble.

"I'm not cold-hearted Nathan. I'm a good person. I have friends. I have people in my life who love me." Emma rose to her feet and dusted off the seat of her trousers. "I apologize for what I said. It was uncalled for. You always worked hard for Caleb. You deserve to be where you are, and let's face it, Lucy couldn't have run Winfrey Farms. She didn't have the interest or the skills."

Nathan stood with his back to her. His hands were once again shoved deeply into his pockets.

"This isn't how I wanted things to go this evening," he said. "I don't even know how to talk to you anymore. Everything with us always seems to end in an argument."

"I'm not sure what you mean by that. We've only had two conversations in twelve years."

He turned around and stared at her. "Who are you?"

"What kind of question is that?"

"You're not the Emma I knew. You're not even close."

"I consider that a compliment."

"It wasn't meant that way."

"Good night, Nathan."

"I can't leave you out here on your own."

Emma crossed her arms. As far as she was concerned the conversation was over.

"Good night, Nathan," she repeated.

Nathan stomped off across the graves, paying no heed to the paths that fell between them. A few minutes later his truck's engine rumbled. She tracked his taillights until they disappeared beneath the trees that arched over the road. Only then did she set off toward home.

# 13

Macy held her phone up to the dawning sky. There was no signal. According to the map coordinates Lou Turner had posted in a group e-mail, she was where she was supposed to be. It didn't feel right though. She'd not seen a single soul since she parked Aiden's pickup truck near a trailhead a half hour ago. She was starting to worry that she'd been sent the wrong information. There was no sign of the other officers who'd set out an hour earlier to search for Joel Edwards in a homeless encampment located near the Flathead River.

The area was just north of town but felt like it was miles away. Morning sunlight filtered through the low-lying mist clinging to the wide river basin. Stands of slim-trunked aspen trees flashed like cut glass and a solid-looking red barn stood alone in a sea of white cherry blossoms. Macy was so busy taking in the view she nearly tripped. The track had been churned up by dirt bikes. In some places the soil was deeply gouged. She glanced over at the river to check her progress. If Lou and his team were nearby she should have heard something by now, but the woods and riverbanks were empty. As she rounded the next bend, she spotted a footbridge that sagged across the Flathead River like a crooked smile. Careful to avoid brambles and poison ivy, she picked her way forward. Thin wicks of wood smoke rose into the air. Snatches of conversation drifted through the trees. Following the sound, she ducked under tree branches and headed down a steep slope. The path took her to a clearing not more than twenty feet wide. The only other way out was a low, dark opening in the trees. The earth was damp from recent spring rains. There was a heavy smell of damp vegetation and dried clover in the air. Off to her left, branches snapped and cracked. Macy turned toward the sound. Something was moving through the dense undergrowth. She searched the gloom for lumbering shadows. Bears were common in Montana. After a long winter they'd be hungry.

Keeping her eyes on the undergrowth, she eased her gun from its holster.

"Is anybody there? Lou? Gina?" she called hopefully.

Macy turned in a slow circle, scanning the trees for movement and the ground for animal tracks. The path leading to the river was marked with shoe prints, all of them human and all of them much larger than hers. The clearing was filled with waist-high grass. None of it was tamped down. She relaxed. It was probably nothing more dangerous than a rabbit.

In the distance a train whistle blew.

Closer still, something growled.

Macy turned in time to see a large black dog emerge from the undergrowth. Hackles raised, the animal bared its teeth before letting out several sharp barks. Macy picked up a stone and threw it. It landed near the dog's front paws.

She held up her gun and took aim.

"Get out of here! Shoo!"

A man stepped into the clearing carrying an armful of firewood. One of his hands was bandaged. Blood seeped through the gauze. He let out a sharp whistle and the dog backed off.

"Down boy! Come here!"

The man was older, probably in his fifties, and had a dark complexion and sad almond-shaped eyes. He looked as if he'd been knocked sideways; the bones in his face didn't quite line up and a wide scar ran along his jawline. His trousers were stained at the knees and the thick fleece he wore hung awkwardly from his slim shoulders. The deep timber of his voice didn't square with his slight frame.

"Sorry about that," he said, motioning for his dog to sit. "Leroy can be a little territorial."

Macy pulled out her badge. "Keep your hands where I can see them."

"I said I was sorry."

"Your dog was about to attack me," said Macy.

"No harm done. You're fine." The man crouched down so he was eye level with his dog. "You can put your gun away. I'm not going to hurt you and neither is Leroy."

Macy backed up a step but kept hold of her gun. "If you can't control your dog you should keep him on a leash."

"Your opinion has been duly noted." He smirked. "You lost or something?"

"I'm not lost."

"I think you are."

Macy caught something sharp in his voice and stopped short before speaking her mind again. The last thing she wanted was an altercation. The forest had fallen silent. Conversation no longer drifted through the trees. She was alone. She decided it was in her best interest to soften her tone.

"I'm heading for the footbridge," she said, gesturing to a low opening cutting through a tangle of brambles. "It's just through there."

His voice was low and lazy. "You don't seem too sure about that."

Macy looked beyond him toward the track that had brought her to this place. He was blocking her way. It made her uneasy. He seemed to sense this. He backed off a bit and moved to the right. Leroy followed him and stood obediently at his side. The man threw her a crooked smile.

"You're a little late for the party," he said. "The rest of Walleye's finest left twenty minutes ago."

Macy holstered her weapon. "They were looking for Joel Edwards. Do you know him?"

"Joel cleared out a few days ago. Near as I can tell he gave away everything he owned. I guess he doesn't think he'll need much once he gets to wherever he's going. A bad sign if you ask me."

"Why do you say that?"

"Joel didn't own much to start with and now he owns nothing. Makes me think he might be checking out."

"As in suicide?"

The man shrugged. "It's a possibility."

"How well did you know him?"

"Well enough to know he's not right in the head. He's been wandering around the last couple of weeks muttering to himself."

"Did he say anything that made sense?"

"He went on and on about his sister's death. Blamed the system."

"Any names mentioned?"

"Not that I heard. I lost interest when he started spouting his conspiracy theories."

"Are you camping out here?" asked Macy.

"You can call it camping if it makes you feel better."

"I'm sorry. That was insensitive." Macy pointed to his bandaged hand. "That looks serious. Have you had someone take a look at it?"

He nodded. "Some church people drop in on us once a week. There's usually a doctor. He'll take a look."

"Have you ever come across someone named Kyle Miller? Young-looking guy in his early thirties. Blond hair."

"Yeah, everyone knows Kyle. When he found out I served in Iraq he made a point of looking after me. He likes to hear all my war stories. He makes sure I get my VA benefits, so I can't complain. He's trying to get me into housing."

"I hear there's a shortage around here."

"Depends on your price range. A new subdivision is going in less than a half mile away, but it's nothing I can afford." He scratched his dog's ears. "Seriously though, you really should watch yourself. There are addicts living rough out here. If they thought you had anything of value your gun wouldn't stop them from trying to take it."

Macy knew he was right. She'd already decided she'd walk back to her car instead of crossing the river. He made a move and she almost reached for her gun again.

"Look," he said, flashing her a smile. "I just want to get back to my campsite before someone takes my stuff."

Macy backed away so he and his dog could pass. Leroy growled at her one last time before running ahead.

"You're not going to shoot me in the back, are you?" he said.

"I'm not going to shoot anybody." Macy flicked through the photos on her phone until she found one of Carla. "Hey, quick question. Do you remember seeing this woman out here talking to Kyle Miller?"

He took his time. "I've never seen her."

"She's Kyle's aunt. You may have seen them speaking to each other. She would have been with a guy. They were both on dirt bikes."

"Seeing a beautiful woman like that wouldn't be something I'd soon forget."

"Are you absolutely sure you haven't seen her? It would have been a few weeks ago."

"I'm positive."

Macy tucked her phone back in her pocket.

"Are you coming this way?" he asked. "If you stick with me no one in the camp will hassle you."

Macy shook her head. "I think it's better to head back the way I came."

The man had to duck down low to get through the opening.

"You take care," he said. "I'll get in touch if I see Joel."

"You didn't tell me your name," she said. "I might need to speak to you again."

"Mike Samson," he said. "I'm always here."

Macy watched him amble away. It wasn't just his face that was crooked. His whole body tipped to the right. Keeping a sharp eye on the surrounding forest, she hurried along the trail she'd taken earlier. Ten minutes later her phone lit up with several messages from Gina. She was worried that Macy had headed out to the river on her own. Macy called her back once she had Aiden's pickup truck in her sights.

"Gina," she said. "It's me."

"Where are you? You sound like you're out of breath."

"I've just got back to the car. I must have just missed you guys."

"Sorry about that. I heard you had a late-night trip to Kalispell. I thought you'd want to sleep in."

"It's okay," said Macy. "Heaven knows I needed the exercise. Did you manage to find out anything about Joel?"

"They were pretty tight-lipped out there, but the general consensus is that he took off a couple of days ago," Gina said.

"I was told he gave away all his belongings before leaving. Sounds like he's not planning on coming back."

"Who did you speak to?"

"A homeless vet named Mike Samson. He knows Kyle Miller from when his church group visits the camp. Stands to reason that Kyle Miller will have also come across Joel Edwards."

"Lou is looking into the church group. Hopefully someone knows where we can find Joel. Did you ask this guy about Carla Spencer?"

"He doesn't recall seeing her out here."

"It's possible he missed them."

"True," said Macy. "Where are you? I'm starving."

"Just about to head for the diner next to the hotel for some breakfast. Meet you there?"

"I'll be another twenty minutes."

"No worries. I've got plenty to do to keep me busy."

Aside from a couple of busboys clearing up tables, the diner was almost empty. Macy had moved to another booth to give Gina some privacy, but it was difficult not to eavesdrop on the phone conversation Gina was having with her husband. They were discussing their finances. Money was tight. They both had to continue working full time if they wanted to keep the house. Finding more money to pay someone to look after their two children was going to be difficult.

Macy scrolled through her e-mail messages. There was one from the coroner's office in Helena. They'd finished cross-checking the list of patients who'd died of accidental overdose. She took a sip of coffee as she waited for the attached file to download onto her computer. Seconds later she was reading.

In the past three years eighteen of the patients on the list had died after taking painkillers prescribed by Dr. Whitaker. It was the second highest overdose fatality rate for any practicing physician in the state of Montana. The state coroner had liaised with the Montana State Medical Board. Despite having three malpractice cases pending against him, his record was clean and he was licensed to continue practicing medicine and prescribing medication. In the past three years he'd settled out of court with patients' families on six separate occasions, paying out an estimated $2.4 million. All the families had dropped their wrongful death suits against his practice. According to records obtained from pharmacies, he and two other doctors were responsible for nearly fifty percent of all opiate-based painkiller prescriptions in the state of Montana over the last ten years.

Macy went back over the accounts of patient fatalities listed in the first anonymous e-mail, now that she knew which cases involved Dr. Whitaker's practice. In some instances Whitaker was the only prescribing doctor and in others he was one of many. Four of his patients who died had histories of mental health problems and drug addiction.

Macy threw her pen on the table. Not one of the accidental overdose deaths had been ruled suspicious, and Whitaker was out of the country the night Philip Long died. Unless someone talked, it was going to be difficult to figure out how Whitaker might be tied to Philip Long's death.

Her phone rang at the same time a patrol car flew past the diner's windows with its sirens on. Lou Turner sounded like he was running for his life.

"Macy," shouted Lou. "We just got a call. Joel Edwards was just spotted entering a doctor's office. Shots have been fired."

"Dr. Whitakers clinic?"

"Yes, that's the one. It's a block east of that big church on Main. Forty-five Elm."

"We're right around the corner."

"Officers are in route. I'll be there in five."

Macy gathered up her papers, threw her laptop into her bag, and rushed over to Gina's table. Outside another patrol car screamed down Main Street.

Macy put a hand on Gina's shoulder. "Time to get back to work. Joel Edwards was just spotted entering a doctor's office around the corner. Shots were fired."

By the time Macy and Gina drew near the glass-fronted building there were already three police cars parked out front and Lou was heading inside. A dozen people loitered in an empty parking lot across the street. A few were on their phones. Others wandered about looking shell-shocked. A woman knelt next to a man who was seated on the curb. His hands covered his face. There was blood on his pant leg. Another woman clutched a young dark-haired boy tight to her chest. Macy held her breath. For a split second she thought it was Luke. An ambulance pulled up outside the clinic. The pitch of the sirens was deafening. An officer ran outside to meet the paramedics.

"Dr. Whitaker is bleeding heavily," he said. "Not sure about the other guy . . . He's taken a shot to the head. He's unresponsive."

Macy stood amid a confused trail of bloody footprints that fanned out in all directions on the pavement. Inside two paramedics kneeled on the floor next to a man wearing a pair of dark slacks and sensible shoes. A little to the left, another man was sprawled out on the floor with his legs bent at awkward angles. No one was working on him. Two more paramedics rushed past Macy. They were directed to a woman sitting on a chair next to the receptionist desk. She was talking to the responding officers with her hand clutched to her chest.

Lou Turner came over and stood next to Macy

"It's definitely Joel Edwards. It looks like he shot Whitaker before turning the gun on himself," said Lou. "He was already dead when the first patrol units arrived. The receptionist is being treated for a suspected heart attack."

"How is Dr. Whitaker?" asked Macy.

"Looks like he got clipped in the collarbone. He's bleeding heavily but still conscious." His eyes flicked to the security cameras. "I'll get the security video as soon as possible."

Macy turned to Lou. "I never got the name of the doctor Joel Edwards attempted to rob. Was it Whitaker?"

Lou closed his eyes. "It was. I didn't think he'd be stupid enough to try robbing him twice."

Macy shrugged. "He's an addict. His behavior isn't out of character."

Lou took a deep breath. "It's been nearly three years. Why did Joel come back now?"

"That's a question that's begging to be answered," said Macy. "What gun did he use?"

"A thirty-eight," said Lou. "It wasn't yours."

"Good to know," said Macy. She called Gina over and they headed outside. She kept her voice low. "The state coroner got in touch this morning. Dr. Whitaker prescribed painkillers to eighteen of the patients who were listed in that first anonymous e-mail. This is all still speculation, but if Philip Long was about to publicly accuse Dr. Whitaker of gross negligence, Whitaker would have good reason for wanting to keep him quiet."

"But that makes no sense," said Gina. "If Edwards is our third kidnapper, why would he try to kill the guy who might have given him the job?"

"They may have had a falling out," said Lou. "Things didn't go as planned."

"This may also be a tragic coincidence," said Macy. "Carla was very supportive of Joel Edwards in rehab. Her death may have caused him to relapse."

They watched the paramedics for a few seconds. It looked as though they were getting ready to make a move. Dr. Whitaker was propped up on the gurney. His eyes were open, but he was very pale. He gave them the thumbs up and a weak smile.

"Whitaker was on a cruise ship off the coast of Baja when Long was abducted and murdered," said Gina.

"He still could have arranged Philip Long's kidnapping as a way of scaring him off the story," said Lou. "That man has a lot of money."

"How much money are we talking?" asked Macy.

Lou pointed to the glass, steel, and brick building that dominated Main Street. "Enough to pay for that church."

Macy stared at the building. "Is that the church where Philip Long's prayer service took place?"

Lou nodded.

"Philip Long called it *the church that pain built*," said Macy.

"Who told you that?" asked Gina.

"It's something Emma said in passing," said Macy. "She assumed it was a reference to her father's feelings about organized religion, but there may be more to it. Dr. Whitaker specializes in pain management."

"Do you think he's been selling painkiller prescriptions to addicts?" asked Gina.

"He wouldn't have been the first doctor to do it," said Macy.

An ambulance helicopter circled overhead. Its wide body blocked out the sun.

"They're taking Dr. Whitaker to Collier County Hospital," said Lou. "He's going straight into surgery, so it will be a while before we can question him."

Macy moved out of the way to make room for Dr. Whitaker's gurney. For a few seconds he was situated between her and Lou. He reached out his hand to Lou.

The doctor's voice was weak. "Lou," he said. "It was Joel Edwards again. He should have been kept in jail where he belonged. I warned everyone he was still dangerous."

"Did he say anything to you?" asked Macy.

Whitaker grimaced as the paramedics started wheeling him away.

"It was just a bunch of nonsense," he said. "I wouldn't be surprised if the man was high on drugs again . . ."

The rest of Whitaker's words were drowned out by the sound of sirens.

"I'll make sure Ryan gets started on Joel Edwards's car immediately," said Macy. "We need something concrete tying Joel to Philip Long's kidnapping. Gina, I want you to head back to the homeless camp with a couple patrol officers. I want to know if Joel Edwards has been talking to any outsiders over the last couple of months, Philip Long in particular. Try to find a guy named Mike Samson. He seemed to have his shit together."

"If we assume Carla and Lloyd Spencer kidnapped Philip Long on Whitaker's behalf, there must be something that ties them to the doctor. They wouldn't have known each other socially," said Lou.

"I'll look at Lloyd Spencer's medical files. He may have been Dr. Whitaker's patient at some point," said Macy.

Lou lowered his voice. "We'll have to tread carefully. Peter Whitaker is a highly respected member of the community. Until proven otherwise, we have to give him the benefit of the doubt."

# 14

Emma found a note from her mother on the kitchen counter. Francine wouldn't be home until after lunch. The newspaper was lying open on the table. Carla and Lloyd Spencer's involvement in her father's kidnapping was the lead story. Emma skimmed the article, wincing when saw that Kyle Miller's name was mentioned several times. He'd refused to return the reporter's calls, but that didn't stop them from publishing his picture and getting a statement from his employers. They'd interviewed his mother as well. She'd blamed Lloyd Spencer for her sister's downfall, rehashing every miserable moment of their marriage, including the physical abuse. There'd been an incident when Kyle was ten. He'd been left with Carla and Lloyd for the weekend. Lloyd had come home drunk and found Kyle in the kitchen drinking milk straight from the carton. Lloyd twisted Kyle's arm right out of its socket before knocking him unconscious.

*I warned my sister Lloyd would come to no good, but she stuck with him anyway. I never understood what she saw in that man.*

The article ended with a brief statement from Macy Greeley. She'd been quick to point out that the investigation was far from over. The authorities were certain there was a third party involved in Philip Long's kidnapping and murder. She'd appealed to the public. While Carla and

Lloyd's son, Sean Spencer, was not considered a suspect, he was wanted for questioning. Anyone who knew his whereabouts was asked to contact the authorities immediately. They were also interested in tracking down an individual named Joel Edwards who'd attended rehab with Carla Spencer and had failed to check in with his parole officer two weeks running.

Emma set the paper aside. Now that Kyle's family's involvement had made the news, Kyle would be viewed with suspicion everywhere he went. Emma pictured Kyle standing over the man in the parking lot with blood dripping from his nose. In the near darkness Emma hadn't seen everything clearly, but it was obvious that Kyle had nearly beaten the man senseless. If Kyle was recognized from the photo in the newspaper, the man might file a complaint against Kyle for using excessive force. Emma looked up the phone number for the bar she'd gone to the previous evening. It rang several times before she was redirected to the manager's voice mail. She hesitated before speaking. It wasn't like her to get involved in other people's business.

"Hello," she said, feeling increasingly awkward. "My name is Emma Long and I'm calling about the incident that occurred in the parking lot outside your restaurant yesterday evening. I'm afraid one of your guests had too much to drink and followed me outside. He tried to stop me getting in my car. I just want to say how grateful I am that you had a security guard patrolling the area. I also wanted to make it absolutely clear that the security guard acted responsibly. If he needs someone to vouch for him I'm quite happy to make a formal statement."

Emma left her cell phone number and hung up. She was already having regrets about getting involved. Nathan had said that Kyle had just been doing his job. He'd accuse Emma of overthinking things like she'd always done. Emma checked her phone. She hadn't had any new text messages from Nathan, but it was still early. They'd once cared for each other deeply. The affection may have been gone, but the connection was still there. It made her sad to think that after all these years they'd only managed to retain the ability to do each other harm.

Emma put her father's coat on over her pajamas and wandered out into the backyard with a bag of peanuts for the crows and a cup of coffee for herself. The crows cawed and circled, some so bold they practically pecked at her bare feet. She dumped the remainder of the peanuts on the ground as she made her way to the back fence where she sipped her coffee and stared at the roofline of Caleb Winfrey's home. She still had the keys her mother gave her. Nothing was stopping her from going over to take a look. She'd been told that Caleb had burned everything Lucy owned, but Emma was hopeful there might still be something in the house that would help make sense of the night Lucy died. She just wasn't ready to go over and find out what it was yet. Emma tossed the dregs of her coffee on the ground and headed back inside her mother's home. She needed to clear her head. She hung up her father's coat and went upstairs to change into her running gear.

Emma didn't hit her stride until she was two miles south of Walleye Junction. The wide gravel road followed the slow curve of the Flathead River. The banks were dotted with boulders, cottonwoods, and clumps of crimson and yellow wildflowers. A row of fishermen, spaced at varying intervals, wore hip waders and stood in cold water casting their lines. Their cars were parked along the hard shoulder near a popular trailhead. She jogged in place as she looked over the notices posted on the sign. She and her parents had often hiked the trails together. They'd have picnics up above the tree line. As she set off running again a springer spaniel, soaked through with river water, raced up to greet her. In its excitement it nearly tripped her up. Its owner whistled and the dog turned tail and ran back down to the riverbank.

A half mile on Emma stopped to admire the view. From her raised position she could just see the outline of her hometown. Directly across the river from where she stood a new subdivision had sprung up in the middle of a hay field. Rows of colorful flags flew over model homes and empty streets. Tall fences flanked small patches of lawn, and slabs of slick concrete foundations mirrored the midday sun. Walleye Junction's only high school was closer to town. The large gymnasium's brilliant blue roof and the surrounding playing fields were visible, but the classroom blocks, library, and administration buildings were hidden behind a dense wall of pine trees. The nursery, elementary, and middle schools were on adjacent pieces of land and further up the hill a long tree-lined drive led to the municipal cemetery she'd visited the night before. In a matter of miles you could be safely transported from cradle to grave. Emma checked the time. If she was going to get there and back she needed to be on her way. She set out again, once more relaxing into her stride.

A car came along the road and fell in behind her. She took a quick glance over her shoulder. Blinding sunshine bounced off the windshield and front hood. She couldn't see the car or the driver properly. She waved the car around, but it stayed on her tail. The track was wide and well paved, but the drop down to the river was sheer. She couldn't move any closer to the side, but there was still plenty of space for a vehicle to pass. She increased her pace up an incline. The rumble of the vehicle's engine and the pounding of her heart were all she could hear. She was growing anxious. All sorts of possibilities circled in her head. None of them were good.

Emma spotted an opening in the trees and veered to the right. The vehicle sped by as she headed down the steep slope toward the river. The terrain was uneven and she had to hold on to low tree branches for support. Insects swarmed around her. There was a sharp bite as a horsefly stung her inner thigh. By the time she reached the river's edge she was hot, sticky, and in tears. She checked the road. The car was gone. Thinking there'd be safety in numbers, she headed upstream toward the men she'd seen fishing. She picked her way across boulders and traversed fallen trees. She found a narrow animal track and scrambled along it until it opened up onto the rocky shore she'd been looking for. The dog that had chased her was lazing in a patch of sunshine. As she stepped into the light, its ears pricked up. A man with his back to her was kneeling down as he dug something out of a tackle box. He turned as the dog ran over to greet Emma. He smiled and waved. Emma blinked into the sun's glare. She didn't recognize him. He pulled off his hat and smiled again.

"Kyle?" she said.

He rose to his full height. "Emma, what are you doing down here?"

She glanced up at the road. Other than a haze of dust there was no sign of the vehicle that had followed her. The dog was at their feet, circling like a satellite.

"I was running," she said.

Kyle touched her arm. "You're shaking. Are you okay?"

Emma started crying again. She pointed to the road.

"Someone was following me in a car."

Kyle watched the empty road for a few seconds.

"Are you sure?"

"As sure as I can be."

Kyle looked as if he was about to say something but stopped.

"Kyle?" asked Emma. "Did you see something?"

He scratched his head. "Emma, I saw Nathan go by a few minutes ago. Could it have been him?"

She shook her head. "The sun was in my eyes. I can't say. Did you see anyone aside from Nathan?"

"No, I'm sorry. Did you guys have a falling out last night?"

"Yes, but that doesn't explain why he might have followed me."

"Even by his standards it would be pretty low to scare you like that." He closed the tackle box. "I'll give you a ride home."

"You don't have to."

"I want to."

They walked to the road together. He'd removed his hip waders and slung them over his shoulder. His pickup truck was parked in the shade near the trailhead. He threw his gear in the back.

"Drink this," he ordered, handing her a bottle of juice he'd fished out of a cooler. "You look faint."

Emma thanked him. He opened the door for her and she climbed inside. It smelled brand new.

"Nice car."

He blushed. "I just bought it."

"Security must pay well."

"It's been a good year so far, so I got a nice performance bonus."

"What did you mean when you said that Nathan's standards were pretty low?"

"It was nothing."

"Tell me."

"There are things you don't know about Nathan. Stuff that came out after you left town."

"What kind of things?"

"It was just rumors, but given what happened to Lucy maybe there was something to them. People were saying he was dealing drugs . . . that maybe he and Lucy were working together."

"That's nonsense. I would have known."

"Did you know what Lucy was getting up to?"

Emma hesitated. "I knew she was doing drugs. I didn't know she was dealing."

"The amount of drugs available around here didn't drop after Lucy died. If anything there were even more going around."

"I'll talk to Nathan," said Emma. "I need to ask if he was following me this morning anyway."

"I don't want any trouble," said Kyle. "Don't tell him I'm the one you spoke to."

"Don't worry," she said. "I'll keep your name out of it."

Emma waited until they were on their way before mentioning the newspaper article.

He winced. "I'd been warned so I knew it was coming."

"If it's any consolation, your mother was pretty convincing. Lloyd Spencer comes off looking like a bully."

"I had my doubts about letting her talk to the reporter, but I think she managed it well. It should help ease people's minds about the rest of the family."

"Did you take today off work?"

"I thought I might hide by the river with my fishing pole until it blows over."

"You might be by the river for a while."

"Then I'll catch lots of fish."

"It's nice that you still have a sense of humor."

"The company helps," said Kyle. "How are you doing otherwise? Last night was pretty intense."

"It was the last thing I needed. It's probably why I freaked out about that car. There's only so much more I can take. Anyway, I'm glad I ran into you. I wanted to thank you again for looking after me yesterday. I was worried that you'd gotten into trouble. You roughed up that guy pretty badly."

"It wasn't a problem. I went in and explained what happened. He admitted what he'd done and they kicked him out." Kyle shrugged. "No big deal."

Emma was cold. Goose bumps had formed along her arms.

Kyle kept his eyes on the road. "What did you and Nathan get up to after you left?"

"We talked. It wasn't pleasant."

"So, you're not getting back together?"

"I find it hard to believe he ever thought it was a possibility."

Kyle pulled up in front of her mother's home. Emma's red hatchback was the only car in the driveway. She checked the time. It would be a few hours before her mother returned.

"Come in for a coffee," she said. "You've gone out of your way. It's the least I can do."

"I don't think your mother would be too happy to find me sitting in her kitchen."

"She won't be back for a few hours." Emma laid her hand on his arm. "You've done nothing wrong. You shouldn't have to hide."

He switched off the engine and removed his sunglasses. His eyes were tinged black and blue and his nose was slightly swollen.

"Oh," said Emma, touching him lightly on the cheek. "That looks bad."

"It's a little sore, that's all."

He took hold of her hand, and they sat quietly for a few seconds.

"Are you sure your mother won't be back for a couple of hours?"

"I'm sure," she said, slipping from his grasp. She looked back at him before opening the door. "Come in for a coffee. I don't feel like being alone."

# 15

Macy snatched a bag of potato chips off Gina's desk and paced the office, trailing crumbs in her wake. It was coming up on one o'clock and the police station was nearly empty. Lou was still at Dr. Whitaker's clinic and Gina had gone with some officers down to the homeless camp to interview anyone who may have come across Joel Edwards. On her third lap around the office Macy stopped at her desk. She needed to speak to Francine Long again. There was a high volume of painkillers coming out of Dr. Whitaker's practice so there was a possibility that he'd been acting more like a dealer than a doctor. Francine had worked for him for thirty-four years. She couldn't have been completely oblivious to what was going on. It was also possible that she confided in her husband.

Kyle and Emma stepped out onto the porch at the same time Macy was parking the car in front of Francine Long's house. Emma was dressed casually in jeans and a T-shirt, and Kyle was wearing fishing gear. Macy checked the car's mirrors. The street appeared to be empty. She grabbed her bag and opened the door. Given his aunt and uncle's involvement in her father's murder, Kyle Miller was the last person Macy expected to see with Emma Long.

Neither Kyle nor Emma waved as Macy walked up the driveway. Emma leaned in and said something to Kyle. Macy thought she may have said *be brave*. Kyle smiled slightly.

"Detective Greeley," said Emma, holding out her hand. "You've met Kyle Miller."

"I have," said Macy, noticing that Emma's hair was wet. "Emma, I need to speak to your mother again. Do you know when she'll be home?"

"I'm expecting her anytime now." Emma tilted her head to the front door. "We just heard the news about what happened at Dr. Whitaker's Clinic. Do you think he's going to be okay?"

"He's in the ICU. The prognosis is very good."

Emma looked relieved. "They're saying it was the same man who'd tried to rob him for drugs on a previous occasion. You'd think they'd have more security."

Macy noticed Kyle seemed to be a little uncomfortable. He kept glancing up the road toward town, probably fearful that he'd see Francine's car.

"The world would be a very sad place if doctor's offices started needed security guards," said Macy. "Kyle, I know you get asked this a half dozen times a day by someone at the Walleye PD, but have you heard anything at all from your cousin Sean? We really need him to come forward. The longer he stays away the more guilty he looks."

"It's really upsetting for me too," said Kyle. "I don't understand what's got into Sean. I've sent him a dozen texts begging him to come home, but so far I've heard nothing."

They all looked up as a car passed by the house.

"I best be going," said Kyle. He turned to Emma. "Thanks for the coffee."

"I'm the one who should be thanking you for the ride home," Emma said.

"Anytime," he said, shaking Macy's hand once more before moving away from the front porch.

The sunlight caught his face. Macy noticed bruising around his nose and eyes.

"Looks like you've got quite a shiner there," said Macy.

Kyle cracked a smile as he headed toward a new pickup truck that was parked along the road.

"Entirely my fault," he said. "I accidently ran into a drunk guy's elbow."

Emma and Macy sat at the kitchen table drinking coffee while they waited for Francine's return. The back door was open and a fresh breeze blew through the house. A wet bath towel hung on the back of one of the kitchen chairs. The remnants of what looked like breakfast for two were stacked next to the sink. Kyle had not only given Emma a ride home, it appeared that he'd stayed in the house while she showered and then sat down for breakfast with her. Macy wanted to ask why Kyle had been in the house but knew when to keep her mouth shut. Kyle wasn't a suspect. Emma's private life was her own business.

"I know what you're thinking," said Emma.

Emma had a cup of coffee in one hand and a smartphone in the other. Macy was pretty sure this was her standard pose. Macy picked up her own cup and took a sip.

"I'm in no position to judge other people's choices," said Macy.

Emma cracked a smile. "You think we're seeing each other."

"It crossed my mind."

"We're not. We're just friends."

"I'm just telling you how I saw it. How other people will see it."

"Two people can talk," said Emma. "It doesn't have to mean anything."

Macy wasn't sure where this conversation was going. For some reason Emma felt compelled to explain the situation to Macy, when she really should have been talking to Kyle. There was something about Kyle's demeanor that made Macy think that he might be interested in being more than friends with Emma. He'd tried to hide it, but he'd been hanging on her every word and gesture.

"Like I said," said Macy. "I'm in no position to judge, but I saw how Kyle was looking at you. You may only see him as a friend, but I'd guess his feelings are stronger."

The front door opened and Francine bustled into the kitchen. She went straight to her daughter, holding her tight in a long hug.

"It's over sweetheart," said Francine. "The man who died at Peter's office was wanted in connection to the investigation."

Emma glanced over at Macy. "Is this true?"

Macy frowned. She'd hoped Joel Edwards's name would stay out of the public domain for a little longer, but as Francine was once employed at the doctor's office, it wasn't surprising that she'd been told the news already. Macy chose her words carefully.

"Joel Edwards was wanted for questioning because he was a convicted felon who'd become friendly with Carla Spencer in drug rehab. He'd not checked in with his parole officer in the two weeks since your father was kidnapped. As of yet there's no physical evidence to link him to your father's murder."

Francine put her purse on the table and took off her jacket. Her cheeks were flushed. It almost looked as if she'd been running.

"Everyone was saying that he was the third kidnapper," said Francine.

"I'd like this to be over too," said Macy. "But we have to make sure we get this right."

Macy apologized to Francine for coming to see her without making an appointment.

"There have been a few developments," said Macy. "I thought it best that we speak again."

"I need to get to the hospital to see Peter," said Francine.

"Peter Whitaker is in the ICU. I'm not even allowed to see him. It's come to our attention that your husband may have been working on a feature about prescription painkiller abuse. We've received two anonymous e-mails on the subject. The source implies that this story is the reason your husband was kidnapped and murdered."

Francine unwound a scarf from around her neck and sat down in the empty chair.

Macy continued. "According to Emma, it was a subject that interested your husband greatly."

Francine nodded. The color in her cheeks was quickly fading.

"Over the past three years, eighteen of Dr. Whitakers patients have died from taking drugs he prescribed to them. It is the second highest fatality rate in the state of Montana. He's settled out of court with patients' families for $2.4 million."

"I didn't know," said Francine.

Emma finally spoke up. "But this seems so straightforward to me. It's clear that Joel Edwards was involved. He probably wanted money for drugs. The fact that my father's story might have been about Whitaker is irrelevant."

"At this point I'm still considering all options," said Macy. "From a legal standpoint, Dr. Whitaker has done nothing wrong. None of the deaths of the patients under his care were ruled suspicious. At the moment I'm trying to establish whether this morning's events at his clinic are linked to the kidnapping or just a tragic coincidence. According to their drug rehabilitation counselor, Joel Edwards was highly dependent on Carla Spencer's support in rehab. It may be that her death pushed him over the edge."

Francine looped her scarf back and forth around her hands as Macy spoke.

"Mom," said Emma. "Is there something you're not telling us?"

Francine spoke softly. "Sometimes I got a little frightened working at that clinic. Some seedy characters came through that office. They were always trying their luck. I think it's called 'shopping.' They'd go to multiple offices looking for a doctor who was willing to prescribe them painkillers even when they didn't need them. They could be very intimidating. Peter had a lot of cash at the office so he could never be too careful."

"Why was there so much cash?"

"A lot of patients paid in cash." Francine's smile was limp. "Sometimes I felt more like a bank teller than a receptionist."

"What does Whitaker do about the patients who are *shopping* for drugs?"

"He always sees them. He once told me that it's impossible to tell whether someone's pain is real or imagined until they've been examined thoroughly."

"And does he give them what they came for?"

"If Peter felt their pain was genuine he wouldn't deny them relief."

The doorbell rang.

"That will be my friend Sarah," said Francine, rising from her chair. "If you'll excuse me, I have to go. She's giving me a ride to Collier. I may not be able to visit Peter, but I feel I should be there for him." She wound her scarf back round her neck and grabbed her jacket. "Emma, I'll give you a call later and let you know when I'll be home."

Macy picked up her phone and called Lou Turner as soon as she was in her car.

"Are you still at the Whitaker's office?" asked Macy.

"Just wrapping things up here."

"I just spoke to Francine Long. According to her there were a lot of seedy characters moving through Dr. Whitaker's office. She said that they were 'shopping' doctors to see who'd prescribe them painkillers."

"Might be why Whitaker normally has a security guard on duty."

"Where the hell was he this morning?"

"He had a flat tire and called in to say he'd be late," said Lou. "Showed up an hour ago with a spare on his car, so I don't have reason to doubt his story."

"We should still check. What company does he work for?"

"Flathead Valley Security."

"Kyle Miller works for the same company."

"Kyle Miller isn't a suspect. He's got a solid alibi."

Macy started up the engine and pulled away from the curb.

"I'm just leaving Francine Long's house," said Macy. "You should know that Kyle was on his way out the door when I arrived. He and Emma appear to be close."

"I'm surprised Francine let him in her front door."

"Francine didn't get home until after he was gone."

"Did he do or say anything suspicious?"

"Maybe. When Emma asked about what happened at Whitaker's office, the question of security came up. Emma was surprised that there was none. Kyle was standing right there and said nothing. He must know that his company handles Whitaker's security."

"Might be something else," said Lou. "Kyle would have realized then and there that someone at Flathead Valley Security screwed up big time, and he didn't want to admit his company's culpability."

"I hear you, but he has ties with the kidnappers and Dr. Whitaker, and he may know Joel Edwards through his church group visits to the homeless camp. We should look into it further. Did the security guard have any reason to believe that his car was intentionally vandalized? He may have heard something. Someone may have been seen in the neighborhood."

"For all we know it was Joel Edwards that flattened the tire," said Lou. "Delaying the guard's arrival at Whitaker's clinic would have cleared the way for him."

"Anything from Gina and the patrol officers we sent to the homeless camp?"

"Nothing so far, but I got word they're on their way back into town."

"Okay," said Macy. "Let's meet up at the station in a half hour and compare notes. I still need to read the witness statements from the clinic."

"I'm going to be a little late coming in," said Lou. "I think I'm going to pay the security guard a visit. Give me a call if Gina has any news. Last I heard Ryan was waist deep in Joel's car. He may have something to report as well."

Macy checked the messages on her phone as she wove between the desks inside Walleye Junction's police department. Aiden had been trying to get in touch since the previous day, but she hadn't had time to return his calls. Her phone rang as she was writing him a message.

"Just a second, Mom," said Macy.

Macy ducked into the incident room. She slumped down into a chair and closed her eyes for a second.

"Macy," asked Ellen. "Are you there still?"

"Barely. I closed my eyes for a second and almost drifted off."

"I've just returned home from Luke's doctor's appointment."

Macy's eyes popped open.

"Is he okay?"

"Yes, it was a routine visit. Flu vaccine."

"I forgot that was scheduled for this week. How'd he take it?"

"Like a trooper," said Ellen. "All was forgotten by the time we arrived at the ice cream parlor."

"That's my boy," said Macy.

"Any chance things are winding down with the investigation? It would be nice to have you home."

"We're running out of suspects, so it's just a matter of time now."

Ellen laughed. "Do you always arrest the last one standing?"

"Something like that." Macy looked up. Ryan was out in the hallway making faces at her through the glass partition.

Macy was dead tired but smiled anyway. "Mom, I gotta go," she said. "I'll call you later. Give Luke a hug from me. And don't worry. I'll be home soon."

"I love you sweetheart."

"Love you too."

Ryan swept into the room and grabbed the chair next to Macy. He took a sip of coffee from a large takeaway cup. The barista had written IAN in capital letters across the side.

"Someone out there loves Macy," said Ryan, cozying up to her. "Was that Aiden on the phone or have you already moved on?"

"Ryan, don't be awful. It was my mom."

Ryan looked disappointed. "That's no good. I can't make fun of Ellen. She won't invite me to your place for Thanksgiving anymore."

"We've never had you over for Thanksgiving."

"An oversight that I'm hoping will be corrected this coming November."

"Duly noted. So what news from the impound lot? Did you get a chance to have a look at Joel Edwards's car?"

Ryan retrieved a file from his bag and smacked it down on the table in front of Macy.

"If we don't start dealing with a better class of criminal I swear I'm quitting," he said. "The man's car was a hellhole. He lived like a pig."

"He was homeless," said Macy. "I'm sure he did the best he could." She flipped through the file before setting it aside. "I don't have time to read the whole thing. Did you find anything I can use?"

Ryan set a plastic evidence bag out in front of her. It contained Philip Long's business card, which had been checked for fingerprints.

"This doesn't prove they actually met, but I found Philip Long's business card in Joel's car. Both their prints are on it."

Macy noticed Gina was standing in the open door and held up the card for her to see.

"What do you think?" said Macy. "Did Philip and Joel actually meet?"

Gina nodded. "Your contact down at the homeless camp seems to think so."

Ryan cracked a smile. "Oh, Macy, you do move in interesting circles."

Macy ignored him. "You spoke to Mike Samson?"

Gina came in and leaned against the wall. "He says he introduced Philip Long to Joel Edwards."

"Well, that trumps my business card discovery," said Ryan, pushing his chair away from the table. "I have a ton of paperwork to get through, so if you don't mind I'm going to find a quiet cafe."

"Call me if anything comes up," said Macy.

"I'd rather invite you out for a drink," he said as he headed out the door. "If anyone is interested, I'll be at the hotel bar at eight."

"You have to admire Ryan's energy," said Macy.

"A fluffy pink bunny comes to mind every time I see him." Gina took the seat Ryan had vacated. "Philip Long was seen at the homeless camp about a month ago looking for Edwards. They talked for about an hour, but when Mike asked Edwards about it, all Edwards would say was that it was about his sister."

"The same sister who died of an overdose?"

"I assume so. Are you thinking she might be on the list we were sent?"

"I don't remember seeing anyone named Edwards, but she may have been listed under a married name."

Gina sifted through the files laid out on the table until she found the information they needed on Joel Edwards. "Does Wendy Martin ring a bell?"

Macy grabbed the e-mail she had been reading earlier.

"It certainly does," said Macy. She flipped through the pages of the first anonymous e-mail they received. "I found her."

Joel Edwards's sister Wendy had only been thirty-five years old when she passed away.

*Wendy Edwards Martin was severely injured in a car accident. Following lifesaving surgery and several follow-up operations that included skin grafts, fusing two of her vertebrae, and facial reconstruction, she was in constant pain. As a last resort Dr. Whitaker prescribed fentanyl patches. Wendy was grateful as it was the first time she was pain free since the accident. Three months later she went for a routine appointment in Dr. Whitaker's clinic. On her way home she filled prescriptions for Xanax and hydrocodone at her local pharmacy. Later that same day she was found dead on the living room sofa. According to the coroner's report there were high levels of Xanax, fentanyl, and hydrocodone in her system.*

"Do you think Joel Edwards went to the clinic to confront Dr. Whitaker about his sister's death?" asked Gina.

"I haven't seen the witness statements yet, so I have no idea what was said."

"I'll give Lou a quick call and see if he knows anything."

Macy scrolled through her unopened e-mails, stopping when she saw that she'd been sent a video link from the clinic's security cameras. She opened it and watched. The sound was too distorted to make out what was being said. She could see Joel and Dr. Whitaker at the top right corner of the screen. It looked as if they were arguing.

Gina put down the phone. "The receptionist was the only one in the waiting room with Edwards and Whitaker, and she's not been interviewed yet."

Macy rotated the laptop around so Gina could see the screen and pointed to the video that was playing. "There was definitely another witness in that room. See that woman seated near the doors? She was standing out front with the others when we arrived," said Macy, picturing the boy who at first glance had so resembled Luke. "She was holding a child."

Gina picked up the phone. "We can get her name from Whitaker's appointment book. We'll find her."

Twenty minutes later Gina and Macy were on their way to an address on the outskirts of Walleye Junction. They pulled into the driveway and parked behind a minivan. The driver's-side door was wide open and the keys were still in the ignition.

Macy rang the doorbell and waited. Through the window she could see a woman sitting in the living room. She rang again.

"Mrs. Butler," Macy yelled. "I'm detective Macy Greeley. I need to speak to you about what happened at Dr. Whitaker's office this morning. I know you were there."

The door opened slowly. The woman look dazed. She barely looked at Macy's badge before opening the door to let them in.

"I can't stop crying," she said.

"Where is your son?" asked Macy, searching the room for any signs of the young boy.

"I put him down for a nap."

"Is it okay if my colleague Gina checks on him?" asked Macy

"I suppose so," said Mrs. Butler. "His room is upstairs."

Gina headed upstairs and Macy followed Mrs. Butler into the kitchen.

"Mrs. Butler, did a police officer try to interview you this morning?"

The woman leaned against the counter. Her hair fell across her face as she dipped her head.

"I don't know," she said. "It's all a blur. I just wanted to get my son home safely." Her hands trembled. "I don't remember driving here."

"That's understandable," said Macy. "You're in shock."

Gina appeared at the bottom of the stairs carrying a little boy. The child reached out for his mother.

"Let's sit in the living room," said Macy.

Macy took Mrs. Butler by the elbow and guided her to the sofa. Gina placed the child on his mother's lap once she was settled.

"Before I ask you anything, I want to know how you're doing?" said Macy. "Are you or your son hurt?"

Mrs. Butler pressed a tissue to her eyes and shook her head. She was struggling to breathe. Macy put a hand on the woman's knee.

"It's okay. You and your son are safe now."

Hot tears ran down the woman's flushed cheeks. She couldn't get any words out. The little boy stared at Macy openmouthed and confused. He was too young to understand what was happening, but he sensed that something was wrong. He buried his face in the crook of his mother's arm.

"What's your son's name?" asked Macy

"William," said the woman.

"He looks like he's about the same age as my son."

"He just turned three."

"Luke is two and a half."

The woman brightened. "My older son is named Luke."

A long sob escaped from somewhere deep within the child. His mother held him even tighter.

"He's still scared," said Mrs. Butler.

Macy pulled a red lollipop out of her bag that she'd been saving for Luke and started to unwrap it. The boy's eyes followed her every move.

"Under the circumstances I'd say he could use this more than me." Macy glanced at the boy's mother. "I hope you don't mind. I should have asked first."

The boy grasped the lollipop tight and tucked it in his mouth.

"Seems like a little sugar is the least of our worries. What is the world coming to?"

"I know it's the last thing you want to think about, but I need you to tell me what happened this morning."

The woman brushed the hair off her son's forehead and kissed him there for a long time.

"I didn't notice when he came in. I was sitting in the waiting area reading a magazine while William played in the children's area near the receptionist's desk. The guy sat down next to me and started talking like he knew me. I remember being annoyed because the waiting room was empty. There were plenty of other places he could have sat."

"Did he say why he was there?"

"He said he was there to speak to Dr. Whitaker about his sister, Wendy, I think."

Macy pulled out Joel's photo.

"Is this the man you spoke to?"

The woman flinched. "That's him."

"I want you to tell me what you remember. Nothing more."

The woman adjusted her son's position on her lap.

"He seemed harmless enough, but he did go on a bit. He said he didn't have any family left in Walleye, that his niece had moved to Denver with her father." She paused. "I may have that wrong. It may have been Chicago."

"That's okay. You're doing great."

"The man's sister, Wendy, had died at some point. He made it very clear that it wasn't an accident. Last I remember he was rambling on about a government conspiracy." Her voice trailed off.

"What happened next?"

"Dr. Whitaker came in and the guy hurried over to meet him. I remember thinking that he was being incredibly rude. I'd spent all that time listening to him go on and on and then he just up and leaves without saying anything."

"Did he have a gun?"

The woman's eyes widened a fraction. "Oh my God, he must have had it with him all along. It was right there in his hand. Clear as day. He walked up to Dr. Whitaker and shoved it in his face."

"Did he say anything else?"

"I'm not sure I can recall everything correctly . . . I was so scared. William was practically crawling at their feet. I couldn't take my eyes off him." The woman pressed the tissue to her eyes. "The guy accused Dr. Whitaker of killing his sister."

"How did Whitaker respond?"

"He said something about her death being a tragic accident, that he'd done his best. The guy went crazy. He started yelling and waving the gun around. He said Dr. Whitaker's name was on the bottles of pills that killed his sister and that Philip Long had said that it had happened before."

"Are you sure he said Philip Long?" asked Macy.

"Yes, ma'am. That's when the shooting started." The woman grabbed hold of her son's T-shirt and started crying again. "Oh my God, my boy still has blood on him."

Macy, Gina, and Lou met in the incident room. It was nearly ten and they'd been going nonstop since dawn. Macy was so tired she could barely think straight.

"It's official," said Macy. "I am now thoroughly confused."

"The tech guys just gave me a call," said Gina. "Sean Spencer and his girlfriend Kristina are definitely back in the Flathead Valley."

"How can they be sure?" asked Lou.

"A photo came up on her Twitter feed from a bar in Collier. Manager confirms they were there last night."

"We need to speak to Sean Spencer as soon as possible," said Macy. "I'm convinced his mother passed Long's files to him."

"We'll keep an eye on Kristina's social media accounts," said Gina. "There's a buzz building about another rave. If she throws one we'll find them."

"I've had word from Collier County Hospital. Dr. Whitaker is awake," said Lou. "We can drive up in the morning to interview him. His statement contradicts what you learned from the witness, Mrs. Butler."

"He's lying and I want to know why," said Macy. "What about the receptionist?"

"She claims not to remember anything," said Lou.

"That's convenient for Whitaker," said Gina. "First thing in the morning I'm going to head down to Missoula to take another look at Kyle Miller's alibi. I'm sure the guys were thorough the first time but it wouldn't hurt to interview Kyle's friends again."

"I appreciate that, Gina," said Macy. "I know Kyle has checked out up to this point, but I still think it's worth having another look. Lou, what did the security guard say when you interviewed him again?"

"He thinks it's possible there was someone outside his house last night. Neighbor's dog was going crazy at around one. The same neighbor confirms seeing the security guard changing his tire this morning."

Macy got out of her chair and walked over to a wall where they'd hung up photos of everyone attached to the investigation. She pointed at Joel Edwards's photo.

"There is not a shred of physical evidence that puts Joel Edwards at any of the crime scenes other than the clinic. He was a homeless drug addict who lived out of his car, a car that Ryan referred to as a hellhole. This isn't a man who is highly organized, so I have difficulty believing he wouldn't have left physical evidence in the house where Long was held captive. We know he's had at least one meeting with Philip Long and we know they spoke about Joel's sister, Wendy Martin, who died while under Whitaker's care. A witness has stated that Joel was in the clinic because he blamed Whitaker for her death. Joel knew Carla from rehab, but we have no idea whether their relationship went beyond an occasional coffee. In my opinion it wasn't in Joel's interest to silence Philip Long."

"Maybe he spoke to Carla about his sister," said Gina. "Carla may have recognized Wendy Martin's name from Philip Long's computer."

"This is all speculation," said Lou, throwing his hands in the air. "We don't have anything on Joel that ties him to Philip's murder, and we have even less on Sean and Kyle."

Macy stared at the wall of photos. "If we're still going in circles at the end of the day tomorrow, I think we're going to have to start this investigation from scratch again."

"Don't be so disheartened," said Gina. "We may get something off Finn Crawley's sweatshirt, and Sean Spencer is finally within our reach. Plus the tech guys are still combing through the file attachments we received with the anonymous e-mails. Something will come up."

# 16

Macy and Lou drove up to Collier County Hospital together. It was still early, and the hospital's lobby was relatively empty. Lou's face was etched with worry. Macy pushed the button for the elevator, and they waited in silence. She'd stayed up late going through Lloyd Spencer's medical files and financial records. At around two in the morning, she opened an e-mail from the tech people in Helena. They'd found something in the Word document that was attached to the first e-mail. The original document had comments that had been erased but were still visible when the file's revision history was accessed. One of the notations was particularly interesting.

*Need more data from Whitaker's clinic. Must risk hacking into Francine's account again. It's hard to believe my wife didn't know what was going on.*

Macy showed the e-mail to Lou Turner on the drive up to Collier. While it proved Philip Long had been investigating Whitaker, it did little to ease Lou's troubled mind.

"Lou," said Macy, once they were alone inside the elevator. "Even if Whitaker is guilty, he may never be charged. Since you have to continue living in the same town as him, I suggest you let me do the interview on my own."

Lou was visibly relieved. "Thanks, Macy. I owe you one. This is not going to be an easy interview. Aside from the e-mails we've got nothing solid that ties him to the kidnapping."

"We may have more than you think. I went through Lloyd Spencer's financial documents again last night. Until two weeks ago he owed Whitaker's practice thirty-six grand in outstanding medical bills. It's all been written off. I think we both know why."

"What's your theory?" asked Lou.

"Philip Long was planning a radio show that would have exposed Whitaker's high patient fatality rate and possibly implicate him as a dealer. Whitaker made a deal with Carla and Lloyd, promising to write off their outstanding debt. Along with another individual they were contracted to silence Philip Long, but not necessarily to kill him. I'm guessing that something went horribly wrong the night he died."

"Nice, but we still need to prove it."

"I'm painfully aware of that," said Macy. "You know Whitaker well. Any tips before I go in?"

"Whitaker is a smart man, but he's got a messiah complex layered with an ego the size of Texas. I'd be careful about cornering him. He'll clam up and call the lawyers."

"I'll keep that in mind," said Macy.

The doors opened on the sixth floor, and they stepped out into the corridor.

"Come find me when you're done," said Lou.

Dr. Whitaker was propped up in the hospital bed wearing a dark blue robe over his hospital gown. His left arm was in a sling. Although his tan had faded his strength had not. He shook Macy's hand firmly and looked her straight in the eye.

"It's a pleasure to see you again, Detective Greeley."

"I'm relieved to see that you're on the mend, Dr. Whitaker."

"I've had excellent care. Are you familiar with Collier County Hospital?"

"My son was born here," said Macy.

"Then you know it doesn't have the best reputation. I can't say I've had any reason to complain." He repeated himself. "Excellent care."

"I'd like to thank you again for agreeing to speak to me. I know it's been a difficult twenty-four hours."

"I understand Joel Edwards was of interest in your investigation. Hopefully, this incident has brought closure. Do you really think he was the so-called third kidnapper?"

"It is a possibility, but we'd like to make sure we've exhausted all lines of inquiry before closing down the investigation."

"Of course," said Dr. Whitaker. "I'll do what I can to help."

Macy cleared her throat. "We've had some anonymous e-mails sent to us over the past week concerning prescription painkiller abuse. The sender implied that the contents of these e-mails are somehow related to Philip Long's death. We've since discovered that one of the attached documents was most likely created by Philip Long."

"I don't understand how that could be the case. Philip was adamantly opposed to taking pain medication of any sort. I doubt very seriously he was abusing prescription drugs."

"You misunderstand me, Dr. Whitaker. The attached file lists eighty-two cases over the past five years where patients have died despite being under a doctor's care. We ran the list by the state coroner in Helena. Your name came up in many of the cases."

"I'm sorry," said Whitaker. "But what does this line of questioning have to do with what happened in my clinic yesterday?"

"I'm trying to establish Joel Edwards's motive for confronting you."

"He wanted drugs."

"According to a witness who saw the exchange, Joel wanted justice. His sister, Wendy Martin, was one of your patients."

"This is out of order. That man marched into my clinic and shot me. If not for the grace of God I'd be dead right now."

"Dr. Whitaker, I've come here as a courtesy. Philip Long made some very strong assertions about opiate-based pain medication and doctor culpability in patient's deaths. The state has assured me that there will be a full investigation. Consider this a chance to tell your side of the story."

"I feel like I should have a lawyer present."

"You're free to stop at any time," said Macy. "But the sooner I'm convinced that you have nothing to fear from the release of information found in these e-mails, the sooner I can move on with the investigation."

Dr. Whitaker gave a terse nod. "Detective Greeley, I understand there is a need to be thorough in an investigation such as this, but it's obvious that you suspect me of some kind of involvement in Philip's murder. For the record, I strenuously deny it. As a gesture of goodwill I'm going to volunteer my DNA and fingerprints." He held up his hands. "I have nothing to hide."

"That's very much appreciated. Someone will come by today if that's okay." Macy took a quick look at her notes. "Did Philip Long ever approach you about a story he was doing on prescription painkiller abuse?"

"He most certainly did not."

"Have you always specialized in pain management?"

"No," said Whitaker. "But I've worked in the field for the past twenty years."

"Would it surprise you to learn that eighteen of your patients have died over the past three years by overdosing on prescription medication?"

"Are you sure that number is correct? It seems high."

"I'll send you the documentation if you like," said Macy. "Aren't you afraid to prescribe such powerful medication given the inherent danger to your patients?"

"Of course, I'm fearful," he said. "I tell my patients that these are powerful drugs. I educate them, and they are all required to sign a patient contract. They promise to only take the medication as directed and to not seek medical care from any other doctor without my approval. In follow-up examinations I remind them to be careful. They are well aware that these drugs can kill them."

"How are your patients assessed?" asked Macy.

"Determining a patient's pain state is incredibly difficult. You follow them closely and eventually develop an understanding. In the beginning I believed everything my patients told me. It was only with time that I became skeptical. Patients will lie to you. You have to have your guard up all the time."

"If you're so careful, why do you think so many of your patients are dying of overdoses?"

"If a patient starts to misuse the medication, they will soon become dependent. At that point it's difficult to judge whether the pain they're feeling is legitimate. If they are convincing enough they may slip through the net. They may also start mixing their medication with alcohol or other drugs that they've bought on the streets or gotten through prescriptions from other doctors." He paused. "Every pain management practice will have patients who die of overdose. The more a patient takes without having problems, the more they will think they can control it, but they're playing with fire. They never know when one extra pill will kill them."

"Why risk treating these patients if it's so difficult to monitor their behavior outside of your clinic? According to Montana State Medical Board there are three malpractice cases pending against you. In the past three years you've settled out of court with patients' families on six separate occasions, paying out an estimated $2.4 million."

"Someone has to take care of these patients. Who are we to say that they are not entitled to a pain-free life? I'm not going to play God. Pain may not be quantifiable but it is real. I'm sad that we've lost a few patients, but I have helped so many others over the years. I suggest you go to my Web site and have a look at the hundreds of testimonials. I really have done my best for all the right reasons."

"Can I ask you about your relationship with Kyle Miller?"

"Kyle is a member of my prayer group at church."

"He's also works for the company that provides security for your offices."

"They don't provide security for me anymore," he said. "I made the call this morning. I wouldn't have been shot if the security guard had shown up for work on time."

"I understand he had a flat tire."

"They were supposed to send a replacement," said Whitaker. "They've apologized for what they've said was a clerical error. That's simply not good enough."

"Did you know Kyle's uncle Lloyd Spencer?" asked Macy.

"The kidnapper?" asked Dr. Whitaker.

"He was once your patient. Until two weeks ago, he owed your practice thirty-six thousand dollars. Why did you forgive his debt?"

"Kyle came to me a month ago to plead his aunt and uncle's case. Lloyd's wife, Carla, was in rehab, but their debt was putting them under a considerable amount of stress, which made it difficult for them to stay away from drugs. It was clear that I was never going to see the money anyway, so I wrote off the debt."

"Tell me about Wendy Martin."

"That was an unfortunate accident and a terrible loss for the community and her family."

"Fentanyl is one hundred times stronger than morphine, and yet you prescribed it along with Xanax and hydrocodone," said Macy. "I understand that you've settled with the family out of court so no charges will be made against you, but surely you must see yourself as responsible."

"As I stated earlier, pain management isn't an exact science. I take comfort in the fact that I get it right ninety-nine percent of the time, and not one of my patients' deaths has been ruled suspicious. I'm fully qualified, certified, and licensed to practice medicine in the state of Montana, and I stand by every prescription I've ever written. If the state has a case against me they're certainly taking their sweet time making it."

Macy gave him her most benevolent smile. "I realize time is short but I have one more question to ask. How is it that a doctor practicing medicine in a town of less than sixteen thousand souls ended up writing nearly thirty percent of all opiate-based painkiller prescriptions in the state of Montana over the past ten years?"

Dr. Whitaker's face went red. "I've committed no crime Detective Greeley, and unless you can prove otherwise I suggest you leave me in peace."

# 17

Emma found Nathan in the middle of a cherry orchard surveying buds for signs of rot. He turned away and headed back to his pickup truck without saying a word. Emma had to jog to keep up with his long strides.

"Nathan, I need to speak to you."

He didn't slow down. "I thought we covered everything the other night."

"I get that you're upset with me, but that's no reason for you to follow me around Walleye like some kind of stalker."

Nathan stopped walking, but still wouldn't look at her.

"For someone who has taken ownership of their issues, you sure like to pile all your shit on other people."

"I know I'm right. Someone saw you in your truck."

Nathan started walking again. "When and where did this supposedly happen?"

"Along the river around noon yesterday."

Nathan stomped along the farm track toward where their cars were parked next to each other.

"Please don't run off," said Emma. "We need to talk about this. You really scared me."

"Emma, can you just shut up for a second?" Nathan opened the door to his truck and grabbed a clipboard off the seat. He thrust it in Emma's direction. "Read this," he said.

Emma studied the top sheet of paper. It was an invoice for a shipment of crates. A credit card receipt was attached.

"I was in Kalispell yesterday," said Nathan, pointing to the transaction's date and time. "I was nowhere near you or the river."

Emma stared at the paper. Nathan's signature was on the bottom. "I'm sorry," she said.

"I want to know who's been saying shit about me."

"I'm sure it was an honest mistake."

"You seemed mighty convinced it was the truth a couple of seconds ago."

"I'm really sorry."

Nathan leaned against the bed of his truck and adjusted his ball cap. "Emma, if someone is following you, you need to talk to the police. Whoever murdered your father is still out there. You can't be taking chances."

Emma pressed her fingertips to her eyes. "Maybe it was all in my head. I've been so willing to think the worst of people these last few days."

"Well, you can stop thinking that way about me. We may have had a fucked-up relationship in high school, but I have grown up a lot since then." He hesitated. "I'm not one of the bad guys anymore."

"You're not all good either."

"Neither are you."

"I've decided to get help," she said, not quite believing she was admitting aloud that help was what she needed.

"Help for what?" asked Nathan.

"I have an eating disorder."

"That's not exactly a state secret."

"I've never accepted that I have a problem."

"Why the change of heart?"

"Something my dad said to me the last time we were together," said Emma.

"Do me a favor," said Nathan. "When your therapist asks about the boyfriend who messed up your self-esteem, try to think of something nice to say about me?"

Emma shielded her eyes from the sun. "There was plenty of good."

"Why don't you talk about the good times more often, then?"

"I suppose I'm trying to get past the bad times first."

"Anything else on your list?" asked Nathan.

"That whole thing with Lucy dealing drugs, were you involved?"

"I'm not proud of it, but yeah I bought stuff from her. Got in so deep I ended up owing her a shitload of money." He shrugged. "But then she died."

"How come I didn't know about this?"

"Emma, I hate to break it to you, but half your friends were using."

"Seriously?"

"You were this perfect girl—straight As and always in control. Meanwhile the rest of us were going off the rails. There was an unspoken agreement among us. *Don't tell Emma. She won't get it.*"

"I don't know what to say."

"There's really nothing to say. After Lucy died most of us never touched the stuff again."

Emma leaned on the bed of the truck next to Nathan. She was tempted to rethink every interaction she'd had in high school. It had always felt like she was on the outside looking in. Now she knew why.

"I need to go," she said.

"You'll tell the police about the guy that was following you?"

"Yeah," she said, heading for her car. "I'll call Lou Turner from the house."

"Emma," he said. "You take care."

"You too."

Emma stood in the middle of her mother's kitchen staring at her phone. There were several new messages. Her heart sank when she saw the text from Kyle. He'd signed off the message with kisses. She keyed in his phone number and waited for him to pick up.

"Hi, Emma," he said. "I was just thinking of you. Do you feel like getting together?"

Emma hesitated. He sounded a little too eager.

"Emma," said Kyle. "Is everything okay?"

"We should talk."

"Sure," he said, dragging out the word like he was anything but sure. "I have plans later on, but I have a couple hours free now."

"That works for me," said Emma.

"You could come to my house," said Kyle. "We'd have the place to ourselves."

Emma stepped out onto the lawn. The grass was soft underfoot, the sky an endless blue. It was coming up to five. There were still a few hours of daylight left.

"I feel like being outside," said Emma. "Let's meet at the park near the fairgrounds."

Emma walked along a paved bike trail that overlooked the Flathead River. Where the river widened, shallow slate-gray water tumbled over half-submerged rocks. Someone upstream must have been throwing wildflowers into the wash. They swirled around in the whirlpools formed by the rapids. Emma noted that she wasn't alone. She'd already spotted a few joggers and a couple of dog walkers. A group of youths played soccer on a nearby field. There were plenty of people around, but it wasn't crowded. It would be a good place for them to talk. She'd been rehearsing what she was going to say. She'd let Kyle down gently. She'd be careful to blame herself. She'd been lonely and emotional the previous day. It made no sense for them to get involved. After her father's funeral she'd be leaving for San Francisco. Aside from her mother there was nothing left to keep her in Walleye Junction.

From the west a lone figure slowly appeared through the sun's glare. Kyle was walking across the open fields. He stopped and kicked a soccer ball back toward the players. He was wearing a ball cap and sunglasses and heading straight toward her. She held up her hand and he waved. She was so angry with herself. She'd acted without thinking things through and now she was going to have to hurt him.

Kyle gave her a nervous peck on the cheek.

"It's a beautiful evening," he said, touching her arm. "It was a nice idea to meet down here."

Emma couldn't look him in the eye. Worryingly, the spot she'd chosen had turned out to be the kind of place you'd come for a romantic picnic. There was a bandstand, a wildflower meadow, and picnic tables tucked back under the trees. She'd remembered it as a dump.

"It's nicer than I remembered," she said.

He put his arms around her waist and pulled her close. She was about to say something when her phone rang.

"I'm sorry," she said, pulling away from him. "It's probably my mother. She was in a bit of a state when I last spoke to her."

It was an unknown number. She gave Kyle what she thought was a convincing smile and lied. "It's my mom," she said. "I'll just be a second."

The woman's voice was too quiet. Emma pressed the phone closer to her ear and put more distance between herself and Kyle.

"I'm sorry," said Emma. "Can you please repeat that? I was having difficulty hearing you."

"You called and left a message on my voice mail. I'm the manager of the restaurant up at the ski resort."

Emma turned to face Kyle. He was a good fifteen feet away. He wasn't watching the river. He was watching her.

"Thank you for getting back to me," said Emma.

"We're very sorry you had a bad experience when you were our guest here at the resort. I've spoken to the bar staff who were on duty that evening. We believe the man who followed you to the parking lot was a member of a wedding party that has been staying here over the past few nights."

"You must know who he was. From what I understand he was kicked out of the restaurant when you found out what happened."

"We don't have any record of that."

"I'm just going by what your security guard told me."

"Ma'am," said the woman. "I'm afraid there's been some misunderstanding. We don't have any security guards working for us."

"That's not possible. He was patrolling the parking lot."

"That may be the case, but he doesn't work for us. I'd appreciate it if you could give us his contact details. We'd like to get to the bottom of this as soon as possible."

Emma didn't know what to say to the woman. Kyle was walking toward her. She hung up.

"Kyle," she said, standing her ground. "That was the manager at the restaurant up at the resort."

He looked confused. "Why . . . why would she be calling you?"

"Do you even know her name? You supposedly work for her."

"They've had a lot of turn . . . turnover recently." He shrugged. "What's this all about?"

"I called the restaurant because I was worried you were going to get in trouble. I wanted them to know that your actions were justified."

"You shouldn't have—"

"Why did you lie about working for them?" asked Emma.

"I didn't think it through."

"Why were you really there?"

"I was meeting someone," said Kyle.

"Who?"

"A friend. Does it matter?"

Emma glanced over at the soccer field. The game had ended. The players were dispersing. There wasn't anyone on the paved walkway. As the sun dropped behind the western range the valley fell into shadow.

"Did you follow me up to the resort that night?"

"Don't be ridiculous."

"I'm going to leave now," she said, turning toward the parking lot.

"I wasn't . . . I wasn't following you." He grabbed hold of her arm. "Emma, don't do this. Don't walk away from me."

Over his shoulder she caught sight of two men jogging along the walkway. One of them was pointing in their direction. She raised her voice.

"If you don't let go of me I will scream."

He dropped her arm and backed away. His eyes were cast downward. His face rigid.

She stared at him. The realization came slow, but when it hit, it hit hard.

"On the road near the river . . . it was you in the car that was behind me."

"No, that's not true. I'd been fishing all morning."

Emma hesitated. She hadn't seen the driver or the car that followed her on the road. She retraced the steps that had brought her face-to-face with Kyle. He'd been hunched over his tackle box, wearing waders and a jacket. They'd walked to his car together. She'd drunk the juice he'd offered. He'd parked so he was blocking the sign to the trailhead. It was the same sign she'd stopped to read as she made her way up the road. He couldn't have been parked there all morning if she'd stood in that same spot twenty minutes earlier.

"I don't believe you," she said. "You followed me on that road then tried to blame Nathan. I spoke to him today. He was in Kalispell yesterday."

Kyle backtracked. "I didn't know it was you on the road."

"So, you admit to following some random woman? And then lying about it? That doesn't make it better, Kyle. It actually makes it creepier. You scared the shit out of me." She folded her arms around herself protectively. She felt as if she might be sick. "It's one of the reasons I invited you back to my house. I was still scared." She shook her head. "I'm such a fucking idiot."

"No, you're not. I'm the idiot. I should have said something."

She backed away. "Kyle, I'm leaving."

He took a step in her direction. "Let me explain."

"Not now. I'll call you tomorrow once I've had time to think."

He kept coming.

"Kyle," she said, holding up a hand. "I told you I'd call you tomorrow. You need to respect that."

The two men she'd seen jogging on the path were now heading in their direction. One of them shouted.

"Is this guy bothering you?"

Kyle turned his back on Emma and started walking away.

"Everything's fine," said Kyle. "I'm going."

Emma arrived home as darkness was falling. She locked the door behind her and stood at the front window watching the road. There was no sign of Kyle's car. Full of nervous energy she went around collecting the stray dishes that were scattered through the downstairs rooms. The phone rang as she was starting the dishwasher. Her mother sounded tired but relieved.

"I finally spoke to Peter," said Francine. "He's very weak, but he's going to be okay."

"That's good news. Will you be home soon?"

"I'll be another couple of hours. My friends said they'd drop me off once we've had something to eat."

Emma sat down at the kitchen table. Her predominant emotion wasn't fear. It was anger. She should have told Kyle to fuck off then and there. She'd never met someone who was so socially awkward. What was he thinking?

"Emma?" said Francine. "Are you okay?"

"I'm fine," said Emma, pushing all thoughts of Kyle to one side. "I've just got a lot on my mind."

Emma took her father's coat down from its hook and stomped across the orchard with the keys to Caleb's house in her hand. Clouds veiled what little moon there was and the cherry trees rose and fell with each gust of wind. All the windows of the farmhouse were dark. Emma cleared the cobwebs that draped across the back porch and unlocked the door. The ceiling lamps flickered for a few seconds before settling into a steady glow. The air smelled faintly damp, but she was sure that was a trick of memory. The water had long since retreated. The house was empty, silent, and bone dry. Emma stepped into the kitchen and tried to imagine what it had been like when she was a child.

When Beverly was alive it had been cluttered with everything from cats to coupons to cake tins. There were always a few long-tailed dogs crashing about the place, baying above the Motown records that were playing on the turntable. That all stopped after she passed away. The records were boxed up and the turntable consigned to the back of a cupboard. The cats and dogs died one by one and nine years later Lucy was gone too.

Held in place with yellowing tape and corners curled up like fists, old snapshots of Lucy covered the front of the refrigerator. It was a carefully curated collection. Lucy and Emma had been inseparable for years, but here there was only an occasional glimpse of Emma—an arm, a tanned leg, or strands of stray hair but nothing more. It was just like the paintings of the girl at Dot's house—the parts could not make up a whole. Some of the photos had been torn in half. Others were folded back. She removed one and pried the stiff card open, revealing her childhood self. Flat chested and freckled, she and Lucy stood arm in arm in the shallows of Darby Lake. They wore matching grins and homemade bathing suits. It was the summer after Beverly died and they'd spent the day picnicking on Darby Lake with Emma's parents. Lucy's hair was a mess. In a sign of things to come, she'd tried to re-create something she'd seen in a magazine using her mother's sewing shears. The result had left her looking like a porcupine for weeks. Caleb had insisted she wear a hat to cover it up, but she'd refused. It was the first of many battles he was destined to lose.

Trailing her fingertips along the textured wallpaper, Emma climbed the stairs to the first-floor landing feeling increasingly apprehensive about what she'd find in Lucy's room. She needn't have worried. Caleb had left nothing to chance. Lucy's room had been stripped back to the floorboards. Everything that she'd once held dear was gone. Emma wandered down the hallway opening doors, but all she found were vacant rooms dotted with a few stray pieces of furniture. Emma saved the bathroom for last. It was the only room that hadn't changed at all. The claw-footed tub and the gilded bathroom mirror were exactly as Emma remembered.

Caleb had been out of town the night Lucy died. Earlier that same day Lucy had cornered Emma in the hallway of the high school between classes. It was clear that Lucy had taken drugs. She couldn't stand still. She'd grabbed hold of Emma with both hands. Her face was inches away. Her pupils were so big her eyes looked black.

*Come to my house tonight,* she'd said. *Caleb's away. It will be like old times.*

Emma had said she had other plans, but Lucy insisted.

*Emma, please, this is important. You have to come.*

Emma hadn't made it to Lucy's house until the next morning. After letting herself in the back door, she'd found a stream of water pouring through the living room ceiling. She'd opened the door to the upstairs bathroom thinking she'd find nothing more interesting than an overflowing toilet.

It was the first time Emma had seen a dead body.

Water lapped over the sides of the claw-footed bathtub. Lucy's lifeless hand rested on the side of the tub, palms up in a gesture of surrender. Her eyes were open, lips slightly parted. Her black hair drifted around her pale face like storm clouds. The note Lucy had written in lipstick on the mirror left no room for doubt. As far as Lucy was concerned Emma was to blame for not being there when she was needed most.

*Emma, sometimes the heart breaks and the broken do not live on. You should have come when I called. Always yours, Lucy*

Emma knelt down next to Lucy and felt for a pulse, but there was nothing. Lucy's skin was as cold as the bathwater. A line of bruised needle marks checkered her arm. A syringe balanced on the edge of the bath like a seesaw. Emma turned off the faucets and looked around the room. A candle Lucy had lit the night before had burned down to the base, and there was a good inch of water on the floor. For a long time Emma stood in front of the mirror rereading the note Lucy had left. Emma had known anger before, but never like this. Lucy had no right to blame someone else for something she'd so clearly done to herself. Emma opened the cabinet under the sink where the cleaning supplies were kept. She'd been careful to wipe clean any trace of Lucy's final words before phoning the police.

Emma retraced her steps through the farmhouse, turning off the last of the lights as she made her way into the kitchen. Halfway across the darkened room, she noticed a faint thread of light bleeding out from beneath the door to the basement. She opened the door and reached for the chain hanging down from the bare bulb above her head. Her father must have left the light on when he last came to check on the property. According to her mother and Nathan, he was the only one who'd been in the house recently. She was about to turn off the light when she noticed there were shoeprints marking the thick dust coating the narrow wooden steps going down into the basement. It dawned on Emma that Caleb's basement would have been the perfect place for her father to hide his journal. There was a distinct buzz as Emma flicked a switch at the base of the stairs and the rest of the lights flickered to life. About ten feet ahead there was a large metal cabinet. The footprints, presumably her father's, stopped right in front of it.

The cabinet door was secured with a padlock, which looked new. Emma sifted through the key ring until she found a key that fit. A large metal box sat alone on the empty shelves. She brought it out into the light and pulled open the lid. Alongside a handgun and a few cartridges there was her father's journal, a portable external hard drive, and a leather pouch containing several glassine bags stamped with a bull's-eye, a syringe, and other gear. She picked up her father's journal and flipped through it. One of the pages was folded back. She opened it to find a photograph of Lucy standing on the steps of Dot Whitaker's house. She was wearing shorts and a halter top. She blew the photographer a kiss. There was a digital time stamp in the corner. Emma's father had written some notes beneath the photograph.

*Photo taken over Memorial Day weekend when Dot and the kids were away in Helena visiting family. I'm convinced Peter took the photo and he and Lucy spent at least two nights together up at the house, but I need more than this to prove he was supplying Lucy with drugs. Given the large stash of drugs found when she died, I'm convinced she was dealing on his behalf. Unsavory to consider, but very likely that he was supplying her with drugs for her personal use in exchange for sex. Lucy was an addict. I know from experience that she would have done just about anything for a fix. Must talk to Dot.*

# 18

Gina slid onto the empty bar stool next to Macy. She was wearing a pair of slacks, a blouse, and a jean jacket. It was the first time in years that Macy had seen her out of uniform. Gina pushed her glasses up on her nose and picked up the wine menu.

"After spending the day in Missoula chasing down Kyle's friends I could really use a drink. Fancy ordering a bottle of red to share?"

"Don't be so negative. Missoula is nice."

"Oh, I've got no issues with Missoula, but I wasn't in town. I was out in the hills with the rednecks. Kyle Miller runs in some interesting circles." Gina flipped the wine menu over and traced her finger along the list of wines on offer. "I've spoken to the friends he was with the night Philip Long was murdered. Their stories line up."

"Anything make you doubt they were telling the truth?" asked Macy.

"No, it all checked out."

"How long has Kyle known them?"

"They met through some weekend retreat set up by Kyle's church last year."

"Criminal records?"

"One served two years for beating his wife. Another has convictions for dealing. Nothing recent. They're all born-again Christians." Gina put the menu down and took off her glasses. "Kyle was born on the wrong side of the tracks. Hanging out with deadbeats must come naturally to him."

"I get the impression he has aspirations to rise above all that," said Macy.

Gina waved at the bartender to get his attention.

"You may want to hold off on a whole bottle," said Macy "I just got word that that rave Kristina has been planning is kicking off tonight somewhere in the Flathead Valley. The tech guys are tracking her social media activity. Once a phone number is posted they'll call in for the rave's location."

"Maybe we'll get lucky and find Sean tonight. So far he and Kristina have been inseparable." Gina swiveled her bar stool around and had a quick look at the barroom. "I'm starting to see why Kristina's raves are so popular. Friday evenings in Walleye are pretty dead."

The bartender placed a pair of martinis in front of Gina and Macy and told them it was compliments of the gentleman sitting at the corner table. They both turned. Ryan Marshall tipped his large-brimmed cowboy hat in their direction.

Macy tried to keep a straight face. "Gina, it appears we have an admirer."

"What's with the hat?" asked Gina.

"I think he's trying to blend in with the locals."

"It's not working."

"Should we go say hello?"

Gina picked up her glass. "One drink isn't going to hurt. It's going to be hours before we find out where that party is."

"Just don't get sucked in," said Macy. "My friend Ryan is a hangover waiting to happen."

The heavily rutted track turned sharply to the right and within seconds dipped down into a dense pine forest. The headlights caught tree trunks and little else. It was pitch-black outside.

Macy checked the coordinates. "According to the GPS we're not even on a marked road."

"Maybe we should double back," said Gina. "We may have missed a turn."

Macy pointed out the front window. "There, through the trees. Are those lights?"

The road dead-ended at a sagging chain-link fence topped with barbed wire. Gina killed the headlights.

"What is this place?" asked Gina.

They looked out over a mile of broken tarmac. Shrubs and grasses grew from the cracks. The rusted hulk of a twin-engine airplane was tipped on its side. One of its wings was snapped in two.

"It's an abandoned airfield," said Macy, shutting the door and heading over to the fence for a better look.

The airplane hangar had been transformed into a nightclub. The big doors were open and people crowded into the floodlit interior. A sound system was positioned on a flatbed truck that had been parked in the middle of the building. Cars and pickup trucks were scattered across the runway. It looked as if some people were staying the night. Tents had been erected on a grassy area near the perimeter fence.

Gina squinted her eyes. "Looks like a few hundred people, but hard to tell how many are inside. I wonder how much she's charging per head."

"The tech people didn't say."

"We need to get in there and have a closer look," said Gina.

Macy moved along the perimeter. "There's a break in the fence up ahead."

The music was deafening. The ground beneath their feet vibrated. The airfield's gated entrance was to the north of the hangar. A line of cars waited to get in. Macy pointed to a bumper sticker on a pickup truck that was parked nearby—NO BETTER HIGH THAN A WALLEYE HIGH. Even though Gina was right next to her, Macy had to shout.

"What happened to the bumper stickers that said *my child is an honor student*?" said Macy.

Gina craned her neck to get a better look. "God this makes me feel old. There are more people here than I realized. How many, would you say?"

"I'd say close to a thousand." Macy fiddled with the keypad on her phone. There was hardly any signal. "We'd better give Lou a call."

"That's a big crowd. I imagine we'll need more than just Lou."

"He's going to have to handle this carefully," said Macy. "Someone could get hurt if the police come in too heavy-handed."

"People will get hurt no matter what we do. Those kids look like they're tanked up on more than just warm keg beer. I'll go back to the car and radio it in. If you spot Sean or Kristina, come find me."

Two girls emerged from the hangar and staggered toward where Macy was hiding. Oblivious to the cold night air, they only wore tiny denim shorts and crop tops. Every few steps they doubled over and went into hysterics.

"I'm going to pee my pants if you don't stop making me laugh."

The shorter girl grabbed her friend's hand and dragged her toward some shrubs growing at the base of the chain-link fence.

"Let's go over there. No one will see us."

"As long as there aren't any snakes."

"Or bears."

"Or perverts."

They laughed again.

"Justin is so messed up. They carried him off somewhere."

"He's such an idiot. Ket is nasty."

"Got any more Molly?"

"That depends." Another laugh. "Got any more money?"

Macy watched them walk away, their tiny shorts disappearing up their backsides. They couldn't have been more than sixteen. She turned in time to see Gina moving along the fence. She was barely visible beneath the overhanging tree branches. She squatted down next to Macy.

"Lou agrees that the first priority will be to keep these kids safe," said Gina. "Events like this are pretty rare up this way. They're still learning how to deal with them."

"By the time they've figured it out, kids will be doing something else."

"The youth of today—"

"Are no worse than the youth of yesterday."

"You speak the truth. I was a nightmare." Gina checked the time. "How do you want to do this? Soft touch or not, when the cops show up those kids will scatter. If Kristina and Sean are in that crowd we'll lose them."

"I'm going to head over and see if I can find them."

"You're just going to walk in there?"

"I'm counting on them being too wasted to notice me," said Macy.

Gina gestured to some low windows running along the western wall of the hangar. The side door was ajar. A man stood outside smoking a cigarette.

"That guy standing by the doors looks like security," said Gina. "There will be more where he came from."

"I know," Macy said, tugging her hair out of its band and pulling it down around her face. She scowled like a teenager for Gina's benefit. "I'll do my best to blend in, and if that doesn't work, I'll run like hell."

A group of youths in their late teens were gathered around a pickup truck. A petite girl with dark hair sat on the shoulders of the tallest boy. She had her eyes closed and was swaying back and forth to the music. Stripes of neon green and pink paint glowed on her cheeks. One of the boys caught sight of Macy and stepped into her path. Macy stumbled on purpose and laughed. Keeping her eyes focused on the middle distance, she pushed him aside and kept walking toward the hangar.

He asked her name.

Macy waved him off, but he followed her anyway.

"I'm looking for my friends," she said.

Warm breath smelling of whiskey and cigarettes was right up against her ear.

"Maybe I can help," he said. "Tell me their names."

Macy took a chance. "Xtina and Sean."

"You're not going to find them in there." He pointed toward the cluster of tents and took hold of her arm. "That's where you want to go. I'll take you."

Macy looked over at the tents. A few glowed in the dark. She didn't think Kristina was the type to hide away in a tent when there was a party going on.

"Do you even know them?" asked Macy.

"You're just going to have to trust me," he said, pulling her along.

"I'll find them on my own," she said, yanking her arm away. "Let go of me."

He threw her up against a nearby car and pinned her down.

"You're going nowhere," he said.

Macy's knee came up like a piston, hitting him hard in the groin. He cried out as he doubled over. She was tempted to pull out her firearm but kneed him in the side of the head instead.

"I don't have time for your bullshit," said Macy, taking a handful of his hair and twisting his head around so she could get a better look at him. "I'm looking for a girl with bleach-blond hair with black tips. Tell me where to find her or get the fuck out of my way."

He glared at her. "That fucking hurt."

"I'll do worse if you don't tell me what I need to know."

"Around back behind the stage. There was a girl who looked like that in the VIP area."

Macy leaned in closer. "I know what you're up to. Fuck with any of the girls here and I'll come find you."

Macy headed for the stage. Strobe lights pulsed above the sea of dancers and music pumped out of speakers the size of refrigerators. A DJ wearing headphones stood in a booth that sat on the back of a flatbed truck that was surrounded by a low barrier. Macy kept to the edge of the dance floor, her eyes scanning the crowd for any sign of Kristina, figuring she'd stand out more than Sean. Glow sticks and face paint aside, most of the girls looked like your average Flathead Valley teenagers.

Macy dodged a group of wasted youth who were clinging to anything that would keep them upright. One toppled to the floor, taking his friends down with him. Elation was soon followed by panic. They grabbed the legs of other dancers as they tried to get up. More fell into the pit. Macy pulled a girl free. She wrapped her arms around Macy's neck and kissed her on the cheek before staggering away. Two boys rolled around in the chaos pummeling each other with their fists, oblivious to the fact that they were crushing anyone who was stuck beneath them. The crowd closed in, and Macy was swept off her feet as a pair of arms locked around her from behind.

By the time she recognized the smell of whiskey and cigarettes it was too late. The boy she'd encountered outside was back. He shoved Macy up against the barrier and pulled up her shirt with one hand while tugging at the waistline of her jeans with the other. She reached over her head and dug her thumbs deep into his eye sockets before twisting around and throwing several punches. The third one was a direct hit. His head snapped back and he dropped like a stone. Macy gave him a final shove and watched as he disappeared into the crowd.

Yards of dank plastic sheeting hung from a latticework of scaffolding that had been erected to block off an area at the rear of the hangar. She pulled it to the side and stepped over the metal frame and yards of thick power cables. Flathead Valley's version of a VIP section was no more than a couple of trestle tables covered with booze and a few dozen beanbag chairs thrown onto the floor.

It was difficult to see anything clearly under the fast-pulsing lights. Most of the kids were crowded around the bar area mixing drinks in large plastic cups. To the right, a set of double doors was propped open with a chair. Outside there was a floodlit area adjacent to the gated entrance to the airfield. She'd counted two security guards so far.

Macy spotted Kristina in an office located at the rear of the hangar. She was pacing back and forth, smoking a cigarette, in front of a window that faced the building's interior. She stopped to gaze out onto the crowd gathered around the trestle tables. She looked as if she'd been lifted straight from the pages of a graphic novel. Her bleached hair was piled high on her head and dark makeup outlined her eyes. Her lips appeared to be painted black. Macy had never seen anyone like her before. For a few seconds she was transfixed.

The girl next to Macy threw her arm sideways and the contents of her cup soaked the front of Macy's jacket. She looked Macy in the face and burst out laughing.

"Sorry, Mom."

"Go home," Macy said, pushing past her. "It's past your bedtime."

Macy double-checked that the safety was on before sweeping into the office with her gun drawn. She kicked the door shut behind her.

"Police," she yelled. "Put your hands up where I can see them."

Kristina stood on the opposite side of a large metal desk, leaning out a window that was a few feet away from the airport's perimeter fence. She flicked her half-finished cigarette outside before turning to face Macy. She didn't look alarmed. She looked bored. Her hands hovered between up and down like she was unable to commit to either of the two. She spoke with a distinct accent, but her diction was spot on.

"Why are you pointing a gun at me?" said Kristina. "I haven't done anything wrong."

"Keep your hands where I can see them. I need to see some ID."

Kristina shook her head.

"Suit yourself," said Macy. "I'm still going to arrest you."

Kristina leaned back against the window frame and took a quick peek outside. It looked like she was deciding whether she should make a run for it.

Macy raised the gun higher. "Don't even think about it."

"You cops are such fascists. Kids should be able to have a good time. We're not hurting anyone."

Macy ran her eyes over Kristina's features. The dyed hair and thick makeup couldn't hide everything. Kristina had put in some miles.

"Hate to break it to you, but you're no kid," said Macy. "I'm guessing you're older than I am."

"That doesn't mean we can't have fun. When was the last time you had a good time, Detective Greeley?" Kristina's tone was withering. "I'm guessing it's been at least a decade."

"How do you know my name?"

"I'm old like you. I read the papers."

"Then you know I'm looking for your friend Sean Spencer in connection with Philip Long's kidnapping and murder."

"I haven't seen Sean in weeks."

"You were with him yesterday. You posted a picture online."

A slight smile. "Yesterday was throwback Thursday."

"Kristina, quit bullshitting me. Sean is only nineteen. He's already lost his mother and stepfather. He stands to lose much more if he doesn't come forward soon."

"You really don't have a clue what's going on," said Kristina.

"Enlighten me."

"Sean wasn't involved in Philip Long's murder."

"That's for the authorities to decide."

"We sent you the files from the story Long was working on. It's all there in black and white. We can't help it if you're incompetent."

"Kristina, we're in the middle of a major investigation. You don't seem to realize how many tips we receive from the public over the course of a day. We can't cover everything. Your e-mail could have been much clearer. Why didn't you tell us from the beginning that the files were Philip Long's?" Macy's words came out in a rush. "Who gave the files to you? Was it Carla?"

They both glanced at the back window facing the perimeter fence. A long line of patrol cars was heading up the access road with their emergency lights on.

"We need to know what happened at that house where Long was being held captive," said Macy. "I'm thinking that Carla contacted Sean and gave him the files. Sean has to give us everything. We need more evidence if we're going to make a case."

"You'll have to work with what you have," said Kristina. "The memory stick Carla used was corrupted. We salvaged what we could."

"Why won't Sean come in and talk to us?"

"I know how things work in this country," said Kristina. "Sean is a poor kid with no family connections. You'll twist the facts and he'll end up getting the blame. I won't let you do that to him."

"That's not how I do things. I'd never let that happen."

"This is bigger than you. The pharmaceutical companies and doctors are behind what happened. It's a government conspiracy."

"Kristina, this case is neither global nor glamorous. I believe a local doctor paid Sean's parents a lot of money to kidnap Philip Long before his story on prescription drug abuse could be aired. The story would have ruined the doctor's career. Someone else was involved in Long's murder and I'm pretty sure Sean knows who it was."

Kristina stared at Macy but said nothing.

Macy raised her voice. "Why is Sean so hell-bent on protecting the man who murdered his mother and stepfather?"

"What are you talking about," said Kristina, matching Macy's tone. "Sean's parents died of an overdose."

"Someone held Carla down and put a gun to her head," said Macy. "She and Lloyd didn't die by their own hands."

Kristina took a few seconds to respond. It was the first time she seemed uncertain.

"That wasn't in the papers," said Kristina.

"As you're so keen on government conspiracies, it shouldn't come as a surprise that the police don't tell the press everything."

"I'm not saying anything more until I talk to Sean."

"You're smart, Kristina. You know we'll track down Sean eventually. He's withholding evidence. Right now I can protect you, but if you leave it too long he'll be charged with obstruction. Someone has already murdered three people. They'll go after Sean if they think he knows something." Macy lowered her gun. "He needs to come in and talk to us. Can you make that happen?"

"I don't know."

"Kristina, do you really think a life on the run is what's best for Sean? He's just a kid. You need to give him a chance to—"

Several shots rang out. The windows behind Macy shattered into sharp fragments that flew across the room. Macy dropped flat onto the floor and shouted at Kristina to do the same. Gunfire raked the wall above their heads. Broken glass and splintered wood showered down on them. Macy crawled behind the desk and sat next to Kristina. The lights went out at the same time as the music. Macy looked up in time to catch a flash of Kristina leaping out the back window. Macy checked the door one last time before holstering her firearm and following Kristina out into the night.

Macy caught glimpses of Kristina as they ran along the runway's perimeter. She was a good fifty yards ahead and moving fast. Macy followed her through an opening in the fence and headed down a narrow track that twisted through the dense wood. She was just beginning to lose her way when she rounded a bend and stumbled out into open terrain. Ahead of her the Flathead River glowed under a sky straining beneath the weight of stars. Upstream nothing moved among the low shrubs dotting the flat gray river stones. Downstream, Kristina climbed up a steep slope to where the land plateaued. As she leaped across boulders the size of cars, Macy could see her body was in silhouette. In the distance, a thin line of headlights marked the course of Route 93.

Macy stood still and listened. It was faint at first, but she soon recognized the guttural roar of an engine. A dirt bike tore out of the trees a few dozen feet from where she stood. It skipped across the uneven terrain heading south along the shoreline, the whine of its engine fading with distance. Macy checked the plateau. If it weren't for the soft glow of Kristina's cigarette, Macy wouldn't have spotted her. Seconds later the light went out and Kristina was gone.

# 19

Macy checked the time. It was coming up to three in the afternoon and she'd not slept in two days. She ordered another cup of coffee from the waitress and tried to shake herself awake. It had been nearly two hours since she spoke to Sean Spencer on the phone. She'd still been at the abandoned airfield and had to scramble to get to the diner in time for their meeting, but after waiting for almost an hour, she was worried he'd changed his mind. The diner's front door swung open and Sean stood in the entrance looking uncertain. He appeared older than Macy expected. Taller too. When he spotted Macy, he shouldered his backpack and slowly made his way to her table.

Sean dropped into the empty seat opposite her and removed his baseball cap. His dark hair hung across his eyes, and he had the beginnings of a beard. Macy pushed a menu across the table and told him to order something if he was hungry. He was polite when the waitress came to the table.

"I'm relieved you came," said Macy. "I was worried you wouldn't show up."

"I didn't have much choice. Kristina said it was either this or never seeing her again."

"Do you have any questions for me before we get started?" asked Macy.

He began to speak but stopped. "I'm sorry," he said. "This is harder than I thought it would be."

"I imagine it's been a rough time for you."

He cleared his throat.

"You told Kristina that my mom and Lloyd were murdered. Is that true or were you feeding her some bullshit line so I'd talk to you?"

"I'm afraid it's true. Do you want me to go into detail?"

He looked away. "Not now."

"Sean, someone else was involved in Philip Long's kidnapping and murder. It's probable they killed Long and your parents as well. I think you know who I'm talking about."

There were tears in his eyes.

"It was my cousin, Kyle," he said.

Sean looked up as their food arrived. He'd ordered two double cheeseburgers, French fries, and a Coke. Macy's salad looked anemic in comparison. She pushed it to one side and ordered a cheeseburger for herself.

"We've had our suspicions about your cousin, but we have four people swearing he was in Missoula when Philip Long was kidnapped and murdered," said Macy.

"Don't believe anything Kyle or his friends say. I'm sure they're all involved in what's been going on. My mom and Lloyd knew Kyle couldn't be trusted, and they still fell for his bullshit."

"I saw your house. I know what kind of debt your parents were in. They were pretty desperate."

"Kyle told my parents they'd kidnapped Philip Long because of the radio show he'd done on the local militias. There were people who wanted to teach him a lesson. My mom says Lloyd threatened to kill her if she didn't go along with it. I don't know why she didn't go to the police when she had the chance. It's just one of the many stupid decisions she's made over the years."

"How were they compensated?"

"Initially some of their debts were paid off, but they'd been promised some extra cash if everything went according to plan. My mom realized what was really going on when she looked at the files stored on Philip Long's laptop. I don't know why she risked her life to save a man she hardly knew, but I'm proud of her for taking a stand. The next time she was alone in the house with Philip Long she set him free."

"He didn't get very far."

Sean talked between mouthfuls. "Kyle showed up at the house just as he was making a run for it. My mom gave Kyle some bullshit line that she'd been overpowered, and he took off after Long on his dirt bike."

"Kyle said he doesn't ride one."

Sean finished off his first cheeseburger.

"Like I said, the guy lies all the time." Sean set a memory stick on the table. "My mom downloaded some of Philip Long's files and gave them to me for safekeeping. Unfortunately, the drive was corrupted. I already sent you all the files I could."

Macy studied the memory stick. There was always a chance the tech department could get more information off it. She'd been hoping for more, but this would have to do for now.

"Sean, when did you meet with your mother?"

"I got a call from her the day after Philip Long was murdered. We met at a turnout near here. She didn't think Kyle believed her story about what happened. She was scared of what he might do to her. I tried to get her to come with me, but she wouldn't leave Lloyd."

"Did your mom mention a doctor named Whitaker?"

"Philip Long told my mom that Whitaker was the reason he was being held captive."

"Did he say anything else?"

"She was trying to get him out of that house alive. They didn't have time to go into detail."

"We'll need to take a formal statement from you at the police station."

"Will I be arrested?"

"Not if I can help it."

"What happens to Kyle?"

"I'll get a warrant to search his home," said Macy. "We need to find hard evidence that ties him to Philip Long's death."

"Don't worry," he said. "You'll find what you're looking for."

"How can you be so sure about that?"

Instead of answering Sean Spencer started in on his second cheeseburger.

"Sean?"

He wiped his mouth with his napkin. "Let's just say that I've made things easy for you."

Kyle Miller stood in the rain outside his home with his hands deep in his pockets. His oversized jacket gave him the appearance of someone who was being swallowed up by events. An officer was stationed next to his front door. The cul-de-sac was crowded with minivans and children's play equipment. Macy and Gina exited the patrol car and went over to speak to Kyle.

"I don't know what you're expecting to find," he said. "I had nothing to do with Philip Long's death."

"We have a witness who says otherwise," said Macy. "Unless you want to take the blame for everything that's happened, I suggest you start talking."

The house was swarming with crime scene techs and police officers. Macy found Lou staring out an upstairs bedroom window. The rain had set in an hour earlier and didn't look like it would stop anytime soon. The garden was a rectangle of freshly laid lawn. Kyle had all the trappings of a suburban homeowner—lawn furniture, a barbecue, and a shed. All that was missing was the wife and kids.

"I hope this pays off," said Lou.

"Me too," said Macy. "Have you seen Ryan?"

"He was in the kitchen earlier. By the way, where did you park Sean Spencer? I don't want to risk losing him again."

Macy squeezed Lou's arm. "Don't worry. He's at the police station. I told them to arrest him if he tried to leave."

Kyle's kitchen was small but practical. The window faced the cul-de-sac. Neighbors were gathering across the street. Children raced back and forth on their bikes. Macy pulled her phone out and called her mother.

"Hi, Mom, is everything okay? I noticed a missed call."

"Sorry, I didn't want to disturb you at work."

"Don't be silly, we'd never talk if you didn't."

"I just felt like hearing your voice," said Ellen.

"That's the best reason to call."

"How's it going?"

Macy wandered around the kitchen opening cupboards.

"There have been some developments. Things may be winding down sooner than we initially thought."

"Oh, that's good to hear. Everything okay with Aiden?"

"I'm not going to lie. It's been difficult."

"That's a shame. He seems like a nice man."

"Mom, I should get back to work. Chat later?"

"Of course, give me a call when you're free."

Macy slipped the phone in her pocket and opened the refrigerator. The contents were sparse but well organized. She picked up a can of Red Bull and held it in her gloved hand. It didn't mean anything. It was only a few cans. There'd been nearly a case in Ron Forester's refrigerator. She started to close the door and stopped. Condiments lined the inside of the door—barbecue sauce, butter, cream cheese, dill pickles, honey mustard, ketchup. She checked the other kitchen cabinets. Everything from spices to breakfast cereals was alphabetized. It was a shame they couldn't use it as proof of Kyle's involvement.

Macy went into the living room and opened the sliding doors that led out onto a small wooden deck. The rain was now falling in thick sheets. The garden shed sat in the corner of the yard. Its door was secured with a padlock. Ryan came over and stood next to her.

"Lou said you were looking for me," said Ryan.

"I was just wondering when you were going to have a look inside that shed?"

"I was waiting for it to stop raining."

"If there's a dirt bike somewhere on this property, that's the only place left it could be. What do you think?"

Ryan held up a key. "Kyle gave us the key voluntarily so it's hard to believe there's something in there that would incriminate him."

"Then I think we should ask Kyle to open it," said Macy, thinking back on her conversation with Sean Spencer. "I doubt he'll mind."

Kyle slid the padlock off the catch and dropped it and the key into an evidence bag Macy was holding. He stepped away and crossed his arms. Rain was streaming off his hood.

"This is a total waste of time," said Kyle.

Ryan swung the shed door open and stepped away so Macy could see what was inside.

"Seems like time well spent to me," said Macy.

A dirt bike was parked in the middle of the shed. The wheels were caked with mud. A helmet, leather jacket and motorcycle boots sat on the shelf next to it.

"Is this your bike, Kyle?" asked Macy.

Kyle didn't answer.

Ryan used a flashlight to get a closer look. "There's a serial number," he said. "We should know whether it's his soon enough."

"It's not mine," said Kyle.

"Are you sure?" said Macy, making a point to check the shed's exterior carefully. "There's no sign of a break-in and a few seconds ago you stated that there was only one key."

"They . . . they must have picked the lock."

Ryan pointed to the leather riding gear stashed on the shelves.

"What about all this stuff, Kyle?" said Ryan. "Do you recognize it?"

Kyle closed his eyes. "Sean did . . . did this. He's trying to set me up!"

"Kyle, during your initial interview you said you didn't own or ride a bike," said Macy. "I'm asking you again. Is this stuff yours?"

"I said it wasn't."

"Why do I have a feeling the DNA will say otherwise?" said Macy.

"Nothing should be in here," said Kyle. "Someone plan . . . planted it."

Ryan held up a handgun he'd found in a flowerpot.

"Macy, is this your SIG?" He placed it in an evidence bag before handing it to her. "Looks like there are some nice prints on it."

Lou Turner came up and stood behind Kyle. "What do you think Macy? Is that your gun?"

Macy studied the firearm carefully. It felt heavier than she remembered and there was damage to the barrel and handle she didn't recognize. She held the bag close so she could make out the serial number. She read it twice to be sure.

"It's mine," she said, blinking back tears. For a few seconds all she could see was Philip Long. He'd looked so lost and alone on the road that night.

Lou twisted Kyle's arms behind his back and slapped a pair of handcuffs on in one easy motion.

"That's always been my favorite part," said Lou. "I'll read him his rights and take him to the station. You coming?"

Macy tilted her head up to the sky and let the falling rain wash over her face. She didn't want anyone to see that she was close to crying.

"I'll be along in a minute," she said.

Ryan came and stood next to her.

"I kind of feel sorry for Kyle. His surprise actually seemed genuine." Ryan nudged her. "Are you okay?" he asked.

Macy handed him the evidence bag.

"I'm not now but I will be," she said, heading back toward the house.

# 20

Emma sat in a small office waiting for Lou Turner and Macy Greeley. She placed a folder on the desk in front of her and plugged her father's external hard drive into her laptop. News of Kyle's arrest for kidnapping and murder had spread quickly. She'd also heard that a police officer was standing guard outside Dr. Whitaker's hospital room. She was hopeful his arrest was also imminent.

Lou Turner followed Macy Greeley into the room. Emma stood up to say hello and shake their hands. Neither looked as if they'd slept recently. They sat down in the chairs on either side of Emma and listened quietly as she opened the folders on her father's hard drive one by one.

"My father has been investigating Dr. Whitaker for years," said Emma. "He was very thorough. He listed names of sources that were willing to go on record, dates that they met with Whitaker to get prescriptions filled, and amounts of cash exchanged. There are also transcripts from over thirty interviews he conducted with Whitaker's former patients and several dealers who claimed to have used Whitaker as a source of drugs in the past. Some of Whitaker's patients' medical records are also on the hard drive. They all either died under his care or had been massively overprescribed opiate-based painkillers."

Macy read through what was on the screen in front of her, occasionally asking Emma to scroll down so she could see more.

"Emma," she said. "There's a lot of detailed information here, and some of it appears to have come directly from the clinic's mainframe."

"My father hacked into the system using my mother's work account," said Emma, hoping she was right. "My mother is useless with computers. She wouldn't have known how to help him."

Lou pointed at the screen. "What is this folder up here that's labeled AUDIO?"

"It's mostly interviews he'd recorded, but there are a couple of files that are especially interesting. One is a conversation my father had with Dr. Whitaker shortly before he was kidnapped. After attempting to bribe my father, Whitaker threatened him with financial ruin if he aired the story about painkillers on his radio show."

"And the other recording?" asked Macy.

"A friend of my father's posed as a patient and recorded his visit to Dr. Whitaker's office. At first he pretends to be in pain, but then admits he's looking for Vicodin, OxyContin, and methadone because he has a habit. Whitaker agrees to write him a prescription, but the transaction never takes place because my father's friend didn't have enough cash on him."

"I wish we'd found this hard drive sooner," said Macy. "Where was it hidden?"

"In Caleb Winfrey's basement." Emma glanced over at Lou. "My father has been looking after the property since Caleb went into a nursing home. A light was left on in the basement, otherwise I'd have never thought to look for it down there."

"Did you also find your father's journal?" asked Macy.

Emma laid her hand on the folder containing the pages she'd torn from the journal. "It was with the hard drive," she said. "I'm only giving you the pages that relate to Dr. Whitaker. I've destroyed the rest."

"I'm not sure that was wise," said Macy. "You may have missed something."

"I read it from cover to cover. Everything that has to do with Whitaker is in this folder."

Macy pulled on a pair of latex gloves and started going through the pages.

Lou cleared his throat. "Emma, even though Kyle Miller has implicated Dr. Whitaker, it may be a while before he's arrested."

Emma said, "I think I may have uncovered something that might speed up the process." She turned to face Macy. "I told you about my friend in high school, Lucy Winfrey?"

"I read her file," said Macy. "She died of an overdose. As I recall there was an unidentified fingerprint found on the syringe."

Emma lowered her voice. "My father was convinced Whitaker was supplying Lucy with drugs in exchange for sex."

Lou sat up. "Can that be proven?"

"I'm not sure. There was a whole section on Lucy in the journal. I think her death is what made my father so interested in Dr. Whitaker in the first place. He spoke to Whitaker's second wife, Dot, and she confirmed that Lucy and Dr. Whitaker were having an affair. It started when Lucy was working as Dot's assistant. It's why Lucy was fired. I'm pretty sure it's why she died."

Emma found the journal page that had a photograph of Lucy attached to it.

"This was taken on the steps of Dr. Whitaker's home on Memorial Day weekend not long before Lucy died. Dot was out of town with the kids. He'd continued seeing Lucy for months after Dot caught them together."

"It's not enough to implicate him in her death," said Macy, looking over the notes from the journal. "Based on what I'm seeing here, the most we can get him on is supplying her with narcotics."

Lou pushed his chair away from the conference table. "I'll be back in a sec."

Emma flinched at the sound of the slamming door. "I've upset him. He's known Dr. Whitaker for a long time."

"You should give Lou more credit," said Macy. "He's the one who's been cleaning up Dr. Whitaker's mess all these years. A lot of the drugs Whitaker prescribed ended up on the streets. The results have been devastating for communities like Walleye Junction—broken homes, child neglect, traffic fatalities, suicides, domestic violence . . . I could go on."

For a few seconds neither of them said a word. Emma pressed her hands flat on the table. Kyle Miller was going to haunt her thoughts for a long time. She'd never forgive herself for getting it so wrong. He'd killed her father. It was inconceivable that she hadn't seen him for the monster he was.

"I can't believe I let Kyle fool me," said Emma.

"Don't be so hard on yourself. I interviewed Kyle. He has a higher than average IQ, is well-mannered, reasonably attractive, and very articulate. He is also a very convincing liar who'd managed to get four people to provide him with a false alibi. I'm not surprised he managed to fool you as well."

"I honestly thought he was socially awkward but otherwise harmless." Emma hesitated. "I want to know what happened the night my father died."

Macy rolled a pen back and forth between her fingertips.

"It's early days, so we're still piecing together various versions of events."

"You must have an idea though."

"I know certain things. The rest is conjecture. The plan to kidnap your father appears to have been ill conceived from the outset. Kyle presents himself as someone with special ops training, when he's really just a computer technician with delusions of grandeur. At this point we can't prove that Dr. Whitaker requested his assistance, but we believe that's what happened. Your father had to be silenced. Kyle would kidnap him. They'd only release him if they were sure he wouldn't go public with the story about Dr. Whitaker's clinic."

"But that's ridiculous," said Emma. "My father wouldn't have been intimidated that easily."

"Emma, it wasn't just your father who was threatened. They made it clear to him that if he didn't cooperate, they'd go after you and your mother."

Emma didn't know how to respond. She closed her eyes for a few seconds. When she opened them the room was brighter, the chatter in the outside offices a little louder. Macy tilted her head.

"This is upsetting you," said Macy. "Are you sure you want me to go on?"

Emma said a quiet yes.

"Kyle recruited his aunt and uncle to help him. He'd duped them into thinking they were sending your father a warning because of the program he did on the militias. It was agreed that their debts would be paid off as compensation. We're not entirely sure why, but Carla grew suspicious and started digging around your father's laptop. When she realized what Dr. Whitaker had been doing all these years, she let your father go."

"Why would she do that?"

"I'd like to think she had a change of heart. This is a woman who lost everything because of drugs. She knew firsthand how much damage Whitaker was doing. You have to give her credit. Letting your father go took a lot of guts. She even downloaded what she could onto a memory stick for safekeeping. Unfortunately it was corrupted and most of the files were lost." Macy picked up the external hard drive Emma found. "That's why this is so important. It's a game changer."

"Is Kyle cooperating?"

"He's confessed to killing your father as well as Carla and Lloyd Spencer, but we still don't have any physical evidence that proves Whitaker is guilty." Macy sat back in her chair. "Whitaker played Kyle perfectly. He appealed to his ego and his aspirations. . . . Kyle would have done just about anything to move up in the world. So far Whitaker has managed to make it look like Kyle acted independently."

"We have him on tape threatening my father," said Emma.

"We'll hand over everything we have to the state's attorney. I certainly think it's enough to make a case, but it may take time to get an arrest warrant. Dr. Whitaker has powerful connections in Montana."

There was a sharp knock at the door, and Lou stepped into the room holding a file aloft. He slapped it down on the table in front of Macy and opened it.

"This is Lucy's case file," he said, jabbing his finger at the relevant information. "I ran that fingerprint we found on the syringe through the system again. There's a match."

"Dr. Whitaker?" asked Macy.

Lou started pacing the room. "He volunteered his DNA and fingerprints so we could eliminate him as a suspect in Philip's kidnapping. After all these years, he's finally in the system."

"Lou," said Macy. "This is good news. We can arrest him on suspicion of murder."

Emma pictured the syringe balancing precariously on the edge of Lucy's bathtub. She'd almost thrown it out along with the lipstick-smeared paper towels.

"I don't understand why Dr. Whitaker killed her," said Emma.

"She may have become a liability," said Lou. "His practice brings in millions in revenue, and she was spiraling out of control. There was a lot at stake."

"I was supposed to be there with her," said Emma, her eyes shifting to Lucy's photo. "She invited me over that evening, but I lied and said I had other plans."

Lou put a hand on Emma's shoulder. "This was never your fault. You need to stop blaming yourself."

Macy gathered up Lucy's file, the pages from Philip Long's journal, and the external hard drive. "Lou, what do you say we head up to the hospital and have another word with Dr. Whitaker?"

"I just need to make a couple of phone calls first," said Lou.

"Come find me when you're finished," said Macy.

Macy shook Emma's hand. "Thank you for bringing this in. I promise that we'll do everything we can to secure a conviction."

"Will you be coming to the funeral service tomorrow?" Emma asked.

"I'll do my best. I need to get back to Helena. I haven't seen my son in a while."

"Oh, I'm sorry," said Emma. "I had no idea you had children."

"Just the one. My mother has been looking after him, but it's time I took over. I think she wants her life back."

"I know the feeling."

"When are you heading home?" asked Macy.

"Within the next few days. I just need to make sure my mother is okay. She is very fond of Dr. Whitaker. It will be a real blow when she finds out he was responsible."

Emma tried calling Dot Whitaker before stopping by her house, but there was no cell phone reception. In the end Emma decided to show up unannounced. She parked her car next to the fountain and walked across the gravel drive. The shadows were long and a chill had settled in for the evening. Emma rang the doorbell and waited. Receiving no answer, she went around back, where the conservatory doors had been open onto the garden the day they'd had lunch. Everything was closed up and the house was dark.

Emma slowly became aware that classical music was playing somewhere nearby. She followed the sound through the garden, down some stone steps, and onto the path that led to Dot's studio. The studio door was open wide. Emma stood on the threshold. The lights were on and music played out of a small radio that sat on a workbench. Splattered paint coated the wooden floors, works in progress sat on easels, and canvases leaned against the walls. She knocked several times.

"Dot, are you here? It's Emma Long," she said.

There was no answer. Thinking Dot must be out in the garden, Emma turned to leave. She was almost out the door when one of Dot's paintings caught her eye. The style was so similar to the ones she'd seen up at the house on her previous visit, she first thought it was another painting of the girl in the red dress.

Emma studied the painting with a mixture of curiosity and revulsion. Dot had captured details that Emma's memory had missed. Lucy appeared to not only float in the bathwater but in the canvas as well.

Her eyes were open, her lips slightly parted. Her black hair drifted around her pale face like storm clouds. The syringe that delivered the fatal dose was balanced on the edge of the bathtub and the needle marks on her arms were painfully vivid. Emma's eyes rested on the mirror. She'd not expected to see her own blurred reflection painted on the glass. She flinched. Red lipstick lines of text looped across her features.

*Emma, Sometimes the heart breaks and the broken do not live on. You should have come when I called. Always yours, Lucy*

The music stopped and Emma turned around. Dot stood next to the workbench with a bouquet of wildflowers in her hands. She walked over to the utility sink and filled a jam jar with water.

"I told you I'd developed a morbid fascination with the macabre. What do you think?" said Dot. "Did I get the details right?"

"I don't understand how you could have done this without a photo," said Emma.

Dot turned and smiled. She held the bouquet up like an offering. There was a little jump in her voice.

"I don't always work from photos, but in this case I wanted to get it absolutely right."

"Dot," asked Emma. "I need to know where you got the photo."

"Would you believe I bribed a police officer? The only addition I made was your image in the mirror." Dot pointed to a small settee. "Come and sit. You look like you've seen a ghost."

Emma studied the painting. "They're going to charge Peter with Lucy's murder." Emma pressed her fingertip into the canvas. The paint was tacky to the touch. "They found his prints on that syringe."

Dot placed the jar of wildflowers on a small table and sat down in an armchair opposite the settee.

"It seems a little late for justice," said Dot. "Come and sit with me, Emma. There's no reason for you to stare at that painting. You were there."

Emma remained standing.

"You couldn't have gotten the photo from the police," said Emma.

"Oh, but I did," said Dot. "I just didn't copy it exactly. You could say I put things back to the way they were supposed to be. I believe in painting the truth now."

"I erased the note Lucy left on the mirror, so it wouldn't have been in any of the photos the police had. The only way you could have known about the note was if you were there on the night Lucy died," said Emma. "Tell me what happened."

"There's really not much to say. Lucy was already unconscious when I arrived. I could have either called an ambulance or helped her finish what she'd already started. I chose to be helpful."

"You murdered her?"

"I wasn't the one feeding Lucy drugs in exchange for sex, and I certainly didn't pay her to sell drugs to high school students. Peter is the one who did all those things, not me." Dot folded her hands in her lap. "As far as I'm concerned, he is the one who murdered her. My conscience is clear."

"Lucy could have gone to rehab. There's always hope."

"Lucy wasn't responsive. Her breathing was impaired, and her pupils were fixed. I'm a nurse, Emma. I've seen what happens to people who've suffered brain damage after overdosing on painkillers. Even if she'd survived she would have had no quality of life. I wasn't fond of the girl, but I wouldn't wish that future on anyone."

"Why were you there in the first place?" asked Emma. "Did she call you for help?"

Dot shook her head. "I'd gone over to Lucy's house because I was desperate. I'd had no luck reasoning with Peter, so I was hoping she'd listen. They were both out of control."

"Dr. Whitaker was using drugs as well?"

"Oh, it was worse than that," said Dot. "He's clean now, but back then he was a full-blown addict. His affair with Lucy was embarrassing enough, but his behavior was putting patients at risk. He'd gotten so sloppy. I was finding his used syringes and empty prescription bottles everywhere."

"Did you use one of his syringes to inject Lucy?"

"The syringe was from Lucy's room. She must have shared it with him at some point. The fact that his print was on it was sheer luck."

"I doubt he'll see it that way."

"At this point I don't really care what that man thinks. Your father was one of my dearest friends. Peter may yet manage to get away with what he's done to Philip, but he won't get away with what he did to Lucy."

Emma sat down on the settee and put her head in her hands.

"Emma," said Dot. "If you go to the police with your concerns, you'll have to admit to destroying evidence. The crime scene will be considered compromised. Peter and I get off on a technicality, and nobody will pay for what happened to Lucy except you." Dot adjusted the flowers so they stood up straighter in the jar. "My ex-husband deserves to go to jail for this and so many other things. Think of how many lives may have been lost because of what he was getting up to in that clinic."

"You worked there. You must have known what was going on."

Dot sharpened her tone. "Are you sure you want to go down that road, Emma? Your mother worked at that clinic longer than anyone else."

"Are you suggesting—"

Dot held up a hand. "I'm suggesting in the gentlest possible way that you let things take their course." She plucked a cornflower from the bouquet and held it up to the light. "There's a lot of beauty in letting go."

"And what about the truth?"

A shrug. "*Beauty is truth, truth beauty.*"

Emma rose from the settee. "I'm not sure Keats had this sort of situation in mind."

"You never know," said Dot, a smile playing on her lips. "People say he was addicted to opiates. He may have understood better than most."

Emma stood in front of the painting. "Will you ever show this in public?"

"I'm not planning on it, but who knows what the future holds. Maybe someday my grandchildren will stage a retrospective of my work."

"I read my father's journal. He was very interested in you."

"I'm an interesting person."

"How much do you care about your reputation?"

"Not as much as I once did."

"Do you want people to know that you were having an affair with my father?"

Dot remained silent.

"I want you to destroy this painting," said Emma.

"I will."

Emma picked up a bottle of white spirit and handed it to Dot.

"I want you to do it now," said Emma.

# 21

Macy handed Gina an industrial-sized bag of potato chips, a box of doughnuts, and a bumper pack of Snickers bars.

Gina laughed. "I was hoping for a cash bonus, but this will do nicely."

"I thought I should restock your reserves. You've been a big help this past week. I couldn't have done it without you."

"Don't be silly," said Gina. "We both know you would have muddled through. Ryan and I are going for a drink to celebrate our last night in Walleye. Feel like joining us? I asked Lou, but he already has plans."

Macy sat down at the desk she'd been using for the past week. She'd already cleared out everything that was hers. All that was left were a few paper clips, a couple of pens, and an open box of chocolate chip cookies that must have migrated from Gina's desk.

Macy lowered her voice. "Sorry, but I actually have a date."

Gina swung her chair around to face Macy. "You are a dark horse. Tell me everything. Who's the lucky guy?"

"Aiden Marsh."

Gina raised her voice several octaves. "Well done, Special Investigator Greeley. He's seriously hot."

Macy felt the color rise in her cheeks. Even though she was mortified, she couldn't stop smiling.

"Gina, do you think you could speak a little louder? I'm not sure the guys across the room heard you."

"Is this a first date?"

"No," Macy admitted. "We've been seeing each other since last summer."

"Why all the secrecy?"

Macy puffed out her cheeks. "That's a tricky one. I'm not really sure why I've been so hesitant to take it public."

Gina cocked her head to one side. "You've recently had your private life on show. Your apprehension is justifiable."

As usual Gina was spot on. Prior to Ray's arrest, Macy was obliged to give investigators a detailed account of their relationship. She couldn't fault them for their professionalism, but it still felt like she was being judged. After word of her relationship with Ray was leaked to the public, things got a lot worse.

"You're right," said Macy. "But it's not just that. Aiden wants to live together. It would mean moving up here."

"That's a tough call. Seems like you'd be giving up a lot."

"He actually suggested that I cut back on my hours or change careers altogether. He doesn't seem to understand how much I love what I do."

"You could always get a transfer to the Kalispell office," said Gina. "It's not too far from Wilmington Creek. If it doesn't work out, you head back to Helena with your tail between your legs."

Macy pushed her chair away from the desk. "I should make a move. I'll give you a shout if our plans change. Aiden mentioned something about going to see some live music."

"Ryan and I have exhausted all the entertainment possibilities around here. A change of venue would be most welcome."

"I'll let you know. Otherwise I'll see you in the morning."

Gina nodded. "Just be honest with him, Macy. Aiden needs to know where your head is."

"Thanks for the advice," said Macy. "I'll call you later."

. . .

Macy found Aiden sitting on the back porch sorting through his fishing gear. He shielded his eyes from the late afternoon sun and smiled up at her.

"How's my favorite special investigator?" he asked.

"Exhausted, but satisfied."

He held out his arms and she settled onto his lap.

"Did you finally get your man?" asked Aiden, pulling her close.

"It was a good week. I managed to get two men."

"You are clever."

"I am."

She laid her head on his shoulder.

"I need to say something," he said.

"I think we both have things to say."

"You're going to have to let me go first this time."

Now that Macy was with Aiden, everything felt crystal clear. Given time, she thought, she could love this man.

"I'm listening," she said.

"I spoke to Charlotte Crawley yesterday."

Macy raised an eyebrow. "Small world. I just spoke to her a few minutes ago," she said.

"About the case?"

Macy nodded. "Kyle Miller admitted to being with Lloyd Spencer on the day he planted the evidence in the fire pit and threatened her children. They were hoping to frame Bob for Philip's murder."

"Did you figure out how Stacy Shaw factored into the investigation?"

"The detective Charlotte hired to tail Bob works as a subcontractor for Flathead Valley Security. Everything he found out about Bob went through their system. Kyle decided it would be easy to set Bob up. He even went so far as to create an online profile using the name Max to lure Stacy down to Kalispell for a week. I'm not sure what his plans for Stacy were after that."

"Thankfully, she's still breathing."

Macy hesitated. "So, what did you and Charlotte talk about?"

"A lot, actually. Bob has moved back in."

"Seriously?"

"That was my reaction too, but aside from giving her full access to his phone and computer, he's promised to go to therapy a couple of times a week. Maybe there's hope for them yet."

"You have to admire Charlotte's determination to keep the family together."

"Charlotte asked how we were doing, and I told her you weren't as enthusiastic about the idea of moving up here as I hoped you would be. I was expecting Charlotte to be sympathetic. Instead I got an earful."

"I'm liking her more and more," said Macy.

"Anyway, I wanted to say that I'm sorry. I shouldn't have put so much pressure on you. Asking you to give up your career so you could move in with me was out of line." He held Macy a little tighter. "I don't want to lose you, but I also don't want to change who you are."

"But where does that leave us? You're tied to your job here, and I'm in Helena."

"I'm handing in my notice on Monday."

Macy sat up. "But you love your job."

"Yes, but I love fishing more."

"Fishing doesn't pay the bills."

"Have a little faith. There is a master plan."

"I'm listening."

"Charlotte has decided to invest a great deal of money in my fishing lodge. The plans have expanded to include a hotel and spa, which she will manage. Think about it, Macy. I'll have much more flexibility. The lodge will shut down for much of the off-season. It will mean I can come down to Helena to be with you for months at a time."

"Are you sure about this? It's still a far cry from living together full time."

"I'm willing to wait if you are."

Macy didn't know what to say. No one had ever been willing to sacrifice so much to be with her. Aiden wasn't asking her to change a thing.

"Now," said Aiden. "I know I promised to take you out for some live music tonight, but I figured we'd go down to the river instead. It's time you had your first fly-fishing lesson."

"What about dinner?"

"All packed up and ready to go."

She raised an eyebrow. "Wine?"

"One red and one white."

"It's going to be dark soon."

"We'll build a fire."

"You've thought of everything."

Aiden hesitated. "Macy, did you have something you wanted to say?"

Macy pressed her lips against his and held them there, but Aiden wasn't going to let his question go unanswered.

"Macy," he said, pushing her away. "You're not going to distract me that easily. I need to know what you're thinking."

"I'm thinking you're almost perfect."

"Almost?" he said.

"Well, there is one little problem."

"Oh, yeah? What's that?"

Macy cracked a smile. "I'm going to miss seeing you in uniform. Any chance you'll get to keep it?"

# 22

It was late when Emma crept into the kitchen and found a roll of garbage bags. She spent the rest of the night quietly dismantling her past. She finally turned off the light at five in the morning. She slept through her alarm, only waking when her mother knocked on her bedroom door. Francine eyed the empty walls and overflowing garbage bags as she sat perched on the edge of Emma's bed. The day had barely begun and Francine already sounded exhausted.

"Lou Turner called me an hour ago to tell me they've charged Peter with Lucy Winfrey's murder. They identified a fingerprint on the syringe as his."

Emma couldn't look her mother in the eye. "He was giving drugs to Lucy in exchange for sex."

Francine's voice broke. "She was only a child."

"They're also going to charge him with dealing drugs out of his clinic."

"Was he responsible for Philip's death?"

"Yes, but they may not be able to prove it." Emma paused. "You'll probably be questioned again."

"Why would they need to speak to me? I've already told them everything I know."

"Dad knew things about Dr. Whitaker's practice that weren't in the public domain. It looks like he hacked into the clinic's computers using your account. When you're asked, I want you to tell them that you knew nothing about what was going on. Do you understand?"

"Emma, I was telling the truth when I said I didn't know what your father was working on. There is something I've been keeping from you, though."

Francine slipped a small black cell phone out of her pocket and put it on the bed between them.

"This was dropped off at the house the same day your father was kidnapped," said Francine. "It's how the kidnappers contacted me. They threatened to hurt you and Philip if I said anything to the police. It's why I didn't call you to tell you what happened to your father. More than anything, I needed to know you were safe."

Emma wrapped her arms around her mother and held her close. For a long time neither of them spoke.

"I really thought you didn't love me anymore," said Emma.

Francine stroked her daughter's hair. "I've missed you so much."

"I've missed you too."

Emma leaned back on the pillows and stared at the phone.

"When was the last time they contacted you?" asked Emma.

"Friday morning. They always called me at the same time of day. When I didn't hear anything over the weekend, I thought it was finally over."

"It is over," said Emma. She picked up the phone and placed it on the bedside table. "We need to put the past behind us and move on. I thought we could start with my room."

"Seems like you had a long night."

"Once I got going I couldn't stop," said Emma. "What time is it anyway?"

"Half past nine."

"I've overslept."

Francine took Emma's hand. "I'm afraid we have to get moving. We need to be at the cemetery by eleven."

"Isn't there a service at the church beforehand?"

"I spoke to the reverend after I got off the phone with Lou," said Francine. "I can't mourn your father in a church Peter Whitaker paid for. We'll have a short service at the cemetery."

"And the wake?" asked Emma.

"It will take place at my friend Mary's house. It's all settled."

Francine was silent during the drive up to the cemetery. Her hands were folded neatly in her lap, and she stared straight ahead. Emma tried to concentrate on her driving but there were too many conflicting emotions coming at her at once. She was worried her mother might be charged as an accessory. All it would take was one person at the doctor's office pointing a finger in Francine's direction. As it was Francine's husband who brought all of Dr. Whitaker's crimes to light, it was probable someone might be vindictive enough to want to bring Francine down.

Sunlight barely pushed through the thick canopy of trees that lined the drive to the cemetery's parking lot. There was already a crowd of mourners gathered near the entrance gate. As she pulled into a space, Emma spotted Caleb among them. She was so nervous she dropped the keys between the seats.

Francine took hold of her daughter's hand. "Emma, it's going to be okay. Pretty soon everyone is going to know what really happened the night Lucy died. Caleb can't hurt you anymore."

"Has someone told him?" she asked.

"Maybe, but I doubt he understands. If he says something, do yourself a favor and ignore it."

"Easier said than done."

Francine fingered the cross at her throat. "This is a hard day for both of us."

Emma watched Lucy's father from behind the windshield. As usual he was leaning heavily on his cane. The woman who'd buttressed him so efficiently at the church reception was standing nearby. Emma hadn't realized until that moment that the human buttress was none other than

Nathan's fiancée Cynthia. Cynthia had stationed herself next to her intended, but Nathan had his hands wedged deeply in his pockets and was turned slightly away from her. As far as Emma could tell, it didn't seem like Nathan wanted to be anywhere near Cynthia.

Francine's voice was as crisp as new bills. "Emma, it's time."

Several of Francine's friends came forward as they stepped out of the car. Dot Whitaker stood apart from them. She wore dark sunglasses and an oversized hat. As they made their way along the main walkway, Emma risked a quick peek at Lucy's grave. The flowers she'd left were still there. Ahead of her, Caleb's white head bobbed up and down, glowing like a halo in the late morning sun. He shuffled along, talking to Nathan while Cynthia tottered after them in her high heels. Beside Emma, her mother sniffed quietly, occasionally needing a supporting arm, but for the most part making her own way to her husband's final resting place.

As Emma stood above her father's open grave, a sense of vertigo played games with her balance, and the smell of newly cut earth pinched her nose. She imagined the gravedigger's blade slicing through the soil, cleanly dissecting everything in its path. The sides of the hole were sheer, almost polished smooth. When the others bowed their heads in prayer, Emma kept her eyes level with Caleb's. His jaw hung loose and tiny, thread veins snaked around his nostrils like flames. He held her stare, his lips quivering nervously, his words ready to spring like arrows from a bow. He shifted his weight, muttering something only his neighbors could hear. Emma watched shocked ripples move through the sea of heads. Someone put a hand to Caleb's arm, but he only grunted defiantly as he hobbled over to stand next to Emma.

"Emma, have you seen Lucy?" he said, his voice quaking. "I've been looking for her everywhere. She runs off sometimes."

Emma put a hand on his arm to steady him. This was unexpected. She looked across the gravestones, seeing if she could pick out Lucy's, but a tree stood in the way. Her secret was safe.

"We can look for her together if you like," she said.

Caleb scanned the crowd. "Why are we here? Who died this time?"

"My father," said Emma.

"Oh, I'm very sorry to hear that," he said, drawing out his words. "Philip Long was a good man."

"Yes, he was," said Emma. She took the handkerchief he offered and dabbed the tears from her eyes. "I'm going to miss him."

# 23

Macy answered her mother's phone call as she drove toward the Walleye Junction municipal cemetery. Gina was sitting in the passenger seat nursing what she'd referred to as a Ryan-sized hangover. She wore a pair of sunglasses that covered half her face.

"Calm down, Mom," said Macy, switching to speakerphone. "I can't understand a word you're saying."

"Someone tried to snatch Luke from the day-care center at the gym," said Ellen.

The right front tire hit the curb, and Macy almost lost control of the car. Next to her, Gina shook herself awake.

"Is Luke okay?" asked Macy.

"He's absolutely fine. It's the adults who are upset. The manager called the police. I told them to speak to your old colleague Brad Newman. He's on his way."

Macy pulled over at the next turnout and climbed into the passenger seat while Gina went around. Seconds later Gina was at the wheel, and they were heading toward Route 93 with the sirens wailing.

"Mom," said Macy. "We're on our way back to Helena now. I know you're upset, but you need to tell me exactly what happened."

"Just a sec. Luke wants to say hello."

"Mommy?"

Macy started crying. Gina grabbed hold of her hand and squeezed it hard.

"Hi, baby," Macy said, steadying her voice. "Are you having a good time with Granny?"

"I made a drawing. It's for you."

"I bet it's beautiful."

"A puppy. I drew one."

"You drew a puppy for me?"

"Yes."

"I will be home soon," said Macy. "Will you show it to me when I get there?"

"I love you, Mommy."

"I love you too."

Macy was left listening to silence.

"Mom?" she said.

"I'm here," said Ellen. "The police are pulling up outside now."

"I'll want to speak to them. What do you know so far?"

"A young woman came into the gym claiming to be you and said she'd come to pick up Luke from the day-care center. The woman at the desk became suspicious when she failed to produce any identification."

"What did she look like?"

"Eighteen to twenty years old, blond, white, and very thin. She was wearing a hooded sweatshirt and jeans."

Macy's mind went into overdrive. "It could have been Nicole Davidson."

"Shouldn't she be in Chicago?"

"They'll have security cameras at the club," said Macy. "Tell them to look at the feed. They should be able to send me the link."

"Did she say anything in her last letter about coming back to Montana?"

"I have no idea. I haven't read it yet."

Macy searched the side pocket of her bag for the letter. She ripped the envelope open and scanned the text.

"Macy, are you still there," asked Ellen. "Brad's here now. He wants to speak to you."

Macy's heart sank. It was all there in black and white. Nicole wanted to come live with them in Helena. She was miserable in Chicago and wanted to be with her little brother.

A man's voice came over the speakerphone.

"Macy? It's Brad Newman. I understand you're up in the Flathead Valley. How you holding up?"

"I've been better. You need to look at the video footage for confirmation, but I'm pretty sure we're looking for Nicole Davidson."

"Ray's daughter?"

"I have a letter from her. She wanted to come back to Helena so she could be with her little brother."

"Christ," said Brad. "They're just bringing up the video now."

"Would you recognize her?

"Depends on how much she's changed," said Brad. "It's been a while since I last saw her."

"What do you see on the video?"

"Hooded sweatshirt and sunglasses. Difficult to say."

"See if you can get a photo to show to the receptionist," said Macy.

"I'm on it. Someone at the office will have something on file. I'll call you back when I know more. Meanwhile, don't worry. Luke and your mom are in good hands."

Macy watched cars pull to the side as Gina sped through the traffic crowding Route 93. Nicole's letter had been in her hands for over a week.

"I should have read the damn thing when it arrived," said Macy.

Gina gave her a sharp look. "Don't beat yourself up. Even if you had read it, you couldn't have known the girl would do something as stupid as this."

"Nicole is troubled, but I never believed she was dangerous."

"If she figured out where your mother's gym is, she probably knows where you live."

"I'm afraid that may well be the case," said Macy.

Macy's phone rang. She held it to her ear.

Brad sounded out of breath. "It was definitely Nicole."

Macy pictured Nicole as a child. She'd been so open and full of life. Ten years on and there was a good chance she'd be charged with attempted child abduction.

"You have to be absolutely sure," said Macy.

"Ray's old personal assistant sent us some photos she had on file. The receptionist at the day-care center confirmed that it was Nicole."

"I'm really worried about her, Brad. She must have been desperate to try something like this. Put out an APB and track down her friends and classmates. We'll need to speak to her therapist in Chicago."

"Will do," said Brad. "We're in touch with her mother. Nicole ran away two days ago."

"I should be back in Helena in a couple of hours," said Macy. "Have some units check my mother's house thoroughly. I'm worried that Nicole may have figured out where we live."

Macy read through Nicole's letter in its entirety. It held no clues as to the girl's whereabouts. If Nicole was as clever as her father, she could keep Macy guessing for years. Macy sat back and closed her eyes. She had a feeling it was going to be a very long ride home.

# Sources

An incredibly well-researched article entitled "The New Heroin Epidemic" was published in *The Atlantic* in October 2014. Though it focused on my home state of West Virginia, it opened my eyes to what's been going on throughout America for the past fifteen years. I followed the sources, eventually finding an equally enthralling piece of journalism that was published in the *Los Angeles Times* in November 2012. "Legal Drugs, Deadly Outcomes" made it clear that many Americans were dying after being overprescribed powerful opiate-based painkillers by their doctors. I knew immediately that this was the story I wanted to tell.


http://graphics.latimes.com/prescription-drugs-part-one/

www.usatoday.com/story/news/nation/2013/08/20/doctors-licenses-medical-boards/2655513/

www.youtube.com/watch?v=r8MaITKJJEI

www.miheadlines.com/2014/08/04/partyers-weekend-rave-vow-projectp-happen/

www.theatlantic.com/business/archive/2015/01/rural-americas-silent-housing-crisis/384885/

www.theatlantic.com/features/archive/2014/10/the-new-heroin-epidemic/382020/